Visitor's Blood
Book One

by
Sahreth 'Baphy' Bowden

Chapter 1: John

Somehow the usual open feel of the high-ceiling room had become rather crowded tonight, and it wasn't for the presence of more workers either. Other than having both myself and my commanding officer on duty at once, the staff was its typical collective. Men and women in uniform huddled about steel desks neatly arranged around the perimeter and then in rows through the center of the tiled floor.

Their attention was on their individual computer monitors with minimal spoken dialogue. My own focus was on the screen before me where the tiny white light causing all the fuss shone. It was surely the intensity of everyone's mindset in determining its reason which was spawning my awareness of all surroundings and therefore creating this perception of being cramped.

"It looks like it's heading for the deserts in New Mexico," I informed. "We can't pinpoint its exact trajectory yet, but that is still within our jurisdiction, so we can handle this personally."

I looked over at the colonel, letting his demeanor soak into my senses. The older man stood only a few feet away, his weight shifted onto one foot and hands straight against his side as he pursed his lips and stared blankly at my presentation.

I knew how easily one could upset him if he felt intimidated. He disliked having his authority questioned and working with him for nearly ten years had taught me an extreme use of tact. After a brief pause without him moving or saying anything, I noted that he was probably waiting for me to continue, so I did.

"If the object stays at its current speed, it will reach the surface within the next two hours. Right here," I stepped a pace to the left and rested my finger on another monitor, "The computer has calculated the time and just below," moving my finger, "Are the coordinates for its approximate landing destination; granted that it doesn't somehow change course."

I let another few moments pass while my superior's brain adjusted to the information. In all my memory of him, I believe this was the longest he had ever been quiet. Not that he was talkative by any means, but generally when there was a call for action, he would always almost immediately have assessed the situation with orders for what was to be done.

Admittedly, it was a bit unsettling for me to see someone of his strength and accomplishment having such a lack of answers. I suppose it was just the thrill of my dream possibly becoming true that dulled my senses to the danger this ordeal might also bring. I had always been called an eccentric by my peers, yet after learning of that little light spotting its way through our system, had lifted a silent prayer they would no longer see me that way.

Although I wanted to sneak off for a second to call my wife, I first awaited orders, or a response of any kind really, from the colonel. She would be equally excited even though it wasn't actually allowed for any of us to disclose data to others, no matter our relationship. However, Connie had previously been a doctor and medical researcher working in the base and Col. Jean was fond of her...for the most part.

In fact, he had let her come to see the station on more than one occasion after her transfer elsewhere- something he could have been given a lot of grief for. Fortunately, he knew enough people to keep himself clean. In those cases, it was especially nice to consider him a friend whether or not he shared our enthusiasm for extraterrestrial life.

I couldn't say he was always pleasant or agreeable and he had made his share of decisions with which I didn't agree. Nonetheless, he did his job well and his highers favored him greatly for it. I should never call him evil, only a man with a mission and a strict way of thinking, to put it kindly.

Breaking away from my thoughts, I looked up at the still mildly frozen form beside me. He moved his arm a few inches to rest it on the machine in front of him as his eyes shifted up from the screen to me. He remained there for an uncomfortably long amount of time before speaking, which had begun to make me feel fearful for the first time that evening.

"Send for teams," he started off shakily, pausing only a moment, then finishing as if he were back on battle grounds, "I want land to leave in twenty minutes and air ready upon call." As he turned his back to me, starting his departure from the area, he gave one last command that triggered goosebumps along my skin, "You shall personally escort them, John, since you seem to enjoy this so deeply."

He halted briefly, likely to be certain I had heard. Despite understanding that he meant it as an insult, like I was the 'alien dreamer' and wasn't taking matters seriously, I couldn't help being eager to move forward, albeit nervous.

Only when I saw he had reached the entrance to the room and had turned on his way down the hall, did I spin around, glancing across the room before acting upon the instructions given. Being of a strong military background myself, I was accustomed to having a voice that would still a group on its own. Nonetheless, with this unsettled bunch, I had to resort to an over speaker.

"Hello, people! People? Hello!"

That worked.

"This is Major Shinn. I just wished to remind you what your job here is. Do you remember?" I asked with rhetoric sarcasm as I looked around at everyone to make my reprimand appear severe.

Some of the employees hung their heads, refusing to make eye contact as they returned to their desks, while others casually tapped away on their keyboards as if they had never ceased working. Noticing that I had actually received a few nods, I decided that my point had been properly made so I removed myself to finish my own tasks.

As I turned, my ears detected the hum that was filling the space again. Instead of paying too much heed, I rushed directly across the main hall to a more compact version of the room I just left and picked up a receiver hanging on the wall in my usual office, instructing four teams to prepare themselves for immediate leave and then another five to await in case there was need for reinforcement.

Once completed, I promptly clicked the machine off and with one stride, reached an identical one, using it in the same fashion to relay orders for those specializing in air-borne maneuvers. When I stopped to think about it, times such as these when I was focused on what I was doing rather than why I was doing it, I realized that I did very much appreciate my career.

True, it took me quite some time to get here and it had been a rough path, however, the end results were definitely worth the effort. The sense of power and control was a responsibility too great for many, yet for me, it gave stability and a sense of peace. The call ended soon and before my head caught up with my body's actions, I was already out of the room, halfway to the end of the hall which was exactly where I wanted to be heading...for at the end and on the right, was a nearly forgotten storage closet that would be perfect for calling Connie without any distractions or interruptions.

Upon reaching its door, I hesitated. Visually scanning to make sure nobody was about, I pulled a key from my pocket and put it into the lock. As it settled into the slot, I gave another scope of the area and then rapidly slung the entry open and slipped myself inside, shutting it tightly behind me without even bothering to switch on any lights.

I sighed as the darkness enveloped me. It wasn't that I needed to see; my cell phone lit up well. It was only that I was sometimes a bit paranoid, or so my wife said. I liked to think it was the right amount of precaution, but the teasing by others had me doubt this every so often. Sensible or not, I didn't feel comfortable calling her before making sure the space was empty. Not that I thought there would be anyone else hiding in the closet...

I swiveled to put my hand on the wall at my rear, feeling for the light switch which wasn't difficult to find. The bulb made a subtle clicking sound as it illuminated the space.Just as I figured, I was alone. Slipping my hand into my slacks, I retrieved the outdated flip phone from its pocket. Perhaps I was overly cautious at times.

I certainly didn't like the idea of being easily tracked. In the growing world of technology, the older the device, the easier to hide from the rest of the electronic and radio webs. I made a simple gesture that threw the device open and without the slightest thought, dialed my wife's number and slid the phone up to my ear. I tapped my foot impatiently with having to wait mere seconds for the ringing to stop and hear her voice on the other end.

"Hello?" she finally answered.

"Connie?"

"Hey hon, I'm on my way home right now. Sorry it's taken me so long," she continued calmly.

I paused at this unexpected reaction, then blurted, "Huh? Where are you at?"

"I left you a note on the-" she started.

"Oh yeah yeah," I recalled the paper I had seen next to the one that I had put up for her on my stop home, "I actually left you one too. I'm at work, sweetie," I explained.

"Oh," she paused. "What's up?"

I glanced down at my watch, failing to realize the time, "I have to hurry, but I wanted to let you know what happened."

"Alright, so tell me," she laughed.

"Well, there is an unidentified craft heading toward Earth," I spat.

She kept quiet. I could hear the leather of her car seat rubbing against her clothing as she shifted position. I should have expected this response. "And?" she finally prompted.

I sighed, "We believe that it is an alien craft."

Now I heard her sigh and could sense the aggravation in her tone, "John...are you sure it's we and not just you?" she spoke harshly even though I knew she didn't mean to be.

"Connie I'm sure of this," my own voice lilted, the echo of it in the closet reminding me of my sensitive position. I cleared my throat and reverted my tone, "It's not just me. I didn't even suggest it first."

The woman let out a long breath. Of the two of us, I was the controlled one, yet my excitement had gotten the better of me once again and I had brought her in prematurely. It was done now though. Babbling further would be pointless and do nothing to show her I was rational about the whole ordeal.

"You know that I believe in them- the ETs- just like you do," her words sounded sullen, "I...I just don't want you getting disappointed again."

I nearly dropped my phone as the sound of someone pounding on the wooden door next to me, the sudden noise producing a jump in my heart and sending my ears ringing. "Hold on, Connie," I whispered into the phone, then immediately lowered it to my side.

Cautiously pulling the door open, I was met with the face of an uncertain private. He came to attention at the sight of me, swallowing hard, his Adam's apple bobbing. I gave him a nod, allowing him to be at ease, "Yes?" I raised an eyebrow.

"Col. Jean wants to see you, sir," the man barked.

"Thank you, Private," I nodded again, otherwise motionless until I saw him off.

The young man clicked his heels and pulled attention once more before marching down the hallway and back from where he had come. When I judged that he was far enough away, I lifted my arm and returned the device to my ear, "Connie?"

"Yes, John, I'm still here," she seemed fatigued rather than genuinely agitated.

"I have to go. Keep your eye on your phone. I'll be in touch," my commanding officer persona had overtaken brain and body, diminishing my anxiety almost instantly.

"Okay, sweetie," Connie replied, losing any hint of annoyance, "I love you. Be careful."

"Alright, I will. I love you too," the words were true even though my voice was cold.

I dropped my arm, pushing the handheld back into its pocket. With a deep breath, I stepped out of the closet, shutting and locking it behind me. I took a moment to be sure I was collected and then took off in the direction of the young soldier. Perhaps fifty feet or so down the gray painted walls of the wide corridor, past the offices and where I had conferred with the colonel initially, there was a set of elevators.

Upon reaching their pristine steel, I pressed the up button, making the passage slide open and allowing me to step in before it sealed. One floor up, I walked out of the lift and a few yards down to the colonel's office. Forcefully, I rapped on the oak door and then politely waited for a response. After a few minutes passed without one, I pushed on it lightly, causing it to fall open just enough for me to catch sight of Col. Jean sitting behind a plain desk of medium size that matched his door.

He was leaned backward in his chair with a finger idly playing with the cord to the landline whose receiver he held to his face. He reached a hand out in my direction and motioned for me to come inside fully. I kept forward and came to attention just inside the oddly cozy room, eyes peering down at the man who had sat up in his seat upon my entry.

I stopped the salute when he repeated the gesture, my shoulders relaxing as I took a pace toward the smaller chair meant for guests. My vision remained trained on him the entire time and I noticed that for whatever reason, his age was showing poorly.

His brow was furrowed, creating deep creases in his forehead and his mouth was fixed into a permanent frown. I wondered if my perception was off now or if it had been before because I had known the man was getting along in years, yet had never really taken true notice of it until now.

The colonel had been staring off to the side as he listened to the person on the phone, grunting occasionally. Finally he spoke to them, saying, 'Of course. You've got it,' then slammed the device down and momentarily turned a stern glare on me before placing his focus on a set of papers laying on his table. "Sneaking off to call your wife, I see," he murmured, sight not directly on my person.

I said nothing while my brain tried to remind me that he didn't care. However, my emotions seemed to be winning over this evening.

The colonel suddenly burst into laughter, dropping the pen in his hand and smiling up at me,

"Hah! Relax yourself, John! Just because she doesn't work here anymore, doesn't mean she doesn't have clearance," he winked, well aware it was ill-advised that he had given her these permissions.

I was relieved. Like I said, I knew this, but a large part of me was always fearful of going against protocol or breaking rules, I guess you could say...something that obviously didn't affect my boss.

"Sit, John, sit," the man had retrieved his pen, keeping his eyes on the files between us, "So tell me, is Connie going to lend us a hand if we need it?" he mused.

Only with this, did I plant myself in the seat I had inched toward, rubbing my palms on my pants to be sure they were clear of any sweat and somehow managing a smile. "I suppose she would love to if this turns out to be what I hope it is," I answered absentmindedly.

Col. Jean stopped writing, lifting a brow, "What you hope it is?"

"Think, sir, think it is," I quickly rephrased.

"Mhm..." he brushed his bearded chin, "Well, I suppose we will see," he was jotting again, vision downward, "Prepare for the worst then, John. Let's have at it."

"Yes, sir," I rose from the chair and headed for the door. The two of us had known each other long enough that precise wording was not always necessary. It was obvious that he meant it was time to head out.

"Oh and John?" my boss caught me just as my hand hit the doorknob.

I twisted around, "Yes, Colonel?"

The man hadn't looked up to speak, "Don't get too excited," he said, starting to sift through the papers. Once more, the words unnerved me, but I proceeded.

Chapter 2: Connie

It wasn't that I didn't have every bit of faith in my husband, it was just...I really didn't want him to set himself (and me) up for disappointment, as he had done many times in the past. John was normally of a highly logical and rational mindset. However, occasionally, the dream that had been close to his heart since he could remember would get the better of him.

It was strange, considering I was the one known for letting my emotions control me. I guess we all had our moments. I was equally enthusiastic about extraterrestrial life and having careers in military and homeland security as he did currently and I had previously, we were closer and more likely to come across such discoveries. Even after leaving my positions in these fields, I retained many contacts who shared with me more than they were supposed to, including John's superior, Col. Jean.

John and I had actually met at work eight years ago. I had been serving as a physician and he had just received his first promotion as major. We met each other on happenstance. There was a battle overseas in which we were involved and I was caring for a wounded soldier.

Well, I was caring for several, but it was the one in particular that allowed the two of us to meet.

His name I only remember because my husband still spoke of him from time to time. Charles Leroy.

The new major had come by to check on him as the two had apparently been close for a couple of years at that point. John's friend had been caught in a pursuit that totaled his convoy yet somehow he managed to remain hidden in the wreckage, passed over by the eyes of enemy troops.

My confidence in his recovery had been shaky at best. Alongside severe lacerations on his abdomen, torso, and face, he endured massive head trauma. He had been floating in and out of consciousness for the past hour since his arrival.

John had found the time to come see the soldier and asked me for the prognosis. Immediately switching to a stoic doctor persona that was more for keeping me calm than the others, I shared the details of his bleak case. John had nodded gravely. Beneath his solid demeanor, it was clear he was upset.

"You should marry this one, John," the patient had awoken again. His voice was weak yet still loud enough for the both of us to hear.

John's eyes widened and he had rushed to his friend's side, kneeling next to the bed, "What the hell kind of nonsense are you talking about now?" he grinned.

Leroy slowly pushed his head over to face the major. Even such a simple movement caused strain on his body, and his chest began to rise and fall more quickly and laboriously. The man's eyes fought to stay open and he forced a smile.

"She's been-" he inhaled sharply, "Telling me stories to cheer me up," the cheery expression faded as he failed to keep his eyelids from dropping shut.

John said nothing. He only watched as the soldier in the bed beside him fell unwillingly into slumber once more, the breath in his chest gradually relaxing.

Charles never woke again.

I ended up telling John about the stories my patient had been referring to, which were all about alien theories and yes, how I very much believed in the idea of sentient extraterrestrial life. It seemed that both the major and I had dealt with degradation and mock brought about by our firm beliefs in sentient extra-terrestrial life.

After that realization, we began seeing each other quite often. We didn't officially begin a relationship until after both of us were able to return home from deployment, which took several months longer. The major immediately filled a new post, but I took a brief leave.

Afterward, I was stationed in the same area as John, working at a few different outposts; one of which was where he currently worked under Col. Jean. When our intimacy became too obvious, I decided to quit and instead open up my own practice nearby.

"I think it would suit you nicely," John reached his arm around my shoulder and pulled me closer to him in the booth at the restaurant we had chosen for date night that week.

"Yeah, I mean I didn't start my career wanting to be in the army anyway," I leaned into his embrace, simultaneously setting my fork down next to my half-eaten salmon.

"We wouldn't have to worry about compromising our jobs, you'd be your own boss, set your own hours," he pointed, taking a moment to kiss the side of my head, "And it'd be a more relaxed environment too. I know how much you hate stiffs," he chuckled that last observation.

"Alright, then," I laughed, nuzzling my head into the curve of his neck, "It's decided."

Suddenly, the man sat straight in his seat again, "I'm so glad you said yes."

"What?" my expression grew quizzical as I turned my torso so I could better face him.

Instead of simply rotating to match, John got up from the booth and stood at the end of the table with a sly smile on his face, "Well, the only reason you haven't married me is because of work, right?"

I cocked my head to the side. For a woman with her doctorate, I could be incredibly slow sometimes. As I gazed dumbly, the major pulled a palm-sized black box into view, setting it on the table in front of him. My first reaction was to mutter an obscenity and place both hands on the wood as if holding it for support.

Vision looking from the present, to the presenter, and then glancing around at the various other customers in the dimly lit building, I finally settled back on the gift as he opened it to reveal a dazzling diamond ring on a gold band. Its beauty was accentuated by the dark fuzzy velvet that lined its case.

"You already said yes, so," John cooed, carefully sliding the jewelry closer to me.

It'd been over four years since that day and we'd undergone many ups and downs, but one thing had never changed: our desire to discover life on other worlds. Sitting in my car, I wondered if it was the real thing this time.

I wanted to be excited and at the same time, didn't want to feel that pang of disappointment when it was found to just be a satellite or glitch in the system or one of another hundred possibilities. So I did my best to keep my hopes from rising.

In the silver sedan right behind my work building, I realized I was exhausted. I allowed myself a stretch and a yawn as I took in the darkness of the clinic now, both inside and out. I had been the last to leave. Walk-in day was always our busiest because for some reason, everyone decided they were ill on those days.

I appreciated the business, but I couldn't understand why people never made appointments anymore. Even so, it had been the mountain of paperwork on my desk that I hadn't made time to finish for days that had finally pushed me over the edge. I gave in, staying hours after closing to finish it all. But at least it was done now.

Rubbing my eyes and sighing, I realized I wouldn't be able to rest until the situation with John's

UFO was resolved. The constant cycle of getting excited, forcing myself not to, and then growing hyper again would not allow my heart to settle long enough for sleep.

I slipped my hand into my purse, retrieving the car key before cranking the machine to life. That really didn't matter though...not quite yet. I still had a half hour drive to get home anyway. Pressing my fingertips into my eyes, I re-situated myself in the seat.

I briefly glanced across my mirrors and then threw the car into reverse, pulling out of my spot and driving forward to the exit, taking a moment to turn the volume on my radio up. The late night host was talking about current music news. I switched to another station. Bleh, a slow song. I flipped to my next preset.

There was a classic rock song playing that I had heard a thousand times yet still couldn't get all the lyrics right. Looking up and down the side road where my office as well as several others were located, I waited for a couple of vehicles to pass before driving out onto the main highway. But I couldn't get my stomach to stop turning.

Ugh!

Inhaling deliberately, I cranked my stereo as high as it would go. I continued down the highway onto the interstate, constantly pushing down thoughts of what was actually occurring in the sky. Aliens? or just another letdown?.. I shook my head, letting anger take over any curiosity. This was not what I needed tonight! The day had been long and tiresome, but it had been productive. I didn't need and I couldn't handle this extra stress right now!

Hitting the interstate, I sped up to five miles over the speed limit and tried to keep my focus on the road. There were very few other vehicles out. We weren't in a densely populated area, but even so, it all felt too quiet.

It was as if everything was begging me to think about those frustrating matters...about something out there bigger than my own existence. I managed to get lost in thought while also remaining calm. Why was I letting this bother me so badly? Either it was or it wasn't. I knew they were out there. It was just a matter of time before everyone else knew it too.

The next twenty minutes were gone quickly. I had finally reached the end of my time on the four-lane and was on that last, long stretch of road to my home. As I journeyed through the seemingly endless rows of trees to either side of the pavement, I turned the music down until it was no longer audible. Cracking the windows, I let my hair out of its tail and slowed my pace, allowing myself to actually calm entirely.

My heart and stomach had settled; the night air sifting in and out of the vehicle was very soothing. Subconsciously, I took a hand from the steering wheel and started stroking my long brown locks. Pausing for a moment and smirking, I kept running fingers through the soft strands. It was another thing that I preferred about a civilian career: having my hair however I wished.

After a few moments, a yawn and droopy eyelids made me feel I was relaxing too much so I stopped playing with my hair and set my hand back onto the wheel, sight forward. A shiver passed over me and I realized just how cold that sweet evening air had been.

My fingers left their post again to press the buttons that closed the car windows. Then they moved on, to turn the radio back up. However, just as my hand touched the dial, my pocket vibrated and started to ring. I retreated my hand from the stereo and sent it to my jacket to retrieve the cellular.

My heart regained its excited pace as my eyes read the nickname 'hubs' on the small illuminated screen. John thought it was a bad idea to put obvious tags in your phone. Something about if a criminal captured the device, he could easily link people that way and find out too much about them. I had used the nick anyway.

A smile reached my face but my eyes rolled out of frustration. I inhaled and answered, "Hello?"

"Hey, Connie. It's me again," John sounded unsure of himself.

"Yeah?" I responded, trying to act neither eager nor aggravated.

"Hey, I-I want you to come up here," he continued.

I took a second to remove the phone from my ear and look at the time. I don't know why, though, since that detail wouldn't change anything. I returned the phone to my cheek, "Why?"

There was a pause and I knew John was trying to decipher my mood, "The colonel thinks that you could lend a hand if this turns out to be...well, you know, only if you feel up to it, that is..." he trailed.

We both knew that it wasn't my help that the colonel wanted. It was my company. For whatever reason, he wasn't entirely fond of John's ET love, but he liked to flatter me by waving his privileges as the boss around. Not that he ever intended on flirting with me nor did he dislike my husband in general. In fact it was quite the opposite.

He very much liked John, but I suppose he preferred me for not being a coworker...and for being of the female persuasion. At any rate, I was fully aware that John wanted me around for support and, if he did believe this was real, to take part in the experience...so it was really irrelevant whether Col. Jean desired my presence or not, just so long as I was allowed on base.

"Honey, I..." I wanted to say I was tired and didn't feel like all this tonight, but I hesitated to use the excuse because I also wanted to be there just in case, and of course, wanted to support my husband in either outcome.

"I know what you're going to say," John spoke up, "But please, I really do believe this is something."

Another pause. I looked down at the speedometer and realized I had slowed down to a crawl after starting the conversation. I looked off to the side of the road. There was a turn that led into a long gravel driveway with a quaint little home at its end. Lights were off and it didn't seem to have any activity about it.

"And even if it isn't...then it will be something interesting, I have no doubt," John resumed his speech as I pulled into the empty drive. I could almost see him winking at me.

I put the car into park and leaned back in my seat. My driving hand was now free and rubbing my temple. "Alright," I relented, "I'm just a few minutes from home. I'll be there in about-"

"Well, actually, we're heading out now," my husband interrupted, "I thought you could meet me nearby our destination?"

"Where do I need to go?" I formulated rapidly even though my train of thought had been thrown off.

"I'll send the map to your phone," John's voice had heightened and I was glad that I hadn't wrecked his mood completely.

There was a soft beep on his end and then a louder one on mine. I took the phone from my face long enough to see the file that was sent. I opened it and nodded to myself before talking into the device once more, "So just a bit farther from the walking trail in the desert then?"

"Right," John affirmed.

"Good thing for you all that it's night then, huh?" I poked, trying to show I wasn't upset with him.

He laughed somewhat nervously, "I suppose. Anyway, gotta go, we will be there before you. Don't get off the trail," he warned, "I'll have someone waiting there."

"I can take care of myself, you know?" I shot. The protest was automatic for me at this point.

"I know, honey," John cooed, "Just do this for me, alright?"

I sighed, "Fine."

"Are you rolling your eyes at me?" he asked.

"No!" I blurted and then chuckled at how well the man knew me, "I'll see you there."

"Okay, hun," he was smiling at my attitude, no doubt, "Bye."

Click.

I pressed the button on the side of the phone to turn off its screen and slid it down to my lap. The night was eerily still. I stretched out into a yawn, but as I readied my hands to steer again, I took a better look at the house whose drive I was in.

It was a home I saw and admired often. Its tidy yard was covered with bushes and flowers, some of which seemed to glow in the moonlight. The building itself was wooden. A simple log cabin style yet nice enough to show that it as an eloquent place to stay.

My eyes wandered to the swing set in the front yard to the side of the building. I always liked passing by that house during the afternoon for the simple reason of that swing set. The two young children, a girl and a boy of perhaps seven, who lived there would always be out either swinging there or making leaf piles at the bottom of the slide. I smiled at the thought of having children of my own one day...

My grin vanished as I remembered what it was I was supposed to be doing. I looked around me before reversing back onto the street behind me, traveling down the way I had come. This trip wouldn't be so bad. At the end of the road, it would be a different route to the desert than what I would take to get to my clinic.

Not more than a forty-minute trip...actually it was probably even shorter than that. Yawning, I decided to turn the music back up and absentmindedly reached for the empty coffee cup sitting below the stereo dials.

I tilted it back for a drink. Only then did I remember I had already consumed it all and I groaned. Oh well, there would be coffee at the base. Surely I could make it that long without the sweet nectar, I chuckled to myself.

Chapter 3: John

I found myself entirely too ready for this venture. Thankfully, an equal amount of nervousness had set in and the two emotions seemed to be properly counterbalancing each other.

I had already sent off a pair of armored personnel with their own teams, as well as readied an actual tank and its necessary crew. I was now huddled together with the corporal who served under me. We had worked together for about three years and she was excellent at her position: always prompt and thorough with orders.

Around us, a handful of black SUVs were being filled with heavily armed and shielded soldiers. As the troops finished piling in, Corporal Hewitt, in rapid succession, saluted me and jumped into one of the vehicles. I followed suit, scanning our current area and taking a seat in a separate van.

Just as my ass hit the seat, the machines were all off, traveling as if in a race. The troupe of military grade vehicles roared out of the guarded battery garage and onto the rocky drive, where their noise settled into a loud hum that could be heard over anything else in the nearly deserted outpost.

Our group passed more guards on their way out of the fences and after a few minutes, we were finally on the highway. If timing was correct, we would get to the landing spot just after the unidentified craft did.

Thinking of this, I told the driver to hurry more, which in turn caused the other drivers to speed up. I expected a great jump in pace, however, it hardly changed at all. I found that mildly disappointing and actually even felt that we ended up slowing down.

For a split second, the discouraging action made me worry that Connie would get there before us. All the thoughts and emotions in my mind immediately shifted their focus to my wife and concern outweighed any excitement I previously had.

What was I thinking? Sending her to meet us at the desert where a fucking UFO would be landing?? Putting it into words at that moment made me realize what an utterly imbecilic move it had been.

What was I thinking? The inflection on the question changed in my head. I knew what; my thought had been she would want to be near the operation and would probably protest if she hadn't been given word. Of course she would want to see this first encounter.

It wasn't like I sent her the direct coordinates, I had sent her to wait a few miles away and I had thought out the times beforehand, knowing we should be there prior to her at any rate. I said these things to reassure myself, but I couldn't keep visions of many horrible scenarios that could happen, and that did happen in multiple alternate realities.

"What the hell, Connie?" I barked at the woman as I approached the scene of the crash. The passenger side of her sedan was completely crushed, pushed off of the highway several yards from the massive RV she had rammed herself into while trying to switch lanes.

"I'm sorry!" the woman sobbed, cowering where she stood beside the wreckage of the car I had just bought her a few months ago for Christmas. She curled into herself, staring at the floor and refusing to gaze at her furious husband.

"What was the rush? What the hell could have been so important that you didn't see a damn camper before switching lanes? You know how badly you could have been hurt? Your vehicle is minuscule next to that thing!"

Every question flew from my mouth more heated than the last. I didn't care about the damn car, I just couldn't stand the thought of losing her. My parents had been my only living family except for her and they'd died just a year prior. She had a flighty sister, but besides that we were all we had and she meant absolutely everything to me.

At first, I didn't realize she had moved at all, but as her hands gradually kept lifting under her hung head, my eyes laid sight on what she was trying to show me. My heart began to slow, my posture easing as I took a step forward and took the ornate shadow box from her.

The borders were mahogany, carved with intricate designs, and beneath the glass were two title

31

cards, each with my parents' names written in perfect calligraphy. The placards divided the display into two parts, proudly showing the medals that my mother and father had earned while in the service.

"I knew the anniversary of their death was yesterday," Connie finally breathed, shyly looking up, but to the side and not at me, "But your birthday is tomorrow. I wanted to-" I cut the woman off by pulling her into a tight embrace, trying desperately not to allow my own tears to fall.

I shook my head violently all of a sudden, forcing my mind back to the present and bringing the attention of the soldier I sat beside. I ignored his glance and he politely returned to his stance. After his eyes were off me, I looked around the vehicle.

Everyone was tense despite the fact that most of these men had experienced brutal war scenes during their career. It had to be something about the great unknown- the many variables here that set them all at unease, which did nothing to help my inward crisis concerning my wife.

I took a deep breath in and slowly exhaled. No. Of course she wouldn't get there before us...she couldn't... Even if it didn't seem so to me anymore, we were going much faster than she would be although she was just a bit closer to that side of the desert than we were...

I shook my head again, both out of frustration at the thought, and out of determination that would not be the outcome. I opened my mouth to order the driver to increase speed again, but closed it as I leaned over his seat and saw the speedometer turned as high as possible.

I settled back down into the cushions and cleared my throat. Calm down, I told myself. Connie knew the dangers of such a situation. She knew procedure. She wouldn't put herself in any danger. She would know to remain rational and...

Shit. Grunting loudly as I remembered how reckless my wife could be, I moved, situated, and re-situated myself in the leather chair. This time I drew the gaze of the same man as well as the woman sitting in the passenger seat up front. I grabbed the handle above my head and tried to stare out the window whilst acting as calm as I could. But it was too late for that.

"Major?" the officer in the front questioned.

I swallowed and gave a curt nod which she returned, though her eyes lingered on me a few moments longer before hesitantly looking in front of her again. This was ridiculous. It probably wasn't even a manned craft...or armed...or even alien to Earth for that matter...

It struck me that it was, in fact, the most probable outcome for it to once again be some kind of misunderstanding. It did work to lessen my anxiety about my wife, yet it also gave me a familiar depressed feeling.

Exhaling, my heart started to calm; my thoughts quit racing. I allowed myself a sad chuckle, leaning back and observing our surroundings. Everything always seemed the same in the desert:

expansive amounts of nothingness and sand...lots of sand.

There was the occasional passerby and sometimes a spindly wire fence. Perhaps a cacti or two. Gazing out over the dunes, you could almost feel the heat even with a beautifully functioning AC. I mentally slapped myself for getting so worked up.

Connie was indeed the type of person to put herself in danger though, and I should have just let her meet me back at the base or better yet, not have told her anything until it was all figured out. That way there would be no questions. She'd have had no anxiety or aggravation...and no disappointment. Damn it. My inability to refrain from haste in the light of my personal interests was my worst character flaw. Had to be.

I found myself leaning forward to peer over the driver's shoulder again, just to be sure we were keeping up speed. Confidence in the revelation of the origins of this UFO gone or not, we still needed to get there as quickly as possible.

I wouldn't be perfectly settled until I saw my wife safe and could feel her in my arms. And with that short thought, I once more became nauseous with the fear of Connie arriving on site before us, and getting harmed or in some other sort of trouble. I swear if something happened to her, I'd never forgive myself...even after releasing a bullet inside my skull...

The groan that left my lips then was ignored by the others in the SUV even though I was sure they had heard it. I must really seem like a great leader to them right now, huh? What with squirming like this and all...

Suicidal ideation was not something I should be entertaining ever, whether it was an idle threat or simply a joke; not considering I had been down that road before...wanting so badly to end it all. Yet Connie gave me something new to live and fight for.

I might not be a romantic person, but damn, I loved that woman and it was my job to protect her. I have no doubt that I would resort to killing myself if I had allowed her to be subject to any sort of mistreatment that led to her death...because before then, I would suffer everything trying to get back to her and have her safe again.

With that in mind, I replayed every detail over and over, assessing every angle of the situation. It was still greatest probability that this was a slip-up and not an actual ET occurrence. Admittedly, it was my coworkers' out of character suggestions about it being so, that had fueled my earnest.

But like me, they could be mistaken as well. Indeed, they would only concrete their disbelief once it was proven to be something simple, I would be laughed at again, and perhaps I would also become mildly depressed.

However, I realized that knowing my wife was safe and that we were together would trump the feeling in the end, as it always did. At the very least, she was armed and not stupid enough to approach a group of strangers in this scenario, or attempt to board the craft herself. Everything would be alright. Mundane, perhaps, but fine.

Chapter 4: Connie

With a military background as strong as his, my husband had molded an outward persona that was both stern and stoic. However, the one thing that always managed to break through those defenses was when extra terrestrial life was involved.

In a professional environment, his demeanor would still express discipline, but just underneath, his entire being would be tickled with excitement. To those who were close enough to know this about him, like the colonel and myself, small changes in the tidiness of his work could be observed...unsettled noises or an occasional rushed thought...

Over the years, there had been discrepancies and misunderstandings regarding the discovery of ETs. Meteors, faulty machinery, compromised computer systems. An incident about two years ago concerning another country's spacecraft was even on the list. Apparently, Russia had launched a prototype vessel to conduct a few tests.

During these, the craft's navigational system had failed, and backup systems didn't boot up afterwards. Project workers were unable to fix either the primary or secondary controls, so instead attempted to manually override commands to bring the ship back home. However that didn't work either.

After the course of several hours, they were finally able to remove the machine from its path, landing it in the same desert that I was heading toward now. The prototype had shut down power just as it became surrounded with military vehicles including large weaponry apparatus, readying to fire.

Obviously since it was remotely operated, nobody was in real danger, though I suppose I had somewhat hurt in a sense, as John had given me a similar call on that day to the one received tonight. The only difference was in that past instance, I hadn't doubted his presumptions. Also, I had made it to base and had taken Col. Jean's company where I was told about the message from Russian officials about the mishap prior to the major.

When the matter was resolved, John's spirit had greatly fallen. He wasn't so much upset that there hadn't been an encounter with aliens as much as he was bothered in letting me down. When he came home that night, I had made him a cup of his favorite hot tea and sat on the sofa, holding him tightly and reassuring him that everything was alright.

He couldn't have known, and I would have had the same reaction...because even though I was disappointed, I knew he felt it more so than me. I was also aware that when he returned to work the next day, there would be jabs at him from those both on his level and above, including the colonel himself.

Even though he was a grown man who was not only used to these jokes, but knew that his associates meant no harm, they still struck a soft spot at times...especially after a failed possibility, whether he had made his thoughts about it open or not. At those times, it all came down to a repeating mantra in our heads:

Your stupid obsession with aliens has done nothing except hurt you.

John was a bit depressed for a while afterward. It had been the strongest of these false encounters that either of us had experienced. Of course, he was tough and intelligent so nobody except me ever caught onto his mood. I had begun to feel worried for his well-being just at the point that he snapped out of it and became his upbeat self once more. I remember him coming home, oddly cheery, and grabbing me, pulling me into a forceful, yet slow kiss.

"You know, if it weren't for this interest in aliens, where would the two of us be?" he smiled while carefully letting us fall into a loose embrace.

I returned the grin with one more devious, and threw myself back onto him, my lips locking passionately with his. As we both closed our eyes, our hands moved up and down each other, feeling out the most sensitive areas. Exchanging our tongues between moans and sighs, it was as if we on the midst of a sexual dance.

A coy smirk grew on my face as I looked out onto the dark road in front of me. Remembrance of those events seemed to have removed any worry or aggravation. Whether this was or it wasn't, we would be there together for the experience and see each other through whatever was to come. Besides, since that time, I had noticed that John had become more thorough when it came to these sorts of things.

His excitement hadn't died down; he just thought things through more carefully, it seemed. I, too, had been trying to be realistic. Even so, butterflies were fluttering in my stomach again and I felt something was really going to be different about tonight. I put my attention back on my journey and realized I had already reached the outskirts of the desert.

It seemed that the trip had gone by much more rapidly than it should have. Dropping my eyes to the speedometer, I saw that I was currently eleven miles over the posted limit. I slowed down to just under it as I nervously checked around me, wondering if I had been speeding even more while lost in my memories. It wouldn't have surprised me if it were true.

John had his flaws or as I preferred to say 'character gimmicks' and of course, then there were mine. One of which was an unintentional lead foot. I had been pulled over numerous times for speeding without even realizing I had been. Probably should have worked harder to make monitoring myself frequently a habit, but that was another thing about me. I was bad with planned acting, as a rule, tending to be a 'live in the moment' type of person.

"You have reached your destination," a computerized female voice informed me.

When it sounded, I stopped driving and glanced around the area. There were no lights anywhere. I peered hard into the dark, scanning for the outline of any people or vehicles. There didn't seem to be anything nor was there any movement. All I could make out were the stars dotting the sky down to the horizon, blacked out in places by the outlines of the dunes.

My high beams were on, so if there was someone, they should have been alerted to my presence. I flicked the switch to the left of the wheel, flashing my headlights a few times. Still nothing. Looking over to the GPS mounted on the dashboard to my right, I studied the path, wondering where exactly this meeting was going to take place.

Knowing my husband would have sent me to a location well enough away from everything anyway, I kept on driving down the path past the beginning of the walking trail. Maybe I was just too far out of sight that whomever was supposed to come out to me wasn't able to see my vehicle.

Ugh. I sighed after several minutes, slowing the car and pulling off the side of the gravel and parking. My sight remained clear of any new shapes, moving forms, or lamps. No doubt now that I had been speeding excessively and had arrived sooner than the soldiers. Although...my vision rested on the radio clock and processed the math.

Hm...perhaps a bit sooner, but not enough to make much of a difference. I did another visual search. Nope. Oh well. I would just have to lay back and wait. Most of the physical manifestation of the excitement and frustration concerning the night had stopped, so I might even be able to grab a nap during this low-time. It would certainly be better to have some rest before anything else happened, even if it was just a call letting me know of a failed experiment or whatever.

I put the lights on dim, cracked all four windows, and locked the doors. Reaching down below my seat on the left, I found the position controls and pushed it into a recline. Then I unbuckled myself and lay backwards, adjusting my arms and legs until I was fairly comfortable. As I closed my eyes, I remembered the P38 that I kept in the glove box.

With a grunt, I sat up again to reach over to the small compartment in the front passenger area. The curved door fell open the instant I pressed the release, exposing the oddly shaped handgun that resembled a toy. I picked it up, sliding its chamber to make sure it was loaded before closing it and placing it upon my lap. I slammed the glove box closed and returned to my previous resting position.

A handful of different half-thoughts and musings floated around my head as I tried to fall asleep. They ranged from acknowledging how tired I was to fantasizing about meeting an extra-terrestrial, to realizing it was time to clean the oven already. I wondered what aliens really looked like. Maybe there were many different races or species. Did I turn the coffee pot off that morning? Oh I think it had an auto-off function. I couldn't believe I finished all that shit today...

I hoped John was okay...

"Huh?!" the word came out more a choked breath than an actual question or exclamation.

I jumped forward in my seat, jolted awake by the sound of powerful rapping on the glass next to me. Still partially asleep, I extended my arm to open the door and greet whatever personnel had finally arrived. However, the moment my fingertips grazed the handle, my brain finished waking up and I remembered that I was still in the middle of the desert and why.

So I ordered my hand to get ahold of the weapon in my lap instead. Taking a more controlled breath, I squinted through the tinted window and into the darkness. Whoever had knocked, had immediately retreated a few steps backward to stand watching for any response from the vehicle's passenger.

I looked harder at the person. It was a man. He was a a bit over an average height: 5'11" or so, and his skin was extremely dark, making the deep hue of his hair seem light. I couldn't really make out any other details other than he wasn't wearing a uniform. I only knew this because his clothing was loose rather than fitted.

He stood there silent and motionless. I could barely see the whites of his eyes against his shadowed features and they showed that his vision was resting upon the car. I was aware he couldn't see me directly due to the high tint of the windows. It was a bit heavier than was now legal, but I'd never been given trouble because of it.

Studying the space behind him and then the rest of the desert around us, I saw that there were yet to be any vehicles, lights, or other people besides this one guy. Was he even a soldier? Maybe he did wear a uniform and my eyes were failing me in the night. But from which direction had he come?

I suppose he could have walked over the horizon to me...or once more perhaps my eyes were failing in the dimness... He shifted position then, turning to look back behind him. He paused as he stared and then took a couple uncertain steps away from my vehicle. It looked like he was about to leave. I inhaled and took tighter hold of the pistol in my right hand, using my left to pull the door handle and throw it open, before curling that hand on the gun as well.

Rising from the vehicle in my strongest stance, I placed my attention on him and set every nerve in my body on high alert. As I stood, the man spun around to face me. I had my weapon aimed, body situated behind the door for extra protection. The stranger kept the same stance as when I first saw him. Slowly, he extended his arms all the way down to his fingers at his sides, and then just as deliberately, lifted them up and formed a 't' with his body...then he stopped moving entirely.

I blinked awkwardly at this gesture and applied a slight pressure to the trigger under my fingertips. It took a moment for me to understand he was only doing this to show he lacked any defense and therefore to comfort me, though his expressionless face was still a bit unnerving.

"Who are you?" I demanded.

Chapter 5: John

Of course...Of course this would happen. Fucking damn it! And I knew it was my fault entirely. There was no pinning this on another one of the personnel or even simple happenstance. Despite determining that it was hasty to have alerted my wife of what was going on so soon, and even more reckless that I had asked her to meet me out in the field instead of safely inside the base, I had continued to stress about reaching the destination before Connie so much that I had ended up distracting the driver.

Instead of remaining patient and waiting for us to get there in due time, I had once more acted in earnest. It only added to the list of stupid mistakes I had been putting together in my head from this evening alone; this one probably being the worst, since we absolutely could not have traveled any faster. A younger man, he might have been, but our driver was excellent at what he did. Nonetheless, his age and the fact that he was fairly new to his position at our station was clearly causing this incident to upset him deeply.

Not in the sense that he was bothered by the actual events themselves, rather he believed he was to blame for them, and furthermore felt the accident would be seen as a lapse in performance on his part and therefore might affect his career. Worry showed through his attempts to remain calm and keep the situation from progressing, and I was too focused on my own guilt to offer him any sense of peace or stability, knowing it was my doing and not his. He was just too fresh to realize the truth.

We had been informed only moments before reaching it, that there was a block to our pre-determined route due to an incident involving a semi that swerved to avoid hitting another vehicle. It had swung too violently and caused a collision between its trailer and two cars in the opposite lane. Like dominoes, three more oncoming vehicles piled up into the mess, two on one side and one on the other.

The funny thing was that the car that had pulled out in front of the truck...the one he had fought to keep from hitting...had gotten away scot-free, not even stopping for the crash behind him. Instead, he simply carried on his way...what an ass. Emergency ambulatory, police, and fire teams were soon on site, the flood of vehicles and workers making it difficult to traverse the area with enough speed to properly stay on target.

If it had happened anywhere else, our convoy may have been capable of bypassing the crowd and off-roading past the mess. However, the small stretch of road, known for congestion, was lined with fences and trees, so with the added bustle, we were forced take an alternate route. Due to our proximity, this meant that we had to turn ourselves around and travel several minutes back to find said route.

Admittedly, this was bad enough in increasing my stress about Connie, but still, it wasn't what had really set me into the near frantic state that I was currently in. No, it was the following occurrence that had me losing my shit directly below my perturbed exterior. There had been two different paths we could have taken after returning to the main thoroughfare.

One, I had traveled many times to get home, so I instructed the driver to use it. Without arguing, he informed me that the other way was slightly faster with a brief explanation as to his reasoning. Rather than relent to his expertise and letting him do his job, or even simply using my power to order him in continuing on the route I had chosen, I started in at him angrily about my own experiences on his supposedly quicker path.

I had leaned forward in my seat, putting my head next to his, and basically barked at him about how horrible the road there was and how dangerous and so forth, though I suppose that my voice hadn't honestly been too loud, just harsh. Regardless, none of it had been necessary. I could have just left it alone...could have spoken my piece and carried on.

But I let my own fear and frustration overcome me, allowing it out on the driver who had done nothing wrong. It was my idiocy in doing so that took his attention, causing us to fall victim to a wreck ourselves, delaying us from reaching Connie in any sort of timely manner and concreting it in my brain that she would be there before us, possibly in danger.

We managed to ram heads with the only other vehicle coming on that highway probably for miles, when the man in front of me had jumped into the opposing lane to pass a slow moving truck because of my shouting at him about going too slowly. Nobody was hurt, thankfully, except maybe my pride. I had ceased growling as soon as our SUV hit the oncoming car, watching the rest of our team move forward without us, though they slowed their pace.

Right when the passengers and myself recovered from the jolt of the impact, the radio clicked. One of the other members from ahead was checking in as to our status and seeing if there had been any change in orders. I answered the call, instructing them to carry on without us. While I did so, our driver rapidly hopped from the SUV, rushing to confirm the safety of those in the truck before handing them a card from his pocket which I knew to contain a number for them to contact about the collision.

He had returned to his seat, reversed, and then pulled around the scene and off onto the path I had traveled on many occasions...ironically in order to get home to my wife sooner. I hadn't needed to command him to do any of it, it was basic protocol that should such an incident occur where the civilians were unharmed, we were meant to push onward after sharing the appropriate information for them to get help.

And, since he surely saw the accident as his own mistake, he didn't question my word about which way we should go any longer, opting to just take the route I had preferred. I didn't really care at that point about the argument yet neither did I relent and take his judgment, still certain that my own choice was better. The rest of the trip was completely silent and I sat staring out the window for its duration, wondering if I was imagining the disapproval in the minds of those riding alongside me or not.

Of course, they weren't going to voice it at that moment if they did feel so, seeing as I was their commanding officer. At least I had that in my favor, I thought as I continued gazing outside with the demeanor of a reprimanded puppy. My concern for my wife worsened, yet I remained quiet and barely moved. I had to, since I had already created this extent of havoc; I wouldn't be responsible for any other problems.

My mind did briefly leave its focus on Connie's well-being to plead silently to whatever spirit or force of fate may be out there, that the night did end up holding something...something fascinating and something positive. In the case that it did, nothing else that had happened this day would matter.

Although the largest desire should have simply been that my wife was unharmed and left alone, my brain had eclipsed that and realized I needed her to be happy as well...pleased by the events of the night so that there couldn't be any reason for for me to dwell on any of the negativity.

Chapter 6: Connie

"I'm called Malook," the dark-skinned man answered me calmly, his arms still outstretched in the air at his sides.

Without turning my head, I rolled my eyes around in their skull to scan for any sign of others out in the desert. Once again, there was nothing to find. As my vision settled back on the strange man, I studied him. I had been correct about his clothes: they were no uniform.

In the darkness, it was hard to make out their colors, but my best guess was a pale brown and they appeared to be all one piece; like robes, almost. There seemed to be a few different layers of the cloth folded over upon itself and it was free-formed, flowing just past his knees.

His facial structure was strong except for his thin, pointed nose. His jawline was prominent as was his chin. His hair was long and pulled back into some sort of a loose bun and was just a shade lighter than his flesh. He was neither tall nor short, fat nor thin. He definitely wasn't a soldier, however was far too clean and well-kept to be a homeless wanderer.

The fabric he wore was strange, yet it was his odd assortment of features that really had me boggled. His look was quite unique to anything I'd ever come across, specifically the green orbs he'd been focusing on me with.

"I don't intend for any trouble," he stated plainly, "I'm only looking for help." The man seemed to speak perfect English despite his exotic appearance, though he did bear an unfamiliar accent. He had to be a foreigner of some sort. But why the hell would he be alone out in the middle of- my curiosity burned greater then. Was he from whatever craft it was that John had seen earlier?

"Mull-" I started questioningly.

"Malook," he repeated.

"Right," I gave a curt nod, not bothering to hide my scrutiny, "What are you doing out here?"

"I-" Malook's head turned slightly to the side like he was looking behind him for support. My gaze followed; it was just the two of us. "I apologize if I've broken any of your laws," he spoke nervously, "It wasn't our intention to land, but we've had trouble with our equipment."

"Our?" I barely caught the wording.

The man hesitated, "Yes...my companions and I," he said finally.

It wasn't our intention to land, the words repeated in my head. He had to be part of what all the fuss had been about this evening. Now to tell where he- they had come from. Were they extraterrestrial aliens? Or just aliens? Even with his unusual appearance, he still looked entirely human. "Where are you coming from?" I tilted my head, weapon still aimed firmly upon the stranger. Except for to turn his own head and shift on his feet, he had remained unmoved at the other end of the P38's barrel...until I asked that.

He took a handful of small, quick steps forward, arms falling a few inches from their strict positioning. In my mind, it was the beginning of a dart in my direction so I shook my gun at him, simultaneously trying to backpedal. I had always had the heart of a healer and viewed offense as a last resort. Therefore, it wasn't much of a surprise that my body's natural response to retreat failed, as I was already backed against my vehicle.

With the attempt, I tripped, falling into my car and hitting my head on the frame at the roof. The collapse caused me to lose hold on the pistol, and it dropped somewhere on the ground just outside my door. On my way down, my brain caught up to the fact that Malook had not bound for me. Those couple of paces had been all he had taken until he saw my accident; and only then had he rushed forward.

The moment it was over, I lay on my butt, my back halfway reclined and my legs in a scramble, hanging out the open vehicle. The man was towering over me, his almost luminescent emerald eyes staring downward, stirring fear in my being for the moment. But then, he reached out, offering an open palm with a subtly concerned expression. Although I furrowed my brow, I still returned a thankful smile, albeit a weak one, upon realizing his kind gesture.

Grabbing hold of his hand, I let him help me to my feet. When I was lifted enough that I was able to grab onto the sides of the frame I had fallen through, I let go of him and pushed myself up the rest of the way. Standing once more, my mind returned to the fallen handgun, however as I turned to find it, I saw that the man was already bent over, picking something up off of the sand...surely my weapon.

Before I could formulate a plan, the man was upright, the steel contraption in hand. He stared at it for several seconds as if it was telling him something important, but eventually he just shook his head and put his attention back to me, "Here," he said, holding the gun out.

I reached with the utmost caution and retrieved it, dithering internally about what to do next. The man had been compassionate, helpful, and even chose to remain defenseless. I probably should have kept him at a distance despite. Nonetheless, instead of turning the pistol on him, I slid it down to my side. "Your name is very unusual," I said, completely unsure of the situation.

The alien chuckled, taking a few calm strides away from me and the vehicle, "I suppose you would think so."

"I'm Connie," I introduced as I stretched out my empty hand. He blinked twice before finally raising his own, and joining it with mine in a handshake. I hadn't been sure if he would know what the greeting was, as I had begun to think that he was, in fact, an ET. "So," I spoke as our arms fell at ease, "Where is it you and your crew are from?"

He inhaled sharply, swallowed, then exhaled. His head cocked to the right with me in its sights, "I feel like you may not believe me."

I froze, heart rate jumping for the umpteenth time tonight. The statement was the only confirmation I needed: he was from a different planet...a different galaxy maybe, somewhere in the cosmos. This was it...this was the day John and I had dreamed of for years...had countless conversations about and fantasized over. It was happening now.

Excitement overtook upon the realization that I was standing in the middle of the desert with a sentient extra-terrestrial life form. And he looked human! And spoke our language? Knew our greetings? Or at least the handshake. So Earth had been studied by aliens...but for how long? And to what end? I stepped forward, mimicking his movement until I was next to him. I twisted my face to his and beamed, looking him dead in the eye, "I might surprise you."

He put his head straight again, "Our planet is called Galdelier; its system, Trinnd." His vision narrowed while reading my expression to confirm my belief or disbelief. He must have seen that I trusted his words, because his demeanor relaxed, "Your people have apparently not made the discovery of us yet," he finished the thought as he turned around to overlook the horizon like I was.

I walked sideways, stopping a couple of feet to his left. The desert was still dead. Where the hell was John? Where was anybody else? "You've been studying us?" I asked quietly, not letting any concern show.

Malook nodded, "Your 'Milky Way' and Trinnd are actually very close...in respectful comparison to how large galaxies are," the man laughed softly at the last part, "Besides Galdelier, Earth is the only other planet we have found with beings of a similar evolutionary status to our own. We've been studying it for the better part of a year now, in your time," he explained, "Like I said before, we weren't meant to land. We had a problem with our computers."

"I get that..." I responded in a low voice, recalling how many times faulty equipment had disappointed us. The alien cut his eyes at me and I almost snorted at how he could tell that there was a bigger story behind my simple affirmation, "We've had crafts from other countries on Earth unintentionally land around here because of issues with their computers."

Malook nodded in acknowledgment, then shook his head and steered the conversation back to his original point, "Do you have people who will help us?" he inquired almost shakily.

"We...um," logic suddenly caught up with me and I was afraid the friendly man and his companions wouldn't be treated well by our fair Earthlings; more so I knew they wouldn't be, "My husband is on his way..." I trailed. "He works for our government. They'll...they should be able to help, but-"

"Would you like to see it?" Malook interrupted me suddenly, inciting an awkward pause in our dialogue.

"Huh?" I gaped.

"Our ship," the alien chuckled. "Would you like to see it?"

Of course I want to see it! my mind screamed...but the more rational part of me questioned his abrupt change of subject when I was struggling to explain what might happen. Did he understand my trouble? Maybe he realized during my tries to answer his simple question that I really didn't know if our people would actually help him, so he had decided to just stop me and wait for them, since he knew now that they were coming anyway.

Or did he think I was covering up what they would do to him and his allies? He could have caught on to the possibility and thought it best to capture me in case it could play to his advantage. I shook my head at that last thought. No, I really didn't believe that. "I would love to," I answered at last.

His lips curled into a polite grin and then started the trek into the distance where both of us had been gazing. Before following after, I glanced down to the gun in my hand, tightening my fingers around it. Walking on sand was annoying and somewhat difficult. Fortunately though, this particular batch was combined with a fair amount of dirt to give a stronger push-back. The mixture allowed for our feet to have a firm enough foundation that it didn't feel like falling every time we put a foot forward.

After two, maybe three minutes, we came over a small dune. I figured it wasn't far past that point where the craft would be, so I peered intently into the new surroundings. There, fifty or so yards out, I saw what appeared similar to one of our own space shuttles resting in the distance. It was of an incredibly dark gray color that could have been easily confused with black.

I wouldn't have seen it at all if it hadn't been for a tiny light on the side of it next to what looked like a door, complete with a small ramp leaning between the bottom of the closed entrance and the sand below. It struck me as funny because it somehow resembled a porch light.

Malook hadn't spoken the whole way except to tell me to be careful or watch my step. Likewise, I remained silent save to respond with a 'yeah' or 'thanks.' The stranger seemed awfully well-mannered and I had quickly become fond of his personality. I did hope for the best possible outcome for him and his counterparts. Even so, as we neared the spacecraft, an unsettling apprehension began to grow in my belly.

I recounted the sudden shift in conversation earlier and reminded myself that I had only just met the man. That, in addition to his being, or at least claiming to be, an alien from outer space certainly meant I shouldn't have been entertaining his company like this.

I heard John's voice in my head: What in hell's name were you thinking? You're going to get yourself killed one day!...I don't know what I would do without you. With those thoughts, I halted. My husband had always told me I had no sense of self-preservation and maybe that was true. I looked at where I was and chastised myself for ever daring to say something about his excitement getting the best of him.

"Are you alright?" Malook's calm voice broke through into my brain. He was a good many paces in front of me and turned to the side to face my direction.

"Yes, it's just..." I tore my eyes from the space ship, over to the man, then glanced back from where we'd come. I couldn't see my car anymore even though I knew it lay just a short walk past that dune. The coldness of the night sunk in rapidly in that moment, giving me a shiver. I was alone in the presences of strange extra-terrestrial aliens with human bodies. How eerie it was finally dawned. Where are you, John?

"It's okay," the soothing voice sounded again, "I understand if you're nervous. You don't have to come any further."

I just stood there, entirely still except for eyes blinking in rapid succession while darting between the man and the spacecraft. I gripped at the handgun I had been holding low, and felt the grooves of the handle while I rubbed its butt with the tip of my thumb. The truth was that I didn't know what exactly would happen when John and the others arrived and thereafter.

This might end up being my only chance to see the machine and maybe meet the other aliens as well. Even if it proved dangerous, I don't think I would ever be okay with passing the opportunity up. Besides, I had a weapon. It wasn't like I was helpless, right And I had come this far...

My expression crept into a beam and I stepped forward to the man, who then continued leading the way. When we reached the outside of the ship, right outside what I had already presumed to be the entrance, Malook held up his hand, signaling me to stop. He then raised the other one and put it on top of a panel that I hadn't noticed before, beneath the light.

The door began sliding upward at his touch. My grin grew wider, but only for a moment...only until an unforeseen roar of engines sounded behind the two of us. Bright lights bounced up and down, shining in our direction. Both our bodies spun simultaneously to their source.

Chapter 7: John

Our tires spun out in the sand as we finally reached our destination. The rest of the team had made it there only moments before us, judging from the spirals of dust in the air. It somewhat relieved me that they had, yet at the same time I wished they would have arrived much earlier so that someone was guaranteed to have located my wife in time.

As it stood, I knew she was on the scene since we had driven by her vehicle already, though it was farther down the trail than I had asked her to go...figures. Her car was there, but she was not, so my apprehension was still left unsettled as I didn't yet know if something had happened to her or if she was with one of the troops who had carried on without us after the crash.

Our driver had looked at me in the rear view mirror when the sedan was in view, seemingly uncertain about saying something after spotting the empty vehicle. He did, however, but only my name. It was enough for me to understand he meant it as a question about if I wanted him to stop or not. I answered by simply shaking my head and instructing him onward with a pointed finger.

Connie, where the fuck are you?

Tearing over that first dune, we all laid eyes on the unidentified craft resting just beyond...the source of the night's frustration, uncertainty, and excitement.

"Oh...my...god..." the soldier in the front seat was the first to spot two figures standing beside the huge machine. Leaning forward and peering closer, I made out the form of dark-skinned, dark-haired man in strange brown clothing. Within a friendly proximity of him was a woman...my wife.

"Dammit, Connie!" I couldn't contain myself from complaining aloud.

The outburst had drawn all eyes in the SUV to me, but I no longer cared. What the hell was she thinking? The fuck was she doing out there? and with a stranger??? Why couldn't she listen to me or even consider how dangerous her actions could be? Where was the handgun I had bought for her? Had she even pulled it out before leaving her car? The angry thoughts rushed in my head, the emotion amplified by how frightened I was that the person I cared about most had quite possibly been placed in the midst of a lethal ordeal.

The vehicle I rode in skidded to a sudden halt. All passengers including myself jumped from it, though I was the only one to run past the safety of its wide open doors. Looking at the spaceship I was prowling towards, I studied its appearance without even the slightest twinge of excitement. My focus was on Connie. My only reasoning in gathering details about the machine was to ensure familiarity with the territory I was approaching.

The thing looked strikingly similar to something I had seen in a science fiction movie but never in reality...not exactly, anyways: perhaps a mesh of fiction and actuality. Imagine an ovular shaped ship with a pointed bow and small wings on either side that also ended in sharp tips. The entire machine was incredibly sleek...silverish and dark, appearing to be constructed from some form of metal, though I couldn't be sure. Altogether it wasn't too large considering what it was. Perhaps fifty feet in length and another thirty or so in width. A small white light shone between where my wife and the strange man stood.

"MAJOR! What are you doing?" the corporal's voice sounded behind me.

I had assessed the UFO's exterior before making it even a few feet past our convoy, which had piled into a defensive half-circle. All of its soldiers had gathered themselves in arms and were awaiting orders. I stopped right there in front of them all. I hadn't even fully realized that my hands were already on my 9mm and had it halfway raised into the air. My ears fell to the men and women behind me; my eyes stayed put on the scene in front.

"That woman is my wife," I informed the corporal with loud yet somehow calm words, "You stay here and take command," I continued. "Roger 2, Charlie 3," I ordered five different men from two different teams to walk toward the craft with me.

While I had been talking, my sight had remained focused, picking up that both Connie and the man I assumed to be from the spaceship, were both looking at me. I noticed that she was, indeed, carrying the P38 I had gifted her. The two remained motionless, though we were too far apart for me to see what expression either wore. I had barely been able to make out the vague description of the stranger, and just enough to know that it was my wife with him.

I wondered why she, at least, didn't begin leaving his side upon seeing me coming. Not that it would have been a good idea- in case we hadn't spotted who she was or he took such an action as threatening. If he had, the soldiers might have attacked if I weren't able to instruct otherwise. However, even though Connie had full knowledge of these things, running to meet me or any of the other soldiers would be the kind of ill-thought thing she would do. I mean, look at where she was now.

The small team and I kept on, the men with me all had assault rifles and two more carried shields. We all wore bullet proof armor under our clothing and the others had helmets adorning their heads as well. When we neared the man and my wife, I suppose Connie finally began to understand what was going on, because she actually started walking then.

After she had come a few yards closer to us, I saw the stranger glance at the ship behind him before placing his hand on the side of it for a brief moment. The motion caused the partially open entry to seal. Once the action was complete, he dropped his arm and followed Connie, but at slower pace.

First instinct made me tighten hold on the gun in my hand to better my aim. And even after I put together that he had waited and made his stroll casual in order to not raise suspicion of intended harm, I kept my weapon ready. Just as Connie and my little group reached each other, the rifles shifted and clicked, seeing that it was now only the stranger in their path.

I quickly threw my arm up to signal the soldiers to wait, lowering my own gun as I grabbed my wife's wrist and shoved her behind one of my shielded companions. I knew doing so would piss her off, but sparing her feelings was not high on my priority list at the moment. I mostly ignored her squeaking my name, my vision remaining intent upon the oddly-dressed man that had been beside her up until that point. He stopped then, carefully lifting his hands and looking at me with the same intent I had placed on him.

"Is this your machine?" I demanded.

As he nodded his response, I heard my wife emit a grunt and felt her hand on my arm, "John," she spoke hurriedly, tugging at my wrist, "Everything's okay. This is Malook. They just need help."

"They?" my eyes leapt from the man to look just above him at the ship.

"My crew and I don't want to cause any trouble," he said, drawing my sights down again, "We've had a problem with our computers and were forced to land."

"Where are you and your people from?" I didn't miss a beat with my interrogation.

"He says a different solar system or galaxy, I think," Connie was whispering at my side, just loudly enough for the stranger to hear, "A planet called Galdelier."

Oh shit, the exclamation echoed louder in my head than my other worries ,which had gradually started to wane upon having my wife once more. Was this a truthful confirmation of sentient alien life standing with us?

"Are any of you or your craft armed?" I somehow managed to continue. My wife was still holding onto my wrist, though she had ceased pulling on it. I glanced over at her, narrowing my eyes and giving a low growl. She frowned and grunted, but let go of my arm.

"Yes," the alien admitted and I could feel tension in the men beside me build at his answer, yet the stranger himself seemed to remain calm. His arms were out to the sides, palms open, "I have a gun inside my tunic," he elaborated, "It's held against my chest on the left."

I twisted my neck and nodded at one of the soldiers who, in turn, threw his SCAR over his shoulder by its strap and walked toward the alien. The man, the creature, whatever he was, kept his stance unwavering as the soldier retrieved the weapon and handed it to me, before returning to his position next to my wife.

I finally lowered my own pistol which seemed to please Connie. Turning the alien weapon over in my palms, I observed that it, just like the man and the spaceship, looked extremely familiar to things our own knew or had conjured up on multiple occasions. It was much lighter than the 9mm that I was accustomed to carrying, but was of similar dimensions. Rather than the typical black color, though, it was a deep shade of maroon.

"Careful," its owner said cautiously as he watched me fiddle with the device.

For some reason, I took offense to this polite warning. Instead of responding to show such thought though, I simply looked for a way to open the pistol to see what kind of ammo was inside. However, there didn't appear to be anything comparable to a chamber on it.

"On the bottom of the handle," the man spoke in the same soft voice.

I lifted my gaze long enough to see that he almost brought his arms down to illustrate, but caught himself before he did, and kept his submissive position. I rotated the weapon around to see a thin indented line around the base of the butt. Twisting it failed at first. However, when I applied more pressure and tried again, the hidden chamber responded, a long slot shooting out of the handle.

Inside were no bullets of lead or any other familiar material, but a cylindrical glass container holding something that looked like crystal in its casing. Around the gem were several tiny wires sparking with electricity. Despite how interesting it all was to me, this wasn't the time for curiosity. I kept the 'ammo' and the gun itself apart, carefully placing them inside deep pockets on my vest. I settled the alien in my vision again, "What instructions have you left your crew?"

He opened his mouth, yet hesitated to speak, "I don't understand."

My vision narrowed. The word had stuck out to me: understand. He understood English. I had already figured they were simply studying us, learning about us and our planet for whatever end they may have in mind. However, his mastery of our language was impressive. "I'm assuming you're the one in charge," I clarified, noticing that he blinked his eyes into a lifted brow at my presumption, "What have you told the rest of the passengers on your ship to do in your absence?"

"Only to wait," he answered.

"But they are armed?" I prodded.

Another small pause before he responded, "Yes."

"How many more are there aboard?"

His hesitation lasted longer this time and when he finally replied, it wasn't an answer, "Please leave them alone. They're not going to leave the ship. They won't hurt anyone." His expression softened, green eyes pleading silently with my own. He had been nothing other than kind, it seemed. Even with the opportunities already presented to him to attack or become hostile, he had stayed peaceful.

His request for the rest of his crew to be left out of everything, to me, further proved their amiable nature, though we did not know what that ship was capable of overall or what they were doing inside. Nonetheless, what happened to any of them was not my call. I looked from him to my wife. She also knew this, but I could tell she wanted to promise that they would stay safe.

I grabbed hold of the radio that was attached to my vest at the shoulder, twisting a dial on it a few swatches to the left before clicking the button beside it and connecting the invisible lines between the colonel and myself. I summed up the situation with the the UFO and the alien I had been speaking with. Before letting go for his reply, I requested that no attempt be made to enter the craft until further information was received.

There was a pause and I could picture Col. Jean leaning back in his chair, stroking his chin with his forehead creased as he considered what he wanted to do. At last, he returned the call, granting my request for the time being, with the compromise of all current teams staying on site save for the one meant to bring me and this stranger to base.

The rest would stay behind to guard the area and additional troops would be sent in in to assist. The strange human eased up slightly at the end of the communication and Connie offered him a weak smile. She had been silent for the larger part of the meeting because she was well aware of procedure. I also felt she didn't want to belittle my authority.

I leaned toward her and whispered, "What did you say his name was?"

"Malook," she whispered back.

"Malook?" my voice was directed at the alien again.

"Yes?" he replied, his own tone reserved and strong while his demeanor appeared to have become stoic.

"You'll have to come with us. Privates Davis and Chressler will assist you to our vehicle." At my words, the two named soldiers left their spots and stepped toward the alien. Davis pulled a pair of handcuffs from the loops on his pants before grabbing Malook's arms and forcing them behind him.

"Connie, go back to your car with Lewis," I nodded at the man who had been standing beside her during the course of the conversation. "Meet us there," I ordered.

My wife's grin flashed away as she attempted to gain a serious composure. Then, she started off with the soldier, leading the way to her car. I let out a previously withheld exasperated sigh in her direction as they trod off. I should have sent her to the base in the first place. It was reckless and thoughtless of me not to do so. Regardless, it was the extent of her own recklessness that astounded me.

Davis and Chressler went through my view then, each with hands on one of the alien's arms. Malook. His amazing calm during the whole evening had been a blessing. Judging his habits- the way he stood, the way he talked...even where he looked and how he had automatically put himself into a surrendered position at the start of it all...I surmised that he was some sort of military personnel himself.

That would also make sense as to his being part of whatever venture his people were on. After he was loaded into the SUV, the rest of us climbed in, spending the return trip in anxious silence.

Chapter 8: Connie

Being granted clearance didn't mean I could just jump in and roam about, butting my head in wherever I wanted, especially since I shouldn't have been allowed inside the base in the first place. I still had to follow protocol and the chain of command and as a doctor, that meant doing medical work comparable to my status.

There was already a physician employed at the outpost, but his hours were few and far between. He worked mostly on call with a nurse practitioner and a handful of nurses always on hand in his stead. This particular station did not see a lot of traffic in the hospital arena.

I assumed that their own doctor would have been told to come in this night, considering the odd conditions. However, he was yet to show if he had been called in, so I was placed in charge of his staff, which comprised of twelve nurses as well as the practitioner. Thinking more on it, I figured the colonel knew early on that John would want me present and had therefore decided against inciting the aid of the regular doctor. The extra hand might turn out to be needed, but for the time being, Col. Jean would likely see two of us floating about as superfluous.

I had barely made it in the building when John and the others arrived with Malook. I didn't even have time to freshen or adjust myself, though of course it didn't really matter how unkempt my appearance was, as it must have been after my tiring day. Even so, the thought of looking ragged stayed ever present in my mind, especially now under the illumination of surgical grade lights. Another part behind it, equal to the one that was simple vanity, was that I didn't like the idea of appearing unprofessional.

I wore a long-sleeve white, fitted button down, a pair of black straight-legged dress pants, and some basic black flats, but had left my lab coat behind in the vehicle. In my head, I couldn't wear the uniform of one job at another, though now I realized that this small detail didn't matter either.

My makeup must be smudged all to hell if any of it were even still on my face, and I imagined that I seemed very out of place with the orderlies around me who were all clad in perfectly pure uniforms, their entire being straight. I felt I must look like a business person who had been hustling from interview to interview all day in a desperate search for new work. Fuck! Stop worrying about it, Connie! my brain chided.

Davis and Chressler, the two privates who had arrested Malook, brought him into the bright, sterile room were I stood with four of the nurses. They escorted him past us to one of the twenty beds there, gently pushing his shoulders in a silent order for him to sit. The alien followed these gestures without any hesitation or argument while Davis re-situated the cuffs. He let Malook keep one hand free, using the metal bracelet that had been on it to chain the stranger to the railing beside the mattress he had taken a spot on.

My husband had been standing in the doorway with two more pairs consisting of people I had seen earlier in the desert. He didn't acknowledge my presence until the privates rejoined him in order to leave the room. Only then did he give a small nod in my direction, keeping his expression solemn before the trio strolled away, disappearing back into the corridor and leaving the four unknown soldiers behind.

I watched him go, taking notice of these new guards that had taken a place at the door. All were armed with FN SCARs and armor. A man and woman stood on my side of the door, facing our team, and two men stood outside of it, keeping watch over the hall and the elevators. Turning my attention back to Malook, I smiled, hoping it showed respect rather than concern. Procedure instructed for some basic tests: Blood work, general triage, x-rays, and one or two other scans, though he had obviously already been searched before being brought to me.

They would have looked not only for any more weaponry, but for the presence of anything foreign whether it was possibly dangerous or not. It would have been a strip-search and if memory served, a cavity search as well. A nurse had handed me a file with pictures of the prisoner and a few jotted notes while he was being restrained to the bed. Studying the photographs showed that underneath his clothes, his body was still human...at least the exterior.

It would be up to me to determine if the insides matched. I didn't really know what I had expected, with what he had said and how he had appeared during our brief encounter, but with yet another thing about the alien so similar to the known Earth, a little pang in the inside of my brain made me wonder if it all wasn't some sort of elaborate hoax.

"Hello again," I greeted.

The man looked quite uncomfortable in the hospital gown he had been forced into. He gave a slight nod and a larger smile. It was curious to me how he wasn't more nervous or even upset by everything he had endured from the unanticipated landing to the thorough search of his person. He had to be bothered to a degree, yet it didn't show. "What are you?" he asked, keeping the same kindness as before.

I stepped towards him, grabbed the blood pressure cuff that hung on the wall behind, and took my time in wrapping it around the thicker part of his chained arm. I didn't think I would, but I didn't want to startle him with any quick, rigid movements. "I'm a doctor," I answered, taking a stethoscope from the nurse beside me and sliding it into place before pumping the monitor, "Is that what you mean?"

I saw one of the nurses shoot a glance at me as if I had just told an enemy my most precious secret. I understood her shock. However, the uptight behavior aggravated me. I did my best to ignore it as I looked back at Malook, adjusting the scope and counting.

"Yes," he returned in a solemn tone.

"One twenty-three over seventy-one," I said aloud as I lowered the stethoscope and began to remove the rest of the device.

His pressure was normal. Well...normal for Earth humans anyway. Replacing the monitor on the wall, I then reached for the thermometer. I figured he had some follow up question or statement regarding my occupation, but he didn't voice it if so.

I stuck the thermometer gently inside his ear and pressed its button. A moment later, a beep sounded and I removed it, glancing at the screen before handing it off to one of the nurses standing at the end of the bed. He promptly wrote down the temperature: eighty-six point four.

"So...you're very calm," I killed the clinical silence, suddenly eager to know the reason for his placid demeanor.

He tilted his head back, looking up at me, "Should I not be?"

I stopped for a moment, not quite sure how to take his words. I hadn't pegged him for the type to be sly or facetious, but my mind couldn't piece together another way to take the question and tone it had been delivered with. "It's not that," I avoided, "It's just...I think anyone else in your position would be at least a little nervous. Yet you've remained completely relaxed during this whole ordeal."

The alien let out a soft chuckle, "I suppose it's because of my training. I've been taught for quite some time now how to remain collected, to not let any emotion- especially fear- get the best of me. But I am not entirely settled," he admitted.

Training? It only just came together in my thoughts that he had to be in some sort of military position himself. That was pretty clear now. So why would he tell me this? Confess his anxiety? If it was part of how he'd been trained to act, much like our own military here on Earth, then it was to allow him to continue thinking clearly in stressful situations and to not let enemies or other opposition take advantage of him.

"I'm sorry," I mumbled awkwardly, "Is there anything I can do to make you feel more at ease?"

There was a pause. I could see his mind working just behind those green spheres as they locked intently upon me. I saw worry in them as well. His Adam's apple bobbed in a swallow and then his eyes hardened once more, "I don't believe you can," he replied almost coldly.

I shot a compassionate look to him before reaching for my stethoscope once more and placing it on his chest over the thin fabric of the gown. His heart beat strongly...steadily...just as a healthy human's would. When I pointed at the folder where his pictures had been, the nurse holding it easily read my quiet request and handed it back to me.

I opened it to one of the clean sheets of lined paper and started writing down some notes. "You don't have to tell me anything," I said without looking at the man, "But I was just curious...about the others who came here with you."

Malook straightened in his seat. He studied me for a moment, expression quizzical, "What about them?"

"Well, you-" I quickly cut myself off before sharing the observation. Three of the four nurses were still around me. I really didn't want to speak the thoughts with so much company. The guards surrounding the the door, I couldn't help. However, the nurses were under my order. "Please locate the major," I spoke to one of them. The woman nodded and walked off, seemingly happy for the reprieve, "And can the two of you prepare the radiography and sonography rooms?"

One of the two remaining nurses immediately left at the command. The other, I had already picked up, had an attitude. She stayed put, "The ultrasound equipment is always ready," she smirked, "I guess you wouldn't know though since you don't actually work here."

I put the binder in my hand down on the bed and raised an eyebrow at her, well aware of my currently held authority, "It's already prepared, you say? Hmm...Well in that case, you can see yourself home. I don't require further assistance from you." I turned back toward Malook, who was watching the scene, appearing to find difficulty in not grinning, like he understood what I was doing.

The nurse inhaled sharply with a smack of her lips, "I guess it wouldn't hurt to double check," she muttered with a glare before stomping out.

Unsure of how long my assistants would be gone, I instantly threw myself back into conversation with Malook, "It seemed weird to me that you left your ship alone, but moreover that you were hesitant to talk about the rest of your crew, regardless of the fact that you haven't had a problem speaking with us otherwise."

He paused long enough for me to worry that my rushing the nurses out had been pointless, finally parting his lips and answering in time, "They're not really my crew," his voice was hushed as he leaned closer to me, "My family is on that ship."

"Family?" I repeated incredulously, "Why would you bring your family out here? Aren't you supposed to be studying the planet?" I matched his volume, befuddled and exceedingly concerned with this revelation.

Malook glanced to his side briefly, "We're not supposed to be here at all...my family and I, that is...you see, it's actually against our laws to leave Trinnd."

My confusion remained obvious.

"It isn't an every day happening that citizens just fly about our planetary system. It's my position that allowed me to be able to take them on such a trip. We just...I didn't mean to actually leave our system," he attempted to explain, keeping a careful eye on his surroundings.

I nodded fervently, "I get that... So it's like your wife aboard? Or husband?"

The alien took a deep breath as his eyes darted around, "My wife, yes. And our young son...and Sulru." He stumbled on that last name.

"Sulru? That sounds beautiful. This person is part of your family too? Like a cousin or...excuse me, I don't know how your familial system works," I continued speaking rapidly to ensure his comfort as well as my own curiosity.

The man smiled, "Only slightly different than your own as far as I can tell. Um, no...she's not blood. More along the lines of...uh...she takes care of my son, Riven, for the most part."

"Oh, so a nanny?" I prompted.

He scrunched his face, mouthing the word to himself as if he was trying to recall its meaning, "Yes," he agreed, "I suppose she's sort of a nanny."

My lips curled to match his as I formulated a mental image of the four aliens sitting around a television set to spend time together. Our dialogue was impeccably timed as both nurses I had sent to prepare for the scans were just returning. I stepped away from the alien and toward nearby phlebotomy supplies.

The orderlies were at my side once more, informing me that everything was in order as I placed the vials, needle, alcohol swabs, and band-aids onto a tray. I handed it off to the bitchy nurse who grabbed it with a scowl and went to Malook to draw his blood.

"So you're in the military too. Back where you're from," I reverted the subject as I observed the nurse search for a vein under the black skin of our patient's inner elbow.

"Hm?" the man's attention had left me and was on the woman bent over in front of him, clutching onto his wrist, "Oh yes, I am. Military or government: I'm not sure which word you would use to describe my position," he mused.

"It sounds like military to me," my eyes shifted from her to him, "How long did it take you to speak English so well?"

Malook straightened, which startled the woman next to him. He eased again, almost apologetically, causing his handcuffs to clank between the rails of the bed, "Well, actually-"

He was interrupted by the sound of heavy treading in the room's entryway. The first nurse I had dismissed had finally arrived with my husband, leaving his side to move out of the way of the incoming troop the moment their feet hit the bottom of the doorway. Something was up...

"Are you finished here?" John inquired too seriously for my comfort.

"Almost," the phlebotomist spoke casually, taking my place while sticking a needle into the seated man's arm.

He didn't wince. I don't think he even realized it happened because, like me, his sight was fixed on the soldiers off to the side. The nurse attached the five small glass bottles one by one to the end of the butterfly, allowing bright red plasma to flow nicely inside each.

After they were all full and replaced in the basket, she pulled the needle out of his flesh, swaying to the side to dispose of it in the bio-hazard container before returning to her position and quickly covering the wound with a bandage. When she had removed herself, John sent a new pair of soldiers over to Malook.

While they released him from the bed, I spoke up in protest, "Major, we still have tests to perform. We haven't probably assessed his health and therefore the safety of-"

I was cut off.

"You can finish these things later. Right now, he's being transferred for questioning," John returned, emotionless.

As the men made Malook stand, he glanced at me rapidly enough that it appeared I was the only one who had seen it. In that tiny instant, I could feel a growing worry in him, though he didn't openly display it. They began escorting him away and I had an unbelievable urge to say something. I didn't want the kind alien to be treated this way...like a prisoner, a criminal. Remembering his earlier confession of fear, I knew I had to at least try to give him some sort of comfort. Anything.

"Major?" I skipped forward so that I was right behind my husband, who turned to face me, waiting for whatever it was I had to say, "Perhaps I can walk with you? I would like to share my notes thus far so that you may inform the colonel personally," I spoke to him as an associate.

John blinked once. I wasn't sure if he was upset with me or just generally annoyed. Either way he relented, "That will be fine," he said as we continued with Malook and his escorts.

I didn't really have many notes with the shallow amount of testing that had been done. Mostly I informed John that Malook so far appeared to be nothing other than human and a healthy one at that. The rest of the trek, I was quiet, glad that he didn't order me to leave after coming to the conclusion that I had nothing more to add. I figured he knew that I only wanted to be present from the beginning.

Our group walked in a zig-zag line down the corridor, occasionally making slight turns into extensions of the hallway that were mildly inclined. Upon reaching a nearly hidden elevator, everyone stopped, allowing the front woman to press the single button on the wall beside it. When it opened, she turned to the side, letting those holding onto Malook enter the small mechanical room with their prisoner.

Afterward, the woman and one other soldier strolled inside, leaving the rest of us behind as the doors closed. Just as they started to slide shut, I saw a weak grin pass over my new friend's face.

"Just do what you can," he said directly to me before the elevator locked him from my view.

I wasn't entirely certain what he was implying at first, as my focus lay with John. I remained silent and still as the major commanded the rest of the group off, staying behind with me as they left us alone together. I didn't like his current demeanor and I had a good idea why he was carrying it too.

Chapter 9: John

I had always known the outcome if we ever happened to take a sentient extra-terrestrial into custody. I didn't necessarily like that other life-forces of equal or similar intelligence would have to endure such treatment, yet at the same time, I accepted that some things had to take place in order to ensure our own safety.

Rotating to face my wife once we were alone, I read her easily. She knew. Even with my easily-excitable personality when it came to such things, it was she who was the less rational and more optimistic...especially when it came to judging others and their intention. That being said, I could tell that she had already grown fond of this alien, Malook.

Putting my hand on her shoulder, I managed a smile, "Let's go to the break rooms and talk there."

She acknowledged me with a sigh, and spun on her heels to return the way we had come. As we strolled, I grabbed her hand which was hanging down at her side, and squeezed it without turning her way. Although she was aware of where things were going concerning the ETs, I would still have to explain it to her exactly. Not that she was dim-witted, of course. Only so that she was with absolute certainty of the events.

Once we reached the medical wing, we boarded the usual elevator; the one that Malook had been sent away in was strictly for reaching the more restricted areas of the base. Riding in silence, I made sure not to let her hand free and occasionally, I would tighten my grasp of it. We rose a few underground levels higher, to the floor that held the dormitories and other rest areas. It was largely a precautionary setup and wasn't used except rarely...at least not to a large occupancy.

We found our way past a few open doors and into the main room. Inside were couches, cushioned seats, a television set, pool table, and a small kitchen. Near the kitchen was a metal folding table surrounded by matching chairs. Connie let go of me then, and went to the table, pulling out one of its pieces from underneath before plopping down, her head laying to rest in front of her. Poor thing, she had pulled a late shift at work today already and afterward had to deal with all this.

I went past her to the cabinets beyond, "I'm going to make some coffee. Do you want some?"

She flopped her head to the side so that eyes were on me, "Sure," she answered halfheartedly.

I retrieved the coffee grounds and filters and placed them on the counter next to the maker below. It was an older machine. Nobody really paid it much attention, but every time I saw it, I made a mental note to bring a newer model in so that the blends would come out fresher. Obviously, I kept forgetting to make those notes a reality. Exhaling, I made the brew anyway.

"So are you going to talk to me or..." Connie was still staring from her odd resting position.

"Well, your friend is definitely not from this galaxy," I started, causing her to lift her head at the phrasing. Out of the corner of my vision, I saw her expression become defensive. She started to say something, but decided against it. So I continued, "The colonel informs me that communications with the UN confirms no space or avian crafts are missing; nor are there personnel gone with access to any such machines."

Connie sat up as I flipped the coffee maker on and turned to face her, leaning back against the counter, "And?" she prodded.

"And we've been ordered to begin operations to gain access to the UFO," I finished.

"What about the people inside?" she said with sudden and blatant concern.

"They'll be brought in, just like Malook," I continued, "Connie, you know all this. We have to learn the extent of their knowledge and what they plan to do with it, as well as assess the immediate and distant threats they may pose. You should be thankful of Malook's apparent awareness of how such things generally work.

"That, and his cooperation are key factors in this ordeal," I pointed, knowing that she would remain discriminant of whether that was actually true or not. Despite, or perhaps because of, having worked in the military herself, my wife was quite critical of government operation.

"But, John, you don't understand. They-" she stopped abruptly, looking behind her before carrying on in a gentler voice, "They're not soldiers or anything. It's his family on that ship."

"How do you-" my head cocked onto its side, "He told you that?" I changed my tone from one of simple curiosity to that of suspicion.

She nodded.

"Hm..." I hummed.

She definitely believed what the man had said to her. However, it was him who I was skeptical of. Even with his kindness thus far, there could be reasons other than just being friendly fueling both his behavior and his confessing these things to my wife.

I didn't want to think he was attempting to manipulate her, mainly because I was too protective of the woman, but I also didn't want that to be the case since it would lead to the reasoning that his people were malicious. Nonetheless, the possibility couldn't be ruled out, "I guess we'll find out then, huh?"

Connie took offense to that statement, jumping up from her chair and getting close enough to me that there was no room left between, "John, I'm serious. His wife, son, and their caretaker are the only others on that ship!"

How fervent she was in her conviction was not what surprised me; my mind stuck on the strange notion that four people were the vessel's sole occupants. It was daft to believe that in itself, but ludicrous to think, if that were the case, that these few others weren't soldiers of some sort. Not to mention how there had been no mention of other creatures, robots, or anything that would warrant great enough protection for such a small crew.

Thus far, there had also been no explanations of the capabilities of the ship. It could very well be as deadly as a tank or worse. I suppose it was possible that it was indeed only a handful of individuals, if their purpose was to scout or simply gain intel; although they would still require some means of protection while traveling in a realm where there was no way they could send radio transmission to their homeworld or quickly receive aid.

As far as we could tell, this craft was alone. Nothing on our scanners suggested that there were more crafts lying in wait. The possibility remained that this was a trap or that there were others, but with ways of avoiding detection, though it seemed unlikely, given our own technology and the events of the evening.

"Honey," I started in softly, understanding that being harsh would only anger her, "He's still a stranger to us, whether you've talked to him intimately or not. We have to be careful and we have to prove what is real, not solely rely on his word."

She slouched her shoulders, dropping her head to rest on my arm, "I know. It's just...he seems so nice...so innocent. I don't understand why people can't just be honest and trusting."

I put an arm around her, hugging her closely while smiling at the innocence she possessed herself, "I wish things could be like that too."

"I don't want them to get hurt," she muttered, rubbing her forehead against my arm, staring off at nothing, "I know that these 'interrogations' can get aggressive."

I squeezed her shoulders. It was true, and since they were confirmed not to be allies and also not from this planet, our superiors would have far more than lenient rein in their exact handling of these alien passengers, "I don't think anything like that will happen," I offered, unsure as if either of us really trusted my words or not, "You know, with how easy dealing with Malook has been. I'm actually quite hopeful that proceedings will go smoothly."

Ding!

The coffee was ready. We loosened from our embrace, allowing me to reach beneath the cabinet above the coffee maker for two of the mugs that hung there. Grabbing them, I began handing one to my wife before quickly retracting it as a new thought entered my mind, "Maybe you should lie down and try to rest for a while instead."

She stretched into a yawn as if the statement reminded her body that it was exhausted, "Probably a good idea," she agreed, bringing her hands up to her face and rubbing her cheeks and eyes, "What about you?"

"I'll sit with you for a bit," I answered, setting down the empty cups.

On the long wall between the kitchenette and the pool table were a couple of doors leading to rooms filled with rows of cots. They were connected to some of the entrances outside the room that we had passed in the hallway.

Most of the dorms were interlaced like that, actually, though there were ways to close them off from each other in case it was needed. I guided my wife over to one of them and through its threshold, but just as I began to follow her inside, I heard someone call for me from where we'd entered initially.

"Major Shinn!"

I shifted on my heels to see it belonged to a saluting soldier in the doorway, "At ease," I commanded, our dialogue causing Connie to turn abruptly and try to peer out to see the man as well. However, I set firm hands on her shoulders to keep her from getting distracted from going to rest.

"Connie, everything will be alright," I assured, "You'll see. If they aren't a threat, things should be resolved fairly soon."

Her hand was up again; this time its fingers rotating in small circles on her temple, "I know...I guess."

Smiling, I let her rotate so I could give a quick peck on the forehead before releasing her entirely. She returned a flash of a grin, waiting to go on to bed after seeing that I had walked a sufficient distance away. By the time I decided to stop in front of the private, I noticed out of my peripherals that my wife had started to disappear inside the dorm, so I called back to her with one final assurance, "Someone will keep you updated."

There was no reply from the woman, but I knew she had heard me due to her slight halt in the frame of the door when I spoke, immediately followed by her finishing traipsing onward to claim some sleep. Instead of waiting or poking for a response, I simply put my focus on the soldier since there was no need for any affirmation from her. The man didn't seem too enthused with the state of affairs; though that may have just been my interpretation of his professional demeanor. I recognized him, yet hadn't had any experience with dealing with him personally.

"Col. Jean requests your assistance, sir," he informed plainly.

I nodded, "Very well."

The soldier saluted once more before spinning to leave, with me fast on his trail. I did my best to pay heed to my job rather than my wife's bleeding heart, but when she hurt, I hurt. All I could do was hope for the best and try to keep her rational mind working over her emotional one.

Chapter 10: Connie

After John left, I took a seat on one of the small beds, rubbing my eyes before actually pulling my legs up onto it and laying down on my back. I let my eyelids come to a close over my vision and tried to relax, but there were so many thoughts and questions swirling around inside my brain for that to come easily.

The situation with Malook and his family was weighing heavily on my conscious and I wasn't entirely sure why. I knew, and I felt he knew too, that it wasn't within my power to protect any of them. However, not doing anything at all made me feel like I was betraying him.

And to me, betraying anyone, whether we were close or not, was a horrible thing. It was something I had just never been able to stomach. He had placed a certain amount of trust in me, had been nothing except kind...

Just do what you can.

The alien seemed to have excellent intuition. I had never promised him safety or fair treatment or anything of the sort, yet he still somehow managed to see that I wanted to...he may have even seen how greatly not being able to would affect me and offered that last statement as a consolation. I rolled my head from side to side restlessly before finally tilting it upward from my pillow to stare out the door.

I sat there dumbly for a moment, contemplating getting up again. The smell of fresh coffee had traveled from the kitchen just beyond, and had begun filling the dimly lit room where I lay. I groaned and put my head down, eyes on the ceiling without actually focusing on anything. Mind returning to my husband, I realized how his suggestion that Malook might be lying truly bothered me which, logically speaking, it shouldn't have.

At first, I thought it was because I thought poorly of John for saying it. After dwelling on it more, however, I came to terms with the fact that I just didn't want it to be true. John was right; the man was not only a stranger, he was a stranger from another planet.

He came from some unknown world with customs, behaviors, cultures...with everything that we knew absolutely zero about. Due to that, even the smallest thing could be misinterpreted. Say, for a simple example, a handshake. Our greeting could be his middle finger.

More than not wanting such a thing to be true, I honestly just did not believe it, whether the feeling was illogical or not. This conclusion sent me to contemplating the man's family...his wife and son. What were they like? I imagined them to be kind, like their husband and father. Perhaps his son even looked like him. Riven? I think I had caught the name correctly. It sounded like 'river,' which I thought was nice.

I hoped they weren't frightened although they must be...at least a little, right? Even Malook, who was apparently both the leader and the strength of the group, had confessed his own anxiety regarding matters. I rolled over onto my side, gaze still void of intent. The son was probably pretty young, considering they invoked the aid of a babysitter, and he hadn't mentioned his wife having any of this 'training' of his.

What if they didn't know how to react to our soldiers? To being treated like criminals when they had done no wrong? The image of a concerned mother trying to comfort a frightened and crying little boy flashed across my mind. Sighing heavily, I pushed myself back into a seated position with legs hanging from the side of the cot. Nope, I wasn't going to be able to rest. There was far too much going on.

Strolling into the kitchenette, I saw the coffee pot was untouched: full, with steam floating up from it despite it having to been close to half an hour since it was brewed. I grabbed one of the mugs that John had set on the counter and began filling it with the hot liquid. The picture of Malook's wife and son that my brain had conjured remained. Ugh. I guess I shouldn't be beating myself up about it. It wasn't my fault and some things just can't be helped...right?

I tried to recreate something my husband would say to try to make me feel better, but just as if he had said it himself, it didn't help. It wasn't like they were going to be killed or enslaved or something insane like that, I started trying to rationalize like John. After all, it wasn't like we could just keep them hostage either. There were others out there and eventually Malook and his family would be missed.

Nobody wants an intergalactic war, especially with how far behind we must be compared to them. Then again, what if his people had already planned war? They could have wanted to take over our planet from the beginning. Maybe that was the real reason Malook had stayed so calm and cooperative.

"UUUUGH!" I groaned loudly. It didn't matter what I told myself, I wasn't going to feel better, whether feeling guilty made made sense or not. Not even trying to believe that the aliens were the 'bad' guys would work because, like I said, I'd feel shitty for betraying what I really had no reason to take as anything other than simple kindness.

Searching the cabinets for creamer and sugar, I took in a deep breath. All I could do right now is attempt occupying my mind until I heard something further. Some sort of update or orders...anything. Studying the contents of the cupboard I had thrown open, I saw there were a lot of random items, most of which looked vintage, including a can of chips that was completely discolored.

Among the items was a half-used container of creamer and a box of sweetener packets. I grabbed the milk substitute and poured it into my cup until an off-white mountain stood warily atop the java. I then watched as it sunk into the brown lake below before I pulled open one drawer, then a second, to find a spoon. Retrieving one, I stirred my drink.

Sulru. Another interesting name. Was she putting on a strong show to help little Riven feel safe? How old was she? Perhaps she was a teenager, a kid herself. I doubt the poor thing signed up for all this when taking the job to look after the child. I picked up my mug and allowed myself as big a swig as my mouth could handle of the heat before setting it back down. I glared at it for a moment while I thought, my hands resting on either side of the cup and strumming against the granite.

I turned to inspect the digital clock on the microwave set along the back of the wall. It had been longer than I thought since I was left alone. Almost an hour. My mind was foggier from fatigue than I had realized...

Even so, it seemed too soon to shove my nose into affairs, yet I couldn't handle sitting around doing nothing. The thoughts and visions created by my idle mind would kill me. So I trotted to the door, giving a quick glance down both ends of the hall when I reached it, to be sure nobody was around that may have been sent to speak with me.

After recalling which way to to go, I strolled to the elevator, pushed the up button, and got inside. Initially, I went up to the medical wing. The room where Malook's blood had been drawn was empty, save for one of the nurses I had not yet spoken to that night. He was tidying up as far as I could tell, and taking notes at the same time- probably to keep record of supplies, what had been used, what was needed...the usual.

I kept on, passing by both the doctor's and the nurse practitioner's offices, a few supply closets, and then the lab. The ill-tempered woman I had nearly fought with earlier was hunched over a microscope, examining slides. No doubt it was the alien plasma. I considered poking my head in and inquiring about her findings, but after thinking on it, spun around in the hallway and returned to the elevator.

Conversing with her now, when she was still in the middle of her work, would surely only lead to her complaining that I was interrupting and keeping her from finishing her task. It was a dead-end at this point and I could do without the extra aggravation.

On the floor just above, was the colonel's office. I didn't intend on bothering him unless he was alone, so when I made it to that first floor and saw soldiers traversing the corridors, my spirit fell a little, assuming that he was busy. As a pair of soldiers squeezed by me though, I stopped them to inquire about Col. Jean.

"He's in his office," the woman answered, "He's been on the phone for the past hour. I'm not sure if he still is or not; it's been crazy around here."

I nodded politely at the explanation and then asked, "Where exactly is his office?" It had been some time since I was last there, and I wasn't sure if anything had been shifted around. The woman paused, looking to her counterpart.

They both hesitated, which I figured was because they took me to mean I was going to barge in on him or otherwise interrupt, so I added a clarification to my original inquiry, "I'm just going to wait outside until he is free."

The woman's sight rested on me again and she shrugged. The man who stood beside her put a foot forward to be fully in my view, and then pointed down the hall in the direction I was facing, "Second door on your right from here."

I gave each of them a tiny smile, "Thank you, sir, ma'am."

Continuing my journey to the place described, I found his name engraved on a plaque beside the office. Alright. Since it was closed, I twisted around and leaned against the wall beside his door, taking in a few deep breaths. I kept an eye on the wooden slat the whole time, while simultaneously remaining aware of my surroundings. Only after a few minutes of brooding, did I hear feet shuffling and chairs scraping against the floor inside the room.

The door clicked open and an armed soldier marched out, peering across the hallway, and upon seeing me, stepped to his side so that I had to scoot over out of his way. He was clearly protecting someone or something, therefore I didn't fuss. I just politely moved a comfortable distance away- comfortable for him, that is.

Even after doing so, and although his sight wasn't directly upon me, I could tell that he was observing me. Next, the colonel emerged, then a third man who wore a similar uniform. This second official kept walking, acting as if he hadn't noticed me. Going past where I stood, his guard followed perfectly on his heels. I found myself focused on the two as they stomped down the corridor and out of sight.

"Dr. Shinn! There you are!" Col. Jean's voice boomed when he saw me, snapping me away from the other officer and the soldier with him. I smiled at the old man, who approached me with open hands, chuckling, "I was wondering where your husband was hiding you."

I took his hands in a friendly shake and returned his beam, "You know you can just call me Connie."

"Oh, I know," he replied with a smirk.

The man had a grandfatherly-like essence about him. It was warm and kind, and also like many of the elderly, stuck in his own ways and ideas with an air of self-importance. At many times, these things about him made me view him as a bit ignorant, bigoted even, and being in his presence again to remember this feeling made me worry about the alien family to a greater degree.

"I know you aren't the type for sitting around without anything to do," he observed, leading us back towards where I had come, "But don't you worry. Granted there's no trouble: no attacks from them, is what I mean to say, then there will be more work for you real soon."

My head jolted in his direction, squinting in abrupt anger. I had to force a deep breath before I could talk, to ensure that my words came out calmly. His insensitivity infuriated me, as I felt it was fairly obvious that we were the ones being hostile.

"Sir, why can't we just leave the rest of them alone? Just deal with Malook? It's not like they were being violent or even aggressive."

The man laughed, "Same old song and dance from you, I see. You'll be given a list of tests to have completed on each one of them including finishing up on...Malook."

This was the only answer I received. I couldn't tell if he didn't like the alien name or didn't like acknowledging the humanity of his perceived enemy. I exhaled. In the very least, it didn't seem to be so bad from this end...yet. They probably wanted some tissue sampling, possibly some endoscopy.

I only hoped that nothing too extreme was found out about them. Surely, if they were at least mostly human, it would be easier for everyone else to empathize with them. I also hoped that the procedures would be limited to the adults.

Col. Jean sauntered to the elevator, sending me on my way to the break room and dorms with a wink. On the ride up, I suddenly got the sense that something else had gone wrong. Everything felt strangely somber for some reason. I shook it off, concluding it was only the the small-minded old man making me frustrated.

I changed my current course of thought to try and think about something positive, and ended up finding it exciting that I was going to meet Malook's family. I could show them the same kindness that he had shown me and perhaps set them at ease. And once again, my brain rushed to the negative.

I wondered what was going on in that interrogation room. From what I knew, those things could be tiring, painstaking...plain brutal. What was he telling them? Was he even telling them anything? How much did he actually know about the affairs of his own superiors? Or about us here on Earth?...if this trip wasn't done with their knowing and falling to our planet was unintentional?

Chapter 11: Malook

Even though I was the one being practiced on, I found myself amused by these people's procedures. I had wondered how similarly to Galdelierian protocol that they would handle this situation. And the answer was...less aggressive. Though, I suppose they had to be mostly improvising, considering until tonight, they weren't aware that there was any other intelligent lifeforms in the universe besides themselves.

Well, some apparently theorized it, but it didn't go much further than that. Not that I was holding it to their degradation. Not really. We had only recently discovered other galaxies ourselves, and Earth would be the first with sentient life on or near our level. It was a drone that first reported the planet to us. It was a simple device which only shared that the planet was of a chemical makeup close to that of Galdelier.

I remember when I heard the news. As General, I was one of the first to be informed of such discoveries. To actually come here myself and see there were creatures of similar understanding was extraordinary, albeit unsettling that I was forced to meet them directly and unprepared.

"What is your purpose here?" the man sitting across from me repeated himself.

After leaving the kind doctor, their soldiers had brought me to a room smaller than the medical facility; it was also more bare. There was nothing within, except for a steel table in the middle, along with two cheaply constructed chairs.

It was extremely cold too; more so, I felt, than it had been traveling through the stars. The uncomfortable temperature, coupling the echo with even the slightest sound, made one feel paranoid. Though this might have been the reasoning behind the atmosphere.

"I thought I had already answered that," I stated plainly.

The man looked up from the portable computer which he had been inputting information into as we talked, "You told me you were waiting for your ship to repair, but why were you here, at our planet, in the first place?" he clarified, both his words and his face emotionless.

I sighed inwardly. I had known what he meant from the beginning, what he wanted to know, but I wouldn't tell. I couldn't. Official business or not, I'd never reveal whether my people were a threat to them. Not that I thought it mattered what I said. It was my sense that they, speaking generally, would feel intimidated either way.

Such a feeling may be warranted despite that we weren't terribly far above them on a technical level. We had had our fair share of lucky breaks, I suppose. I had already defied law enough by even being here without a direct order from the Empress; I wasn't going to screw myself and my family over more with acting as anything other than a reserved soldier...even if some things these Earthlings wanted to know were harmless curiosities.

I glanced down at the wires leading from his machine to my fingertips. When I had been placed in one of the chairs across from him, I was ordered to remain calm and sit straight while two bands were stretched around my chest. These were also attached to the computer.

I hadn't asked what it was, but was told anyway. They called it a polygraph and it was used for monitoring physical shifts in a person's breathing and heart rate to determine when they were lying or being honest.

We didn't have anything like this 'lie detector' back home. There was only so much that could be picked up through radio and other invisible frequencies from the ship. Fortunately, we'd been able to learn enough of the Earth's language to put together a strong enough data base before the actually landing. We had done well to process that this one, English, was the most widely spoken.

"What is your purpose here?" my interrogator asked again.

Even through his stoic demeanor, I could tell he was aggravated with having to repeat himself so frequently. I cut my vision to peer behind me while turning my head to the side. The two men who had brought me here, now stood a few feet back with their version of rifles ready, not directly aimed at me, just on standby.

I switched to forward face again, seeing the indignant Earthling in his unrelenting stupor. Remaining silent would show me as antagonistic despite my polite cooperation thus far. Normally, it would still be my command to refrain from speaking. However, with my family in the mix, I knew I had to say something, though without talking truthfully about Galdelier, its people, or our leaders.

"To study the planets in this quadrant. We didn't realize there was intelligent life here," I half-lied, wondering if his contraption actually realized it.

As he strummed his fingers against the buttons on the device, I thought back to the doctor. Connie. I suppose it wasn't entirely true what I had said to her about needing help. Actually, we only needed a bit of time to let the system reset itself and it should be up running as usual.

Should be. I had only left it to survey the area since, with the mapping down, I couldn't do so from inside the ship. There was no assistance needed; I only felt it would give the strangers the semblance of holding the whip.

"And what will you do with this information you have acquired?" he continued.

I looked directly into his gaze. It wasn't in my plans to show any aggression or even simple dissatisfaction, so I kept my body fixed and spoke calm, a false hint of pleading in my tone, "I feel I've been very cooperative with everyone. I've been answering your questions. I've asked nothing of you."

The man adjusted himself in his seat. His vision narrowed at me momentarily before typing a few lines into the computer. I watched as he did so, waiting for him to respond to my statements. Finally, he was staring at me once more, and replied with a tilt of his head, "I see...and what exactly is it that you want now?"

I blinked a couple of times while I thought. I wanted them to leave me the hell alone. I wasn't naive though. They were going to do what they wanted regardless, and at this point they'd likely already attempted to capture my family as well. I didn't hide my next exhale as I reached my hands up to rub my eyes.

They never touched. I was held back by the click of the metal bonds on my wrists hitting against the rods of the chair I was sitting in, "Are these necessary?"

The man smirked. It was the first expressive sign I had seen from him since we'd met, "Are they?" he asked, the mock showing obviously through his attempts at indifference. Pausing for a second without any response from me, he removed his gaze and added, "Maybe they are."

I gruffed and pushed back in my seat to stretch my back as best I could manage. I was starting to feel sore from keeping such a rigid pose. Upon doing so, my chair squeaked across the floor, creating a loud echo in the quiet space. In immediate response, I heard the weapons behind me shift, as their handlers shuffled on their feet.

My sight cut backward. It was hard not to display agitation in such a scenario, although I'm sure if I had been without my family, the task would be exceedingly easier. The soldiers settled once more after a few moments without any other movement or action from their prisoner. No doubt their purpose was to make sure I didn't try to start something. Attack or become manic, I guess.

Even knowing the Empress' orders, should a similar situation arise back home, would have been much worse than the treatment I'd received from the Earth government, being treated like a criminal...or a monster, was unnerving and admittedly, a bit depressing. It made my thoughts change from my present predicament to Sulru. I wondered if this was the way she and her people felt back on Galdelier?

I was a known sympathizer of their race, so it was on my brain quite a lot about how it must be for them. However, at last having a small taste of it myself really made it start to sink in. It was definitely not pleasant. Nobody should be made to feel sub-par or worthless when they'd done nothing to deserve the treatment. I never considered the Earthlings enemies, but if their prejudice stretched too far with my son, my wife, or Sulru, that could easily change.

"What will you do with the information you have gathered about Earth?"

Although I steeled my focus on him, my thoughts rested with my companions. Nanny, I recalled the funny sounding word. Another lie. It wasn't untrue that she looked after Riven, but...it was definitely not in the same sense I had made it appear. 'Bodyguard' might have been a more appropriate term. Once again, I had softened the reality for the Earthlings...or at least for Connie.

Our brief research of the planet had shown that there did not seem to be a species here in the likeness of Sulru's. It had been a comforting discovery, seeing as it meant that we held an offense with which Earth could not easily compete. This awareness should have preserved the idea as to the others' well-being: that she was there to protect them. Nonetheless, I remained on edge, contemplating what complications might arise because of maybe not her presence, but her actions.

"Has my crew been left alone?" I didn't expect a clear answer, and I knew that they wouldn't have been let be for long. Mostly I wanted to stall. If he revealed something, that would be a plus.

The interrogator had kept his eyes on me the entire time. I think he had said or asked something that I hadn't caught while my mind was focused on other matters. I was sure I heard him growl before replying, "You are in no position to be giving orders," his head quickly fell downward to the screen before him, eyes darting left and right across it like he had to find his place again.

I didn't bother pointing out that I hadn't been demanding anything- merely asking. Saying anything in the first place had thrown him off and worsened his outlook of me. Besides that, he had given nothing away: a mild, yet expected disappointment. Neither

Sulru nor my wife would willfully open the shuttle, nor would they leave it; and my son was too young to fully comprehend the situation, so he would be under their close watch.

Of course, I would do nothing to aid in their leaving or these people entering. That would leave it up to the Earthlings to make their way inside, which they may accomplish through demolishing part of the craft or using their own technology to break through its servers. Whichever means was employed, I was without doubt that Earth was capable of attaining this goal.

I was also with a hundred percent certainty that this would set into motion an undesirable chain of events, since Sulru's dedication was boundless. She would protect Riven and Soare-a at any cost ,and Earth was NOT equipped to handle her. I kept dithering between believing her involvement would be detrimental, and feeling it was possibly the only way out of this mess.

In any case, I knew not being there to guide her actions toward being beneficiary, would create unnecessary trouble and cost unneeded bloodshed. That is probably what worried me most.

I wanted my family safe, but I also wished to return home with as few negative repercussions as possible. At this point, I would already have to deal with the Earth people's sudden newfound knowledge of our existence. Fortunately, I was able to surmise that their governments were much more chaotic than our own, working as numerous different factions, rather than being consolidated and functioning together.

With that truth, news about us would not spread rapidly, if at all. Even thus, I felt that Sulru would definitely make us appear as a threat, and therefore jeopardize any future of a peaceful coalition with Galdelier when the leaders of the two planets finally faced. This alone could, and likely would, be disastrous. However, what was more dire to me, was that my family and I would be easily linked to the events.

I wasn't concerned for my welfare. I messed up; I would take the consequences when they came. It wasn't even really my wife and son whom I worried for. Riven was just a boy, he had no choice and Soare-a could claim to have gone under duress, in order to be with her son. It was Sulru who concerned me.

Despite the fact I was her boss and she was required to assist me, no matter the reason or price to her personally, in our society, she would not be granted forgiveness for acting illegally, even if only under orders.

Her people were considered less than filth. Indeed, if they didn't prove useful as a means to attack and defend, they'd have been eradicated long ago. That's all her people were in our world: weapons...but not to me. I never felt that way about her kind. Not even as a child. I had tried to get others to understand that they were people like us, equal although different.

It never went so well for me...or for them. And unfortunately, to attain a position of as high a rank as mine, I had to suppress my opinion and my sympathy for many years. In more recent times, however, I had still been found out by others serving alongside me. I never suffered anything negative because of it, thankfully, but the rumor was still out there...a potentially hazardous rumor due to its truth.

Please be gentle, Sulru, I prayed silently.

Chapter 12: John

"What?!? What do you mean you need more men? How many people are on that ship?!?" I yelled at the corporal standing in front of me with her hands on her knees.

She had been the last in a convoy sent back to the site of the spacecraft, and had returned, panting in panic. When we had found ourselves unable to communicate with the alien passengers inside, we'd tried to gain access remotely, but that failed too. The colonel had then commanded forced entry by means of several small, yet powerful blasts along the area that we had seen the alien man close upon our initial arrival.

The corporal had arrived on site just after it had been done. Rather than follow the rest in, her team was meant act as a relay to the base. However, nobody here heard from them until only a handful of team members showed back up, herself included. All were wounded. Through her scattered breaths, I managed to catch that directly after soldiers boarded the vessel, shots were fired.

After waiting a short period of time without radio, the other teams entered. The outcome was the same as the first, except for two men who were seen retreating. Whoever the assailant or assailants were, they followed the survivors out and then attacked everyone within close proximity of the ship.

With such severe anxiety, the corporal hadn't been able to give many details, and I had been lucky to catch that much. Whatever had happened, had her completely spooked, which was a feat in itself. I had served with the woman for quite some time and she wasn't so easily influenced.

This was more than some average troops with guns...or were there just a lot more people aboard than Malook had let on? I felt that being the case was quite likely. At the very least it could be merely wishful thinking that they didn't have some sort of super soldier or what have you. 'Just his family,' my ass.

"Okay," I softened, "Let's get you to the medical wing with the rest."

The corporal straightened her spine in an apparent attempt to regain herself, clenching her jaw, "I'm not-"

"I want you checked out just the same," I ordered sternly.

The woman gave in with a shaky nod, and walked with me in silent obedience. There was more to it than simply worrying about a friend. I wanted her to sit and relax so that she could try to elaborate before I threw any more people into what was now a battle zone. A medical setting was typically good with lulling, even sometimes the ones that had a fear of doctors.

When we reached the next floor, the staff was scurrying about, and several gurneys lined the hall. On the end opposite us, on the other side of the main room's entrance, I spotted the colonel.

"Major, what the hell is going on here?" he barked, gaze following the wounded soldiers being piled inside for treatment.

"An attack, sir," I answered. "There weren't enough men to counter it, and almost all returned with injuries or not at all. I'm still putting everything together," I added.

"Hm..." the old man hummed thoughtfully as he stepped towards me, "I trust you can handle it while I take care of matters on this end? I have another call to make."

I saluted briefly, "Yes sir."

"Good. See to it then," he stomped past me and returned to the elevator.

I was honestly surprised that it was all he had to say. Given the abruptly dire turn, I had imagined many furious words delivered with a fiercer attitude. Nonetheless, I could feel the anger boiling in him, and he was clearly focused on rectifying the situation.

I turned my attention from where he'd gone and finished escorting the corporal to an empty bed right inside the ward. Sitting her down, I guided her into slow breathing as I visually searched the place, finding my wife easily.

She was several cots down on the first row, checking the arm of a young man which was terribly gashed and swollen. It was large enough that I could see it from where I stood several yards away. Connie finished the examination, quickly speaking something to the nurse who stood beside her, and then made her way to the next soldier. This second patient was laying down on the bed in obvious pain. I watched as another orderly hovered close, staying barely longer than needed to inject something into the line in his arm.

After a few moments, the man stopped squirming, though he was still awake, so I assumed the injection was morphine. My eyes fluttered down to his injury to find it was far worse than the first man's. Instead of a simple gash, his right arm was all but torn from his torso. Even at my distance, I could see the bone jutting out through the craggily torn tissue and the shine of surfacing blood.

It seemed to be a few slices up the length of his arm, ending with a shoulder pulled out of its socket. More than just out of place, however, it appeared that it had been yanked violently, in an attempt to completely remove it from his body.

The job had not been finished, which I would liked to have said was fortunate, but looking at the damage, I didn't know if it wouldn't have been better to sever the limb to lessen the discomfort from the rest of its injuries.

I tore my gaze from where Connie was working and scanned the rest of the men and women in the room. Every single one of them had a similar wound on their arm, ranging in intensity between that first patient and the second. The nurse practitioner whose name I always forgot, was on the opposite end of the beds from where my wife was.

Taking a look at the patients he was tending, I noticed that in addition to those on the arms, many soldiers also had damage to their chests, close to the base of their necks. Whatever had attacked, had cut right through their clothes and appeared to have been aiming for their throats. And the enemy had succeeded in doing so with one of them.

I observed the practitioner shake his head, mumbling something before leaving the soldier's side. Dropping sights to the patient, I realized that her neck had been shredded just like her bicep, and the plasma had already stopped flowing. My heart sank as vision settled onto her dead eyes, seemingly fixed in horror. The nurse that had been assisting, slowly pulled a blanket over the woman's body and covered her face.

Still, the activity in the wing did not lessen. The nurse was already with another one of the patients from a section who were in acute conditions, carting them off through the room, past me, and into the hall. Connie ran after them, too focused to even notice me standing there at the doorway. The first to surgery, I guessed.

"John," suddenly the corporal was speaking, drawing my attention.

"How many passengers were there?" I inquired instantly, desperate to learn more.

"Three...just three..." she breathed, head shaking.

"Three?" I repeated in disbelief.

"Yes...there were two women...and a little boy. They seemed normal at first. Human. And the woman holding the kid, she- the two of them were normal, but...the other one," the corporal looked up at me with an expression terror-struck, "I don't know...she's some sort of monster. Claws, fangs, and those eyes? She was too fast for us. All of our men against her and only one bullet managed to hit...in her abdomen."

I nodded once, patting her shoulder before strolling off, giving a final glance over all of the wounded. It was jarring. After meeting Malook, I hadn't truly anticipated such violence...not from them anyway.

I knew that our people's behavior could be seen as aggressive, yet I had pretty much assumed that the aliens, at least this handful, were not an immediate threat. Aliens. Even with its certainty now, I still hadn't gotten used to using the term as reality instead of theory.

Of course, I didn't know beforehand if and when their existence was discovered, how it would be. Peaceful, violent, mildly turbulent? In any case, I expected it to feel validating that I could say it without being viewed as a nut.

However, with the corporal's fearful words ringing in my ears and the vision of my fellow men in their current condition, I felt nothing other than anger and dismay. I needed to accompany my own team to the desert and end this bloodshed.

I found my way back to the control room in quiet determination. When I was once again in the place where it had all started that evening, I grabbed the microphone, clutching it in front of my mouth as I used my other hand to switch buttons to direct where my voice would sound.

"Call for teams Calvin, Devon, Rex, and Marshall," I spoke, "Equip third line, HWP. Ready in five."

After repeating myself, I replaced the speaker in its position and continued my trek to the garage. Upon arrival, I saw that several of those called for had already reported, and I could hear the rest marching in behind me.

Not even two minutes passed until all were standing tall, patiently awaiting the briefing. I presented a precise update, warning them to stay fully alert and to keep a good space between themselves and the creature once it was spotted.

Our SUVs pulled out of the base quickly and sped onto the main highway. Although we ended up taking the same route we had last time, it was a different driver controlling the vehicle. Even though we were going straight into known peril, I was more relaxed on this ride.

My wife was safe inside the base so I could focus on this mission without worrying for her. It seemed we reached our destination more rapidly than before, and as we pulled near the spacecraft, the drivers automatically parked the SUVs in a barricade-like manner.

There were still some troops at the site: the few who had been originally sent to guard the area against civilian entry or alien exit. It was a relief to see that none of them had been harmed. Probably a safe assumption then, that the alien was only attacking those who ventured into the machine.

Good and bad news in that. It meant the assailant was, so far, only defensive and not offensive. However, knowing that we planned to invade the being's space and cause her to act in defense...it wasn't so great.

I flung the vehicle open and slid out, along with those riding with me. They all settled behind the machine's doors, a few behind their own shields, and every one of them armed. Their weapons consisted of machine guns, grenade launchers, and a couple even had flamethrowers. We weren't taking any chances.

I approached one of the men who had been guarding the area and asked for a report. He stated just what I had surmised, that nobody out of immediate range of the craft had been attacked nor had any alien come away from the UFO.

He then informed me that after the wounded were gone, a woman left the ship, closing its entrance again somehow through the blast damage, and had been standing sentinel outside.

When he said this, I gazed over his shoulder to look, "I don't see anyone out there," I argued, squinting to make sure.

He spun around, rifle clicking, and scanned the length of the craft, "She had been standing right outside the door..." he muttered, eyes still searching.

I kept my gaze trained on the ship as I traipsed back to our new barrier. Leaning inside the SUV I had traveled in, I opened one of the under-seat compartments, producing a megaphone. I pulled out of the vehicle, stepping one foot onto the floor board and throwing my left arm over the top of the door so that I was standing taller than the vehicle.

The megaphone reached my lips as I pressed the button to speak, "This is Major John Shinn. I wish to talk to the one who attacked our men."

There was no answer, not that I had expected one. Nonetheless, I carried on, "We don't wish to harm anyone. We only want to speak with you." Although it wasn't a complete lie and even after my years in service, I still found it hard to muster the strength to say such half truths.

I looked around the ship again when it occurred to me that perhaps this alien didn't speak our language. Since Malook could though, logic would say that she could as well. Another possibility lay in that the alien may have retreated back inside. If the guards had missed her disappearing from her stand, then it was equally likely that they had missed her re-entering the craft. The corporal had mentioned its speed.

"Please come talk with us," I spoke once more into the speaker before tossing it into the seat of the vehicle and making my way down from the makeshift podium. I motioned for one of the teams to move forward, and I followed with a second.

We set a path straight for the entrance to the ship, realizing it was only haphazardly closed when we got there. The c4 had shown enough damage that the sliding door no longer fit smoothly within its lining.

"I think we can leverage it back up, Major," one of the men told me as the rest were focusing on our surroundings.

"Leave it be for now, but you, Devon, wait here," I ordered the man and the rest of his team, while motioning for Calvin to follow around one side of the ship and Rex to follow the other side.

After they had begun their walk, I split the remaining team to join either of them. Standing for a couple of minutes with head rotating from side to side in order to watch the progression of the troops, I then took a moment to step closer to the ship.

There was a panel next to the door with various markings. I couldn't tell that there were any buttons, but the writing was definitely separated into specific groupings similar to that of a calculator or a phone. Out of curiosity, I decided to tap one.

"AAAAAHHHHH!!!"

A blood curdling scream shook me from contemplation and the men around me lifted their weapons, flying into high alert. I threw my hand up in a gesture for them to follow me as I started running toward the sound of the cry, simultaneously ordering through my radio for the rest of the soldiers to approach as well.

As we fled toward the source, which was just on the opposite side of the craft, there was heavy gunfire, yelling, and a spurt of flame could be seen over the top of the ship. Then everything fell silent. When we reached the end of the spacecraft, keeping along the curve of its nose, a vision of those men and women slaughtered flashed across my brain...so when my mind was in reality again, I was relieved to find the team standing, huddled around something that I couldn't yet see.

Navigating across the short span between us, my feet carried my body through the quickly parting crowd, allowing me to inspect the situation. There was a solitary man, one of our own, laying on the ground. His throat was slit in the same sliced pattern as the others' wounds had been, yet it was barely sputtering. He was already gone. One of the surviving soldiers was kneeling next to him and had closed his eyes.

Another body was lying beside his fresh corpse. A woman. She was tall, slender, and ghostly white...even her lips, which were barely parted, showing a glimpse of yellowed teeth. She wore a tunic similar to Malook's, except for its pitch black color that matched her short, dark hair and her unnerving coal eyes. The iris, the pupil, even the sclera...they were entirely black.

The only hue on her person was the crimson coating her hands, splashed on her face, and pouring from wounds in her torso- probably the gunfire we had heard prior. Her hands were so crusted with the drying liquid that it was impossible to tell that she had white skin. Her fingers were strangely shaped and ended in points. Claws, the corporal had said. This was the perpetrator?

I neared her, making sure someone had my back as I knelt and leaned in closer. I could hear shallow breathing; her chest was barely rising and falling, and it was the only movement she displayed. My eyes darted to hers, and I wondered if she was observing us. It was difficult to tell with the coloring of those orbs and the fact she wasn't blinking at all. I looked up at those around me.

"She-" I started, but was cut off by a deathly cold grip suddenly crushing my throat.

My head darted back to the woman who had sat up on the ground, clutching onto me with one claw, suffocating me as she pulled our faces close together. Her lips were curled in a snarl, showing that her teeth were indeed fanged.

In fact, instead of a set, they were all sharp. The intimidating appearance of those eerie eyes were heightened by their apparent lack of emotion. I couldn't recall ever being so frightened.

"MAJOR!"

The abrupt shout was succeeded by hands on my shoulder, tearing me away from the monster as rapid gunfire sounded. The beast screeched as it fell to the ground once more, claw ripped from my neck, taking off a good chunk of skin with it, yet fortunately not mortally wounding me. Even after she had ceased moving, the soldiers continued to empty their weapons into her.

"Major, are you alright?" the man that had tugged me out of the monster's grasp asked as soon as his fellow men stopped firing.

I jumped to my feet to get away from the alien, but the movement after having my oxygen supply cut off made me dizzy, almost causing me to fall down next to the creature. Two of the soldiers immediately rushed to my aid, lending support until I regained enough strength to stand on my own.

I nodded, finally answering their concerns before watching as the man, who had closed the fallen's eyes, stepped nearer the alien's body and wrapped his fingers around its wrist. He then put his head over her chest, the side of his face shown to have gained a few spots of crimson when he rose again.

"The bastard's dead now," he informed.

Chapter 13: Connie

Letting out a weary sigh, I slouched down in one of the seats of the medical wing's tiny rest area, and sipped on a fresh cup of coffee. The night had gone from alright to horrifying way too quickly.

The nurses and I had managed to clean up, sew up, and repair all of the wounded men and women brought to us except for one woman, who had passed before anyone could even attempt to help.

Apparently one of the nurses had known her from working in the base because she shared with us how the soldier had been a single mom with two sons, neither older than ten. The dad was an alcoholic and had lost all rights to the kids previously. In light of her death, though, I hoped they weren't were returned to him, since he was terrible, judging by the description given. Then again, I also didn't want the kids to get stuck in the system. It broke my heart to think about, yet my mind kept returning to the tragedy.

I readjusted myself, as eyes fell down upon the beverage in my hands, stopping mid-sip when the realization that Malook had lied to me struck. I had so fervently believed his story. Hell, I had felt sorry for him! And he let this happen; he hid this from us. Although I had only known the man for a period of less than a day...less than half of one, actually, I still felt betrayed, something that I had been in turmoil about the possibility of putting him through.

However, I guess it was because of how easily I had trusted him and everything he had to say, rather than any true fault of his own. I was really the one to blame, right? I didn't know if his family was actually on that ship, but whoever was attacking our people, ripping them up like they were nothing more than old rags, was an exceedingly well-trained fighter.

She looks after my son, mostly. My mind suddenly recalled his words, bringing along another thought which calmed me somewhat. It was this so-called babysitter: Sulru.

Malook had originally said that in addition to his family, she was aboard, and had seemed to have trouble explaining her relationship. Or at least that's what I had thought at the time, hence my suggesting the term 'nanny.' Maybe he wasn't having trouble at all, but rather didn't want to clarify her position.

He had hesitated before even uttering her name. Maybe her job wasn't just to look after his son. Perhaps she was meant to protect all of them. Was she even the same species? At any rate, if that were so, he hadn't really lied to me. It's not like I asked if any of them were dangerous or inquired as to what they were.

I took a drink, the warmth filling my stomach nicely. This hadn't been how I had expected to spend the night after such a long day at work, though I wasn't yet sure if I was completely upset or still pleased about it, ignoring the numerous injuries, of course. Upon first meeting the alien, I had definitely been thrilled, yet all the violence, as a doctor, pained me immensely. It was worse knowing that it could have been avoided.

On the other hand, I had always been aware that when our world finally confirmed sentient life outside of ourselves, at least some bloodshed was imminent, and this long-anticipated discovery had finally been made. So my feelings were mixed, and in the end, all I knew was that the evening had drained me.

Sleeping or even just relaxing was out of the question, with as much as was going on; and although I was usually the type that preferred to stay busy over being left to mull over things repeatedly, somehow I really did want some downtime. Taking another sip, I thought I was getting it, until a man appeared at the door, stepping my way.

"Ma'am," the private spoke politely without his face expressing it, "Your husband said to inform you that he has left to help gather the others from the craft, and that he would speak with you when he returns."

My eyes widened slightly, the news not settling well. Despite John being an extremely intelligent and entirely rational man who would act with the utmost caution. it caused me grave concern, after all I had just witnessed. He was quite the capable fighter himself; Nevertheless, that didn't change the fact that their enemy was unrealistically powerful and vicious.

I took a moment before responding, to reprimand myself for using the word 'enemy,' "How long has it been since they left?"

"Just under two hours ago," he answered. "We haven't heard anything yet."

I slowly nodded, grasping the mug in my hands a bit tighter and lowering it, "I understand. Thank you."

The soldier tilted his head in a small motion of acknowledgement and then spun on his heels, retreating from where he had come. I watched until he was out of sight, afterward bringing my drink back to my lips and sipping, before leaning back in the chair as much as was possible without tipping over. John would be fine.

He would be fine; I tried to convince myself, but immediately, visions of the mangled soldiers flashed in my mind. In a desperate attempt to keep from going insane with worry, and also to see if I could figure anything more about the situation out, I leapt to thoughts of Sulru, Malook, and what had been shared with me.

His initial interrogation had ended and I assumed they would soon be sending him to me to finish studying. Even without those tests, there was no doubt in my mind that he was human or similar enough that it didn't make a difference. That being said, it would seem likely that his wife and son were also human.

At least his son, right? We really didn't know how things worked within their culture. Maybe interspecies relations was a thing. Maybe the son was adopted. Maybe I was jumping the gun in thinking that there was a second species in their world at all.

Really all I had to go on was Malook's word, so that's where I should start: his wife, son, and Sulru were the only ones on the ship. They were armed. Malook was human. Sulru was a guard of some sort. If that were all true, one of them, probably Sulru, was either an insanely adept warrior or superhuman...a super soldier, perhaps.

I planned to question my patient about it when he returned to the medical ward, even though I was sure he had already been pressed on the subject of the other passengers, especially after what happened. I wonder what he said to them, if anything?

An alarm sounded abruptly, shaking me from contemplation. I looked up toward the beds in the main room where the patients lay, and saw that one of them had a drop in their oxygen saturation level. Before I could get up to check on him however, a nurse walked into view and and adjusted the long tubes of the cannula running from his nose to the machine beside him. The monitor almost instantly stopped beeping, but she remained a moment longer, staring at the screen to make sure that was the only problem.

It didn't take much effort to shift back to my previous train of thought. I guess I shouldn't have expected Malook to tell me something like that. I mean it wasn't like we were friends or even knew each other at all, and his crew was his priority. Even thus, I felt a connection with the man.

Maybe it was due to the fact I was the first person he met on this planet, or maybe it was just the novelty of who and what he was. Either way, I wanted to actually talk to him about what had been going on to get his side of it, despite awareness that it would probably be pointless to do so.

I took a gulp from my quickly cooling coffee and then released a long breath. I would worry myself crazy if all I did was sit here instead of doing something to keep my mind otherwise occupied; so I stood up and strolled to a counter down the way. After I set my mug safely atop it, I twisted around to gaze down the row of soldiers recuperating.

Although at first glance, everything appeared fine, I decided to walk to each of the stations and check them individually. Nothing unusual about the first two. The third seemed good as well, yet I stopped upon seeing her, noticing a spot of drool on her pillow from her deep, medicine-induced sleep.

It was an inappropriate time to reminisce, but I couldn't help it, barely holding in a giggle at the sight. The first night John and I had spent together, I had awoken to his smiling face next to me. I started to return it, however my cheeks reddened with the realization that I had been drooling, leftover saliva pooling beneath where my head rested.

As I reached to clean it away, he had held out his sleeve and wiped my mouth for me instead.

You're so beautiful, I could hear him say it now as genuinely as he had back then.

"Doctor?" a voice asked from behind me.

Doing my best to shake into the present again, I twisted at the waist to see that the same soldier, who had spoken to me only minutes ago, stood there, "It's your husband."

I walked away from the wounded woman to give my full attention. A brief silence passed while my brain caught up, and I could ask with brow furrowed, "Is he alright?"

"He just reported over radio. There were two casualties including the assailant. They're on their way in," the man still kept his face flat though his tone was friendly.

"Okay," I offered a small smile, "Thank you." Another killed...two if you counted the alien, which I did. I was just thankful the battle had ceased for the time being, "Wait!" I called after the man, who had already made it halfway down the hall, with an after-thought, "How many passengers were there?"

The soldier halted, hesitating before answering, "Just three, Doctor."

Once more, I was lost. So he hadn't lied about that. By the time I thought to give another thanks, the messenger had already gone. Only a few moments later, another man appeared in his place: a medical worker pushing a gurney. The body atop the thin mobile bed lay motionless, covered with a white sheet as it was wheeled past my vision and to the cold room at the other end of the wing. .

Shortly after, another gurney came into sight, appearing identical to the first. Underneath the blankets, however, one of those corpses was that of the alien which had caused the mayhem. I wanted to go and see it...her...both out of scientific and morbid curiosity. I had to force myself to ignore it, and instead go to one of the nurses who had been silently hanging around the main room with me.

"Excuse me," I whispered.

She spun around in obvious surprise.

"I'm sorry," I continued whispering. "I didn't mean to startle you; I just wanted to be sure that I was called if any of the aliens were brought down for tests."

She grinned and nodded, "Of course. I'll be sure to call you. I'll be here."

"Thanks," my reply was hushed as I patted her on the shoulder and departed.

I made it out the door and was well on my way to the elevators when my brain suggested that perhaps they wouldn't call me.

I felt it was a distinct possibility that the colonel would decide to remove me from my post because, although I had been obedient thus far, he was well aware of my deep sympathy for others, even those labeled as lethal enemies.

I did have a history of insubordination with Col. Jean as well, which was mostly due to him rubbing me the wrong way. Maybe I should have stayed in the ward just in case. My prior assumption of never being able to catch any rest was testing me.

Perhaps more now, since I was no longer fearing for deaths, including that of my husband. Either way, I was exhausted and the only usable beds were in the dormitory where John had tried to get me to sleep earlier.

Standing in front of the elevators and staring at the button, I tried to determine if I was absolutely sure of leaving. After several seconds, I put a foot forward and pushed the up button. Sheesh...why did I dwell so long on such simple things? I would get a chance to speak with Malook again. I'd see the others too. Col. Jean had no reason to pull power from me...not yet. The nurse would surely call.

When the door slid open, I hopped on and commanded the machine to move. As the metal passage closed and the lift hummed to life, I pondered what was going on...the bigger picture behind all these events. I hated being ignorant; it was like having tiny bugs slowly eating away at my brain, a feeling I couldn't stand. Overall, everything was okay. John was safe; whatever had been assaulting them had been killed. Although...to be fair, it was us who threatened them first.

The elevator ceased movement and produced an exit, the machine sighing alongside my own breath. I wished things weren't the way they were. Why couldn't we just approach these people with the same peaceful manner that Malook had done with us? Why couldn't these friendly actions be trusted since everyone was just truthful? I walked out towards the lounge, trying to think of what my husband would say.

We have to be cautious in order to keep ourselves protected. Not everyone is trustworthy, even if they act nice. Connie, would you rather not question them and take the chance they might actually be a danger to us, to our country, or even our world? What if it was your child? You wouldn't take chances at all.

I paused with that last thought. My child. I took a few more steps and it felt to me that a silence had suddenly fallen...an eerie stillness overtaking everything around me. Maybe it was because I was now trying to hold back tears after unintentionally upsetting myself. The attempt was proven unsuccessful when I felt one droplet fall from my eye.

I quickly threw my hand onto my cheek to wipe it away while choking back the rest of the emotion. Placing a hand on the doorknob in front of me, I slowly pulled the entry open: the inside remained empty. I didn't figure on being here long before I was called downstairs to work, but since I was here now, I closed the room behind me and strolled over to the coffee maker.

There were still a few servings left. It took looking up and down the counter to remember that I had left my mug downstairs. I found the cabinet above and reached in, retrieving a green one, and then placed it on the counter. John was right...people were only so paranoid because of how distrustful others were. It made you question why anyone felt the need to be so hateful in the first place.

I tried to force those thoughts instead of the single word that had struck a chord in my soul as I stood there fixing my drink. Another failure at hiding the hurt of the topic, I suppose. I had wanted to be a mother so badly. John and I had tried countless times. We went to fertility specialists, we marked the calendar, we took aids, changed things up... We had tried everything. According to the doctors, neither of us were infertile. Even so, I couldn't seem to get pregnant. Except for once.

I had been off birth control for some time and had missed my period two months straight. I didn't pay the first one any heed because I knew it could just be a fluke. Menstruation could become irregular at times even with someone like me who usually had hers like clockwork. After the second, I took a pregnancy test at work and was elated when it read positive.

It was an answered prayer, if I had ever known one. John, of course, was also ecstatic. We set up a gender neutral nursery, told my sister, who is our only relative, and even set up a savings account for the baby.

I had carried him for almost five months when I woke up to a bed covered in blood. We rushed to the hospital. The next hour or so of tests were pure agony; they couldn't find his heartbeat... Finally, the doctor told us that our son's brain had not formed properly and he had passed the previous night while still inside me.

I underwent an emergency c-section, giving birth to a seven ounce baby boy: Charlie Alexander Shinn. Since then, I had given up hope of ever having a child. I couldn't go through that again, and I wouldn't let another one of my children suffer either.

I raised the cup to my lips. This wasn't the time for that sort of thing. Why did I keep having these intruding memories tonight? I took several more sips within a matter of seconds, trying to brush the recollection off.

Reminding myself how tired I was did little to help, but it was all I had. Having worked all day and then instantly called here to work for hours more had made my feet ache, my back sore, and my whole person just overall weary.

Glancing down the length of the kitchenette, into the room with the cots, I told myself I could lie down for a little while and get some sleep. Who knew how much longer the night would be? I set the cup beside the coffee maker and traipsed into the long room, kicking my shoes off at the foot of one bed before walking to its side and plopping down.

I pulled my feet up onto the mattress and then lifted the cover over me. The last thought that passed through my mind before my head found the pillow and slumber found me was: they better call me.

Chapter 14: John

"Connie...Connie..."

I sat on the edge of the bed where she lay, hardly moving in response to my gentle nudging. Poor thing. It had been the hundredth time I thought it this night, yet it was warranted, knowing how terribly long and taxing her day had been. My wife wasn't a high-strung person or one to cave under pressure, yet considering her bleeding heart, then with this particular, I was surprised she hadn't fallen dead asleep far before now.

She took way too much upon herself and although I had to admire her compassion and even her optimism at times, I hated how much they could destroy her if she let them. That was why I always did my best to keep her grounded. With one more push, the woman started to wake.

"Hey," I whispered, smiling on her, "How are you feeling?"

She stretched and yawned as she began to sit up next to me, her lips curling, "Hey, John. Sorry, I dozed off."

"I'm glad you were able to get a little nap," I replied, "Nothing to apologize for."

I reached an arm around her side and rubbed her back. She leaned into me, completing the hug, then cleared her throat and started in with the questions I knew were going to come, "So what happened? With the family? Someone told me that whoever was attacking had been killed.

"Yeah...one of my men had to shoot her multiple times though: an insane amount. The coroner is going to have a field day removing all of those bullets," I shook my head, thinking back to the incredible beating the creature had taken.

"Really?" my wife's eyes seemed to brighten with interest, "So she wasn't human or, well, she wasn't like Malook? What about the others?"

"No, she definitely wasn't human. Except for a frightening sight, I haven't a clue what she was," I replied, those dead alive black eyes haunting me.

Connie broke herself from my embrace, shifting on the bed to better face me, "What do you m- WHAT THE HELL IS WRONG WITH YOUR NECK?"

Her gaze had fallen from mine and caught on the injury I had sustained, which I had already forgotten about. It had been my intention not to mention the wound, hoping I could cover it or at least wait until later to bring it up. Guess that plan was out the window now.

"The creature was laying on the ground. She had already been severely wounded and wasn't moving. We all approached assuming she was dead or dying."

Connie had taken to her feet and was prodding me to move my head in different ways so that she could inspect the gash properly. I grabbed her hands after a few moments and put them down on my lap, cupping them in my own, "Anyway," I continued, "She jumped me. After the next shots fired and she fell again, we made sure her heart had stopped."

"It's not too deep," the doctor concluded, agitated that I had stopped her from tending to the wound, "Just wide. Does it hurt?"

"Burns a little," I admitted, "But I'm fine."

She didn't remove her focus from my throat, "Okay, so the other two passengers, what-"

"A woman and a young boy. I'm assuming the wife and son Malook spoke to you about," I answered without her needing to go any further, "They're completely unharmed and same species as he is, as far as we can tell. They're here now too."

"What, um, I mean, do they speak English?"

I shook my head, "It doesn't appear so. We've been talking with Malook again. He insists they can't. He also won't say anything regarding that beast that was with them."

Connie scratched her head and lifted a brow, finally meeting my gaze, "Nothing at all? Does he know she's dead?"

"Yeah," I shrugged, "When he was told, he did say something, but nothing useful."

"What did he say?" she prompted.

"He said he was surprised; that's all. He didn't seem bothered in the least," looking back at my wife, I smacked my lips, "He has apparently proven to be quite difficult."

I saw that Connie had taken her vision from me once more and was staring blankly. I tried to decipher what she was thinking, which was an impossible task. Her mind was all over the place, her thoughts too sporadic, and her emotions were a constant roller coaster. I wondered if it would be a bad time to tell her that Malook and the family had already been sent for more medical testing.

She had probably told them to call her so she could assist, however, the colonel thought at this point, she should go home. He had learned by now what things Connie didn't approve of and after what had been ordered to be done with the aliens, even the child, he had told me he 'wasn't going to take a chance on disaster.'

Our new guests were being treated little better than fugitives. The way most of the people in the meeting I had recently left justified this to their own conscience, was not solely by saying they had broken our law by entering the airspace.

The destruction and slaughter they had brought to us was what, on paper, gave none of them grief about treating the rest cruelly. I knew my wife and she would not see it that way, regardless of the atrocity. Even though I was fully aware and appreciative of the actions we needed to carry out in order to ensure our own safety and the safety of our planet, I found myself wondering if nothing bad would have happened had we just left them alone.

That creature had dealt horribly irreparable damage, and yet it was clear that it never ventured away from the ship. She hadn't ever attacked until she assessed a direct threat to her companions. Most of the meeting had consisted of what had been said during Malook's interrogation and how they should proceed with the next session.

He honestly had not spoken much of anything, and the large portion of what he did say was useless. All we knew was that he was some sort of government official on his home world and the three aliens- well, two now- were no threat to us.

I got up and followed my wife, who had gone back to the coffee maker on the other side of the wall. Studying her up and down, I mustered the courage to inform her of this, "Connie, honey, why don't you go on home?"

"What?" she murmured numbly.

"It's late. You're tired and you need your rest," knowing that she would not want to go, I readied myself for protest.

"But Malook, the family- I have to..." she trailed off when I took her head in my hands, tilting it upward to face me.

I gave a weak smile, "They're not your problem. You should go home and relax. Everything has leveled out here."

There was a pause. I could tell she had caught drift of the allusion behind my words and was piecing together what it meant. Upon understanding, she abruptly jerked away, "Not my problem?" she repeated accusingly.

"Col. Jean thinks that maybe you shouldn't have any more association with them," I blurted.

"Oh. I see..." she replied indignantly, angrily rolling her eyes.

I knew I didn't have to say anything else, but I didn't want to just leave it at that, so I reached out and took her hands again, "It's just...you know how you get in these situations."

She nodded slowly with a sharp inhale, obviously trying to control her ire. Ridiculousness notwithstanding, she was likely feeling guilty. Removing her hands from me, she complained about the sleep in her eyes, though I figured she might be trying not to lose her cool. It was probable for her to have been on the verge of tears, knowing the woman as I did.

"Tell you what," I stood up and trotted toward the door, "I'm not going to be doing anything for a little bit. Why don't the two of us sit down and have a bite to eat? Hm?"

A short grin flashed over her face and she managed to look at me, "Alright," she agreed with a sigh, "But what is there?"

I curled my fingers around the door handle, glancing back over my shoulder and waiting for her to take my outstretched palm, which she did, "Well, let's just go on down to the cafeteria and find out."

"Isn't that up on the first floor?" she asked.

I laughed, "Yes it is. You know what I mean," and with that, I led us from the tiny kitchen, through the lounge, and out into the hallway.

The silence of the trip was broken when she breathed a 'thank you' as I held the cafeteria door open for her. Once inside, we saw that there was nothing freshly prepared, not that I had really expected it. More than anything, I was trying to get her to feeling better. Likely nothing new would be cooked until the morning. I glanced down at my watch and time suddenly caught up with me; it was almost daybreak already.

We could sit around and wait to have an actual meal. However, movement from my wife pushed this realization away. She had made it to the bar holding the soda fountain, and had grabbed a banana from the fruit bowl beside it.

I joined her as she strolled to one of the long tables in the clearing and sat. I should have grabbed something as well, but I didn't like eating a snack so close to a meal and I certainly wasn't too fond of fruit. So I ignored my stomach and seated myself across from her.

When I pulled out a chair, I noticed the expression she wore and I didn't like it at all. It was one of frustrated disappointment, of guilt and depression. I knew she wanted to stay involved with the undergoing, even if it was just to offer the aliens kindness herself. I wished so terribly that I could grant her this simple thing, yet it wasn't within my power.

I tried once more to take her hand to comfort her. Unfortunately, when she was feeling so down, she hated that, so she simply pulled away and peeled her banana instead. I had to give her something to hold onto though; had to let her in on things as much as I could. Although I wasn't sure if hearing about it further would further upset her, it was all I could offer.

"Right now the family is in the medical ward, finishing up the basic tests," I explained, studying the woman's each move, every single nuance, "If they all continue to show as human, then they'll be given anesthesia to undergo deeper tissue sampling," I paused, allowing this bit of information to soak in, "Afterward, I believe they plan on talking to them again."

"What if they still don't share anything?" Connie's voice had dropped to a low octave, her eyes focused on the still uneaten fruit in her hand.

"Honey..." I trailed.

"What about Riven?" she asked, finally looking up at me.

"Who?"

"Malook's son. The boy," she clarified.

"Oh," my tone picked up slightly when I realized I could give her a bit of good news, "They've called in a child psychologist. At present, he and the woman haven't spoken. At least not anything we can understand. They figured the psychologist would be helpful in either case."

Her absentminded gaze was back on the banana. It didn't seem to change her mood, and made me unsure about saying anything more, yet I began feeling desperate to soothe my wife.

"Everything will be alright. The whole family will be fine and you haven't done anything wrong, sweetie. You should know that. You'll see," I put my hand on top of her arm, grasping it firmly until she looked back at me. Then I smiled reassuringly. It was all I could do for now.

We sat in silence for several minutes while she actually began eating the snack she'd been fidgeting with. At last she finished, carefully placing the peel onto the table between us, "Not the whole family."

"What?" my vision narrowed, thrown off by her observation.

"You said the whole family will be fine," she pointed, "But one of them was killed, so it's not the whole family."

My breath hitched, "Well, yeah," I choked out, "But Connie, you need to remember that she killed three of our people and gravely injured many more," No shift in her demeanor, "She tried to kill me too, you know?"

The woman's eyes shot up, staring apologetically at me while they filled with tears. I felt a tad ashamed, since the attack didn't bother me; I was perfectly fine. However, I knew speaking of it with how close we were, might resonate better with my wife, and I had been right. She parted her mouth to say something, but quickly shook her head, taking the thought with her as she lifted the banana peel up off the table, abruptly standing and going to discard it into a trash bin.

"What has become of her?" she inquired through a sniffle, though I knew it wasn't what had popped into her mind.

Of course the body had been sent for autopsy. She had to know it. She also had to know that since it was now, just a corpse, there would be nothing holding our teams back from studying it to the full extent.

Nonetheless, inquiring was her way of hiding whatever idea she had neglected to share, and I wasn't going to agitate her by answering defensively, "Her body is with the coroner which I believe is on the same floor as the medical wing."

She took a couple of paces so she could place her hand on the table, then looked intently into me, "I want to see it."

I hesitated, unsure if that was a good idea, "Why?"

She swayed where she stood and dropped her head, "I just want to know what she looks like. You said she wasn't human; I'm curious."

I sensed that wasn't completely it, but ignored the feeling, "Okay," I said, standing and pushing my chair in, "I don't see the harm in that." I went to her, placing my arms around her and hugging tightly, "Are you alright?"

I felt her head rub against my chest, "Yes, just tired."

I kissed her forehead, then loosened my hold. I offered my arm and when she took it, I led us down to the elevators. Just as the metal gateway slid to its side to let us in, I felt a vibration at my waist. My gaze skipping toward the sensation, I saw that it was my pager going off.

Major Shinn to conference. I exhaled heavily. Of course. I re-pinned the small machine onto my belt.

"What is it?" Connie asked.

I stepped into the machine with her, "Another meeting."

"Oh," she muttered.

I pushed two buttons inside the small room and the machine closed before moving again, "I'm going to have to go. Will you be alright by yourself?"

"Yeah," she nodded, vision blank though her lips lilted into a weak smile, "I'm fine."

"Okay," I gave her another hug, a quick one, "If anyone questions your presence, tell them I sent you there."

"Okay."

Soon we were at my stop where I pecked my wife on her cheek before stepping out and beginning down the corridor.

"John!" Connie called, causing me to spin, "Thank you," she said almost under her breath with the same discontent smile.

I grinned warmly for her, "Of course."

Chapter 15: Connie

As the elevator reached the floor of the medical wing, I took in a deep breath and slowly exhaled. I had expected to see the hall alive with the staff on the other side, but instead I stepped out into empty whiteness.

There was not a soul to be seen for the entire length of the walls. Even passing the main room, where the few most gravely injured soldiers laid recovering, seemed strangely still. I kept on down the hall until I reached the last door in that direction, taking a second to study it before entering.

Rather than a name plate or a sign with the word 'morgue' on it, it was simply marked 'freezer.' I thought it weird and a bit comical, yet wasn't in the mood for laughing. I stood there for another moment, listening for anything behind the door and when I didn't hear any movement, gave a polite knock which instantly caused feet to shuffle inside, coupled with a male voice yelling, "Come in."

I swung the entry open and stepped into a large, clear area. There was a man and two women standing a couple of yards from me, huddled around one of the corpses, though I couldn't tell who it belonged to: Earthling or ET. The three were decked out in scrubs, gloves, and masks, but beneath her face shield, I recognized one of the nurses as the one who I had lovingly named a self-righteous bitch.

I hoped that she wasn't aware that I wasn't supposed to be around anymore, because she would surely start something if so. The other woman was hands deep in the abdomen of the person who was lying on the table in front of the trio. Her sleeves were bloodied, but outside of that, her clothing appeared neat.

The man was entirely clean, strolling toward me and pulling his mask down as he approached, "Can I help you?"

He seemed to be somewhere between the ages of my husband and that of the colonel, his hair starting to age into that silver shade that I had always found very beautiful. I allowed myself a glance around the room before answering.

There were two other bodies, dead ones, in the room besides the one being dug into. White blankets covered the larger part of their torsos and limbs, but the faces were exposed. All had been stripped of clothing and I was still unable to spot the alien warrior from where I stood.

"Major Shinn sent me," I replied, grabbing my ID and handing it over to him, "To see if any progress had been made on the attacker."

He took the card, giving it a once over before looking back at me and raising an eyebrow. The action made me feel that he had been told of my denoted status, however either he hadn't, didn't care, or realized that I was related to the major and didn't want to be found sending me away if I were being honest.

"You're a bit early, then," he grinned, leading me past his coworkers and toward the other corpses, "I just finished cleaning up so that I could work on her. I was already having a lovely conversation with Mr. Sanderson's entrails over there when she was brought in," he gestured where the women were standing as he halted at the body against the wall, "But I was told to rush, so I had to cut our words short," he chuckled.

I knew doctors eventually grew desensitized toward death or at least many did. Even so, I had never gotten used to the nonchalant behavior of morticians. The doctor twisted to the wall beside him, pulling out a fresh mask and handing it to me, apparently not bothered in the slightest that I hadn't acknowledged his joke. I took the offered item and held it loosely in front of my mouth as I laid eyes on the corpse below.

She looked human though very pale...sickly pale, but then again, she was dead. Her body was lean, her head topped with short, straight, and silky black hair cut in a few different layers, giving her an odd punk-rockstar look. Her eyelids had been closed making me wonder what color they were.

The other features of her face were rounded yet somehow she looked exotic. I didn't see anything of the frightening appearance John had mentioned until my eyes wandered down her arm and to her hand.

That was definitely not normal. Besides being covered and crusted with blood, her hands came into long, slender fingers not unlike a human, but at the last digits, they seemed to morph into claws. When the mortician saw me staring, he reached over and flipped her hand onto its side. Leaning in more closely, I could see the sharp outline of the blades.

They were extremely thick and completely undamaged, without even the slightest chip. Each one stretched out into a sharp yet still heavy point, ending about five inches from where they began. Underneath the red, they seemed to be made of the same clear type tissue that my own nails were.

"That's fascinating," I murmured.

"Look at this," I straightened my spine to put attention back on the man across from me. He had picked up her other hand, placing the palm upright. I noted that it wasn't as crimson stained as her right, "They retract like a cat," his voice was amused as I watched him apply pressure to the back of her knuckles.

Doing so caused the claws to either pull into themselves or extend. I had fought the urge to touch the first hand, having seen how dirtied it was. However, the one the mortician held seemed mostly clean so I reached out slowly.

When my fingertip lay on top of one of the blades, I found them even sturdier than I had surmised. I had only barely slid my finger down its length when I was greeted with a sting.

"Ouch!" my hand flew from the strange weapon, my mind resisting putting the pricked finger into my mouth like a baby.

"Here," another short laugh from the man as he set her hand down, and grabbed a napkin from underneath the box of masks beside us. He handed it to me with a smile, pointing through the latex of his own glove to a bandage around his index finger, "I had the same problem."

I took a pace backward while pressing the paper against my cut, simultaneously letting my mask down to set it on a tool table. Removing the tissue after a moment, it was rapidly replaced when the brief second showed I was still bleeding. The small cut was deep was as if I had nicked it on razor wire.

"Amazing, isn't it?" the mortician looked from me, back to the body.

"It's strange," I replied somewhat grumpily. A minor twinge of fear flicked in my stomach upon scanning the room and getting a better picture of the two other dead. I suddenly remembered that it was this person...this creature that had killed them. She was the one that had sent all those poor wounded to me earlier in the evening.

"So she's the one that did all this damage?" I muttered, half to myself, as I observed the other woman removing the liver of the first patient.

The man grunted, "Yeah, like I said: amazing."

I shook my head fervently, agitated by his disassociation, "It's awful!"

The man's expression flickered, causing me to become afraid that I had offended him. However, he quickly returned to the morbidly enthused person he had been before, and replied with calm, "I suppose when you're in my line of work, you get used to death too much. It doesn't have the same effect."

His line of work? I hardly contained a scoff. I was a doctor too. I actually witnessed the people dying. But then that, I guess would make me more aware that cadavers weren't simply shells...that a person had once lived inside of them.

My vision returned to the alien woman. I found myself staring at her closed eyes as if I could telepathically lift their lids. I guess I had never gotten used to it...death, I mean.

Compared to others, yeah, but for a doctor with my experience, no. It still truly bothered me. It was worse when the person had been a patient of mine. Someone I had known for days, weeks, even months. It was like I failed not just them, but their entire family.

All their friends. Everyone. Sometimes I even felt that I was the reason of their passing. Thankfully, I had my husband who was always good at trying to console me and getting me to think logically.

Nonetheless, when emotions were set into play, logic liked to vanish. Was that why I was here? Did I feel badly for her being killed even though she had done more than her fair share of damage? I guess so. I still felt sorrow- guilt, even- that she had to die. Of course, I didn't know how intelligent a being she was.

I didn't know if she had family or anything. But I couldn't imagine being stranded in such a strange land, having to fight so hard, and then dying all alone, probably to never be seen again by anyone who knew her. I looked over the body once more, my gaze falling to her hands again. I immediately lifted my own, remembering that I was holding a napkin on the cut. I gently took it off and the saw there was no more plasma emerging.

"Is there a trash bin?" I asked.

He pointed toward the door of the room while showing me a confused expression. I sighed, not bothering to smile. If all this destruction hadn't concerned him, why, then, would he care for such a small act of manners? I spun around and headed toward the container, reaching it after only a handful of steps. Before I could discard the tissue, the sound of a horrid scream and crashing metal made me jump.

I recognized it as the mortician's. My head twisted backward so suddenly I was sure I had given myself whiplash. What I saw there disturbed me beyond anything, and apparently the other women too, for one screeched while the other rushed to the exit, fumbling to open it before succeeding and dashing through. I paid her no more heed than that, as I froze in utter shock at what was in front of me.

The alien was alive?! She stood beside the table where her corpse had previously lain, arms extending over the gurney, now collapsed on the ground, and around the man's sides, where her abnormally sharp and long nails dug deeply into his flesh. Looking up at her face, I saw her mouth was wide open, displaying a set of yellow teeth, all fanged...and they were pierced into the man's neck.

The creature was sideways in my view, her body barely covered with the now draping sheet that had been resting upon her prior. Holding the mortician tightly, sucking on his throat, and licking at the blood coming from the wound, some of the crimson fell past her white lips and trailed down his skin and across her face. Whether he was still conscious or not, I couldn't tell. However, his body was jerking, not in an attempt to free himself, it didn't seem, but rather as his system's reaction to the attack.

I knew that she was going to kill him, yet even so, I couldn't manage to look away from the ghastly scene...to act in his defense in any way, or to save myself. After what felt like minutes of staring at the gore, my sight was focused on her face once more to take notice of the eyes I had been so curious of, and I instantly understood what John had deemed so terrifying.

Fortunately though, she was not yet laying them upon me.

I was finally able to force myself to put a foot in reverse, the noise I made in doing so took the beast's attention away from its meal. I had laid my foot on an instrument that the lady who ran away had dropped in her escape. Those cold black eyes turned on me, and I felt I was being watched by evil. The alien released her mouth from the human, still holding his body, now limp.

Her stare remained on me, unblinking, her body motionless just like his. The other woman realized the shift in the creature's gaze and she, too, began backpedaling toward the door. I tried to gain full control of myself again so that I could run with her, but my mind wouldn't let me pull focus from the horror it was caught on. I couldn't break from that dreadful glare. It felt as if she was staring into my soul and trying to smother it.

I saw her claws begin to loosen from her victim. Just as his body started to fall from her, the nurse to my other side sprinted away, disappearing out the exit previously left open. I heard her yelp as she almost tripped on its threshold, yet the creature did not cease looking into me the entire time.

Right before the last of her scythe-like fingers came out of the mortician's flesh, she gave a final lick to his neck, and then let the body slip to the floor, her only clothing falling with it. My vision darted to the fallen. He was no longer even seizing.

But the alien was moving. Coal eyes still intent upon me, she took a slow pace forward, in my direction. Something struck then, and I finally gathered the strength to run from the morgue. The woman who had gone out in front of me was at the end of the hallway with sights rushing frantically between where she had left, and the elevator whose button she was desperately mashing.

As I went, I saw the machine slide open and watched her disappear into the small room. I tried to yell to get her to wait, but she let the elevator close and take her away...leaving me there to wait for its return...locking me in with the monster.

I pushed the button the instant I reached it. To my surprise, there was a ding almost immediately. My heart fell, though, when I realized it was the start of an alarm over the loudspeaker, warning everyone to find their way to the safe room on the first floor whilst ordering every soldier to arm themselves.

I looked at the lift. It was still closed. My eyes jumped from it, back to the morgue. Sure enough, at the very end of the corridor, the alien was standing, still watching me, but now cloaked in a haggard and black robe-type garment.

Stopping to find the clothes was probably the only reason she hadn't caught up to me yet. My heart pounded even heavier at the sight of her. Then, she lunged into a stride.

It made me decide to give up on the lift and instead find the stairwell. Although right as I twisted to leave, my face lined up directly with hers. She wasn't just strong, she was fast. I started gasping for air, not knowing what else to do. As I did, she suddenly became taller than me.

I guessed that she had been crouched while running. All I could do was stare as she adjusted to her full height. Even with her thin figure, she appeared massive, standing maybe a foot over me.; I also noticed that despite being lean, all of her seemed to be muscle.

Just as she settled herself, the alarms sounded again in the background, and the electricity cut off momentarily, drawing my head to search the darkness in the single moment before the light returned, wondering if I should try continuing to flee. However, when I could see...the being had disappeared.

I looked down both ends of the hallway and saw nobody. There was even nothing on the ceiling when I scanned it. My search ended fruitlessly, which allowed my heart to gain a minor amount of calm. Soon came a friendly beep as the elevator door to my side slid open. Where had she gone?

It was puzzling, but I didn't stick around to find out. I quickly loaded myself onto the lift and commanded the machine to the first floor so I could get to the safe room. It felt as though the short ride took an hour, and I thought that perhaps due to the acute stress, I had begun hallucinating.

Even so, it was equally as insane to believe that. As the car passed a few floors; I heard gunfire, which determined against any hope of psychosis. It was really happening. She must have gone for the stairs... Why would she just leave me like that? I had been so certain of my doom.

My thoughts returned to before...this woman had only fought in defense of her shipmates. Defensive, not offensive, I mused. I hadn't posed a threat, so she let me be. Hearing shouts and flying bullets, every part of me wanted to scream: Don't fight! She wont' hurt you if you don't attack! Yet all I could do was finish the ride with the silent hope that nobody else would die.

It wasn't like the soldiers would actually stop fighting if I said anything anyway. My brain jumped to contemplating her strength: the way she had taken hold of the mortician and fed on his blood; how she had been pelted with machine gun fire; her heart literally stopped beating; and she had remained alive. A vampire? Was she an immortal beast?

I backed into a corner and slid down onto the floor, hugging my knees in dread of what was happening. Directly after I fell, the happy ding of the elevator came, and released me from its hold and into a corridor torn asunder and void of life.

Gradually, I made it to my knees and then pushed to my feet, my eyes shifting nervously about. I was shaken to the core fearing that I would stand up and come face to face with that horrible creature again.

As I strolled cautiously through the mess, I took note that there was no blood, there were no bullet shells, and there were no bodies. I had made it halfway down the hall toward the designated safe room when I heard gurgled choking sounds coming from behind. I was too stunned to look back. Instead, I simply stopped in my tracks, vision widening, swallowing air loudly.

The sounds carried on, and then became stronger like they were getting nearer. The hair on my ears and my neck rose. Whatever it was, it was right behind me. I could feel it. I finally began to rotate...carefully, deliberately, yet before my gaze even hit the wall beside where I stood, something large was chunked past me, landing at my feet. I squealed at the sudden motion, gasping when I realized what had been thrown.

Now stomach down, skull barely lifted from the floor, was a female soldier. Her eyes were huge with terror and there was crimson foam sputtering from her mouth: the source of the gurgles I had heard. She was choking on her own blood! Without a thought to how she had gotten there, my doctor instincts kicked in and I knelt, using my hands to help her lift her head. She was trying to speak.

"Sh-sh-sh! Be still, it's okay, you're going to be fine," I spoke, completely flustered.

I heard a sharp exhale from the direction she had been flung. The woman's eyes rolled back and her head became dead weight in my palms. Another loud exhale. I slowly rose to my feet, warily turning my head, but not my body. There the alien creature stood, staring at me again.

Her face was painted red and her mouth hung open just far enough to show the points of her fangs. I gulped, omitting obscenities as I pounced into a heated run, dodging over-turned tables and various objects while occasionally glimpsing backward. She hadn't moved. She stayed in that stance, simply observing. Still, I fled.

I threw my ID up to the scanner beside the door of the safe room as soon as I reached it. Out of my peripherals, I felt a little relieved to see she hadn't followed, "Come on. Come ON!" I growled as the technology denied my access, "Let me in!" I yelled furiously, "It's Dr. Shinn! LET ME IN!!"

I was unable to control the delirium in my voice. As I pounded on the door again and again, the lights on the scanner flashed a different color, and the door popped open a crack.

I grabbed it and pulled it enough for me to squeeze inside, ignoring the barrel that had pointed out of it and aimed itself at my head. Brain overwhelmed by survival instinct, it barely gathered that my husband speaking as I felt his arms slither around me and pull me inside.

"Are you okay?" he demanded, his tone laden with terror.

I nodded over and over in rapid succession as I kept studying the room. Behind my husband were several other armed men and women. The colonel stood amongst them as well. They all seemed to be as petrified as I was, and fighting not to show it.

Then my sights found Malook. He was standing with two others, unarmed: a woman and a little boy. This was his family? They were all wearing gowns standard to hospitals, save without the opening in the back.

She was about my height with long, mid-length blond hair and skin only a little lighter than that of her husband. She was holding her son tightly against her. He couldn't have been much older than the sons of the woman who died earlier in the evening.

He, too, had dark skin with hair like his father's. There were three SCARs pointed at them. I didn't have time to do anything but stay in John's embrace as everyone's attention rapidly returned to the door that had been shut instantly after my entrance. Someone was pounding on the other side.

"PLEASE!" they begged with a voice that made my blood run cold, "PLEASE OPEN UP!"

The soldiers guarding the door looked to the colonel, who shook his head, making them remain at their posts. Not even a second later, the panel on this side lit up, and the entry popped open just has it had for me.

A human hand reached around it, the soldiers just inside adjusting their weapons in response. Then, it pulled the door wide to reveal a woman. She was panting and her entire self was trembling. As the guard closed the door, trying to quickly grab and pull her to safety as John had with me, another hand took hold of his arm.

It was Sulru's.

She had appeared suddenly behind the woman and took a tight grip of the guard, tugging at him, while simultaneously kicking the passage completely ajar. She kept yanking him until his body ran directly into hers.

Only then did she let go of his wrist, grabbing instead his head and banging it with such force against the entryway that it could have killed him. He was at the very least unconscious as he thudded to the floor.

The moment it registered in the frightened woman's mind, she pushed past the alien and jolted back down where she had come rather than rushing into the room with the rest of us. Sulru did nothing to stop her, didn't even look in her direction. The creature's focus was now intent on the soldiers surrounding Malook and his family.

Regardless of where her attention appeared to be, it was me that had her gaze. Even as bullets began hitting her chest, rumpling her already tattered clothes, it was obvious she was fixated on me. She reached out and jerked the two guns that were shooting her, one with each hand, bringing their owners with them.

As the soldiers fell forward, the alien sank her claws into their backs, making them squeal. Three more stepped forward, growling and readying to shoot when suddenly Malook's voice boomed above everything.

Chapter 16: Malook

"Sulru, stop!"

At my words, the woman ceased her movement, and so did the men around us, even though they kept their weapons aimed carefully upon her. A last, stray shot exploded from one of the barrels and grazed past Sulru's cheek.

I saw her eyes flinch as if they had darted over to take notice of the new, tiny scratch on her face, her expression growing annoyed as she glared at the man who had fired it. Under her heavy gaze, he took an uneasy step backward, managing to mostly keep his ready stance.

I looked from the scared solider back to my friend, giving her a quick once-over. Her clothes were filthy and torn, holes showing her ghost-white skin beneath, that had already healed around the probable bullet wounds that had made the tears in the first place. Judging by the damage, she had sustained numerous shots. Her body certainly hadn't been able to reject all of the metal, so I wondered how much discomfort she was in.

Upon seeing me studying her, she suddenly lifted her long black sleeve, and I barely caught a glimpse of blood droplets around the corner of her mouth, before she wiped them away and let her arm fall back to the side. She had fed, which was good.

Illegal, according to our laws, to do so in this manner, but she needed the strength after such strenuous combat, especially since she had now become our only way to escape Earth.

There was a rustle to my side that caught my attention. Just in front of me, I saw Connie tear her face from Sulru and pull tightly against her husband. Looking back over at my partner, I saw the subtle nuance in her expression that I'd come to know as her contemplating another's thoughts.

She was observing Connie during the shift, so my mind figured that perhaps the Earth woman had witnessed something concerning Sulru, perhaps her feeding. As evidenced by the fact the doctor was still alive, she had not tried to confront my companion.

Both her eyes and mine left from their current focus then, and we both visually scanned the room. After working together for several years, we often found ourselves in sync, and always so when danger was about.

Every individual surrounding us held the same intensity of fear and concern. Most hardly showed it, but I could still sense it. The doctor seemed to be the only one not worried with masking her feelings.

I stepped forward toward Sulru, instantly greeted by the clicks of guns shifting with their owners, who had been aiming them at us. I paused, holding my palms up and open to show I wasn't trying to start any trouble. However, in response to my moving closer to our guard, I felt little Riven brush by my legs, running right past the armed men to the coal-eyed woman.

Before my son could grab hold of her, though, one of the female soldiers released a hand from her rifle and caught the boy by his shoulder, jerking him back.

I immediately stepped up in protest, yelling, "Don't!"

Each gun pushed nearer to my person, making me halt in my tracks. Sulru, on the other hand, pounced forward, ripping the woman's hand from my son and, taking a strong yet careful grip onto him herself, shoved him behind her body and away from all the strangers.

My heart relaxed a might, seeing my young son protected, hugging our ally's leg. He obviously wasn't fully aware of the situation. He took a moment, speaking to his savior in our native tongue, asking her why everyone was being so mean.

Sulru, never breaking her eyes from the soldiers between us, replied in a soft, placating voice, "Echmar," which was the Earthling equivalent of saying it's fine, calm yourself. Riven looked down from her and began peeking from his spot at his mother and me.

I took another step, this time being allowed to do so by the soldiers who had been given silent gestures from the man called John. Taking advantage of this minor freedom, I made a gesture of my own, urging my wife, Soare-a, to go to Sulru as well and stay with our child. She obeyed, but with extreme caution.

Her gaze was darting back and forth among all the people and their rifles as she made her way to join Riven. After I judged that my family was safe, I attempted to follow after them, but just as I came face to face with my friend, she rapidly thrust me to the side and changed her position so that the three of us were behind her and she was facing the leader, apparently directly above Connie's husband on the ladder.

The colonel grabbed a heavy pistol from a holster at his waist, and stomped in our direction. As he neared, seemingly to attack, the others returned to their former battle positions, realizing that the highest commander had taken full control over the group. And he wasn't too eager to just let us go.

Even with Sulru, who had to appear to them as nigh invincible. Our guard remained strong where she stood, unwavering as the short barrel of the man's gun inched close to touching her.

"What the hell is this thing?!" the Earth leader growled, speaking to me, yet staring at my guard.

Sulru tilted her head on its side. She understood what he had said, but didn't lose her collected demeanor, and instead waited for me to answer, "Her name is Sulru," I said, peering around her shoulder, causing her to bring an arm up to ensure my safety.

"I don't care what her name is," he replied in a mock tone, "I want to know what it is."

I barely saw the woman in front of me blink and shrug when I glanced over, motions meant to express her apathy toward the situation. She kept her focus on the others, though. In a last ditch effort at a peaceful relation, I took the moment required to explain, "She's, as best I can describe in your terminology, a vampire."

A brief, quiet murmur brushed over the soldiers. A few of them, I picked up, had repeated the archaic term. Connie had revealed her face again and let go of her husband, though still standing so that they were touching. She was looking at the vampire with an expression of realization and understanding that confirmed my earlier suspicion. Then I turned to Sulru myself.

"You fed, didn't you?" I asked in a medium voice, unsure if I wanted the others to hear me or not. I didn't think that they needed any more intimidation factors and at the same time, wanted to play the upper hand that we had acquired. She didn't move at all save for her lips, that responded in a half-growl, all-annoyed tone, "These people quite drained me with their unnecessary violence," neither of us had bothered to hide our conversation by using our own language.

"Unnecessary violence? It wasn't us who ripped a dozen people to shreds!" the doctor had interjected herself further into the middle of things to voice her complaint. The woman's courage in standing up to the vampire was astounding, bordering on stupidity.

And Sulru didn't miss a beat in responding as she took a pace of her own, momentarily grazing the weapon which Col. Jean still had pointing at her. He fell back a minuscule amount, enough that it wasn't. I was honestly surprised when he didn't fire.

Twisting at her waist to face the Earth woman, she huffed, "I merely acted in self-defense: to protect this family."

"You're nothing but a monster!" Connie spat.

The vampire's brow furrowed at the insult; otherwise, she didn't react. Connie, however, almost jolted forward as if she were ready to start a fight. Sulru wouldn't have critically harmed her, not in this scenario, not if the doctor hadn't come after my wife, son, or myself directly...but of course nobody else knew that. John lunged with his wife and pulled her back as one of their own guards moved in to offer aid.

My friend didn't attempt to fend the overzealous human woman off, however, when the soldier brushed past his bosses with a finger flicking at the trigger on his own rifle, her instinct took over.

Instantaneously, she grabbed him with one hand by the shoulder, the other taking hold of the barrel in her face before jerking it with such sudden force, that it pulled the joints in his arm, creating enough pain that he dropped the gun. Sulru used her newly freed arm to grasp the man by his ear and force his head to the side, exposing his neck, her mouth beginning to open.

"Sulru!" I put a firm foot down, placing hands on her shoulders, "Enough."

I knew she wasn't about to go through with the action. Not only because she had just eaten, but because it would compromise the strength of her position, allowing and begging for assault. No, her reasoning was simply to further unsettle her enemies.

She paused for a moment before obeying my order, loosening her grip and casually pushing the soldier out of her way as she clicked her maws closed. The man groaned, awkwardly searching for his feet as he grabbed his weapon off the ground and hustled away to recover.

"Let us go now," I spoke calmly, yet sternly.

My hand was still resting upon my friend's shoulder. The vampire nodded, gaze on the others. She remained, motionless with her intent glare, as she waited for my wife, son, and I to start heading out of the room and to our escape.

We were a great many yards away before I glanced back and saw that the vampire had only just begun walking away from the crowd, slowly making her way to the door, being certain nobody was trying to attack, at least not until we were at a safe distance.

Chapter 17: Connie

John held me back against him, which, after a moment, I realized was a good idea because surging toward the vampire definitely wasn't. I had become immediately aware every time the creature's eyes were resting on me.

To be honest, I really hadn't paid attention to how much she focused on any other person, but it felt to me that for whatever reason, she had singled me out from the others.

My own gaze had faltered from hers, until the initial shock of the events I had witnessed involving her had worn off. I looked at the vampire, my brow furrowed with contempt as I stared deeply into her cold eyes.

However, while I did so, I could see that underneath her intense appearance and fierce actions, there was a greater pain: an odd softness to her soul. Even with how terribly violent the things she had done were, knowing the things she could do, she was also somehow inspiring.

She had made it perfectly clear that she would do anything to keep Malook and his family safe; she would protect the peaceful aliens at all costs. My mind returned to its earlier distress of wondering who was really at fault here. Her? or us? Some would label me a traitor for it, yet still I was certain the answer was us.

She did have to fight; there was no other option. Just as I felt guilty for not being able to help the aliens, she took it upon herself to take care of them even at her own consequence.

Our people had asked for trouble when they had decided to exert force in order to get what they wanted from the strange newcomers. As I gazed back into those dark spheres, my demeanor relaxed with the epiphany that I did not blame her. Nor did I think she was a monster.

A twinge of regret hit my stomach as I remembered my callously thrown insult. Malook had already left with his wife and son, leaving the vampire behind, where she kept her sentry position several seconds longer before finally beginning to back out of the room herself, her gaze on me again.

"You better be glad I'm not the monster you think I am," Sulru spoke to me in a stern voice with gentle undertones, letting her eyes linger on me only an instant as she turned and lunged out the door, down the path the family had taken.

All of the soldiers shifted in their stead at the amazing speed she tore away with. A few ducked into the hallway, only to realize she was already too far gone. Letting their weapons fall to the side, some faced the colonel and some faced the major...all waiting for further instruction. But even John's seasoned boss seemed to be in a state of shock.

"Are you alright?" my husband's voice soothed as he loosened his hold, tugging slightly in the hope of spinning my body around so he could see me.

I allowed it, seeing he had his head bowed, looking at me caringly. His teal eyes were full of concern. No doubt I had scared him by facing off with that creature...with Sulru. Sometimes, I could really be my worst enemy, "Yeah, I'm fine."

It was amazing that I hadn't been killed, yet then again, it really wasn't. I had put together from the start that the vampire was defensive and that her companions weren't likely dangerous at all.

Although, I wondered if John hadn't have stopped me, if she would have hurt me for approaching her so aggressively. Maybe she would have, but what was more curious to me was this seeming fascination with me.

I don't know. It could just be my imagination. Nonetheless, I felt like she had focused on me a little more than what was normal.

"Unbelievable!" Col. Jean roared, "Just unbelievable! Who trained you monkeys?"

Looking around at the others, I saw nothing except fearful faces. Was it the colonel's rage or the astonishing creature they were up against?

Probably both, but I would have definitely been more frightened of Sulru than the stubborn old man. Either way, someone or someones were going to get their ass chewed if the aliens did end up getting away.

"Colonel, with all due respect," John retorted, little reverence actually showing, "Did you not see what we're having to handle here? We have no idea how to kill that. For all we know, it's an indestructible foe."

"Nonsense!" the elder spat back, narrowing the gap between the two of them, "Blow it to pieces if you have to, but don't let it get away," he barked before motioning two of the soldiers watching him out of the room and following after.

Nervously, my eyes shifted from him to John, who responded by giving me a tight squeeze of a hug. I really wanted our side to just give it up. Let Malook, Sulru...just let them leave. Why were they all so willing to risk more bloodshed? My husband didn't even question it. He simply jumped right back into obedience mode.

"Connie, get him to the medical ward," he said to me softly, his gaze upon the man whose head had been bashed during Sulru's entry.

Luckily, I had noticed the man move a bit, trying to recover, so I knew he hadn't been killed. He'd still need to have his head examined though, since he had to have endured a concussion, and with how powerful the blow had been, he might have internal bleeding as well. Two others in the room ran to the fallen's aid just as the major spoke, carefully helping him to his feet.

The man was obviously dizzy, unbalanced from the attack, as he had trouble walking without wobbling about. So he clung to the two and let them guide and halfway carry him through the hall.

John dismissed the entire room, informing them to be ready should he call for them during the next several minutes. He then watched as all of the men and women gradually left.

The last stopped, steeling herself and returning to her default demeanor as she spoke to us, "Should I stay and escort you?"

My husband declined, "No, thank you."

The woman gave a slight bow before following after the others. I slowly found my way from my husband and to the exit, looking out to see some of the people who had left, had halted their trek to move the body of the gurgling woman Sulru had thrown at me earlier.

Seeing them fumble with her corpse sent a chill down my spine as the scenario from before flashed, in detail, across my vision. I was relieved, even so, that more had not been hurt. Then I remembered the gunfire and screams I had heard while riding the elevator. Maybe there were more.

"Will you go after them?" I spoke to John, deflecting my thoughts from the idea of more injured to be found. I felt his hand on my shoulder then, so I turned to face him.

"It looks that way," he sighed.

I stepped to the side as he eased past me and into the corridor, taking in the scene himself. He tilted his head back enough to see me and offered his hand, which I took before hanging my head and beginning to walk with him. I glanced up as we came to a stop behind the others positioned at the elevators.

We both stood, waiting on the machine, without a single word to each other. I figured that he was thinking about what was to be done next, so I stayed silent because I wanted to know too. I'd probably end up pitching in with the new patients.

Seeing with how everything went down, it was a good guess that the colonel wasn't worried with keeping me from carrying out my doctorly duties and caring for the injured.

While I waited for John to enlighten me to his planned actions, I wondered where Malook and the others had made it to and what their plans were. If they got back to their ship, would they be able to fix whatever had gone wrong with it in the first place?

And also, what would they do about the damage done to the entrance when the soldiers had broken in to take the family? The elevator door slid closed after the three who had been standing in front of us made it inside.

We politely remained calm as it vibrated away and then John reached out and pressed the little arrow button.

"Where do you suppose they are?" I decided to speak out loud, having grown impatient of the quiet, "I mean, Sulru's the only one with that speed, it seems. How far could they have gotten? And in what direction?"

"Hm?" John mumbled with little consideration. He was still stuck in his own contemplation. The lift dinged open again and we stepped inside.

"Malook, Sulru, them," I clarified, raising my voice to demand his attention, "Where do you think they are about now?"

"I would guess that they are trying to find a way back to their ship," John absentmindedly observed, "Probably, Malook remembers the way he was brought in and has led them to the garage."

"But they have to fix the ship first, right? How do they plan to do that?" I asked.

There was a pause that let me hear the elevator humming downwards.

"Well he said the ship needed to repair. He didn't actually say that they needed to fix it. For all we know-" the lift stopped with another small beep, interrupting him.

As the door slid open, John gestured for me to go first. I did, with him on my heels as he finished his sentence, "For all we know, the ship may have just needed a rest...a recharge or reset."

I nodded, understanding the reasoning. I hadn't thought so much on the semantics. My mind was not always very quick with picking up subtleties like that. It also tended to wander.

Like now, a comical vision of Malook plugging in his ship to charge crossed my mind. I let out a small chuckle which gained my husband's gaze. He didn't say anything though, and neither did I. We only continued our trek to the colonel's office.

Just as we reached its shut door, I blurted, "I want to go with you."

John stopped in his tracks, perplexed, "What?"

I inched closer to him, trying to look determined though I probably appeared more like an eager child, "I want to go with you, after them."

He made a movement that was difficult to tell whether it was a head shake or a confused drop twitch, "There are plenty here who need your help. Stay and tend to them," he ordered, "I don't want you ending up in a hospital bed too."

My husband spoke as if his words were the end all concerning what I would and would not do and that, in itself, was utterly infuriating. He waited for no further response as he stepped toward the colonel's door, raising his fist to knock. Before he could, however, I jumped forward and grabbed his hand.

"Like I want you to end up hurt either!" I whined, definitely sounding like a petulant child this time rather than a grown woman with a doctorate.

He lowered his fist with a sigh, twisting to lay frustrated eyes on me. Reaching his arms around me and pulling into a hug, he whispered in my ear more considerately, "Connie, you know this is my job. It's not your responsibility anymore. Stay here; stay safe...for me."

I looked down at the floor as I thumbed his palm, "Okay," I relented.

He leaned in and kissed my forehead. I gazed back up at his smiling face and gave a discontent grin, "I love you," he said, staring deeply into my eyes.

"I love you too," I muttered the words more out of obligation than sincerity.

John pecked my head once more, and then let go of me to fall back into the proper position for approaching his boss, expression becoming solemn to match, "I'll be back soon and safe," he assured, "Now, please go see to your patients."

I shrugged, vision shifting from him and down the hallway, "Yeah, okay," was my only answer as I trudged away.

I could feel my husband's gaze linger on me as I went, but I refused to pay heed. I heard his knocks seconds before I had reached the doors of the lift. As I stepped aboard the machine, I caught a glimpse of him entering the office out of the corner of my eye.

I found my way back to the floor of the medical wing and into the main room that was filled with the newly injured. If I hadn't caught myself in time to fight against the behavior, my jaw would have dropped. Even so, I still gawked inwardly.

Every bed was occupied with men and women suffering worse than the ones brought in prior. I could see from my distance, that the vampire had not held back against anyone that came after her.

The sharp claws she wielded had left all these people with shredded arms, chests, stomachs, and there were even more with potentially fatal neck wounds.

The staff seemed to have doubled since charge had been taken from me. Certainly more medical workers had been called in sometime between then and now, including the doctor who normally ran the floor. I spotted him as he was ordering two of the wounded to be rushed to surgery.

He also noticed me, stopping for only long enough to say, "Dr. Shinn, I'll speak with you later," as he ran after one of the patients being transferred.

Breathing in the realization that I wasn't wanted, I spun around and strolled down the corridor to return to the elevators. The doctor, I knew, wasn't being rude to me no matter how it had sounded.

I had met him on several occasions with John, and he was a very compassionate man. Even so, it was obvious he had his hands full and was without the time to explain anything to me.

So I was at the lift, reaching out to press that stupid little arrow, when it opened to reveal the female mortician from earlier...the one who had run from the room after the bitchy nurse. My appearance obviously rattled her, because she jerked slightly backward, vision widening at catching sight of me.

"Oh, hello again," she stated awkwardly as she paced to the side and around me.

Since I hadn't quite processed what I was doing, I hadn't been polite enough to move and let her by. Twisting slowly to the side, I watched as she made her way to the morgue. Halfway through her trek, I suddenly made the decision to go with her, making quick strides until I was walking beside. She tilted her head at my stance, a puzzled look on her face.

"Can I help you?" she asked, raising an eyebrow and stopping at the closed freezer, waiting for my answer before entering.

"I just..." I began, not actually sure why I had gone after her.

"You're the major's wife, aren't you?" the mortician's tone changed when she asked. It was kinder somewhat, yet I still wasn't able to exactly place it.

"Yeah," I managed a small grin.

"Sorry, Doctor," the woman frowned, "I don't have anything for you."

My brow furrowed at those words, not understanding what she meant, "Beg your pardon?"

She cleared her throat, easing her shoulders and showing what looked like concern, "I know you must be worried about him, but I can't give you anything to occupy your time, and I think they have things covered elsewhere," she glanced back at the main.

"Oh, I- uh, okay," I mumbled, giving her a nod and awkwardly turning on my way.

"Doctor?" she called after I had only barely moped away from her.

I spun around, hoping there was something after all.

"He'll be alright," she smiled brightly.

I sighed, "I appreciate it; I guess we'll see."

The mortician cocked her head slightly, "He will be," she insisted.

Her dedication to this cop-out made my mood switch instantly from worried sadness to agitation, "How would you even know?"

In hindsight, the words came out much too harsh. Either way, she didn't seem to take any offense. Shrugging and blinking, she replied with the same smile, "I just feel it."

She then reached out and opened the freezer, "Think about it, then trust your gut," she added with a wink before strolling into the morgue and closing the entry between us.

I stared after her. Trust my gut? I scrunched my face in thought. I was definitely the act first, ask questions later type of person, but did I act on trusting my instinct, or just in response to whatever emotion I was feeling at the time? or was that the same thing?

I couldn't be sure. John would probably say it didn't matter because you shouldn't rely on anything that was clouded or not completely sound.

Inhaling, rotating, then exhaling, I saw a patient being carted toward me, so I moved and put myself flat against the wall, sight resting on the bed while they passed and went into the morgue as well.

The woman laying there hadn't made it, obviously. Her eyes were shut, barely visible under the sheet that had been haphazardly thrown over her body. I took another deep breath, staying in my position as I put my thoughts on my husband.

They leapt to visions of my meeting Malook; seeing his family for the first time; and of Sulru's dark dedication...

Before realizing it, I was jogging to the elevator with the garage clear in mind as my destination. I couldn't rightly judge if it was emotion or instinct, but whatever it was, it was telling me to go. I needed to be with John and I needed to know more about these aliens.

Chapter 18: Malook

Sulru and I shared an uncomfortable silence as I waited for her to hack into the primitive machine we had made our way to.

Considering we were undoubtedly being chased, it was good to see that the doors of the vehicle were already unlocked and its system was simple enough that my friend could figure out how to rewire it to her control: anything to speed our escape along.

I had made certain Soare-a and Riven were safely inside, before I stood next to the front passenger position with my door open, doing my best to keep a look out for anyone coming near, as Sulru sat in the driver's seat and pulled on different colored wires under the wheel.

My lips kept parting in a desire to speak, yet I simply forced them close again each time so that I wouldn't cause her to remove attention from our best chance to successfully flee the pursuing Earthlings.

Instead, my focus remained on our surroundings. Looking towards the small building from where we'd come, I thought back to the trip there. I had worn a blindfold so didn't recall much of the ride except the sounds from the vehicle and the occasional word among those riding with me.

Sulru however, being presumed dead, had not been masked, and therefore I was trusting her memory and her instinct to guide us to our ship. I glanced away from the base and to her once more, watching as she twisted one of the sets of tiny cords in her palm.

The woman was highly intelligent and intuitive, which made her an invaluable ally. I had grown to really depend on and trust the vampire, sometimes to the extent of forgetting how different our standings were. I viewed her as an equal; something that our world did not see.

My species controlled Galdelier including the modest population of vampires therein. They weren't treated as property in the sense that they were owned by anyone, but the law was far in their disfavor.

They had almost non-existent rights when it came to issues of legality, and because of their physical superiority over us, there was no such way deemed appropriate for them to defend against a human. Not that humans generally went out of their way to attack the creatures or anything like that.

Most kept their noses high, yet refrained from dealing with the vampires at all. So in every matter, Sulru's people were at the lowest tier of our society.

There had even been motions to eradicate the species in the past, yet the government would not allow it. It wasn't per any noble cause, regardless of how it might have been explained either. It was simply that our leaders saw value in keeping them around.

Vampires were required to work within the military, usually in positions similar to hers where the main focus of the job was to protect an officer or group of officers.

As I climbed in rank, my career required less and less field work, which directly affected Sulru's position. We both gradually left handling these regular instances of potential harm, and settled into more easy-going routines.

Mine, now, was doing a great deal of desk work and hers, less about protecting in dangerous circumstances and more watching over my family as I was locked away in my office for the majority of my days. Of course, there still were times when I required her presence; it was just that they were fewer than she had been accustomed to in the past.

Having come to know her well, I knew Sulru viewed herself as equal to any human, though she should have to deny these thoughts or any related actions amidst strangers or the common people.

True as that may be, she had always held her head high, gaining reprimands by many. Not me, just others. That reminded me of something else.

Back inside the structure, which I had surmised was mostly underground due to how tiny it appeared on the surface, there had been several injured people in the hallways as we navigated our way out.

When Sulru had caught up to where Soare-a, Riven, and I were, she noticed my eyes paying the wounded attention. My partner had said that she didn't kill anyone who left her alone. That had been the extent of our conversation and she hadn't looked at me as she spoke.

The woman wasn't a violent person by nature, though this facet was something nobody else was really aware of. She hid it well behind a rough, uncaring exterior formed from a life of being forced to be an obedient assassin.

The years had not been kind to her, and sometimes I felt she was starting to lose herself to this facade. I had never intended on speaking to her about who she had harmed in her mission to get us to safety, since I felt any bloodshed done on Earth the past night was strictly my fault.

This whole experience was my mistake and it pained me horribly to have heard her speak those words just now because it reminded me that I had made her be that monster this time. I had no doubt that more than fighting her way through the humans, she was thinking about how she had fed from one of them.

It wasn't the legal matter of feeding that would be a bother to her so much as how feeding altogether was regarded on our planet. I certainly didn't want to bring that up either, yet at the same time, I needed her to know that I was still on her side; that I understood.

The sound of the driver's door slamming shut brought my mind back to the present. Sulru had already revved the engine by the time I threw myself inside the vehicle next to her.

Closing my own side, I glanced back one last time, still unable to see anyone hounding us. The vampire didn't waste any time in speeding forward to find the path out of the sheltered area and off toward a large, wire gate in the near distance.

As we approached it, I noticed sentry posts on both sides of the exit. I strained my sight, attempting to discern if there were any people inside the boxed rooms at the top of each tower, but the glass around them was far too darkly tinted.

I turned to face my wife and son, offering a smile and readying myself to do whatever I could to keep the boy from knowing we were being attacked, should we soon find guards amidst those posts with such a goal in mind.

Fortunately, the only interference between us and getting on the other side of that gate was Sulru jarring the vehicle into another incoming rover, scraping the two machines together as we continued to speed down the path.

I took my eyes off my family and peered out the rear window at the apparently startled passengers we had collided with. Past that, I couldn't see due to the dust.

Now all that was left was for my friend's memory to do its duty so we could return without further fuss. I knew it was doubtful that it would fail her; the years together had taught me to trust her senses, especially the one of direction.

"Are you two alright?" I dropped my gaze onto the woman and child in the seat behind me. Soare-a, who was holding Riven close to her, nodded, but the expression on her face was one of terror. I reached backward and placed my hand on her knee with a smile, "It's going to be ok."

"Yeah, Mom," Riven piped up, "Sulru will get us home. Isn't that right, Sulru?"

Vision settling to see both those two and the vampire, I saw her smirk while answering, "That's right. The ship will be back to normal now. We'll be there in no time," she lovingly assured the child.

My son had become very fond of Sulru, his age granting him the innocence of ignorance. He was getting older though, and would soon start becoming aware of our world's prejudices. I could only hope for him to keep the compassion I had always tried to teach.

I left my palm laid on my wife's knee, rubbing it gently before returning to face the front of the Earth rover, "Sulru," I endeavored a reassurance after all that transpired, "You wouldn't have been able to save us if you hadn't fed."

She didn't move, keeping her sight on the road ahead, "I know," she replied flatly.

I grunted acknowledgment. Despite its bluntness, it was a friendly response. I understood her meaning perfectly, well aware of the feelings behind her harsh demeanor. There was a stillness that settled then, the affect of her face not changing a bit.

She must have known my empathy, yet as I looked at the bare desert around, she felt the need to speak an actually kind answer, "After all this time, I expected that we understood each other, Malook."

I looked over at her again and although her body was in the same rigid posture, the smirk she held prior had been revived. There wasn't a chance for further interaction, as she turned suddenly and sharply, knocking me against the inside of the machine.

The vampire remained in my vision the entire time, and I could tell by the increased curve in her smile that she wanted to laugh. The startled look on my face certainly didn't help her refrain. Nonetheless, the gravity of the situation did stall her reaction.

My son, however, lacked this consideration. The moment Riven belted, Sulru let out a soft chuckle. I managed to grin briefly in order to keep him at ease, but quickly returned to a solemn state.

Even though we appeared to have made a decent distance away from the largest part of the threat, I would remain extremely worried until we were back in space and out of range of the Earthlings' clutches altogether. I was pleased that Riven wasn't upset. Next to his safety, I was most afraid that the ordeal would traumatize him.

It was another fifteen minutes of silence afterward, with our guard managing her way easily through every other vehicle that we encountered, gaining many honks, glares, and what I assumed was a hand sign for showing distaste.

The vampire never lost her focus and the next time there was any clue she even remembered that the rest of us were still in the craft with her, was when we came to the first bits of desert sand.

"Just over those hills," she announced, sirens sounding immediately, as if her voice had signaled them.

I twisted in my seat, straining to see everything possible behind our vehicle. Several machines identical to the one we had stolen were close, yet thankfully far enough that we should have no trouble with getting back inside the ship before they were able to cause any grief. I dropped my sight to my wife and son, grimacing upon realizing that the blaring alarms had Riven frightened. Soare-a pulled him close to her, unable to hide her own fear.

"Shit," our driver observed, glancing into the rear-view mirror and shifting in her seat, becoming even more intent than she had been, if that was even possible.

My eyes kept darting between the bare sand in front of our vehicle and the dusty clouds enveloping the rovers chasing us. The sun was just beginning to rise, which somehow made me feel worse on edge. Perhaps it was not having the cover of darkness any longer, or maybe it was because it outlined how long we had been there.

This meant the likelihood of knowledge of us had spread, as well as decisions concerning not only Earth's desired fate for us, but how they would deal with our people should we come in contact with them again.

And we would. It was definitely a fucking mess I had gotten us into, though dwelling on the eventual consequences was of zero use right now. I just needed to focus on getting aboard the ship and getting airborne.

Chapter 19: John

Gazing out the windshield, I saw the stolen vehicle turn abruptly off the road and into the desert sand. The soldiers still out on site had been alerted to the situation before we had left, but during the ride, there had been no return contact.

We took it to mean that the aliens had not yet reached them, although momentarily I wondered if perhaps they actually had an alternative plan; something other than heading back to their ship. Maybe a second craft or other unknown technology was even hidden somewhere that would aid in a safer, easier escape, or continuing whatever mission they had.

Upon actually seeing the vehicle in the distance, after counting possibility that we had lost them to an unseen plan, I realized just how confused I was about it all. Whatever my wife may think, I had never condoned the treatment that Malook and his family had received.

I even understood the reasoning for that creature's attacks though, of course, I didn't excuse it. The fact remained that she had killed several people and gravely injured many more when none of the aliens had been physically harmed.

Not even herself, until she refused to cooperate or allow the two she was with to work with us either.

She wasn't even human; she was some kind of monster. Nonetheless, part of me hoped that they did get away.

Whatever good relationship our worlds could have had was certainly gone, or at least very far out of reach, considering these events. I really didn't want the further mistreatment or even death of these people on my conscious.

Yet I simultaneously hoped that we were able to secure them once more so as to increase our knowledge, and make that creature pay for the blood she had spilled. Greater than this inner moral turmoil, was my fear for the eventual outcome of the past night and day.

Not what would happen directly should they escape or were recaptured; not if that creature paid for what it had done; not even if we were ever to learn more about these strangers. No, it was the concern for more violence, for war, for the subjugation or elimination of Earth's people.

That was what bothered me most. These aliens had at least two things over us. One, their technology was advanced to ours and two, they had the aid of superhuman beings.

In the short amount of time that had passed, I had gone back and forth amongst all these feelings and had become an even larger ball of confusion, though it obviously didn't show on my exterior. There, I remained strong and in control. Just underneath however, I was completely uncertain of how this would turn out and moreover, how I wanted it to.

I did my best to ignore these anxious thoughts and focus on my job, which was retrieving them at all cost. There wasn't room for failure in the eyes of my superiors.

This, to them, would relinquish any way to properly protect ourselves against the extra-terrestrials. In another attempt to stay in the present, I forced my brain to actually comprehend where I was looking through the glass at the alien-occupied SUV.

They had just reached the site, not stopping for the men and women standing around. Not even when they began shooting at the incoming vehicle. I flinched as I watched the alien driver take down a soldier who had been adamant about attacking our enemy.

He had stood firm in his place, sending multiple, rapid shots to the SUV's windshield. When its tires revved into him, sending him spiraling to the ground beside his original position, a couple of others abandoned their fire to assist him.

"Uh...Major?" a voice sounded awkwardly behind me.

I glanced to the backseat to see that one of the privates situated there was turned around and staring out the rear window. Failing in my attempt to see past my companions to where his vision rested, I demanded to know what was going on, "What is it?"

The man turned back around and faced me, showing his own uncertainty, "Sir, I think that your wife is behind us."

I strained to see once more, finally catching a glimpse of the fellow government grade vehicle that was not far beyond. My eyes darted to the soldier as I opened my mouth, yet before I spoke, thought better of it and looked again. That was when I realized that it wasn't what I thought. It was a large sedan with similar tinted windows and dark paint, but not black: Connie.

"Goddammit!" I growled at the woman's stupidity.

Her lack of consideration for anything but what she wanted was beyond irritating. She had completely ignored anything I had said. Why the hell would she come out here? She knew she could be killed and she knew of the dangers and yet here the fuck she was.

I took a few quick deep breaths before twisting to the front and remembering what I was meant to do.

Letting out an audible sigh, I waved my hand in dismissal to the others upon seeing their concerned and questioning expressions, "I will deal with it. Stay ahead."

The soldiers settled down, but I was not at ease. I was going to kill Connie myself; maybe that would teach her the meaning of self-preservation. She always acted before she thought. That or she just rarely thought clearly.

Years of this marriage and I still couldn't figure that one out. Just as our vehicles reached the spot of the fallen barrier, I saw that the man who had been hit was alive and pulling himself up to sit.

He wasn't moving his legs and there was a massive gash on one of his thighs made by the vehicle's grill. Our driver spun to a halt and we piled out. Still many yards away, the alien group had stopped and left their vehicle as well, hurrying toward the ship's opening, which was propped open, its door still damaged.

Before I started to run for them with my own company, I felt my wife's hand on my arm. In an instant rotation, I faced her long enough to bark, the words showing every bit of anger and agitation I was feeling, "What do you think you're doing?!"

"Um..." Connie squeaked, obviously startled by my rage.

Shaking my head at her, I continued off after my men, "Wait here," I ordered her as I left, pointing furiously at the ground.

Readying my pistol as I ran, I observed the human alien woman and her son disappearing inside the craft, leaving Malook and the vampire standing outside as we reached them with our weapons aimed. We were a group of about fifteen then, mostly armed with traditional FN SCARs.

The two ETs still exposed, turned to face us, the man yelling something at his family who could barely be seen within the ship's entry. When his wife remained in place, he repeated the foreign words more intensely, causing her and the boy to completely vanish into the shadows. The creature stepped between Malook and our troops as we stilled, the soldiers waiting for my command.

"Out of our way," Sulru hissed, getting closer to me as I readied my nine mil.

"Sir?" one of the women beside me spoke.

I stepped toward the beast, pistol coming to a nice position aimed at her forehead, "You all step away from the machine and come with us."

The creature was undaunted, "Ihc-hahl crahsba, Malook," she spoke to her ally, but kept her gaze steeled upon me.

I clicked my gun in response to the man behind her moving slightly at those strange words. I wanted to fire. To just shoot between those two evil black eyes if only to cause her pain.

However, I had to restrain myself. If making the shot wouldn't slow her enough that the soldiers around me could properly act in subduing her, it would make things worse.

None of us even knew how to take her down or control her. Staring back into those eerie orbs, I was sure I saw them shift and suddenly got the feeling she was no longer looking at me, but past me.

It was hard to know for certain with the entirety of them being a solid color, so I allowed myself a glance backwards only to see that Connie was just beyond our group.

Damn it, woman.

And that fleeting moment was all the monster needed to flip the entire scenario. Before I realized what had happened, I felt that same, freezing hand from my prior encounter with the vampire around my throat once again.

Although my vision returned to my front instantly, I wasn't able to act rapidly enough to keep her other hand from grabbing the one of mine that was armed. She forced my elbow to bend and pointed my weapon to the side of my temple, keeping my head in place with her firm grasp on my neck. I struggled to free myself, but the beast was unfathomably strong.

"Put your weapons down and stand back," she ordered coldly, "Or I'll make him pull the trigger."

I continued the struggle, my gaze peering to the side at the steel barrel of my own pistol with my own hand still holding it, finger ready to trip the trigger. She had my body pinned tightly against her stomach so that my free hand was trapped between the two of us. I tried wriggling its fingers, tried moving it at all to scratch her or anything, yet it proved useless.

"JOHN!" I heard my wife scream and looked up to see her sprint forward, two members of the troop catching hold of her to restrain from a closer encounter.

"Connie! FOR FUCK'S SAKE! BACK OFF!!" I yelled.

The moment I spoke, I felt the vampire's grip tighten around my neck, causing me to choke. I could feel her claws beginning to sink into me and the wet warmth of plasma trickling down my skin. My eyes rolled upward to see her nod at Malook, who finally stepped aboard their craft, disappearing like the rest of his crew.

"John!" my wife's words were a sob as the soldiers retained her.

Vision leaving my captor to lay on the crying woman, and then to the troops around, I gave another order, "JUST SHOOT!"

But they hesitated; doing so for the same reason that I had not shot the beast earlier. Throughout my entire career, I had never been at such a loss for what to do. I wasn't worried with dying. However, if I was going to, I wanted something to be gained from it.

"I'M ORDERING YOU TO SHOOT!" I repeated.

The soldiers still refused to act and this thing that held me obviously picked up that she had won. With a chuckle so low, I was sure I was the only one to hear it, she began reversing onto the ramp, taking me along.

I heard the spacecraft hum to life and despite not having started to move yet, the sound of the engines was enough to throw my wife into a frenzy.

I watched as she pushed against the men holding her in one final, successful attempt to break free and approach. Connie lifted an arm, her small handgun aimed at the vampire.

At that moment, there was a sudden jolt, making me realize that we were finally atop the ship's ramp and had begun to ascend into the air. We were only inches off the ground when Connie opened fire on my captor. I heard the vampire grunt and felt her grasp lessen in response to what I could only assume was my wife's bullet hitting her.

Taking advantage of this, I managed to twist within its arms to the point of half-way facing her, my eyes lingering on her freshly wounded cheek. There was bright red splattered around a darkened hole in the middle of it, that I could see was rapidly healing under my gaze.

I found myself both enthralled and terrified. Breaking away to look into its eyes, she barred her teeth in a growl, showing her pointed fangs, now smeared with the same liquid. Her claw released my neck and took hold of my other arm, twisting me around to face her completely as she opened her mouth wider, letting something fall from it and clank onto the ramp below.

The bullet.

She shoved me forward, her blades cutting fairly deeply into both the skin on the arm she held and my hand that still clutched the nine millimeter which remained aimed at myself.

I felt the floor fall from beneath my feet as she began dangling me over the side of the slowly heightening spacecraft. A quick glance informed me that we were now several feet above the ground.

"SULRU!" The yell came from inside the ship. The vampire tilted her head forward, vision narrowing as she began letting go of me so that I would fall below. But I wasn't finished fighting.

Instead of simply allowing my body to thud back down to my men, a distance that wouldn't cause any grave harm, I focused my attention on my weapon and waited for her to weaken her hold on my hand enough that I could break away and use it.

The creature was smart though. She, too, focused her strength on my hand, relaxing the claw on my other arm first. However, she did finally have to relent.

Just as she did, I used that palm to grab onto her arm, pulling against her to gain control of my gun. She jerked away from our previous standing so that we were both on the metal ramp again.

As we continued to rise into space, my goal was to take the creature back down to Earth with me. I did everything I could to keep within touching proximity of my enemy, for I knew that I'd have the best chance to prevent any severe attacks if I could keep her focused on getting me off of her.

Unfortunately, she was still far stronger than me and it didn't take her long to push my body to the floor, nearly severing my trigger finger with her claws in order to make me drop its weapon.

I lay on the ramp, attempting to regain myself, but the beast wasted no time in bearing down upon me again, crouching and grabbing onto my shoulders firmly. I cried out when those razors sunk into me, and then growled at her glare as she once more shoved me toward the end of the synthetic ground.

Then something happened that I don't think either of us expected. Out of nowhere, I felt a hand on my ankle, but not the cold palms of the vampire I was desperately fighting. The creature's head shot up, eyes darting to look past me, and I looked as well.

There, at the ramp's ending, I saw my wife's hands. One still held the P38 while its arm was working to pull her body up onto the ship, scalp just barely in view. The vampire grumbled, releasing me as it stood, then gave a swift kick to my face before trudging toward Connie.

Enduring the pain of my now broken nose and ignoring the gushing plasma, I resisted the urge to lay back and nurse myself. I couldn't let anything happen to my wife, and we were obviously trying this monster's patience.

I managed to get to my feet, wobbling as if I were drunk. My head was certainly foggy and spinning as if I were. The vampire had taken hold of Connie, pulling her up to our battleground and forcing her into a similar position to the one she had me in when threatening to force my hand in killing myself.

"HEY!" I shouted as I lunged forward without much thought, grabbing onto the beast who faltered under the weight of two humans tugging on her.

It felt certain that we were about to topple over and fall the distance downward, eventually smacking into the planet. However, my wife let out a pained squeak, alerting me to her hand which was now streaming red beneath her captor's claws.

Before either of us could act further, the vampire had full dominion over that hand and the gun it held. She twisted it to face me. Everything slowed in my mind as I watched Connie unwillingly pull the trigger.

My vision was hazy.
My heart was racing.
I felt a jolt;
And a brief but intense pain in my head.
Then everything went dark.

Chapter 20: Malook

I looked across the room to where Sulru was sitting in the pilot seat monitoring the various screens, panels, and dials before her. We had been in silence for more than an hour. She wasn't a talkative person, partially due to our societal rankings, but I could tell there was something on her mind; something I was sure had to do with our previous disagreement concerning the two Earthlings she had beaten.

I hadn't known at first how to react. Dropping the two from the height we were, by the time I was back at the scene, could and probably would have killed them. Yet we couldn't turn back for my family's sake, and that included Sulru. It wasn't that I expected treatment any better than we had been given, just that I refused to actively place us under such conditions.

This matter was what worried me at present. I knew the two aliens, laying unconscious in one of the ship's spare rooms, would receive the same unfair management from our people, if not worse. Regardless of what had happened on Earth, I didn't want that.

I glanced past the pilot to where the room's open entry. Soare-a had retreated to our bedroom immediately, upon seeing Sulru and I transporting our unaware company the rest of the way inside and to their own beds. Before she had left, she gave me that look of utter fury that I was well acquainted with. It seemed she was using it more often, and no efforts I had made thus far had helped in making her love me again.

My wife had never shared my compassion for vampiric people. Neither had she ever approved of the friendly relationship between my guard and our son. The agitation these things brought her only increased over the years, until we had reached this point of near total distaste for one another. I still tried to make it work, though my resolve weakened every day.

Riven had watched Sulru and I, waiting for us to finish our task before asking what would happen to the aliens. I had told him that I wasn't certain, but I needed him to pretend like he didn't know anything about them until I could figure it out. He acted mildly confused as he agreed, turning to Sulru and inquiring if she was okay. It was only then that I realized she had been wincing.

She had thrown herself into her duties without hesitation, ignoring the horrible pain she had to be experiencing. The Earth doctor successfully shot the vampire through her cheek, bullet breaking into the fangs just underneath its thin skin. Vampire flesh and tissue instantly healed itself, however other substances such as their nails and teeth did not repair.

I had offered to inspect the damage, which she refused at first, soon relenting by opening her mouth wide and using a finger, claw retracted, to peel back her lips as far as possible. The metal had not made it completely through her teeth, yet did crush into the core of three of them on that side. I grimaced at the sight, unsure if there was anything that could be done about it.

Sulru dropped her lip and clicked her jaw shut once more while I informed her of the extent of the injury. She sighed and shrugged, turning her attention to the sleeping humans. That was when we had discussed what was to be done when we returned home, our differing opinions causing the discomforting quiet we now sat in.

If we were to speak the truth about our trip to their planetary system, Sulru and I, at worst, would be charged with treason: a crime punishable by death. In even the most favorable outcome, she would be executed, basically for being seen as faulty, and I would be stripped of my status. So that, of course, was not an option. It left us with spinning a tale of only cruising around Trinnd, which was my original purpose for taking my family on vacation. With that, our loss of time could remain blamed on computer failure.

It was only after being out and learning about my wife's interest in the Milky Way that I had taken us there. We flew around its planets, my own interest overtaking me when nearing Earth. It was what to do about Connie and John where Sulru and I disagreed. She felt it was in our best interest to dispose of them prior to landing, justifying their murder with outlining their mistreatment of us.

I had pointed out that they were not responsible for any of it. That it fell on the heads of their superiors. I explained how the doctor had been exceptionally kind toward me and how I never sensed hostility from her husband either. My friend responded with saying we didn't owe them anything and returning home with the strangers would create the highest likelihood of something going wrong. Nonetheless, I remained adamant in my stance against killing the Earth people.

She had then stopped talking altogether. I had sent my son away to rest sometime during the conversation. I didn't want him around all the negativity, especially not to hear Sulru speaking about murdering two people that were right in front of him. He held the vampire in the utmost regard and I didn't want a bad situation coloring a different picture of her in his mind.

In the cockpit, I stared out of the thick tempered glass separating the vampire and I from the coldness of space. We had only just passed Earth's moon several minutes ago, meaning we werr nearing time that my partner would be readying for superdrive to speed us out of the realm of the Milky Way and into the darker space between it and Trinnd.

I released an annoyed breath at the current situation with my dear companion. I knew that she would go along with whatever I decided; not just because she didn't have a choice, but because she wouldn't want to disappoint me. I was well aware of this, although I would never acknowledge it, if only for the sake of her ego. Besides, she didn't truly want to harm Connie and John, I knew. She was only superbly dedicated.

"What is it?" she asked with flat affect, alerting me to how obvious my exhale had really been.

I readjusted myself in my seat with a slightly less noticable inhale, "Nothing."

Sulru turned her head. After taking in the sight of me, she looked down in front of her again, tapping twice on one of the panels before spinning her seat so that her entire body faced me. "You know," she started, "You should probably go and check on your cousin."

"My what?" I sounded oddly as I voiced my need for clarification, swiveling my own seat like she had. I knew the vampire had a tendency for allusion or otherwise being vague and I usually picked up on her meanings easily. However, the intensity of our predicament and my fatigue were fighting against me.

Her large dark eyes narrowed and her head tilted as she rephrased, "Your cousin and her husband have been resting a while. You should probably wake them."

I gazed back, her confident onyx eyes setting me at ease. "My cousin, huh?" I grinned.

Sulru leaned her head further to the side, simultaneously raising an arm to rest on the small counter space in between her and the controls, in order to hold her cheek. Her lip curled in displeasure as she rubbed the skin covering her broken teeth with her knuckles. My smile fell seeing her in pain, but I didn't act on it since it would just bother her.

Instead I thought about the doctor. Perhaps she could do something to help. Cousin? Hm... I pursed my lips in contemplation. I suppose Connie could pass as such, though she was lighter than the flesh color I had inherited from my father. John, with extreme paleness rivaling a vampire's, would never do. His wife, however, was of medium skin, undoubtedly passable as a distant relative.

Grunting, I pushed myself up from the seat. "You're right," I agreed, strolling for the exit.

I left the cockpit and journeyed down the hall to the small room in the dormitory where our guests were. Their battle with Sulru had ended when the spacecraft had become unlevel during its ascent, causing the damaged entryway to jolt and throw them in. Connie had rolled and hit her head against the wall opposite of the ramp while her husband banged his on the doorframe, immediately passing out.

He would have fallen down to the earth had Sulru not caught herself on the other side of the doorway and reached over to grab his shirt, jerking his dead weight up and slinging her arm over his shoulder and around his chest for a better hold. She lugged him into the craft, laying him next to his wife, who had been barely keeping herself awake. She wearily attempted to get to him and it seemed she was trying to speak. Nonetheless, the moment she touched him, her eyes rolled back and she fell into slumber as well.

As I neared the door we had locked them behind, I took another deep breath. I hoped that it would be simple to wake them since we had much to discuss before we arrived on Galdelier. I paused to listen for activity in the room to see if it was safe to enter. If they had already woken, I wanted to be aware of how they were taking their current condition. When I heard nothing, I waved a hand over the panel beside the room, its seal sliding on a curve upward in response.

The open door revealed to my vision that the couple still lay in their small, individual cots. It appeared that they may have shifted slightly from the positions we had left them in, but they were still unconscious. I stepped inside, strolling to the space between them, glancing from husband to wife and watching their chests for movement. Both were breathing easily.

Once we had gotten them lying on their backs in the beds, Sulru and I had given each a quick check for further injury. Beside a few bruises from the fall, the only wounds were those given to them by the vampire. Connie's right hand had a few decent cuts from Sulru's grip, but she was far less damaged than her husband. Both of John's arms were scratched up pretty badly with a couple of gashes on his left.

The knuckles on his right hand and his shoulders were cut deeply. Bone could be seen in places through the exposed red flesh on his hand. The torn skin on his shoulders was terribly deep as well, yet the greater mass of muscle and tissue in the area kept any bone or tendon from showing. He also sustained a broken nose from Sulru stomping on his face in her frustration.

I had washed their wounds and cleared away all the drying blood and detached skin around them while Sulru and I had been arguing. We hadn't done anything more than that for their injuries. Mostly due to our distraction regarding their fate and Sulru's disgruntled end to the dialogue. I heard a moan behind me then. Turning around, I saw that John was starting to rouse, so I slid out from between the beds and stood at the end of them instead. I couldn't be sure of his reaction to my presence or to his surroundings; I needed to play it safe.

"Wh-what the hell?" the man mumbled under his breath as he managed to sit up, rubbing his head. "Tsst!" he made a hissing noise, his hand falling abruptly to his lap. He stared at his wounded trigger and middle finger, being careful not to twitch them. I imagined that the movement felt like a burn.

"Don't worry," I spoke calmly and strongly, "We'll have that tended to."

His face shot upward, still waking eyes realizing who was talking. "What the-" he began to curse as his gaze left me and took in the room around him.

"You're on our spacecraft," I continued, keeping motionless in my position, "We've just reached the outer rim of your solar system."

"What?" he raised his good hand to his head, rubbing again as he forced himself to his feet.

Getting another sweep of yhe area, he saw his wife sleeping on her mattress. He lowered his head to her chest, listening to her heart and then stood to face me. "What happened, Malook? Why are we here?" the words were almost a bark.

I hesitated at the sound of my name. I hadn't honestly expected him to be so informal, even now. "You and your wife took a nasty bump to the head as we took off. We couldn't risk taking you back... I'm sorry."

There was a pause as he returned to his wife and took a seat on the small amount of space next to her. Using his left hand, he caressed her cheek while whispering her name. The woman began shifting at his sound, her own cut up hand reaching up to rest on her chest. John immediately glanced to it, the sight of the scratches jogging his memory.

He stayed on the bed, but spun to address me again, "Where is that fucking monster?" he growled, eyes narrowing in anger.

"I'm right here," Sulru's confident and agitated voice came from the door, bringing both mine and the Earthling's attention.

The man raised himself from where he sat, standing as tall as possible and broadening his shoulders. "You stay away from my wife," he ordered the vampire, who ignored his futile efforts as she walked into the room.

"I have no interest in your wife," she replied gruffly, hardly even taking notice of him as she stopped in a position two feet from my side.

The quarrel, if you could even call it that, aided in waking Connie further. The doctor moaned as John slowly took his place at her side once more, vision staying on Sulru until he sat. Then he looked down at his wife, "It's okay, honey," he tried to soothe, hand grazing across her cheek and forehead. "Her temperature," he whispered with concern, "It's climbing."

He looked at me, his expression a muddle of anger, fear, and worry. I felt as if he was expecting me to offer some sort of help, but I had nothing. Ending the short, awkward quiet, Sulru moved from her stance, sliding gracefully through the tiny slot past me and the foot of the bed, to reach the other side of the cot across from John. The major tensed as she approached his wife across from him. Sulru moved deliberately slowly, lifting her hand, palm up, and offering it to the man.

"Here," she spoke softly, her eyes resting easily on the two humans, "It's quite cold."

Chapter 21: Connie

I awoke to the feeling of something cold on my forehead. Groggily, I pulled myself up to sit as I rubbed my eyes, mind trying to determine what it was. It felt like a hand, but was so chilling that I figured it must have been some sort of material which had been placed to restrain me. However, since I was able to continue rising, I realized I wasn't tied down. Maybe it was a thermometer or other medical monitor?

When the blurriness finally disappeared from my vision, I looked up at the figure looming over me, my heart jumping upon seeing the vampire with her hand resting on my head. Her coal eyes were fully open and situated on me. At my startle, she slowly removed her claw and took steps backward until she was against the wall behind her.

"Connie, sweetie, are you alright?"

I turned to the other side and saw my husband sitting beside me. My body had woken up enough that I could feel his own, warm hand on my lap. His eyes were glossy as they stared at me. John never cried, but I could tell he was loosing his will to resist. I smiled as big as I could to assure him I was okay.

"Yeah, I'm fine," I said, doing my best to keep my attention on him and his obvious concern instead of worrying about where we were. Even so, my eyes had already wandered from him to see Malook standing nonchalantly at the end of the bed.

I remembered jumping onto the spaceship, fighting Sulru, and falling back inside... John lifted his hand from my legs, reaching to place it on my shoulder as he leaned forward, hugging me tightly. I reciprocated the embrace with equal passion, even though my focus had returned to Malook while I rested my head on my husband's shoulder. So we were still on the spaceship?

"I'm glad you're awake and feeling fine, doctor," the dark skinned alien beamed with friendly green eyes.

I pulled back out of my John's grip, my gaze falling to the wounds on either side of his neck. My jaw dropped slightly as I reached out to examine them. Damn, they were way too deep! He pulled my hands carefully from him and placed them back onto my thighs, with his gently atop. The sight of his face revealed that his nose was bent, a bit of blood dried at the tiny cuts of its break. My vision shot toward the vampire, narrowing with anger and mouth snapping open to yell at her...yet she beat me to speaking.

"I can get what equipment we have if you would like to nurse his wounds," Sulru spoke with calm, her face remaining void of expression.

"I-uh," I stammered awkwardly at this unexpected offer.

After taking in my confusion, she lowered those black eyes to the floor, tilting her head forward as she walked past the end of my bed, and headed out of the room without acknowledging the differing looks of the men she strolled between.

"Wait!" I called after her just before she was out of view.

The vampire twisted around, head slanted to the side while she studied me, waiting for my reason in stopping her to be made clear. I noticed she was still wearing the damaged black tunic from before. As she stood patiently in the doorway, my eyes were on the tatters of the fabric, recalling the damage she had sustained herself. Then I remembered that I had even shot her not long prior to blacking out. Attention returned to her face, I saw a vague outline of what had to be the hole my bullet had made on her cheek.

"Are you ok?" I asked with nothing other than the interest of a caregiver.

The strange woman's eyelids twitched, "Yes," she answered hesitantly.

"Your hands," I started, "They're so cold."

I was indeed curious for the truth behind their temperature, and I wondered if she were actually as alright as she appeared. We still didn't know much about her kind. For all I was aware, she could be dying from her injuries. Although...she was a *vampire*, right? How accurate was that description? Was she some undead creature or did our language just not have a better word for her species? Somehow, I disbelieved that she was some immortal, soulless walking corpse.

"They are always so. I have cold blood," she responded bluntly, spinning around and taking two large strides out the door and my field of vision.

John stared intently after the woman. Knowing him, he was no doubt well disgusted with her. The moment she was gone, Malook cleared his throat and addressed us, "You'll have to excuse Sulru."

"Excuse her?" my husband spoke critically, "How the hell do you let your family around a creature like that?"

Malook's eyes grew instantaneously intense in acute offense of John's words. It was odd for me to see the kind man like that, but I suppose that up until now, he'd only shown his best side in hopes of keeping peaceful terms with our people. "Sulru *is* part of my family," his voice grew low and matched the same harsh tone which John had used.

My husband, realizing his mistake, apologized, "I'm sorry. Forgive me for not understanding."

Malook sighed, his demeanor easing, "It's alright," he said, "You should know the people of Galdelier share your sensitivities. It's not normal for Sulru's kind to be treated with anything other than contempt."

"So it's not normal for uh- military officers? Or whatever exactly it is that you are, to have vampiric body guards?" John inquired.

"I'm a General, actually," Malook clarified, "Though I gather our rankings are a bit different. I'll explain that later. As far as vampires- yes, it is quite usual for them to work within the military with a small amount being guards for higher ranking officials. In fact, all vampires are military personnel. The law requires it."

Sulru re-entered the room at that point in the conversation. She was carrying a metal box, square in shape and about a foot in diameter. Traipsing toward us, she held the container out before my husband, standing perfectly still while he cautiously took it from her and twisted to lay it on my lap.

I lifted the top of the box to reveal two strange instruments, along with what appeared to be a cleaner similar to alcohol and several small rags, or pads perhaps was a better term. Either way, they were far too thick to be the typical gauze I was used to dealing with. I picked up one of the instruments, handling it oddly.

It was constructed of something strange. Metal, plastic, glass? I had no clue, but it was fairly weighty and silver in color. There were two closely placed perpendicular rods with what looked like needle points on one end, and a base connecting them, with a third rod running vertically against the first two. It all made the tool seem like some kind of gun.

The vampire had apparently predicted my confusion regarding the technology, as she had not faltered from a position standing behind John. She raised a hand to his side, my eyes barely catching a glimpse of her claws pulling tightly inside themselves although they were already retracted. My husband still acted put off by her presence, but I freely handed her the instrument without pause.

"We've already seen that though our machines are much akin to one another, they're different enough to warrant explanation," Sulru spoke simply while taking the device from me into one hand, just like a weapon, and motioning towards John's arm with the other.

He glanced from her to me and back, obviously unwillingly to have her touch him again. Nonetheless, I reached forward and took hold of his arm, sliding up his sleeve and bending it so that she could show me how the strange tool worked. I could tell my new patient was finding it difficult to comply.

Sulru leaned down over the foot of the bed, placing the needle points lengthwise against one of the gashes on John's arm, taking her time to be sure that I was following along with the actions. She lifted a finger slowly, showing me that upon placing it in a certain spot on the handle and applying pressure, those tips shot up and out of the gun before piercing through each side of his cut and leaving metal pieces behind to cling the wound together.

"Oh, I see," I murmured. The instrument worked much like that of the stapler that we used on Earth to suture injuries shut, yet without the requirement for two pairs of hands.

I remembered back in medical school that the differences between when to use stitches and staples had been one of my first mysteries; one with a rather anticlimactic answer as well. It ended up that it mostly only depended upon the physician's preference. I kept my eyes on the work, expecting her to continue, but she had stopped. I looked up to see dark spheres staring at me.

"Do you want to finish?" she asked me as soon as our eyes met.

"No, it's ok," I replied quietly.

The vampire's attention fell back to John's arm as she completed sealing his cut, her speed increasing as she needn't demonstrate the device any longer. In mere seconds, the first gash was completely shut and she had moved onto the next, finishing all three of the large scratches in under a minute. When she was done, her arm stretched toward me so that I could take the stapler back, so I dropped my grip from John's arm and did so.

"What does this other one do?" I asked, having taken notice that the second instrument in the case looked slightly different.

Sulru rapidly retrieved the other device from its container. This one appeared simpler. It was only one bar, white in color with a shining tip. Compared to the rods of the other gun, it was longer and thicker. The woman held it midways down its length in a tight grasp, her pointer finger lying horizontally with it, ending near the silvery part. "I think this is better suited for your hand, John," her voice was mild despite how her eyes squinted as she looked at the man.

He likewise gave her an expression of distrust before relenting and raising his right hand. It was the first time I had really taken notice of it since waking, and I couldn't help but to coo an 'oh no' when I saw the damage. Glancing with momentary fury at the vampire, I reminded myself that she had only fought to defend her family.

"It may be uncomfortable," she informed, waiting for a signal to go ahead.

"I'm sure it can't hurt any worse," John scowled.

"Hm," the vampire hummed as she angled the gun to point in between his knuckles, using her grip to put pressure on the alien device that was mere centimeters from touching the open wound.

A tiny laser-like beam flashed out of the end of the silver, its red light burning the torn flesh on my husband's hand. His lips curled in a grimace, yet he remained still and quiet...even as Sulru lifted her free claw to squeeze his injured hand together. She continued to press John's knuckles, never acknowledging his discomfort as the tool in her hand seared and melded the tissue.

"Fuck," I muttered as I observed, my mind a mess of wanting to stop her and also blindly trusting the alien's method.

It didn't take long for her to finish with this wound either, and she immediately dropped John's hand to replace the rod inside the metal box. I stared at the scorched flesh, judging the effectiveness of this practice. His fingers were back in their original placement, his hand no longer looking like it was falling apart.

However, the necessity of the damage the technique had done to the previously unharmed epidermis was questionable, as was the efficiency of the coming healing process through the burns. I still had a hold on the original device and shook my gaze to press on and suture John's shoulders.

The vampire had straightened herself and turned back around to take a spot at Malook's side, yet she paused when he gave her a look that I couldn't read. He was silently referencing something that Sulru understood and was refusing to agree with. He seemed to want her to say something, refraining from just doing so himself.

I glanced up and down their dynamic while tending to my husband, who seemed to be focusing on his hand even though he was looking at me. I imagined it had felt much worse than he had first assumed. Sulru ended up winning whatever telepathic debate they were having. I determined so from the fact that she finally continued past Malook, disappearing once more as her friend watched after with a sigh.

"What's the matter?" I asked, only just getting to the second scratch on John's shoulder. Sulru had made using this thing look easy.

Malook shook his head at the floor before looking up and watching me as I worked, "I'm afraid Sulru is very stubborn. She won't ask for help, but...when you shot her, you injured her teeth pretty badly."

John cut his eyes to see the alien without moving the body I was nursing, "I was under the impression that her body healed quite quickly. Immediately, even."

The green-eyed man shook his head again, "Yes, but this capability is limited to tissue, you see."

I nodded my head, focusing more critically on getting through with the lacerations on my husband, "Teeth aren't made of the same substance," I mused, "So her claws?"

"They don't regenerate either," Malook affirmed.

"How bad is it?" I asked, almost finishing on one side and moving to the other.

"Um..." Malook thought, "At least three of them are shattered."

My lips curled in thought, "I don't know what the rest of your medicine and medical technology is like, but I'm assuming that since you're asking me-"

"We're not far different from you," Malook chimed in, "We're also a military power. Our medical knowledge is a might lax," he admitted.

"Most Earth governments focus less on the basic well-being of its citizens and more on war as well," John sighed.

Malook paused in seeming disagreement with John's comparison. However he didn't elaborate further.

"Malook, I'll take a look at it if she will let me, but it sounds like they'll need to be pulled. She'll need it professionally done," I told him, my handling of the alien stapler finally beginning to quicken as I went onward to the next gash.

"I thought you were a professional," the alien responded.

I looked up from the injuries under my working hands to see his green eyes had become quizzical. "Yes, but I mean she'll need gas- uh pain medication? She won't want to be aware during a procedure like that."

Malook's expression grew more puzzled, "I don't understand. If you're worried about her tolerance-"

"No, it's not that," I interrupted to assure, "She's obviously got an incredibly high threshold for pain. I'm just saying it's unnecessary and even dangerous to put her through such discomfort."

Just as I finished up with my husband and replaced the device in its spot, he spoke as if a thought had suddenly occurred him, "Are you hiding us, Malook?"

The alien's face grew solemn. "Of course," he answered simply before returning to his previous questions, "Can you do this for Sulru or not?"

Inhaling sharply, my mind trying to fully comprehend the brief reply to John's question, I relented, "Yes."

"Thank you," he said, spinning to where the vampire had left and making his own way out, "Follow me to the cockpit once you're ready. We have much to discuss."

Chapter 22: John

My mind hadn't left the alien's response to my inquiry. *Of course.* He had spoken in a grave tone and the two simple words felt like a cop-out to me. He also instantly went back to speaking about his vampire, as if trying to ignore the topic I brought up.

Perhaps I was wrong, though. Their other actions toward us appeared kind at the very least, and even though both Connie and I had attacked that beast he seemed to care so much for, neither of us had been treated as an enemy.

We hadn't been restrained or even locked inside this room when they left. Not that we were much of a threat with that- with Sulru around. Especially now that we were apparently weaponless.

"John?" Connie's voice sounded softly next to me after Malook had disappeared.

I looked at my wife. She had shifted out of her previous position and thrown her legs off the side of the small bed, scooting herself next to me until our thighs touched.

"How are you feeling?" she continued.

I paused, looking her over as I thought. Aside from her hair and clothes being a might frazzled, she seemed intact physically, and having a good understanding of how her mind worked, she was probably excited for this adventure rather than fearful of the possible consequences.

She somehow retained a trusting nature into adulthood and I knew this extended to the alien man she had only recently met. Even thus, she'd understand me just as well, which would be why she showed this amount of care in the way she talked.

"My hand fucking hurts. I mean honestly, what the fuck?" I chuckled, giving her a light-hearted opening to feel less like she had to hide her mood.

She smiled and laughed back, "I guess it works? I don't know. I'm concerned it won't heal properly now. Can you at least bend your fingers fine?"

Her eyes dropped to my hand as I took a breath, preparing for the pain before extending my fingers. It hurt like hell, but I managed to only grunt as I bent and wriggled them quickly.

"Yeah, seems fine," I surmised, ready to rest them again. My gaze returned to her and I grinned, waiting for the bubble holding back her eagerness to pop, which I knew wouldn't take long.

"I know I should be more worried, but," she spoke rapidly, "John, we're on an alien spaceship leaving for an entirely new solar system!"

There it was.

"I mean I know they could just like experiment on us or kill us or something when we get there or-"

I thrust myself forward then, grabbing hold of her face in both hands and pressing my lips onto hers, successfully shutting down her excited blabbering.

Bright eyes widened with surprise only a moment before she closed them, parting those soft pink lips that I loved, and letting me kiss her. I teased the woman often about her enthusiasm and even reprimanded her naivety, but the truth was that at the end of it all, these 'flaws' made her even more beautiful to me.

"Calm down," I whispered, easing off of her, "I *am* extremely nervous about what will happen...yet thrilled for the chance to learn more about them as well."

She nodded, coyly tucking a stray waft of brunette hair behind her ear, "We should probably go then, so we can figure out what's going on."

"Yeah, I think so too," I agreed, my mouth falling into a severe line as I changed into my business personality.

I stood from the bed, turning to offer my good hand to Connie which she happily took as she lifted herself from the mattress. After making sure she had proper balance, I tightened my grasp around her slender hand and led us from the room.

The hallway we stepped into was clinical. It was all a very light color, shining in pristine condition. The walls, rather than being straight, curved slightly. It wasn't enough to cause the corridor to be circular or even ovular, but just enough that it couldn't really be called rectangular. I had neglected to ask Malook the direction to reach him, my logic taking over that his lack of explanation probably meant it would be easy to determine.

And I had been right. The hall ended in a curve after a short stroll, at the center of which was an open room almost twice that of the one we had been in. A quick glimpse inside allowed me to see both the black skinned man and his white skinned counterpart sitting there. Before stepping in, I glanced down the other side to see the hall turned sharply, making the path become a circle.

As we entered, neither of us could help except to look out of the window at the front of the pit. We were facing the sight of a million distant stars in the dark and nkthing else. It was breath-taking. Beneath it was an almost counter like top that appeared empty at first, save for a few dials and lit screens in front of the vampire's seat. But under closer scrutiny, I took notice that there were flat panels and what might be buttons on the surface. They were only not illuminated as the ones to the left of Sulru.

Malook turned when he realized we were standing there, "Tap anywhere with your foot," he commanded as my vision scanned for a place to sit.

My wife did as instructed without question, the floor beside where she stood emitting a mechanical sound as a round platform raised out of it, pedestal underneath. The platform folded out into two round, flat pieces, forming a seat.

"How cool," she whispered to me though apparently the vampire heard her, because I saw it smirk.

Still uncertain about this association with the creature, I grunted and copied Connie's motion, the same metal chair rising from the floor. As we settled into our places, me keeping a hand around Connie's in her lap, I heard Malook speak again, but he didn't talk in words I understood.

He had spun sideways to face his body guard, who was focused on a screen directly in front of her. She spoke in the same foreign language, responding without facing him and even though I knew I wouldn't comprehend it, I still strained to make out the words.

I thought back to being briefed concerning the alien's interrogation. When they had asked how he spoke our language so fluently, the only response he had given was 'I studied.' Which, thinking about now was funny.

We had all been certain it was a lie although the polygraph results had been inconclusive. Listening to the strange words the two were conversing with had me interested again in knowing more about it. I glanced at my wife who was obviously on the same line of thought.

"Alright then," Malook's voice subtly changed back to English while he put his focus on us once more. "You no doubt assume your reception on our planet would not go over well," I could tell he was watching for nuances of confirmation or denial from us as he shared these thoughts, "So we will have to blend you in as fellow citizens instead."

I raised an eyebrow, "Why protect us?" I asked accusingly, well aware that they owed us nothing.

Even though it had not been mine and my wife's wish to harm them, we had done so nonetheless.

"He's not protecting you, he's protecting us," the vampire thew back at me, swiveling her own chair just enough to turn a steely glare upon me.

"Sulru..." Malook murmured angrily.

"That's perfectly understandable," Connie chimed in with unmistakable sincerity.

Malook sighed. "It's in the best interest for everyone if your true origins remain a secret. I was without clearance to take this vessel further than the edges of Trinnd and as I tried to explain earlier," his eyes narrowed momentarily on me, "Our leaders are not forgiving."

"Hm. I see," I contemplated the scenario, "Well, however odd it may sound, I appreciate you not simply disposing of us."

Sulru's evil eyes cut over to the man with a grin to match. Malook shook his head furiously at her. I was considering saying something to better judge this exchange but was surprised by a sudden sound and movement behind my wife and I. Looking over as it traveled around us, I saw the young boy I had previously learned to be Malook's son.

He ran in to his dad, completely ignoring us while yelling something that sounded like *leekdi baba*. The man took hold of the child's waist, replying in a stern tone. Riven, if I remembered the name correctly, twisted to the side in his father's arms as he was chastised, presumably.

The boy's eyes caught sight of me and he instantly jerked them away without any further reaction to our presence. Riven spoke again, this time the words sounding like a question as he walked away from Malook and rested himself against the vampire instead. Her name was the only word I understood.

The creature gave her complete attention to the child, leaning down to look into his face as she carefully placed a claw on his tiny shoulder and talked to him in their tongue. Once again, names were all I recognized: Malook and Riven.

Of course, I couldn't be sure, but my impression was that whatever the father had told his son, Sulru was reiterating. Riven shrugged his shoulders, waving arms around in the air the way any bored kid would do before he trudged back out of the cockpit, seemingly singing under his breath as he left.

"I suppose the first thing we need to know is how to speak in your language," I vocally steered the conversation into answering my curiosity.

"Indeed," Malook hummed, "Let's start there."

I glanced over at Connie, who flashed a smile, having been hanging on every little thing that was happening. She wasn't typically so quiet and whether she saw me as 'in charge' or not, when both of us were in a serious environment, she generally allowed me to carry the weight of the ordeal. She had told me before it was because she trusted me to handle such things most appropriately.

"The ship reads different frequencies. Radio waves, sound waves, even lengths imperceptible to our senses," the man continued, "And stores them in a database that translates them into perceptible vibrations. Once we can physically sense them, we set them to be analyzed against our previously recorded knowledge.

"There, people we refer to as managers, translate these amplifications even more, through context and comparison to the workings of our society, to ensure that it has been accurately translated into our own tongue. Hence why we share so many words, phrases, and even other cultural similarities...moreover than there are in reality."

"Fascinating," Connie breathed, then asked in a louder voice, "How did you come to speak English so well, though? Or rather, how will we learn to speak your language quickly enough? How many languages are there on your planet?"

Her enthusiasm seemed to amuse Malook. He chuckled and began answering the rapidly fired questions, "We have one official language. There are still some who are aware of past languages including most vampires, but the vast knowledge of these has been eradicated. It is a crime to speak anything other than the official tongue."

"That seems...strange," my wife frowned and I knew strange was not the descriptor she wanted to use. Wrong, perhaps, or unfair. She must have settled for the most polite phrasing.

"I would imagine it's a means of control," I guessed.

The man scratched the long hair that was tied behind his ears, tilting his head with green eyes wide as if he hadn't thought about this. Or either he was just surprised that I had caught on so easily, "'Yes. Our leaders say such differences divide us and that we must be united to remain strong. But I suppose it is a way to control the population."

Connie was furrowing her brow, making it obvious to me that she was thinking of how to reply. However, it was a pet peeve of mine when a serious discussion derailed. Particularly one that I had an invested interest in. So I rushed to speak first, "How will you teach us this language?"

Malook cleared his throat and stood, Sulru's eyes following his movement as he walked past us and opened a compartment hidden in the wall behind. He rustled his hands in the box and then we heard a clicking sound, immediately after which, he returned to his spot.

Upon reaching the front of the room, he placed what was revealed to be a thin column like container lined with something akin in appearance to SD cards. The man threw the flowing sleeves of his robes back as he withdrew two of these chips and placed them into tiny slots in the stealthy computer I had noticed when first coming into the cockpit.

After hovering fingers over a few spots on the panels there, each illuminating at the sense of him, he stopped and waited for about a minute until the lights were gone again. He then retrieved both pieces and turned around, stepping closer to us.

"This," he held one of the cards out between two fingertips, "Holds our language as translated within the brain."

"You're saying that microchip has brain waves stored on it?" I asked, the idea sounding incredulous to me.

"Yes. I'm aware that our anatomies are exceedingly similar. All of our brains think through electric impulse. It isn't a far leap to put that into electronic devices," Malook's matter-of-fact explanation made me feel dim. "Anyhow," he went on, "This will transfer the waves that understand our tongue into your brain."

"How exactly will it connect?" I furthered.

"I'll place it at the base of your skull, a tiny razor will break your skin so that an equally small metal rod can extend into the stem. You'll feel a shock and that's it."

"I suppose there's no use in worrying about the safety or anything," I sighed.

"Not really...but I assure you, you'll be fine," the alien smiled.

"Alright, go for it," I said without much certainty.

Malook strolled around to stand behind where I sat. I stayed perfectly still, vision forward to realize the vampire's cold eyes were watching me and she was grinning. I scowled, knowing she could sense my nerves. Without any warning, Malook pressed the tiny device against the back of my neck, the actions happening in such quick succession that my mind couldn't keep up with the process.

I felt a shocking sensation in my head so sudden I was unable to resist grabbing my forehead with the ensuing ache. I barely caught a glimpse of my wife becoming startled, pushing a hand against my chest as I curled forward. I heard her voice, yet was unable to understand her words. I sat back up straight and looked at her, getting over the initial jolt of the experience.

"It's ok," I offered, trying to ignore the horrid ringing in my ears, but she just met me with an utterly confused expression. "What's wrong?" I asked, heart rate dropping at the surreal energy I began to feel, "What-"

The vampire belted, interrupting me. It wasn't a sound I anticipated from her, and her enjoyment during the stressful situation angered me so much that I rose abruptly, keeping the creature in my sights. Malook immediately threw his palms onto my chest to hold me back as I let the eerie fear take over.

"What is so funny??" I barked at her and then cried to Malook, motioning back toward my wife, "Why can't she understand me? Can she hear me?"

"Calm down, John," Malook soothed, pushing me to sit in the chair beside Connie.

I took the position without a fight, turning to grab my wife's hands, who had remained as bewildered as before and with concern growing. I looked from her to the man still holding me, now by the shoulders.

"For several minutes after a new language is transferred, you can only communicate with that language," he explained, "She hears you, but no, she can't understand what you're saying. You should recognize the differences between the languages soon."

"Don't you think you should have warned me?" my voice was still panicked.

"We didn't expect you to freak out so bad," Sulru smirked.

"Shut up, Sulru!" Malook spoke with surprising agitation as his head cut sharply backward at her, but quickly returning to face me though his eyes were on the floor.

The vampire's cheer left and she raised an eyebrow at her friend before letting her dark eyes nestle into squints while watching him rise out of his grasp on me. He threw a hand into the air in her direction, seemingly using the gesture as a sort of mild apology. His chest heaved up and down a couple of times and then he dropped the hand down again.

We all remained silent for a while until Malook spoke, calm having returned to him, "You should be fine now."

I hadn't been paying attention until that moment, but after he said this, I tried to communicate with Connie, only to realize that I was aware of two different sets of words for everything I wanted to say.

My strange new bilingual ability was so exciting, I didn't bother in any attempt to stop the beam spreading across my face.

Chapter 23: Connie

"Is he okay?" I asked Malook, even though I was facing John, "Are you okay?"

I felt a bit guilty for my reaction, but John's attempt to relate something to me in the alien tongue had me grasping for an appropriate response. Despite not knowing what any of them had said, his upset was clear. I had done my best to stay relaxed afterwards.

I let Malook diffuse the situation since apparently John was incapable of speaking with me at the time. It appeared now that things had returned to a comfortable mood, the huge grin on his face creeping me out more than the rest of the scenario had.

"I'm good, honey," John laughed. "Sorry, I-" he laughed again, "I'm good," he patted my hand and then squeezed it.

"So I'm assuming it worked," I stated awkwardly.

"Yeah," Sulru's voice cut in, sounding aggravated as she spun around in her chair, placing a hand above one of the panels in front of her and making a couple of taps with the tips of her claws, "I need to engage the drive. Hurry it along."

Malook sighed inwardly and turned from the woman to address me, simultaneously raising one of the tiny pieces in his hand, "Connie?"

I glanced to my husband who squeezed my hand again, "The shock is a bit startling," he said, "But it passes fast."

I nodded at him and then the man standing in front of me, "Okay, I'm ready when you are."

Malook walked around me like he had with John. I kept still, a little frightened after having witnessed my husband's minor freak out. I didn't have much chance to worry though, because the moment he was behind me, I felt this nearly overpowering jolt in the back of my neck. The feeling spread to my head then my ears began ringing.

John was right about how soon it faded. I had been so focused on not letting the discomfort get to me before Malook was even leaving to administer the transfer, that I had somehow blurred past the pain without any outward reaction at all that I could tell. I stayed in place until Malook stood before us again. Then I slowly turned to John, still expecting there to be more to the experience.

"Am I talking different now too?" I asked as I didn't feel any change in my mind.

John grinned, "Yes, but I can understand."

"Alright, you two," Malook began instructing as he returned to his chair, "Stay in your seats for a moment."

The man pressed the last digits of two fingers against something to his side, holding the motion for a few seconds. Afterward, he glanced over at Sulru with a silent affirmation. She replied only by grabbing a small dial that she rotated before pressing it down. There wasn't any blatant change in movement, which made me wonder why we had been told to sit.

The starry picture I had been focusing on through the glass, however, instantly shifted. The white dots became long lines of light and there seemed to be another, brighter and almost flashing ray that enveloped us. I stared at these things for the three or so minutes that the display flickered.

Suddenly, it all stopped. The lines, the lights, the stars had all disappeared and we were left in complete blackness. I inched forward where I sat, working hard to peer into the space around us. I couldn't see anything at all.

There were no signs of planets or moons or suns. There was absolutely no light whatsoever. The idea of being lost in a never-ending cosmic darkness suddenly took hold of me. It was a disturbing concept to think that we may just vanish into nothingness and never be heard from again. And somehow, it was also very romantic.

"Connie," Malook rotated in his chair again, "You are now my cousin. You and your husband will be staying with us while you grieve the loss of your son."

My heart fell, blood running cold at his words. Although he couldn't possibly know about my real son, this story he concocted was so relatable it was eerie. John sensed my tension too, for I saw him look to me out of the corner of my eye while tightening his hand around mine.

"What- uh..." I stammered, hurrying to reply before anyone else caught onto me, "How did he die?"

"Unknown," the man answered. "An infant that stopped breathing in his sleep."

I nodded, working on shaking away the depressing emotions trying to change me. I did think about the son I had lost often without much of an emotional response, but having something someone say force the thoughts to come about was more intense.

"What's the need for such a story?" John asked in an almost rude manner, but if Malook had heard the lilt, he didn't make notice of it.

"Our society does not delve into the personal matters of others who are dealing with tragedy," the green eyed man explained, "Unless you are an investigations officer, it's considered of the utmost disrespect."

"I see, so this would make it less likely for anyone to ask questions," my husband surmised.

I finally was able to think csemi-clearly, my mind gratefully grabbing another detail, "I take it I'm the relative since I'm mixed?"

Malook cocked his head as if it was an entirely new concept, "Your skin color, you mean. We don't separate race on Galdelier like you do on Earth," Malook picked up on my mind's process, "I believe you would call me black? And you are white?" he pointed toward John, who agreed.

"Yeah," he agreed less awkwardly than I would have.

"We separate by species only. We have humans; we have vampires. Then we have what are referred to as 'dumb species' or what you simply say are animals," Malook continued. "So these terms of yours mean nothing. However, genetics work much the same so yes, it's more believable for Connie and I to be related than John and I."

"People have different distinctive features based on where they're from though, right?" John pointed out. "You don't have any words to describe that?"

"Like I said," the alien reiterated, "We don't have races. Galdelier has developed much differently. There are no sets of features shared by any group of people like this. Perhaps far in our history, but no longer. Everything has melded together at this point."

"That actually sounds really nice," I started imagining a world where nobody judged each other based on skin color or country. They even only spoke one language... Then I remembered that we had only been told about the planet as a whole. Surely it was divided further. "Malook," I started again, "You've only mentioned Galdelier the planet, but not any specific areas."

"Sulru!" Riven's sweet giggling sounded, along with tiny running footsteps.

The vampire's head shot backward, seat rotating just in time for the boy to run up to her, reaching out for a hug. I watched Sulru's grim demeanor change into one of sincere care as she bent forward, opening her arms and carefully placed her claws around the young human. I was snapped from watching this oddly touching embrace by another new voice in the room.

"You'll need to get rid of those clothes," Soare-a said over to our side.

Her voice dripped with contempt and even though she was no doubt talking about John and I, her gaze was on her son who had just let go of his vampire friend and was standing with his back leaned against her chest. It made it difficult to come to any conclusion as to what was irritating her. It could be more than one thing though, I guessed. Malook's wife stood with right hand resting on her thigh, elbow jutting outward slightly, and left hand raised in the air to talk with.

"And the names. Don't forget that, Malook," she bounced her head on its sides to take in the sight of every body in the room.

"Of course," he acknowledged, his voice seemingly discontent as well. He looked from his wife back to us and smiled, "Your names should actually be fine though," his eyes went back to Soare-a, "Can you hand me that tablet, dear?"

The woman removed her hand from her leg to show it had been concealing a smooth and slender device attached to a holster around the the side of her thigh. It appeared similar to a smartphone except, as she lifted it from her, I realized that it was entirely clear.

She stepped forward, giving it to Malook whose touch commanded a colorful image to light up on the device. He slid one fingertip in a semicircle on the screen, commanding the background to change to pure white. Then, his fingers popped into view a stylus that had been hidden in the object's rim, also transparent. With it, he scribbled in black for a few seconds before reaching to hand the small computer to me.

I took the heavy-looking glass contraption, only to feel that it was very light with a feeling of almost fragility. Written in a text that seemed an odd mixture of Spanish and traditional Chinese, were two words I could best put down as Ka'ney and Jun.

Staring at them was the first moment I came to awareness that there was a new language in my mind. I shot a look to my husband, whose answer was one of complete comprehension, accompanied by the lift of his injured hand to stroke the back of my hair, his nails scratching my scalp lightly. He, too, studied the revamping of our names on the screen, taking his hand back to rub his chin.

"Should you need to share your names, produce them this way," Malook instructed.

I nodded, still gazing downward at the screen in my palms. I glanced at my husband to make sure he was finished before I turned the device back to Malook. Midway through stretching my arm, however, I looked from him to his wife, recalling that it had belonged to her. Halting in my tracks, I questioned quietly who I should give it to. I didn't have to express this confusion aloud because Soare-a stepped toward me and retrieved it, powering it off and reattaching it to her leg.

"Riven!" she ordered after doing so, "Come help me find them some clothes."

The boy swayed in his stance, looking at John and I for the first time. He had bright green eyes that matched his father's, "So I can talk to the aliens now?" his innocence shone through the words and the incredible beam on his face.

"They aren't aliens, Riven," Malook told his son, "These are your cousins, Ka'ney and Jun."

Riven continued to move from side to side without lifting his feet, staring at us still and contemplating a few seconds before finally affirming the information with, "Cool. I have real family now."

"Riven, come!" Soare-a called again in a harsher voice, keeping me from asking what her son had meant.

The boy skipped away from the vampire, grabbing hold of his mother's leg as she turned to leave the room once more. Upon reaching the doorway, she glanced back and added one final thought to the conversation, "Oh and make sure they know how to treat the vampire before we get there."

Her bitter words sent an odd flush of uncomfortable and angry energy through the room. When the two had disappeared into the curve of the hallway, I put my eyes on Malook and Sulru in front of us. Both kept their gazes after where the woman had left, the vampire's expression having returned to its usual dimness and the man slowly shaking his head. I exchanged an awkward glance with John, waiting for someone to clear the air.

"I've told you that vampires are looked down upon on our world, but I haven't quite stressed the exact extent," Malook was the one to speak and his voice was filled with sorrow. His head dropped, momentarily staring at the floor before looking back up and finishing, "When we're around others, you can't speak to Sulru. You must act as if she's not there. And not just her, but any other vampires you may come into contact with."

My eyes darted over to the woman sitting opposite him. I had expected her to shy away from this dialogue and put her attention elsewhere, but she stayed facing the rest of the circle, dark spheres resting on Malook, who seemed extremely disheartened to have had to say what he did.

"Is it...illegal to associate with vampires? or..." I asked.

"Not so much illegal," Sulru picked up, apparently finding the subject easier to discuss than her boss, "As you will draw too much undesired attention to yourself. Malook has enough of that already because of his pity for my people." I found myself lost in trying to read for any hidden emotion in her expression. "It's dangerous," she added, brow dropping in an almost glare.

I managed to break myself from her gaze to see Malook tilting his head up and down, "It's easy to become an outcast with these sorts of differing views which is *never* a good thing to be on Galdelier," the tone of the discussion had suddenly taken on an extremely grave tone.

"How so?" John spoke up. He had his head tilted to the side, giving him an easy view of both aliens in front of us.

"Here!" Riven's chipper voice was in the room again. The boy had run up to my side and laid some sort of fabric on my lap while grinning up at me, "I got you clothes."

I chuckled and replied over-enthusiastically, "Thank you!"

Riven was completely adorable and obviously very loving. His re-appearance had been perfectly timed to keep my distress over the unpleasant turn in conversation from growing too much or at least too quickly. I was glad that Soare-a hadn't come with him this time either. That woman was not very pleasant.

"Let's just say people who are disagreeable to the appropriate constructs tend to come up missing," Sulru pointed vaguely, clearly wanting to answer in a way that Malook's son would not understand as per her low tone and settling her vision on the boy.

Chapter 24: Malook

I spent the better part of the next hour explaining some more core details about our home. When I had confirmed John's inklings concerning our government being totalitarian, his wife had seemed to be thrown off kilter. She apparently had not picked up on this from anything previously discussed.

Earth's ruling powers and their basic societal rules had been the first details our people sought out after piecing together its primary language. My rank allowed me to be one of the first to know these things. However, there were so many different factions on Earth that it proved difficult to keep everything straight. There were somewhere around two hundred countries, each run in a manner different from the rest. A large number of these claimed to be allies, yet they kept their leaders and laws separate.

According to Connie, freedom was an intense desire amongst the people of Earth and still, she had trouble giving me a direct answer as to what exactly freedom was. The gist of her definition was that everyone should have the right think and believe how they want, and also to care for themselves how they choose so long as it wasn't causing detriment to others.

Grasping onto this concept was problematic for me. Of course, I was adamantly against some things about our society, namely the subjugation of Sulru's people, but for there to be free reign to the extent Connie proposed, I felt it would only be begging for chaos. The Earth woman assured me it wasn't so, with the reasoning that this was how the government of their country did things. Recalling my short experience with these 'Americans,' I simply stated I rather doubted that this worked as well as she felt it did.

Mostly, though, my argument boiled down to two questions: How was it fair that a person should be free to not only hold dangerous ideals against others, but be able to promote them without consequence? Didn't this threaten the 'freedom' of those on the opposite side of these beliefs?

The open prejudice that the vampires experienced was due to their being inhuman and therefore not seen as our equal. Even so, it was not legal to push for violence against them because such an allowance would only further disrupt the peace by letting citizens focus too much on aggression and hatred rather than on standing strong under the law.

Needless to say, our disagreement wasn't resolved. John simply stepped in to politely steer the conversation elsewhere. He repeated the inquiry his wife had made earlier that had never been answered regarding our planet's geography. Galdelier was an almost flip of Earth as far as this was concerned.

Instead of being dominated by water, most of the world was covered in livable land which was not divided, but rather one large mass running through both poles. This accumulation of dirt jutted out into either ocean as rounded shores and was commonly referred to as looking akin to a stomach when outlined. The planet itself was only slightly smaller than Earth, with a diameter of nearly seventy-six hundred miles.

There were two countries, Gelvin, where we lived, and Satel, each having boundaries beginning at the north pole and ending at the south on either side of the globe. They were made up of twenty and twenty-one states, respectively, which were defined by the area's contribution whether this be a natural source such as trees and crops, or one that had been man made like research facilities and factories.

At the highest power of governing, we had Empress Naiker over Gelvin and Emperor Inton over Satel. They were sister and brother, their family having ruled Galdelier for close to a millennium although it hadn't always been an empire. Within their individual domains, seven generals were appointed. Each general was in charge of three states, with up to twenty commanders beneath them, depending upon the density of their states' populations.

The amount of officers beyond that was not strictly regulated and the services they provided ranged from patrol to investigation to keeping the peace. Those of the General rank, such as myself, were assigned a companion to accompany us on ambassadorial missions, such as meeting with others of our status, commanders, or even the Emperor or

Empress themselves. Although it was recommended that these aides be vampiric, we were allowed to opt for a human counterpart.

The duty of these guards was to protect their General as well as any other human of equal or greater ranking. For example, Sulru's job was to protect me while I was away from the secure facility where I performed a large portion of my tasks. If, however, we were at a meeting with another General or Generals, then all assisting would be responsible for maintaining a barrier together around these superiors and not their direct upper alone. In the rare events that our Empress was present, their focus would remain on defending all Generals in addition to her sovereignty, with greatest concern for Empress Naiker.

Unless the Empress was involved to overrule my command, Sulru was legally required to answer to me. Our Lady Naiker had her own protective detail of both vampires and humans, though a greater amount were human. This was meant to level out the the human to vampire ratio in favor of our species.

Despite having developed weapons to successfully fend off these people with grand regenerating capabilities, everything was always planned to keep the number of vampires together to a minimum. Starting with commanders and working down the ladder, there were more inhuman officers because there was a huge increase of humans at that point. Also, these government employees dealt more with physical altercations where the need for vampiric strength was greater.

"That should do you well enough for now," I said when our dialogue had finally begun to lull. "You'll learn more after we get there. Just ask me questions as you have them."

The two earthlings nodded and John spoke up in order to summarize what was probably the most important thing for them to know before we landed, "Alright, thank you. So basically, besides ignoring any vampires, we act as informally as we have been with you?"

"That should be fine, yes," I agreed. "Obviously refrain from asking much of others. I don't anticipate putting you into any situations where you should need to talk too in depth. At least not for some time."

John leaned back into his seat. I saw his vision turn momentarily to Sulru, who had stopped showing interest in the chat long ago even so, I knew she was still listening. Instead, she looked forward and silently monitored the navigational systems. The Earth man had retrieved his eyes from her and put them downward while he studied his burned hand In a way that could have been intent or absentminded, bringing the attention of his wife who stared worriedly at the newly sealed wounds.

"Feel free to move about the place," I prompted them to relax further, less for their sake and more for mine. I hadn't realized until then how strained my mind and body had become.

"We should probably go change," Connie piped, rustling the outfits that had been resting in her lap for the duration of the discussion. It seemed by the tone of the words and John's slow reaction that they, too, were starting to feel their own exhaustion.

The man stood up with a grunt, offering his good hand which the doctor took and then stood as well, "What should we do with our clothes?" he asked.

"Just bring them back here. I'll have Soare-a take care of them," I answered, unwittingly opening up for more discussion.

The two spun softly to face me, both no doubt with the same thought on their minds. John, however, was the one to ask. It appeared to me that Connie allowed him to take the lead the majority of the time.

"Don't take this the wrong way, but your wife doesn't seem to care for us very much," he said, pausing for a second before adding, "I, of course, understand why she would have trouble with it. After everything that you've all been put through in such a nonstop course at that. A lot is happening very quickly."

I smiled at his diplomacy, "She is under a lot of stress, but you'll come to know that Soare-a carries herself in a very strict manner. I assure you it's nothing personal."

John gave a single nod, leading his wife from the room by the shoulders before she had the chance to react. I watched after them as they walked to the very end of the hallway, growing smaller and smaller in my view until they had at last disappeared into the cavity at its end. I then rotated my seat, halfway between facing forward and Sulru, and I let out a heavy breath.

"Strict is what it is now?" my vampiric friend mused, keeping her position except for a lift of the brow.

"Ugh," I groaned, putting my attention on her fully, "Soare-a will get over this enmity once she sees past her pettiness and realizes this is best for her too. There's no need in anyone being alarmed."

Sulru smirked as her chair rolled to face me, "Angry and petty; that sounds more accurate."

I stared back at the pale-skinned woman. I knew I should have defended my wife, yet gazing into Sulru's onyx eyes stayed my mind. Soare-a hadn't always been so hateful. We had loved each other once, hadn't we? There had always been differences between us; I knew that. I just never expected her to stick with the preconceptions she had back then. We were both young when we met, her more than I.

She hadn't had any real dealings with vampires or direct experiences with government at all, actually. My family had always been employed by our leaders, but hers was not known for anything in particular; its working members going for whatever job they could, and trying hard to keep it for any length of time.

That, in itself, was a feat considering that the people she came from were largely uneducated and lazy. Not only that, they had a history of unrest with government officials. Therein, laid Soare-a's only background with vampires. I suppose she grew up seeing them as unimportant and even evil because of these things. She had shared with me memories of officers raiding her home when she was quite young.

Among them was a vampire who had roughed up her father pretty badly as he attempted to flee arrest. She also had stories of vampires coming around her family with police on other accounts, sometimes having to keep the humans from being violent towards each other. Everything she had recalled about the species was how terrifying they were. She never seemed to fault her family, not really. It was always the vampires.

I tried to sympathize; I really did. However, having always been involved in law enforcement, I was well aware that these vampiric officers were only following orders; doing what was required of them. Going on Soare-a's own word, they weren't being excessive in any way. Still, my wife had trouble understanding that it was not the other species that was at fault, and her hatred of them only strengthened over the years.

Even Sulru's kindness wasn't enough to jar her from this bigotry. At some moments, I felt she must realize to some extent her mistaken beliefs; that at least some part of her saw that vampires, as a whole, were not as wicked and destructive as she had been led to think. I wondered if this was true and it was just that she was just too base to admit she had been wrong.

No, I didn't feel sorry for my wife. Not anymore. Her childhood had been difficult, but this was more than a disagreement; it was a core detail that determined the very morality of a person. It's okay to be ignorant of things. But I would not accept someone who outright refused to move past stupidity.

She *knew* better. She had been given more time with vampires. I had shown her how they were forced to be and how it wasn't who they really were, as a rule. I dug into records and proved to her that it had been her father, mother, uncles...*they* had been the ones at fault in those altercations. All my effort only angered her and set me to figuring out how to sever our ties in the best way possible.

She wasn't making it easy.

I didn't want to be the bad guy...but if I wanted, I could easily have her back into that scum life she had been raised in; the one she had been a part of even until the day we met. There would be no question that Riven would fall into my custody. I literally had the power to rip her entire life away. I wanted to settle this to get back to where we had started. I thought that maybe if I could get her to feel for me again, we could get somewhere this time. This trip had been my last attempt in getting her to see, and obviously hadn't worked.

"Malook?"

I shook my head forcefully, throwing my thoughts away. My eyes had been resting on Sulru who looked at me now, brow furrowed and eyes covered with concern. "Sorry," I mumbled. "I'm tired."

"Don't lie to me, friend," she growled back softly.

I chucked my head to the side with a titter, scratching my jaw line, "I'm fine, Sulru. I don't feel like talking anymore. Not right now."

The vampire's expression fell back to numbness after a short, single roll of her eyes. It was an imperceptible movement due to their coloration, but one I had become capable of determining after coming to know her so well. She let out an aggravated exhale, turning back to the front of the pit and gazing into the blackness just outside the glass shield of the craft.

"Get some rest, Malook," she said less softly than her previous statements.

With a deep breath, I rose to my feet. I knew Sulru wasn't like my wife. She didn't take my denial to share my thoughts personally. It was only worriment that she was expressing, nothing else. Speaking wouldn't give her any peace anyway. This situation was far too complicated for a few simple reflections or distractions to fix.

In addition, I was too weary to work on these problems at present. Instead, I strolled over behind the vampire, placing my hands on her shoulders. I leaned down so that my head was level with hers, our cheeks less than an inch from touching. She didn't move. Even her eyes remained in place.

"I will. Thank you," I whispered, turning my chin slightly, resting my vision gently on her dark eyes as I touched my lips to the cold skin beneath those spheres, planting a slow, but small kiss on her pale cheek.

She blinked once and I could feel her chest change its pace under the weight of my palms laying on her shoulder. Sulru gave no further response and the only other action by me was to let go of her before stepping away and leaving the room.

Chapter 25: Sulru

Malook infuriated me. I had told him many times to back off, yet he persisted. Perhaps it was because he knew me better than anyone else...something I should have probably never let happen. He knew I clung to any tiny bit of intimacy he showed no matter how intensely I denied it. I despised how easy it was for him to tease me with his love, knowing that nothing would ever come of it.

The two of us seemed to have shared a connection since our first meeting, but it wasn't for a few months afterward, that it was made clear just how deep that bond would become. There was an underground faction that had been growing for several years on Galdelier. It mostly consisted of vampires, myself included, but there were quite a few human members as well. Everyone involved laid somewhere within the rankings of officer.

Our agenda was the upheaval of the current empire to be replaced by a republic with laws based upon ideals shared by the group. One such agreed upon change to the current political system was the liberation of the vampire species. It had actually been the basis of our group's initial founding.

Other changes included the freedom to choose one's own career and otherwise have the right to be individualistic over being compelled into group-oriented habits, hobbies, and so on. As more people were brought in, though, it was made clear that simply fighting for fair treatment was not enough.

Human members had given the insight that there were many things about our world's society that were, indeed, agreeable. Such things included universal healthcare and the forbidding of certain activities such as Malook had attempted to explain to Connie earlier, in the interest of the safety for all. The problems were less with the written laws of our world and rather with the fact that such supreme rule was given to one family. Two individuals alone to be exact.

This left much to be changed at the whim of the emperors and those beneath them fell in line because it was the easiest and only absolute path to ensure one's own welfare. Many others not part of the government staff remained obedient, solely for believing there was no other way. My people were used in perpetuating the fear of consequence of noncompliance. It was a sickening abuse...but I digress.

It was I who had brought Malook into the fold. He had been called to the site of a double homicide one evening and I, of course, accompanied him. It wasn't his usual work at the time as per his rank. However, the incident happened within the city where we resided and it dealt with two commanders directly under him. He was there for that invested interest. Both commanders had been killed at the hands of another, lower officer.

I knew this third human. A kind man, dedicated to the purposes of our secret order. I had spoken to him at various times and always remembered how fondly he talked about his husband who, although he was aware of our group, did not play an active part in it. It was for his mate's peace of mind that he refrained from attaining membership. Upon our arrival, the man, Dova, was being escorted from the home where his superiors had been slain. He was in an obvious panic.

While passing Malook and I, the vampiric officer who was moving Dova pulled him tighter under control by the two arms pinned behind his back. My former ally, once catching sight of me, couldn't seem to refrain from speaking. "I had to do it. I had to do it!" he yelled, blood splattered face looking directly at me as he pulled against the vampire that held him. Fortunately, these actions weren't seen as connected to me in any way but instead thought to be part of the man's emotional frenzy, having killed two close friends moments ago.

Nobody registered it as more than that. Nobody except Malook.

Malook was known for his great intuition and skills of deduction. It was one of the major reasons the Empress had chosen him to become General. I didn't even realize that he had picked anything up from the outburst, as I knew I had not reacted to it.

We had gone inside the residence and seen the two commanders lying dead on the floor, one with a bullet through his head and the other with three shots to the chest. Malook studied the scene until he felt satisfied that he knew as much as the place could tell him. It was only after leaving the presence of the others there that he brought to my attention any suspicions gained from Dova's cry.

"Dova Forkint," Malook spoke the name as if tasting it, while I parked the rover we rode in next to his home that night, "Met him before, have you?"

"I have not," I lied, my face straight as I slowly turned off the vehicle's engine and rested my vision on him.

"Really?" he hummed, shifting in the passenger seat, "Seems to me he knew you."

I cocked my head to the side, "I don't know what would have given you the idea he did."

"Well, he was silent until he saw you," Malook pointed, raising any eyebrow.

"He was entirely worked up. That was painfully clear," I scoffed.

"Maybe..." my boss glanced to the side and brought a hand to his face, two fingers aimed upward as he rested them against his lips in thought, "Why do you think he did it?"

I hadn't at this point gotten quite used to Malook's casual approach when speaking with me away from prying eyes. It wasn't normal. Even many humans within the faction kept a formal, almost awkward distance when conversing with its vampiric members.

It wasn't generally out of disrespect, rather the setting of our two species in dealing with each other so closely was still highly unusual. Malook, however, had never shown the slightest discomfort around us and was always extremely relaxed with me.

"I couldn't guess it. Could be many things," I answered vaguely. Our group learned later from Dova's husband that the man had gone to the residence in an attempt to recruit the two commanders, who obviously turned on the idea. Like I said, Dova was dedicated. He must have killed the men in order to keep our secret.

Malook dropped his hand then and chuckled, turning back to me, "Sulru, it's been what? Three months since we started working together? Are you still this uneasy around me?"

"I feel fine around you, *Malook*," I had stressed my use of his name to outline that he did not, in fact, intimidate me, "I don't understand what more you want me to say."

But I wasn't daunting to him either.

The man had smiled, raising an arm and placing his hand on my shoulder in a friendly gesture, "Sure, but I do hope one day you will put this ritual aside and actually talk *with* me."

My brow had furrowed as I stared back at him. The odd placement of his hand threw me off. I couldn't recall a human having ever touched me like that. It highlighted everything in my mind of how he had always treated me with respect; as an equal. WhileI tried to gather myself into a response, though, he retrieved his arm and his grin fell.

"It's sad though," he had mused, face forward once more, "Not only are the commanders gone, leaving their families behind, but this man, this Dova...he'll be gone soon as well. What he's done? A capital crime twice over."

I had tried my best to numb my expression, and I had to have semi-succeeded, but there was just too much happening in that instance. My attention stayed intent upon this strange man and I even momentarily doubted his sanity. When I didn't acknowledge his loud thoughts, he added another.

"I wonder if his death will leave anyone alone too," Malook turned to see me again and I knew he was studying me.

I bit my tongue to refrain from any further reaction as my mind flashed with the knowledge of Dova's husband. Nonetheless, shrewd Malook had seen this tiny movement. To me, that was enough to break my silence and input my own means to learning more about my partner.

"The vampire marked with destroying him will learn more about him in a moment than anyone will discover through days of investigation," my words sounded more philosophical than they actually were.

It was well known to our people that the blood of a being was imprinted with that creature's very essence. Their soul, if you will. It wasn't to say that by drinking it, a vampire could perfectly understand another person or know intimate details about them. Rather, doing so gave a strong impression of that being's karmic weight; their intention. Some humans believed this tale and some didn't. Either way, the story was out there.

I hadn't taken my eyes off of the man the entire time and neither had he parted his from me. His head tilted ever so slightly then, his demeanor softening. "Yes..." he whispered. "I feel sorry for the person who has to suffer through knowing this man's true turmoil."

Person.

It was all the answer I needed. Everything I pondered about Malook made clear to me in one simple word. Vampires weren't referred to as individuals, as people or persons, or even citizens. Creatures, animals, beasts, soul-suckers...these were a few of the kinder words used to describe us. But he had said none of them. Person. He spoke kindly of a vampire that he would never even know, and he did so with something greater than a basic respect for another living being.

It was days later that I had shared with him the knowledge of our order. Even with the previous experience with him, I proceeded with the utmost caution. I enlightened him to the idea before the truth. I gave no names as I, too, was willing to give my life for the sake of our mission.

He took it with positivity so I arranged a meeting between him and the only general with us at that time, personally seeing to it that the two were completely alone. Otahn had heard the rumors of Malook's sympathy for vampire kind and, being of equal status, both had already met a handful of times.

From there, Otahn took charge of revealing more about us to Malook.

After it all, I had found myself growing increasingly delighted to be in the man's company. To be honest, I hadn't before taken much interest in his life...in his wife or his son. I had seen them as another job. Just more average humans. But Malook was anything but.

He was the only adult human I had come across that not only believed vampires and humans were equals, but fully acted upon that conviction. Never did he show unease around my kind, even in the presence of other humans. And it wasn't in the typical 'I must prove that I'm not frightened by these creatures' or 'that I'm better than them' that many other officials had. It was sincere.

However, this genuine friendship gradually began turning into something different. Soare-a had the same attitude she had now ever since the day I had met her. She was haughty and she was selfish. But as time went on, she and her husband fought more and fought worse. All these arguments boiled down to their extreme differences in personality. They'd have in depth disputes about inane things, with the most severe verbal sparring concerning their son. Namely how he was being raised and taught to act.

Both of them seemed to like to focus on the vampire versus human aspect of life and even brought me into their arguments several times, which was far from my place in many regards. I suppose it was their mind's reasoning for doing this since it was such a prevalent issue. Nonetheless, their problems ranged greatly from just this one thing.

Soare-a began distancing herself from both Malook and Riven. The latter of which pissed me off to no end. She would often disappear with her friends or even by herself, leaving her son in my care, giving her something to further complain about later, as she truly despised my good relationship with the boy. She hadn't always appeared to be so to me, but she had definitely developed a pretty self-destructive pattern of behavior.

The worse her and Malook's relationship got, the more attention the man gave me and it was far more than platonic. It caused me great concern in the beginning. I felt that he was deflecting his painful emotions and that these advances were not truthful. I did, though, quickly realize that I easily saw him as a romantic partner despite the entirely ridiculous idea. The possibility of such a thing occurring was impossible as anything farther than hidden moments of affection.

Malook was a very disciplined man. That's why it alarmed me when I had received this call from him: "S-Sulru? I need your help." His voice was shaking and stuttering.

"Malook?" I had risen in my bed. It was dark as the night had just changed into the first hours of the morning. The man had dismissed me from his family hours ago as he was home with them, and so I had gone to my own residence, a communal building with other vampires, "What's going on? Are you at home?"

"No, I'm...I'm out on...Do you remember where the forest is?" The words had been mumbled and I strained to hear them.

"Black Forest? Of course. What are you doing out there?" I had already made my way from my resting spot and placed a cloak around my shoulders as I stepped out into the home's hallway.

"Shh..." he whispered, then chortled, "Just come pick me up."

I drove past the outer parts of the city into the dimly-lit bits of nature beyond. The forest was pretty large. Best estimate was a hundred miles on its longest path. It was a popular place for my kind to go in our free time.

Many of us found pleasure in running and often would race one another within the safe confines of the deeper parts of the wood. It was the humans who would traverse the outer rim of the forest for their own relaxation, spending time with the animals that were kept there.

Parking the rover, I jumped out and began walking alongside the trees, looking for Malook. My large eyes easily saw through the dark and after several minutes, I spotted him tripping along one of the synthetic paths. I rushed to his side, grabbing hold of him and putting my weight beneath him for support.

"What the hell have you- are you drunk?" I asked in almost shock.

"No," he groaned, "Not anymore."

I took in and let out a deep breath. There were those who created their own toxic drinks despite the strict laws against the use of these substances, yet I had never known Malook to have partaken in such things and since then, he never had again. I helped him get back to where I had parked the vehicle, leaning him to rest against it while I opened the side door.

"Here, come sit down. I'll take you home," I comforted the man, figuring there had been another fight with Soare-a that had set him off.

"Sulru?" the man had kept his back next to the machine, his eyes had been focused on the ground, but he lifted his face to look at me then, "Do you only put up with me because you have to?"

"Why do you worry about such a thing?" I had said with distaste at the thought of him feeling that way when there were blatant pointers to the contrary.

"Because I don't want be part of a forced union anymore than your people do," he had almost spat the words, glaring at me.

I had stood still, my voice becoming angrier as my aggravation grew, "I have never felt obligated to do anything when with you, Malook."

He had stared back with green eyes starting to shine, as if he were on the verge of crying, but his demeanor remained staunch. The long brown hair that was normally kept perfectly in a tie behind his head was loose and disheveled, with much of it falling into his face. Likewise, his tidy tunic was crooked and dirty to deepen the look of hopelessness he had about him.

He had lifted himself from the vehicle, quickly closing the gap between the two of us. As he grabbed one of my hands with both of his, I instinctively made sure my claws were completely retracted. I could feel the warmth of his blood under the skin, a comforting sensation to my icy hands. My black eyes softened while I gazed back at him. He lifted my hand, placing it against his chest carefully before taking one of his and putting it against my cheek and caressing it.

My heartbeat became shallow at this closeness, my body itching to react while my mind reprimanded me for letting this progress. So I just stood, umoving and silent, waiting to see how far he wanted to push.

The man tilted his head to the side, eyes falling to my mouth, and I found myself looking at his as well. He had beautifully dark and defined lips that contrasted greatly to my own, which were absent of color and thin. The two of us looked so different, yet we were amazingly similar. He leaned in, lids falling down to cover his vision as he planted his face onto mine, removing the last of my inhibition.

I pushed back into the kiss, taking control of my hands and gently placing their palms onto his cheeks. I felt his arms reach my waist, hands wriggling within the folds of my robes to find my flesh. As the tips of his fingers grazed against my side, my brain reminded me how we were out in the open. Although the likelihood of someone coming around at that hour was slim, I still felt the need to take firm hold of the man and shove us under the coverage of the foliage.

Malook allowed me to move him without question, his force coming back once we were better hidden. He threw me against a tree before ripping my robe at either side so that it fell from my shoulders. I was still physically stronger than him, but I had no desire for this to stop. The cloak had been covering the thin tunic that I slept in. I hadn't taken the time to change into appropriate attire before rushing out to find my friend.

The man easily slipped his hands beneath the upper part of my dress, sliding them upward to grab hold of my breasts. Even though my chest was small since I was naturally lean, the arousal was there and caused me to moan. Malook let his fingers crawl around my back, reaching over my shoulders as he pushed his body tightly against mine, his knee prompting my legs to part. I could feel that he was hard when he pressed himself onto me.

I looked at him longingly, as his fierce green spheres stared back, filled with lust. I had not been intimate with another person for many years. I had certainly not felt a connection to anyone like I did with him...not since...

I latched onto his shoulders then, my claws jutting out just enough to scratch him, but I didn't regress. I threw my lips onto his again, eagerly mangling them together as I tugged and sucked, him reciprocating while simultaneously releasing me from his grip, so that he could pull up the bottom of my tunic. We only continued to choke the air from between us, him pushing against me so my spine scraped against the tree, and me ignoring trying to control my claws as I pulled at him.

Malook successfully raised my tunic so that my bare legs and groin showed. He trapped the fabric in the middle of our crushing bodies as he reached to touch himself so that he may be free from the constrains of his own clothes. I stared at him as he did, my body clutching and tightening in sweet expectation. Finally, he was pressing his stiffness against me, his soft tip brushing the lips of my mound. I clenched, my body begging for him to be inside me.

He didn't hold back. After guiding himself to my entrance, he pushed violently, breaking in. I clutched my walls around him, my body beneath him, and my claws into his shoulders. He grimaced and grunted with the pain of my razors cutting him, immediately giving another, even more aggressive shove so that my back lifted barely from where it rested, and then banged against the tree once more. He was completely within me then.

I cried out softly with the pleasure of feeling him as his groin pulled away from mine, before pushing in again. During every repeat of this motion, my body seized with the building ball of pressure at my core. He began moving faster and faster. I looked up to his face to see his expression was stiffening, the need for release growing.

As I felt myself winding, becoming so tight that my body was aching, I realized that Malook had pulled a hand from my side and had placed it directly beneath my neck on my chest, its fingers curled so that his nails dug into my skin. He continued to thrust in and out of me, that hand creeping upward so that it took a loose hold onto my throat. It was unusual to me, but not displeasing.

Retrieving a hand from his shoulder, I placed it on the wrist of his which lay on my chest, causing his grip on my neck to toughen. It became just enough that I could feel a minor change in my ease of breathing. My eyes shot to his.

I don't know what he thought he read in them, but he relinquished hold of me and instead put his mouth on mine again to take another passionate kiss. Just as our lips touched, I felt my core explode. I growled contentedly at the intense pleasure, which was followed by the feeling of his own release inside me.

This had been the only time I had and would ever let myself fall victim to his love. Maybe...maybe one day such a thing could be. But I was well aware of the way humans and vampires alike worked. Even in the world we were fighting for, this kind of relationship would only create problems.

Chapter 26: John

"I hate it," Connie complained after we had gotten changed into the strange garments.

"I'm sure as per their fashion, you look great," I smiled, not really happy with what I was wearing either.

I don't know why not, but it hadn't struck me until then that though they were varying colors, all of the aliens wore the exact same thing, even the vampire. And now, Connie and I matched. The attire was best described as a tunic. It was one loose piece of fabric that cinched just under the waist. The sleeves flowed down to the wrists and hung several inches below the arms. The bottom fell within the area between the knees and ankles.

There were bits of fabric attached to the main body, in lines of different lengths, down the one that Connie wore, seeming to be present only to alter its appearance. Mine, on the other hand, had an inlay at the chest area making the one piece look like two. They were a shade of orange. Hers, a light, almost pastel and mine, a darker 'burnt' coloration. Both were pretty heavily weighted.

"At least they're comfortable," Connie said.

"True," I laughed. "I do feel like I'm wearing a dress though."

"You look it," my wife said under her breath.

"What was that?" I demanded.

"Nothing," she smiled and threw her arms around me to steal a kiss.

Grinning back, I swung her around in the embrace, making her giggle. I dropped out of the movement, keeping my hands curled at her waist, as hers hung loosely onto my shoulders.

"Are you nervous?" she asked, trying to take a serious expression and failing.

"Yes," I admitted, "Even with what we've been told, there's not much definite as to what will actually happen."

Her beam lessened, "Maybe... Even so, I feel like it's going to be alright. I honestly do, John."

I leaned forward and gave the woman a kiss on the head. She wanted to make me rest easy, but only the experience had the ability to do that. Well wishes and prayers had never made me feel better. Solely knowing the truth of things, whether good or bad, would take away this anxiety of uncertainty. Although, I had to admit that it helped to know she wasn't worrying.

"I suppose it's time to present our new selves," I sighed as I fell away from her to grab the brown sandals from the bed beside us, "Plus I'm really hungry," I added, bending down to slide and fasten the leathery shoes onto my feet.

Connie's smile came back as she grabbed the pile of Earth clothes from the mattress, already having put her own pair of clogs on, "Me too."

I nodded my head before turning around and departing the room. She followed closely behind, taking place at my side once we were in the hallway again. Walking with bare feet sliding inside the smooth material of the sandals, I surmised that it must be genuine skin.

It seemed an insignificant detail, but it told that there were industries on the alien planet for the consumption of animal products. This was important to my hungry stomach at the moment because even if there was none on the ship, meat was no doubt part of these people's cuisine.

My mind had just put this bit together, when we reached the cockpit to find that Sulru was the only one still present. I managed to keep myself from groaning outwardly. The idea of asking a vampire for food seemed exceedingly awkward. However, there was something even more so that I wanted to speak with her about.

I had honestly been working to see past my dislike for the creature- the judgement I placed on her for the blood she had spilled. Mostly because in the back of my brain, I knew it made me a hypocrite. Connie kept on into the room after I had already taken a place behind the chairs, still erect from our use of them prior. I rested my hands on the back of one of them while my wife strolled around to their front, stopping a couple of feet from the vampire who swiveled her seat to face us.

"Where should we put these?" Connie asked the other woman, lifting the clothing in her arms just barely enough so that it was apparent what she was referring to.

"Place them on your chair, there," Sulru's only motion was to slightly bob her chin in my direction.

My wife gave a brief smile before setting the pile onto the seat I grasped. She glanced at me momentarily, and then turned back to the vampire. "Sulru?" she asked, "Malook- um... Do you want me to take a look at your teeth?"

Connie was looking at her with those doctor eyes. The vampire blinked at the words and then dropped her head, simultaneously rotating it to the side and grinning. She probably had thought about how Malook had asked for the help that he informed us she would not have. She then rested my wife in her vision.

"Yes, that would be helpful," she answered, face returning to the expression of nothingness that it seemed to most often exhibit.

I watched as Connie approached Sulru again, this time to the point where she could easily lay her hands on the strange creature, "Open your mouth," she softly instructed the vampire, who did so without hesitation, twisting her neck so that her eyes were on me and her damaged teeth were shown to the doctor.

I couldn't tell if Sulru was actually looking at me or if her gaze was just settled in my general direction. Either way, it didn't make me feel uncomfortable, which made me wonder if she wasn't staring at me or if I was just getting used to her. Connie took hold of the pale woman's small lips to pull them carefully upward so that they were atop gums instead of fangs. Even with the deliberate motion, Sulru winced in pain.

"Damn, I'm sorry," my wife whispered as she studied the damage her bullet had done.

The vampire pulled away abruptly, wetting her lips with her tongue, "Don't be," she muttered.

Connie seemed somewhat offended by the harsh reaction. "They definitely need to be pulled," she added quietly, not removing her attention from the vampire.

"Okay," Sulru answered apathetically as she stood, strolling past Connie, then me, and then left the cockpit.

My wife looked from the departing woman to me, with a shrug of her shoulders. I stretched out my arm over the chairs, gesturing for her to accompany me as I followed after the alien. Sulru was still in view as we left, and we easily caught up to her since she apparently wasn't in any hurry to arrive at her destination. We kept on her heels as she led us around the curve of the hallway beyond which neither of us had yet explored.

This previously hidden part of the path appeared to be an exact replica of the other side and it, too, reached into a dead end. About halfway down the corridor, Sulru stopped and turned into an open room larger than both the control room and the bedroom that Connie and I had been traversing. Walking into it after the vampire, I easily determined that it took up most of that side of the ship. It was some sort of storage department.

There were rows of what had to be cases, completely filling the area; their columns stretched from floor to ceiling. Sulru stepped to one of them that was near the far left wall, and slid herself in the slender space between it and the one beside. Connie and I stayed near the entrance waiting for her to reappear. We heard a small sound, similar to the clicking from when Malook had retrieved the devices that taught us their language, and then the woman was back.

"Will this do it?" she asked while producing a pair of silver forceps in one palm.

Looking down at the tool, I could tell no difference between it and the Earth version, other than the two small circles of metal at its ends that were lined with something akin to rubber. Connie took it quickly with a simple, 'yes' as she studied them more closely in her own hand. However, my eyes lingered on the vampire's claws, noticing them twitch a singular time before they dropped back to her side, as if she were anxious of the coming process.

"That is going to hurt like hell," I observed while replacing my vision on eye level with the women.

Sulru glared at me. Just as Malook had alluded, it was obvious she was sensitive to the topic of her strength and durability. "I'll manage," she said in a low voice.

"Alright," Connie sighed, "I need you to lay down, or at least sit, so I can get a good view."

The vampire lifted a half-fist to her side, lightly tapping the wall behind her without taking her eyes off of us. Part of the wall fell into a seat, similar to the folding chairs in an auditorium. The machinery seemed rather crude in comparison to the rest of the alien craft and technology that we had seen thus far. Still, it was smooth and clean to match all else.

Sulru took the seat. Instead of placing her back against the wall, though, she sat sideways, leaning herself backward at a minor angle as if in an invisible recliner. Her head rolled in a way that had to cause a crick, but she only placed her focus on the doctor while one hand held onto the side of the ship for support, and the other clutched onto her knee.

My wife put a hand on the vampire's chin, causing me to twinge slightly as she exposed the fiercely pointed teeth inside. Sulru turned her head to display her injury once more, remaining completely silent and fixed in her position. Connie swallowed loudly before hesitantly reaching the tongs into the creature's mouth, and grabbing hold of one of the fangs.

I hadn't seen them well before, but I was close enough now to realize just how terribly they had crumbled under the impact of the gunshot. The forceps clutched at the base of the first tooth, barely able to catch a grip on what was left. I moved forward, wanting to be able to make a barrier between the vampire and my wife, should the pain prove to much even for this powerful being.

However, I also didn't want to cause further distress. Sulru's lips had already curled into a grimace. I didn't at that point believe she would intentionally hurt Connie, yet should there be a knee-jerk reaction, I wanted the brunt of the retaliation to hit me instead.

"Alright, I'm going to pull the first one," Connie announced.

There was no response, so she went ahead, yanking with full force on the remaining piece of tooth inside the vampire's mouth. I focused on the patient. She began growling at the first hint of pressure, the menacing sound becoming louder as the fingers resting on her leg curled, claws jutting out and ruffling against the fabric of her black tunic. I was amazed that she was able to keep the rest of her body just as it was.

"Got it!" my wife almost shouted.

Sulru shot up to sit straight in the chair as soon as the pliers retreated. She shook her head violently several times while continuing to growl. It took me a few moments to understand that it wasn't just a sound, but she had been speaking...or rather, cursing, in neither English nor the alien tongue we had come to know, "Hatsun efferseth palor!"

The final words were less mumbled than the rest, yet still made no sense. I assumed it was one of the dead languages known to her people that Malook had mentioned during our earlier lesson. Connie and I both stared at the vampire until she quieted, taking a few breaths before regaining her former spot, but not until first raising an open hand for the tooth to be discarded into.

Through a few rapid blinks and another exhale, she made one final statement, "Alright, let's get this over with."

Connie shook her own head, handing off the bit of enamel, which her patient took, and then replaced her hand on knee, parting her mouth to allow for the next extraction. I was pleased to see the amount of self-control that Sulru had, for the better sense of safety for my wife and myself, however it did put the thoughts back into my mind about her battle with our people on Earth.

You better be glad I'm not the monster you think I am.

I remembered her admonishing comment clearly. I *had* thought she was a monster then. It was hard not to. Seeing her now, outside of this threatened guardian role, had gotten me to easily accept her as something other than the villain we had been introduced to. She had been violent, seemingly ruthless, but she could have easily done much more extensive damage. Though gruff in demeanor, she had been kind to us from the moment we stopped presenting as enemies.

Connie had gotten the second fang out sooner, and with less of a reaction from Sulru. I guessed she had gathered a sense of the actual tenderness of the procedure from the first, and therefore was better equipped to handle a repeat. My wife did her best to rush in removing the last one. I wanted to share something with the vampire- the soldier, but I patiently waited for when I could have her full attention so there would be no doubt of her understanding what I had to say.

"Done!" Connie declared, removing herself from the vampire so that she could stand and regain composure.

Sulru opened her jaw into a stretch, kinking her lips and cracking her neck to either side before stilling her body. She turned to face us, having returned to a casual, yet stern posture. The only further movement I could see was her tongue moving behind closed mouth, feeling the now hollow spot in her jowls.

She gave a tiny bow of the head to Connie, "Thank you."

"Of course," Connie replied, her mind obviously not having caught up with the experience quite yet.

The vampire took the last fang from the doctor, examining all three briefly in her claw, before walking between us and beginning to leave once more.

"Sulru!" I called, pausing her just as she had made it a couple of feet away.

She spun around and I expected to see a raised eyebrow or glare, but there was none. Only her bland voice, "Yes?"

Despite having already practiced the speech in my head, I still deliberated while under the cold weight of those dark eyes focusing on me. "I've been a soldier all my life," I started. "My parents were soldiers; my grandparents were soldiers..." I made sure my gaze was steeled upon hers so that the full affect of the meaning behind my words were abundant, "I know that sometimes we have to do horrible things- things we don't really want to do- in order to protect what we are meant to."

Sulru's vision narrowed ever so slightly; otherwise she remained motionless. A few silent moments passed. Our eyes remained locked, and I somehow found it easier to rest beneath her quiet scrutiny, as if I could feel the tension that had been disrupting our relationship gradually floating away.

At last, she blinked once and responded, "I understand."

Her voice sounded compassionate, alerting me to the fact that she did indeed understand what I had wished to relay. I couldn't help except to allow a smile. Connie's hand slipped within mine, drawing me to twist and see she was grinning as well. My confession had done more than diffuse the situation between Sulru and I, it had eased my wife to see that I was growing more confident, or at least more comfortable, with our current bearings.

"Do you need anything?" Sulru asked in the same delicate voice.

Chapter 27: Connie

"Actually, we're both a bit hungry," I answered, delighted that the relationship between her and my husband had progressed to better ground.

I had belted out in anger at the vampire, but I never truly judged her on the things I had been witness to back on Earth, because more than an atrocity, I had seen a woman defending her own. It just so happened that she didn't need synthetic weapons to do so like the rest of us. John on the other hand, was very sensitive to death. It felt weird to say, considering both his background and his strength of personality; nonetheless, it was true.

The man took a great offense to anyone he knew dying, even if only a brief acquaintance; kind of how I was with betrayal. As long as he associated a person with kindness, it was hard for him not to feel deep sorrow or anger when they were harmed. In this way, we were quite similar except I was less bothered by an actual demise, and more on that which was left behind...the emotional aspect, I suppose. In any case, to see that he was moving past his own sensitivities and trying to understand others' place and faults was a big deal to me.

Sulru strolled alongside the shelves and to the other end of the room. She turned back to face us while placing an open hand onto one of the columns,

"Food is kept in this one," she said with shortened claws tapping against the metal with a clink.

As I stepped closer to her, she dropped the extended arm and backed away from me, almost mirroring my movements. I slid within the space she had pointed out, and began looking up and down the vertical metal chest. It was lined with the same simple, flat outlines that comprised the other panels we had seen on the ship.

These perimeters weren't in the same shapes, instead varying to create several different size bins. Along some of them were labels written in the alien text, with an equal quantity remaining blank, which made me question if it meant they were empty. Over the curiosity, I decided to just work on translating the freshly learned words and go from there.

I found that I was reading words like fat, protein, sugar, and vitamin. This sorting initially appeared different than the one I was used to, since it seemed that the Earth food groups were divided more by harvesting techniques such as meat, fruits, and grains. However, it was the way these foods were harvested or produced that gave them the nutritional values, likes proteins or minerals. Generally speaking anyways. Though I suppose naming the groups such as the aliens did was more accurate, being that there were nuts and other legumes in our meat group.

Sliding my hand over the strip underneath the heading 'sugar,' I lightly touched my fingertips to it. The panel rolled upward on a slight curve, and hid itself into the main unit while a grated box popped out, leaning its uncovered top toward me at an angle that kept its contents from falling out.

I had half-expected there to be MREs or something of the sort, so I was pleasantly surprised when I saw what had to be fruit instead. There was only one type in the bin that I had uncovered, but I determined from catching a glimpse inside the large collection of containers, that the places behind the panels around held other fruits.

I carefully picked up one of the brightly colored pieces. It was some manner of purple and orange mixed color, with a pattern not unlike the red and yellow of a gala apple. Contrasting from the typical apple shape however, its contour was almost like that of a kidney, and about the same size as a healthy cucumber. I looked away from my previous focus then, to my husband who had stepped closer to me to take a place at the end of the row that I was in.

Giving him a quick smile, I stretched to peer past him, looking for Sulru. John realized immediately what I was doing and moved aside. Doing so revealed that the vampire had taken a spot watching us, back propped against one side of the room's doorway. I crept past my husband to get within a comfortable speaking distance.

"What is this?" I asked, holding out the fruit.

"It's called an akeban," she answered.

"Akeban," I repeated, glancing down at the thing in my palm and feeling its weight, "It's a fruit?"

Sulru nodded.

"What does it taste-" I cut myself off the moment I remembered I was talking to a vampire, letting out an awkward chuckle as I changed the thought, "I guess you wouldn't know, would you?"

I watched the woman cock her head to the side, her eyes moving slightly from me to John, who was looking equally uncomfortable with the thought, though I guessed it should have been worse for me, considering I had actually watched the vampire attack and drink a man's blood.

Sulru put her head back in place and her vision on me, while keeping a somber expression, "I've never tasted it, no. I am told it is very sweet, but many complain of the texture."

I nodded, wondering how the conversation had felt to her, since it had been pretty odd for me. Glancing over at John, I could tell he was thinking hard upon something. Probably Sulru's diet. I hadn't told him about seeing her drink from the mortician. Not because I was keeping it from him or anything; I only hadn't had the opportunity.

Not knowing absolutely though, I was sure made him more curious to learn. I would have started the inquiries about the vampires' feeding habits myself, if I didn't know that my husband would prepare the questions in a more precise way compared to how they would just spill uncontrollably from my mouth.

So instead, I lifted the fruit to my mouth and waited for him to decide to ask, "Do I need to wash this or...?"

"No, everything is cleaned before it's stored, and the confines are set to spray chemicals to disinfect and keep the food fresh," Sulru answered and then seemed to ponder something before adding, "It's completely safe to consume."

My gaze dropped to the akeban and I took a breath before plunging my teeth into the strange fruit. At first, it felt like biting into a tomato. The outside was firm, but not too difficult to pierce. Once breaking into the inside, the juice squirted into my mouth. It was intensely sweet. I don't think anything on Earth tasted so naturally sugary except maybe the rare occasion that you could find a perfectly ripe fig.

And, just like a fig, I then felt the questionable texture that Sulru had mentioned. Even though I was warned, it threw me off at first, and I wasn't sure if I was going to need to spit it out or not. I persevered though, and decided I liked it. After the first gush of juice, you could feel the roughness of the actual plant against your tongue, but to me, the extreme candied flavor, which was somewhat akin to green grape- tangy yet not sour- was enough to override the odd consistency.

"It's weird, but very good," I grinned, while drying the bits of liquid that had splashed onto my face with the edges of the tunic's sleeve. I looked from Sulru, who gave no response other than to keep her eyes on me, and to John, "You won't like it, hun."

"I didn't figure so," my husband laughed softly before putting his attention on the vampire. "Sulru, can I ask you something personal?"

The woman turned to face John, crossing her arms over her chest, "Only if you refrain from being formal with me when it isn't necessary," she replied with a glare.

He breathed in, "Fair enough. I was curious as to your people's diet? Namely how it is allowed."

"As you should be aware by now, vampires are strictly controlled. Much more so than humans or anything else," Sulru opened, "This extends to feedings. We act as executioners. That is how we are allowed to drink the blood of humans."

"Can you not drink animal blood?" John asked without skipping a beat.

"Yes and no," Sulru sighed, "Their blood is similar, not exact. There were, at one point animals from the same order as humans- primate, I believe is the correct word- with like enough properties to nourish a vampire. However, these species, along with most other primates, have long since been extinct."

"All mammals have comparable plasma. Warm-blooded animals differ from others because their red blood cells lose the nuclei when mature," I mused, "But certain antigens and proteins have been found to only be present in humans, or sometimes their more distant primate brothers."

It took me several moments of staring blankly at the barely-eaten fruit in my hand, to realize that a silence had fallen after my input. I shook myself into the present and looked up at Sulru and John. It was hard to tell about the vampire, but my husband was a mite lost.

"I don't understand all of your jargon," he almost scoffed at me, "Though I suffice it to say that there is a scientific reasoning for why they would need human blood specifically?"

"I couldn't explain it too precisely myself," Sulru interjected, "My only education is from tidbits I have picked up from humans over the years. You can appreciate that teaching vampires mathematics and science isn't of high priority on Galdelier."

Although the vampire woman didn't strike me as poorly educated, what she said did make sense. It saddened me to think about her, a person with an obvious natural intelligence, being denied a proper chance to learn. Furthermore, I felt that she regretted this as well.

"You said before that you have cold blood," John recalled. "What did you mean?"

Sulru paused as if she didn't remember having said it, but then explained the reasoning for saying such a thing had she done so, "Vampires don't have a self-regulating temperature like humans do."

"So you're literally cold-blooded? Like a reptile?" John asked.

The woman's brow furrowed and it looked like she was glaring at him. At first, I couldn't understand why; then I realized that the word 'reptile' might have registered differently in her mind. Many times, people on Earth would use the word as an insult, or a way of invalidating someone's feelings. Nonetheless, it didn't become necessary for this to be pointed out to her because she continued.

"Something like that," she answered.

I didn't bother to correct either of them on their discussion of cold-blooded creatures. It was actually a misnomer that some animals had warm blood and others had cold. The technical terms for these different types of animals were ectotherms and endotherms. The first of which needed outside aide to maintain a healthy temperature, and the second one possessed a body with the ability to control this itself.

"Is it too cold for you out here in space?" I asked instead.

Her lips flirted with the hint of a grin, "It's not preferable. I do much prefer the warmth of the sun."

Even though I knew there were large differences between Hollywood vampires and her kind, just as there were with Earth lore and real animals that were given the descriptive term of 'vampire,' my brain still jumped to the thought of Sulru laying in the sun, smiling contentedly as the star burned away her very flesh.

"Outside of a few things, your people are very similar in appearance to humans," John stated, cutting into my thoughts, "I would think that your two species were related at some point in time."

"I don't believe this is so," Sulru inhaled, "Besides, these similarities seem more prevalent than they are. Having developed bipedal and without much hair are really the only things that make us look alike."

"Hm. I see what you mean," my husband agreed.

The room became quiet. I had been idly thumbing the akeban, but hadn't eaten anymore of it. I took advantage of the lull to take a few small bites, chewing around the core that I had found. It was also like a tomato in the way it looked and felt, so I probably could have consumed it as well. I only couldn't bring myself to do so for the simple hangup that it was the center of the fruit.

"Disposal is over there behind John," Sulru spoke again, as she made the decision to leave the room.

However, while I approached my husband to reach around and activate the trash can, I thought of another thing I wanted to clarify about these alien vampires. In our culture, everyone had varying stories that they preferred to hear about the blood drinkers. Some favored the idea that vampires had to kill to eat. This sometimes was because if they didn't, the one they fed on would also become an agent of the undead.

Now obviously Sulru was not previously deceased; she was just another animal from an alternate evolutionary timeline. This begged to say that there was no virus that could change other creatures into vampires. I also assumed that her kind was not granted the gift of immortality, but I wondered why they killed to eat. Did their fangs excrete some sort of poison?

"Sulru, why do you have to kill people to drink their blood?" I inquired.

The woman twisted abruptly, leaning herself on the door frame once more. Although her energy had felt simple while we interrogated her, it shifted then, the look on her face registering of anger. Initially, I was unable to tell if it was aimed at me or something else.

"We don't," her voice was a low growl, "Our human leaders are the ones that require this. It's a sickening abuse."

"Why don't your people fight all this horrible treatment?" John chimed in, "You're physically stronger and faster by far, if I can judge based on you."

The vampire's brow furrowed and she lifted herself from the wall in order to stand straight, "This is true, but we are also vastly outnumbered. Four billion humans versus a couple million vampires isn't the fairest battle even with our capabilities," Sulru explained, "Especially when you consider that the humans on our world have lived alongside us for centuries so, unlike the people of Earth, they have developed weapons capable of rivaling our talents."

"Four billion?" I repeated, "So there are less Galdelierians- Galdeliers-"

"Galderlierans is the correct form," she told me.

"Galdelierains. There are more people on Earth than on your planet?" I asked. "There's, what, eight billion people back home, John?"

"Closer to seven billion," my husband replied, "But yeah."

The vampire looked from John to me and back, "I suppose so then."

I nodded as I tried to crunch the numbers in my head. Their population was about half the size of ours, but that fact alone didn't make it very easy visualize the amount, since both numbers were incredibly large. Even so, I surmised that it was a grand difference.

We already knew that the planet itself was about the same circumference as Earth. However, the government was totalitarian and had been for quite some time. The whole planet was under a strict, singular rule. It wasn't far off to think there were laws regarding population control.

"Are there laws concerning reproduction? Having children, that is," John and I had been on the same line of thought judging by his being the one to ask.

"There are," Sulru confirmed, "For both humans and vampires. When a person comes of sexual maturity, they undergo a procedure that halts the creation of eggs and sperm. If they decide to have a child, there is a process to undergo so that they may gain this right. The implant that keeps them sterile is temporarily suspended until an offspring is conceived."

"So both men and women have to do this?" I said, "That's interesting. On Earth, it is only women that take birth control."

The vampire cocked her head, "That doesn't make sense. A man is just as necessary for reproduction as a woman is. And having both sexes undergo these procedures greatly decreases any risk of accident."

The beginning of another silence started then. Before it could completely fall, Sulru added one last thought, "I need to check in. The two of you should eat and rest."

Without waiting for any response, she had turned around and was walking down the hallway. I had to admit that her abrupt appearances and departures still caught me unexpected.

Chapter 28: Malook

"I'm not doing this anymore," Soare-a yelled at me, throwing her arms in the air.

"Fine. What do you want to do, then?" I asked, my tone clearly agitated as I sat down on the bed.

The woman paused, her bottom lip dropping hesitantly like she hadn't expected me to give up. To be honest, I hadn't. It was only my intention to end the fight for the time being without having to leave the room, because all I really wanted was to lie down and sleep. It had been my mistake to say anything to her in the first place instead of just crawling into bed.

"I don't know," she finally said in obvious defeat.

Shocker, my mind thought, but was smart enough to not actually say. "Well, when you figure it out, let me know," I grumbled, pulling my legs up and wiggling my way under the heavy blanket that had been beneath me. When I was down on my side, head on pillow, I heard her complain something about my being 'impossible,' to which I gave a full roll of my eyes before closing them and attempting to settle. I was facing the opposite way so she couldn't see any of this to further comment on.

I heard her sigh exasperatedly, her hands probably on her hips, prior to walking by the end of the bed and presumably out of the room. Lifting my lids, I found I had been correct. The door was closing behind her, so I ordered the lights off and turned over onto my back. I didn't know if she was truthfully ready to quit this relationship since I had no idea where she thought she would go. I knew I was ready for it to be over...just not yet.

Soare-a definitely had a propensity for being selfish with complete disregard to the effect her actions would have on anyone and everyone else. Often I wondered if she even truly loved Riven. I had no doubt that she would do whatever would make her happy, at least in the moment, even if it harmed him.

Therefore, I knew there was no concern in her being for these aliens. That was why I had to explain that keeping them hidden and safe would be the only way to keep her safe as well, although I hadn't anticipated her agreement coming this easily.

Generally, such a conversation would unravel thusly: expressed frustration at inconvenience by Soare-a; her desire to end the immediate problem, no matter if it created more problems in the long run; attempt by me to reason the better option; Soare-a continuing to argue about what she wanted and how life was unfair to her.

Then would come another attempt to get her to see the bigger picture, this time by appealing to her personal well-being; more of Soare-a's distasteful views; repeated arguments on my end; and finally she would pout, but go along with what I had proposed, though usually without verbally relenting.

However, this time was different. We seemed to stop at the point where I said why doing things my way would be best for her. She had then jumped to fighting with me about our marriage overall. I was only half-listening, but she started off on something about how I disregarded her feelings.

It was extremely unfortunate that I now had to continue our relationship in order to ensure she didn't do anything stupid and rash like revealing the truth about our trip and our new friends, just to get back at me. Times like these made me question how I could have ever fallen for her. Despite already having given up on us, I had wanted to give one final swing at piecing our lives together; hence the reason for this trip.

I had pulled some strings to be able take her and our son into space, so we would be away from any force to distract us from our family. Admittedly that premise should have excluded Sulru; however that wasn't a possibility. As my guard, her presence was required for any venture into unprotected areas, on command of Empress Naiker.

She had ended up saving all of us anyway, and there was little I could do to repay such a deed. The vampire and I already owed each other our lives time and again, and in more ways than one. Now...she had saved my son too. The only thing left for me to do to regain lost ground was to save her daughter.

Sulru kept mention of her girl to a minimum. Soare-a didn't even know about her for the longest, and I had only met her a handful of times. Teylof was her name and she was close in age to Riven: a year or two older, if I remembered correctly. The father had been killed in service only months after her birth, and Sulru struggled with the idea of sending their child away. This was why she rarely spoke of the daughter she loved so dearly.

Law required vampiric children to begin training as soldiers and learn proper etiquette for human contact once they reached a certain age. The year wasn't specifically stated because the vampire species developed differently than humans.

It was only set forth that they should be sent to the training facilities once of an age that they could understand easily and had full control over their physical capabilities. This was to lessen the strain on the academy staff. Just as any other creature, the vampires had to grow into their claws, their balance, and even their feeding habits.

If she wasn't there already, Teylof was certainly approaching this time in her life. She already towered over my son and she'd always been extremely intelligent, just like her mother. Even though talk of the subject was scarce, I knew Sulru's dread at losing her.

Perhaps calling it a loss would seem a bit dramatic, but the girl would be removed from all contact with her mother and any others she had known, unless they were also at the same academy at the same time. This would last for the duration of training, which was anywhere from five to ten years.

After that, she would be placed wherever vampires were needed. Whether that would be near her mother could not be predetermined, however, at that point, she'd have the freedom to travel to see Sulru...if she made it that far. Many vampires never saw past the walls of these facilities and even more left being a completely different person...not ever in positive ways either.

If one was judged to be incapable of properly performing, they would be seen as a risk and executed. A student could easily be sentenced too. The humans who ran the academy very much had free reign over those children.

In my younger days, I had gotten a glimpse of the barbaric nature of their teaching methods. Exactly what went on within wasn't common knowledge to anyone other than vampire kind. Equal treatment wasn't something the majority of humans were concerned with.

In addition, nothing about the functioning of these places was ever made public or even really relayed beyond its workers. Vampires, of course, had no place in sharing this information with humans and doing so with others of their kind changed nothing.

I had been racking my brain about how I could delay Teylof's induction, but could see no way around it. Sulru and her mate, just like everyone else, had to gain birthing rights. That meant their daughter's existence was not a secret. If too much time passed without Sulru bringing her in, officers would be sent to their home to inspect.

They reserved the right to put in for the child's removal, should they determine she qualified to begin training. Unless our rebel faction was able to make some bold moves between now and then, I would just have to focus my attention on keeping tabs on Teylof while she was undergoing this conditioning.

That would be difficult.

Ideally, I'd only need send my personal interest in the girl and she would be looked after. As General, many times such a thing was all that was required; often because the common man attributed more power to this rank than it actually held.

Unfortunately, such a thing would not work in this case. To invest interest in a vampire like this would paint me dimly and would likely give her even more trouble. That was if I wasn't able to ensure she was sent to a specific camp where I knew one of the lead officers.

Ansel Luten: an utterly despicable man. Just thinking of him made me want to vomit.

He was cruel, vile, and if given the chance, I would take delight in ending him. He despised vampires, his mindset constantly ricocheting between wanting them hunted into extinction, and desiring their never-ending torture for merely having the audacity to exist. He was even brutal towards many humans and, at the very least, easily disagreeable. I would never wish for poor Teylof to be placed under his care.

Although, having no real control over the academies, my brain kept returning to the fact that the past relationship between Ansel and I might allow me to stay in the know regarding Sulru's daughter. If I was able to manipulate it properly, this would mean always having up to date information on her. Making a deal and associating with this scum was something I would have never even considered doing again, if it wasn't for Sulru.

I flipped back onto my side and stared through the dark at the door. Soare-a obviously knew nothing of these thoughts, and I hadn't yet shared them with my vampire companion either. I wasn't the type to offer any hope, or deliver bad news, until a final decision was made. Right now, my prime objective was to keep our adventures on Earth a secret and make certain that we all remained in the clear.

Babying my wife and keeping her content in our partnership was part of achieving this. Even so, I hoped moreover to be able to give her an easy out, since it would be easiest for me as well. I'd gladly set her up with her own home, portion of my earnings, and even time with Riven and some control over raising him, if she would just leave me and keep hush.

Rolling to my other side, I sighed, then grunted. I really didn't want to have to deal with all this, especially not now, yet my brain couldn't seem to stop turning. When my mind finally managed to stop stressing about my marriage and son, the aliens and Earth, the rebel faction and my conflicted vampiric lover, it began bringing up things from my past.

It was like every part of me was doing its best to highlight what a real piece of shit I was. I couldn't stop from thinking about absolutely everything, and I found myself in such an overly frustrated state that I was certain I wouldn't be able to relax. Sleep...all I wanted was some sleep...

Just shut down, I silently prayed, *just let me rest...*

Chapter 29: Connie

I'm sure she had other things to do, and I didn't imagine she was the type to enjoy sitting around teaching two adults the names for commonplace things, but I had wished that Sulru would have stayed around longer while we thumbed through the contents of the food bins.

John and I ended up finding vegetables, grains, and what had to be dehydrated meat, before we settled on a few items. I nibbled at a perfectly square slice of dense, yet soft bread as he attempted figuring out the package from the proteins container.

"Why don't you just cut it open?" I suggested.

"Because it might need to be prepared while still sealed," he sighed, "I don't want to take a chance on ruining it."

"But there's no instructions. Maybe it's supposed to look that way and there is no preparation needed," I replied, watching him flip the small log for the hundredth time.

"Just because there's nothing attached telling what to do, doesn't mean there aren't instructions for it," he returned, sounding harsh, though I knew he was just tired and hungry.

"You could eat something else," I picked up one of the cucumbers, or at least that's what I was calling it, and gestured, "Your diet is atrocious."

John placed the stick of meat onto the little table in front of me, and then sat down on the opposite side. We had found more chairs, and even a couple of tables, identical to the seat Sulru had knocked down in the room earlier, to let me remove her teeth. My husband looked up at me, took the vegetable, and groaned.

"Have you tried this thing yet?" he asked.

I shook my head.,"No, but you go ahead. This could be fun," I grinned, taking another bite from the bread.

He chuckled, "Fine."

My gaze grew increasingly intent as he lifted the food to his mouth. Just as his lips parted, however, Soare-a stormed into the room, taking both our attention from the meal. She trotted determinedly to where the food was kept, and angrily tapped at two separate containers simultaneously, before reaching a hand in and grabbing one of the other fruits. As well, she retrieved a package similar to the one that had been frustrating John.

I felt that she would have easily kept about her business without taking notice of us, if it hadn't been for the brief moment where she caught us watching her. She stopped when it happened, right after closing away the bins. She stood still as she faced us, giving the scene a once over. The sudden situation caught me off guard, but fortunately John was with it enough to react.

"Hi," he greeted, rising from his spot politely, "Are we in the way?"

The woman continued staring momentarily, with a quite critical expression, and then emitted a small scoff, followed quickly with a smile. She lowered her snacks and loosened her posture.

"No," she answered in a sweet voice, "You're alright."

She said the last words with a look down my husband's person, and then back up to his face. The movement came across as flirtatious, but I tried not to read into it. I trusted him. Even so, I *was* the jealous type. I guessed that most of my insecurity came from not having been able to have children, because I knew John had always wanted his own family, which made me feel like less of a woman since I had struggled with giving this to him.

"John can't figure that thing out," I interjected, mostly to put myself into the conversation, though the words had come off in a rougher manner than I had meant.

Nonetheless, I pointed to the dehydrated food Soare-a held to her side, causing the woman to take her eyes from John and place them on me. I had already been studying her, so the instant she turned, I was taking in any nuances in her demeanor. I knew I hadn't imagined the change from coy to indifferent.

"There's nothing to it, really," she said, stepping towards us and picking up the cylindrical meat item from the table, "But do you even know what this is?" her judgmental eyes bore into me.

"We figured it was some sort of meat," John stepped in, Soare-a's vision fluttering over to him.

"It is... What are you having problems with?" the woman's vision was rested once more on my husband as she returned to her kittenish behavior.

"Well," John, as quick as he was, was yet to pick up on Soare-a's shifting persona when talking betwixt us, "We have what are called MREs for situations where keeping food fresh, or stored for extended periods, is needed. Situations like space travel. MREs are just dehydrated foods in pouches. You add hot water to them and they become actual meals."

"Oh, I see," Soare-a swayed her hips in a motion that put her closer to John as she casually handed the package back to him, "I mean you could hydrate it, I guess, but it's not necessary."

"Thank you," my husband smiled, accepting the food back, and then carefully taking hold of a plastic flap at one end of it, in order to slowly tear it open.

I watched as he pulled out the piece of meat, seeing that it looked much more like a bratwurst than I previously realized. John was a finicky eater, his diet consisting mostly of meats and potato chips. He wasn't much of one to try new things, so the look of uncertainty he shot both the alien woman and myself before taking a nibble from the dog, was fully expected. His expression stayed blank for several moments while he chewed awkwardly.

"So?" I prompted with a chuckle.

"I'm not sure that's meat," he finally spoke with a swallow.

The force of Soare-a's laugh seemed overdone, "It's meat, sweetheart."

"Is it a bird or?" John eyed the food, contemplating whether or not to take another bite.

"It's mostly bavar," the woman almost muttered, her tone leaving its fake cheer, although she was still focused on my husband.

"I'm sorry," John offered, "I suppose there are still some words to be learned. Not everything can have a translation, right?" he half-laughed.

"Bavar is a type of cattle. Definitely not a bird," Sulru's voice sounded suddenly from the room's entrance, drawing everyone's gaze.

"Uh, thank you, Sulru," Soare-a spat, allowing her hips to graze against John, lightly pushing him back with her fingertips on his chest as she took steps closer to the vampire, "I'm quite capable of explaining the differences between *animals*," she stressed the last word angrily, subtly pointing out her feelings concerning Sulru.

"Yes, I'm sure you're well acquainted with them," Sulru crossed her arms, her lip curling into a smirk, "They are the *dumb* species after all."

Soare-a scoffed loudly and stomped toward the vampire, halting mere inches from touching her despite how Sulru's height had the other woman peering upward, taking away from the threatening behavior, "You watch yourself, *vampire*. You may have Malook's sympathy and these people might not understand," she threw a hand backward at John and

I, "But to the rest of the universe? You're still just a filthy soul-sucker. You are nothing."

The words angered me and I wanted to step in, berate Soare-a for being so cruel, but John held me back once more and hushed me. I knew it would have been pointless to do anything anyway. Nothing I could have said would diffuse things, nor would it have helped Soare-a to see past this prejudice.

John probably realized before me, as he always did, that I'd have to get used to this sort of thing. On Galdelier, I wouldn't be able to object to such hateful acts. I'd even be pressed to go along with them. This was going to hurt my heart.

After staring down an unabashed, yet unresponsive vampire, Soare-a took her leave as furiously as she had entered. I was still getting used to judging her expressions due to those coal eyes, but as Sulru turned her neck to watch the bully depart, I thought I saw her return the look of arrogance that the woman had shown her.

Before I thought too much on it, her eyes were back on us, "It's interesting to me that some things have evolved so similarly on Galdelier and Earth, yet we still have many organisms you don't and vice versa," Sulru had kept with the discussion she had walked into, completely ignoring that Soare-a had ever been present.

"I agree," John stumbled, trying to ignore it as well, "What are the differences between a bavar and a cow or other cattle, then? Do you have cows and buffalo?"

"We have cows, but neither buffalo or bison. Bavar are basically small cows with a lot of hair. Cows are not generally slaughtered for meat either," Sulru explained, "Bavar can provide meat, leather, fur, and are are much easier to breed and handle due to their size."

"What are cows used for then?" I asked. It hadn't taken much to catch my interest.

"Pets, " the vampire answered, "Some people consider them dangerous, yet others keep them as companions or for show. Otherwise, they're not bred for anything. I also hear they're extremely expensive."

"Show?" It seemed like an odd thing for cows to be part of, though I guess people did put them in fairs on Earth, which was kind of the same thing. However, in that they were mostly judged based upon their attributes desirable for use on a farm, "What about horses?"

"There are horses not like yours, and there are far fewer kinds," Sulru informed, "They used to be the same as those on Earth, but have evolved past that. They more or less look the same; the only real difference is their snout. It's longer, curved, more pointed, and it's mostly muscle rather than bone and cartilage, therefore, it has a wider range of movement. They also have teeth similar to your own now."

"Did their diets change?" I questioned, doing my best to put together a picture of the creature inside my head.

"Precisely," Sulru confirmed, "They're natural omnivores. Mostly they are also pets. Government offices do keep many on reserve for certain ventures, or in the event of technological failure."

"Fascinating. You'll have to show us one," I blurted.

Sulru paused and John joined her in staring at me. He gave me an odd look, making me wonder what I had done wrong. I remembered at that moment that she was treated little better than a slave on her home world. Had I sounded bossy? Or did I assume a freedom she didn't have? Or-

"I will," she finally answered, keeping me guessing at what had happened, "If I can."

I smiled weirdly at her, my mind having gone back to the skirmish with Soare-a. I kept trying to justify her hatred for the vampire in less of a condoning way, and more just trying to understand. Talking with Malook made it seem that vampires were forced to act overly violent, to do what was expected of them.

Sulru had done nothing except prove this point by how she acted outside of a situation where protecting this family-not-family of hers was needed. So I ended with the conclusion that Soare-a was the one at fault.

"Sulru?" I started timidly.

The vampire said nothing- only kept her eyes resting easily upon me.

"I know on Galdelier, we're going to have to...be okay, I guess, with treating you as, well, less," though it was hard for me to get the thought out, I pushed on, "I just want you to be aware that I'm not okay with it."

She took in a breath and exhaled sharply. My husband reached his hand out, putting it on my shoulder, giving a brief smile before turning back to the woman, "The same goes for me, Sulru," he agreed.

We watched the woman, who seemed mildly confused, as she continued gazing back at us without speaking. I could feel my heart quicken as I waited eagerly for any sort of reaction.

"You're both very kind," she said in a flat voice, "You'll find that Galdelier is less so...not to my kind alone either. I suggest not wasting your time with concern for others. Protect yourselves and be careful who you trust."

She dropped her arms, spinning her body to the door, letting her sight linger momentarily first. Then she was gone again, her final words leaving a knot in my stomach.

Chapter 30: John

I had expected the new planet to be a fairly hostile territory, given the details from Malook about their governments, especially that of it concerning the vampires. However, something about the way Sulru warned us, and her rejection of our extended kindness regarding how the planet and its citizens treated her, left both Connie and myself with a deeper sense of unease...as if we weren't having enough trouble with that already.

We finished our food in quiet focus, save for the occasional smile or yawn. Afterward, we stepped back into the empty halls, strolling toward our room. We had planned simply to go to bed and discuss everything, or perhaps only spend some moments in each other's arms in an attempt to relax. This would be greatly appreciated, should our arrival in the alien world be met with confrontation, which was an ever-present fear in our minds.

When we once again reached the cockpit, I peered inside just barely, and saw Sulru sitting in the same seat as before, but facing the door, arms crossed over her stomach to rest in her lap. Our eyes caught one another, prompting me to show an awkward acknowledgment. She didn't react, something apparently commonplace for her, yet I knew she had seen us and was watching now. I could feel the weight of her black eyes as I shrugged at my wife and entered the pilot room.

"How long have we been on the ship?" I asked casually.

"You slept for quite some time," her monotone replied, "It's been almost a day in your time."

My eyes widened a bit, "Really?"

No response.

It seemed what we had said to her in the store room, had triggered her into returning to this detached demeanor. She had become friendly when we first were kind to her, so why had furthering that kindness reverted our relationship? Perhaps something to do with placing us on Galdelier, switched her back to the persona she had to portray there.

"Our time?" Connie stepped into the conversation, "The days are different on Galdelier?"

"Yes," the vampire blinked, otherwise remaining unmoved, "They're shorter. Not by a large amount...a few hours."

"But are hours the same?" My mind was still getting a grasp on how their translations were able to account for differences in words and phrases between languages, that even with Earth's best translators, would normally create a cultural barrier.

"The system of dividing days into hours and minutes is the same. The actual amount of time each is, however, is slightly different...and there's twenty hours to a day," Sulru answered plainly.

"I see. How long will it take to get there?" I continued.

"From here?" she uncrossed her arms and spun in her seat to quickly look out the window, and then down at a monitor before her, "I'd give it just under a week if all is smooth," she twisted back, eyes narrowing on me as if assuming my next inquiry, "Which is ten days."

I nodded, thankful for the unprompted answer. Glancing at Connie, I could tell she wasn't thinking upon the new topic...most likely still stuck on the vampire's warning and subsequent shift. Her urge to say something specific about the incident was so strong, it was as if invisible hands were reaching out and grabbing me.

She was able to keep her refrain, though she did change the subject to Sulru in a different way, "Have you been awake this whole time?"

The vampire's eyes twitched at the question, which I assumed was her looking from me to my wife, "I have."

"You must be exhausted," she was the compassionate type for certain, though knowing her well, it was obvious to me that the observation was less sincere. It was more an offer than anything, letting the other woman know subtly that regardless of what she had said, that Connie still cared.

Sulru tilted her head and paused, at last answering with, "I will rest later."

Connie shifted in her stance, glancing awkwardly from the vampire to me, to her feet, and back. After the previous conversation, she was nervous to upset the woman or drive her away, and Connie generally took it as a fault within herself when others didn't like her.

My wife was, as well, fully aware she was not very good with properly placating. In order to relieve her, I inhaled sharply and started a casual, if not friendly, conversation- remembering the almost demand Sulru had given us about formalities when speaking to her away from judgmental eyes.

"Do you require as much rest as we do?" I put bluntly, "Or do the humans on your planet even sleep the same as us?"

She blinked a couple of times, straightening her neck, "I would assume that people like Malook and yourself sleep similarly. I *can* go longer without sleep while still functioning well, but being part of the same society and schedule as humans, vampires have long adapted to a pattern that mimics theirs."

Sulru's last few words lost strength, tapering off as her head fell back just a tiny amount. I realized she was putting her gaze on the entrance of the cockpit, so I turned my head and looked as well. There was a noise growing closer to us that sounded like a steady beat.

"SULRU!" Riven's cheerful voice sounded, instantly prior to his form appearing in the doorway, "Sulru!" he called, tiny thudding feet taking him past my wife and I and up to the vampire.

The boy stopped in front of her seat, smiling as he held out a bag with crackers or something of the like in it. He held it both by the top and bottom, pulling it tight and waiting patiently, while simultaneously catching his breath from the run. The vampire gently lifted a finger, extending the claw on it to carefully tear through the plastic. Riven then happily took the snack, eagerly grabbing a cracker and munching on it.

He spun around quickly, beaming at Connie and I, "Hey," he said sweetly between bites.

Connie returned his enthusiasm, switching to her 'child voice', "Hey!"

"Do you want one?" Riven offered the bag to her.

"Oh, no," she grinned, "Thank you, though."

After I gave the same response, he turned around to face the vampire, putting the snacks in front of her at first, but then retrieving them, "Oh, I forgot."

He seemed disappointed that he couldn't share his food with her. The scenario created an odd energy in the room. It was both touching and eerie. Somehow it seemed strange that such a young child should be aware of a topic as grim as the diet of a vampire who was, more or less, his caretaker. Yet seeing that he felt safe and loving of her was refreshing. Truly innocent. The thought struck my mind how I wished the world he was to grow up in would not change his accepting nature.

"Shouldn't you be in bed, Riven?" Sulru spoke in a low, yet warm tone.

"No..." the kid mumbled sarcastically.

"Your mother is going to be upset if she sees you're still up," she continued.

Riven kept looking at the ground and shrugged his shoulders.

The vampire opened her mouth as if sensing the boy's thoughts, but she hesitated to speak, finally opting to lean forward and raise a carefully concealed claw. Placing it over the child's shoulder and pressing her palm into his chest, he fell backward onto her to allow for a half-hug. His cheek rested briefly against her jaw, causing her to wince, though she ignored the pain as he put both his hands onto her arm to reciprocate the embrace.

She let go after only a moment, "Go to bed, Riven," she whispered and he reluctantly obeyed, leaving the room with a somber feeling.

"Just like his father," Sulru mused as soon as Riven was out of sight.

"He's a sweetheart," Connie agreed, then admitted, "But he did get me wondering again..."

The vampire set her eyes on the woman and waited for clarification.

"Do you- Is there blood on the ship for you?" my wife's floundering was adorable.

"A small amount, yes, but use of it is prohibited, unless under extremely specific situations," she answered, returning to a harsh voice, "Distress, length of time, reasons behind why the duration of the trip changed... Like explained before, feedings come with intense regulation. Relaxed meals are nonexistent for vampire kind."

"Have you been able to eat since-" Connie cut herself off, once more beginning to speak before thinking through what she wanted to say.

Sulru raised an eyebrow, gaze scanning my wife as she shied away from the topic, "If it hadn't been for Earth, no, I would not have eaten. Law actually prohibits me to do so at all during this trip, except in the case the ship malfunctioned and we became stranded for a period of more than a hundred days."

I took charge again in place of my saddened wife, "Your metabolism is very slow then."

The vampire shifted her eyes to me, "Yes. Also," she looked down and pulled at her tunic, scrunching her palm on either side of it in order to show that it was much thicker than the clothes we wore, "We talked previously about my blood. This tunic is lined with heat pads to keep me at a better functioning temperature while in such a cold environment. Before that time could pass, protocol commands their removal, which would further lengthen my survival time."

"I had thought about that earlier too," Connie spoke again, "When you said you preferred it to be warm and all."

Sulru let go of her shirt and nodded, and everything started to get quiet and still. Our pilot at last moved her sight onto the controls beside her, eyes darting across the monitors and buttons several times, until she was satisfied with whatever she had been checking for.

Her gaze then cut backward and to the side, only long enough to see that we were still present. Connie had to be right- the vampire, despite these physical differences- must be wearing down after all that had transpired.

"Well, I'd like to go lay down myself," I informed politely, rather than just leaving.

I took my wife's arm, who whispered, "Thank you, Sulru," as I turned to guide us out of the cockpit. The alien, however, made no acknowledgment of our departure other than to act as though we had already gone.

Chapter 31: Malook

As we entered through the air station, my heart skipped in a near panic. I wasn't one to fluster easily, but with such an unprecedented situation, I'd be a liar in saying I wasn't entirely worried for all of us.

This initial introduction with landing, and the legal fraud I'd have to handle with conjuring paperwork to account for the alien's existence as Galdelierians, would be the most difficult part. After that, it would just be a matter of gradually integrating them fully into society.

I looked over to my new family members, who were busy with Riven as he proudly showed off his favorite toy. Connie exaggerated an excited response when my son held up the metal animal, pressing a tiny finger at the back of its long neck, causing it to make a screeching sound.

John also tried to show enthusiasm, however clear it was that he was not so simply distracted. His focus was on the same concerns as mine. Even with the high risks, I did not regret my decision to hide the couple.

The last handful of days on the ship had been...okay. Soare-a mostly ignored me, keeping her usual behavior toward Riven and Sulru, while she seemed to suddenly develop an interest in the aliens. I saw her multiple times in conversation with John, each time seemingly happy, though part of me wondered if she was keeping with him in order to piss me off. It really didn't matter either way, because I was just glad she wasn't acting irrational about how we were dealing with our company.

Each of us seemed to take turns in teaching the Earthlings more about our people. The culture, the history, the science, and even many small details that were vastly unimportant, such as stories from our lives and our hobbies. Riven, of course, being the largest proprietor of needless tales. Nonetheless, both Connie and John remained enthralled in all that was shared.

They were both highly intelligent, on par with the intellectuals of Galdelier, despite their own planet's slower progression. It seemed that Earth had experienced many drawbacks to their acquirement of knowledge. Largely something that was called the 'Dark Ages.'

It made me curious should they have even surpassed Galdelier's development, without this setback period. They were, after all, near in age to us...older, actually. Still, the woman's personality made her prone for acting prior to thought, which definitely worried me.

Fortunately her husband was more than aware of this, his own traits complimenting hers in a way that I felt the two would remain safe, as far as this was concerned. Of all that was taught, I tried to steer things towards our culture since I felt it would be the most important part of their blending. John seemed to agree.

Our greeting, for one, was not a bow nor a handshake. One hand was held head high with an open palm facing the other person as the other hand was held straight out from the waist with palm toward the sky. It was meant to address, while showing that nothing was being hidden, in an offer of good will. Although, like on Earth, this formality was not necessary when meeting friend or family, it wasn't replaced with a hug or kiss. At least not away from an intimate setting or with children.

The thing that the pair seemed to take most interest in was always science. The wormhole technology that we used was something only theorized on Earth. The major found it especially amazing that we had been able to locate several natural wormholes, one of which was within Trinnd and led to that dark space just outside of the Milky Way.

Our scientists had developed routing systems that detected the path of the wormhole, in order to guide ships safely through the temporal fold. In addition, there was a substance called Ahlversian, named for our ruling family, that allowed for accelerated travel. I had shared all this because there was no point in hiding it from them, considering what they knew, but this information was not yet public to our people. Space travel? Yes, just not out of our planetary system, and certainly it was unknown that there were other inhabited planets.

I turned my gaze on Sulru. She didn't seem bothered by any of it...she never seemed bothered by anything. Even thus, I knew better. Stiff and stoic, undaunted by struggle, the vampire had one affliction. Right about now she would be driven for us to succeed, so she could focus on her daughter's safety and future. And I would be focused on Teylof as well...as soon as everything was settled.

As we neared the city's structures, the Earth doctor was able to remove her attention from Riven, when prompted by her husband to look out of the fore window on our vessel. The couple stood tightly against each other while they gazed beyond, to the enormous skyscrapers lining our view. Buildings on Galdelier differed from the ones they were used to, in the sense that they were typically a rounded shape instead of box like.

At least on the outside. Inwardly, the rooms were often cut into rectangles or squares, the hidden crevices of the curves being used to hide electrical components and other such things. Groups of buildings were also arranged in a more precise pattern than theirs, usually in a wave, with the tallest places located toward the middle of a given city and smaller structures around the edges.

"Welcome to Galdelier," I grinned, watching the excitement grow in both their eyes, temporarily relieved from anxiety, "This is Contuin, where we live."

"It's beautiful," Connie breathed.

I nodded my head, turning back to look outside. I was glad to be home. The warm sun glistening off the metal of the city, with the Black Forest barely visible in the distance, was an extremely inviting sight after the taxing trip, which had lasted far longer than originally intended.

Another thing to be explained, though the malfunction that actually occurred of the ship's computers would easily suffice for it. I thought a brief reminder of our our cover stories was called for. John must have thought the same, for he spoke was the first to bring it up.

"So Connie is Malook's cousin and I her husband. We're staying with you because our infant son died in his sleep. And you're going to try and set me up to work as an officer of some sort to match my supposed job back in...Calfere?"

I noted that the man skipped through the bit about their son more quickly than the rest, and although I wondered why, I didn't ask. I, too, held to our world's ideal that others' personal affairs were not to be casually spoken of, without their own initiation of the topic.

"That's correct," I agreed, "Calfere is quite large. No worry for you to come across others from there who don't recognize you. It shouldn't be a problem for me to place you with a career either. First level officer...it's a lot of work, but not hard to learn. You'll pick it up without trouble."

"Alright," his eyes were solemn, "What about Connie?"

I inhaled, "For the time being, let us just leave her as a stay-at-home like Soare-a."

"You may find it best to sit down now," Sulru cut in, not tearing her vision from away.

I obeyed, stepping to take my own seat, as they did likewise. Riven skipped toward me, sitting on the floor at my feet and balancing himself between my calves. Sulru angled her head slightly to take in that everyone had settled, before setting the final course to pass through the tallest of the skyscrapers, working the ship around the spiral of its destined resting space.

The changes in momentum around the curves and the semi-abrupt twists were soon over, and our pilot slowly let the ship fall into a stop, where it hovered for a minute or two above the landing platform and then eased itself onto the ground. Riven, of course, was the first one up and I was barely able to grab hold of his arm as he began to run away.

Pulling him back to my side, I reminded him to stay quiet and, pointing to Connie and John, asked him who they were. Without hesitation, he answered by saying they were his cousins. *Where are they from?* Once again, he gave the appropriate reply. I gave him a smile and kissed his head before letting his arm go.

The others in the cockpit had stopped to observe this interaction, so I was the next to stand, "You two just follow after me. If there is any talking to be done regarding who you are, let me handle it," I instructed the couple as they also rose to their feet.

They both nodded, while Sulru took her position behind me, my son also falling back, so as to stand with the vampire. I led the way out of the cockpit and down the hall, where I saw that my wife had left not only her room, but the ship as well. The entrance was already open and the ramp out, by the time we reached it. I successfully managed to hide any inner distress, even upon seeing that someone was outside waiting for us.

His name was Cartef and, by all accounts, was my assistant. He kept me on schedule, helped with moving and filing paperwork, and otherwise was a go-between for me and those requesting my attention. He must have been in office today, and came around when the ship entered air space. That or had someone on site notify him of our return. Either way, Soare-a had met him, and the two were speaking until I showed with the rest of our company.

"My friend," the man gave the customary greeting in brief, his eyes scanning all of us, down to my son, who had taken a tighter grip on Sulru's leg, his head hardly reaching her midriff, "I see your young one still has an attachment to the vampire. You really should discourage it, Malook."

Despite being used to the ill-treatment of her people, his words were still offensive and utterly disrespectful. Moreover because of his obvious distaste for how I raised my own son, however, and less, in that moment, for anything to do with vampire kind. I took in a deep breath and raised my brow, eyes sitting low in mutual disdain.

"I agree," Soare-a spoke up, "But he won't listen to me."

I almost growled my response, "Soare-a, nobody should ever discourage their children from being kind."

My wife made a loud, obvious scoff, as she rolled her eyes and changed the subject, "I was just telling Cartef that your cousin Ka'ney was going to be staying with us a while," she raised a knowing brow: a silent reminder that she hadn't been on board with this deception.

I almost scoffed myself. It wasn't that it was fraud either. She was on no moral high ground here. Her prime concern was her own safety and comfort. In that case, I knew the secret was safe. Going along and informing Cartef of this was enough to make her a criminal, should the truth come about. Nonetheless, it remained an attempt at threat on her part and she was petty enough to be stupid.

I caught sight of Connie beginning to step forward instinctively with a handshake, when John interceded, snatching hold of her hand and clutching it next to him for a moment. He then released it, raising his hands in the correct greeting. Connie copied him, but neither spoke, just as I commanded.

"It's been a long trip," I started, "I'll be here to write a report tomorrow. Right now, we're just going home."

"Actually," Cartef smiled at me, "I have a couple of things that need your immediate attention. You were gone longer than expected."

I sighed, a fatigued smile on the medium-toned, short haired man grinning at me. I really didn't feel like this, but I wasn't going to put off my duties. In the position we were in, that would be begging for trouble. I guess I would have to trust Connie and John to Soa- no, to Sulru. The vampire, I could trust. My wife, not so much. Besides, home wasn't far. There should be no problems.

"Take the family home," I told Sulru with my professional demeanor, "Make sure they're safe before you leave."

The woman blinked in complete understanding of the simple order. She waited for any of the three human adults she was to escort, to begin the trek. When Soare-a stepped away from my assistant with a wink, Sulru glanced at Connie and John, waiting for them to go as well. Connie didn't catch on as quickly as John did, which I had already picked up on being normal for her. The major, having taken hold of his wife's hand once more, pulled the two into a stroll after Soare-a, their guard following closely behind.

Chapter 32: Sulru

I had always viewed Cartef as a shifty individual, even if Malook didn't seem to think so. My feelings had nothing to do with his blatant hatred of me either. Being despised was not something new to me, so I took no offense to it. There was something more...

Perhaps it was just how well he and Soare-a got along. It was more than a shallow, self-serving relationship, such as I had observed her having with most others. To me, this spoke that Cartef was, as well as the woman, little more than a slimy bottom feeder. I certainly didn't trust him with anything, and had made this more than known to Malook, who assured me that his assistant was no worse a man than the rest of the blindly prejudiced rabble.

Even thus, I did not appreciate that he was there waiting when we returned. He stuck too close to Malook for my liking and yes, I was aware of this being part of his job. Nonetheless, the man liked to butt in when it was not required or wanted, and had reached an equally unsettling familiarity with my boss's scathy wife.

The General was an extremely intuitive man. It was one of, if not his most notable, assets so it could be a mistake on my part...or Cartef's own skill might lie in deception. Either way, Malook was both intelligent and trustworthy, and I would have to leave it at that. At least with him, I didn't have to worry for the overly-trusting, slow to process nature that Connie had.

I watched the Earth woman fumble in greeting Cartef, and then in taking the way before me, now being her body guard. Kind as she was, the thing was a bit daft. A stay-at-home was certainly the best option for her for now, maybe always. If I wasn't fully trained in the art of hiding emotion and shielding reaction, I would have definitely rolled my eyes. As it was, I kept my sighs inward and silent.

Disregarding what had been said, Soare-a left her son at my feet. The boy also appeared to dislike Cartef, though from his perspective, it was likely to do with how I was treated. I wasn't sure why, but Riven had taken a great liking to me. He was definitely his father's son, so whatever attracted the man to me, he might have seen as well. As I stepped to follow after his mother and the Earthlings, he let go of my leg, remaining close beside me as we walked.

We went down the pristine metal platforms, past all the air vehicles kept at the station, and made our way to the lifts that would take us to ground level. These elevators were larger and rode more quickly and smoothly than the ones I had seen on Earth.

Soare-a, Connie, and John strolled into the moving room, the couple taking a position next to the large glass piece on the opposite side, while Malook's wife retrieved the device strapped around her leg. She then put every ounce of attention on whomever she was talking to through it, with furious taps on the screen.

As the door slid to a close, I hovered my finger over the tiny arrow on the wall inside the lift, then turned and looked at the Earth people while the machine began its descent. Both had eyes plastered to the view of the city in the windowed wall next to us. Riven had left me in order to peer through the glass with them, tracing the shapes outside with his fingertips. No one uttered a word, and I found myself gazing outward, along with the couple.

It had been nineteen days since I last saw Teylof. Although she was quite mature enough to fend for herself, I had left her in her grandfather's care. Speaking of children being like their fathers...Teylof definitely favored hers. Lotac had been the epitome of brave, his soul the most adventurous I had ever known. He loved his job and he was never worn down by the world.

So what if we are hated? If we let them crush our spirit, then that's on us for giving it away.

He had told me it numerous times, and I had always admired his strength. Even until his last day, the day what he loved finally killed him, he never bowed. And though Teylof was a fighter for sure, she still wasn't properly aware of just how cruel life could be. I certainly didn't want her to have to find out...not without me there with her. I wanted to protect her, keep her with me always, yet I knew it couldn't happen. The moment the representatives saw her, they would take her. She was far past the point of leaving. I only hoped they had not come in my absence.

I snapped from my thoughts as the picture in front of me grew dark. We were almost to the base floor. Turning around to face the entrance, I glimpsed that Connie and John had done the same, their wondrous reprieve overtaken by uncertainty. However, I couldn't dwell on their discomfort. I would deliver them to Malook's home, where they'd be as safe as possible; then I could see my daughter.

The upper level of the station where we had landed, had been mostly void of life other than our own, but this first floor was filled. Not altogether crowded; it was still fairly open. The presence of more people alien to them created a noticeable shift in the energy about Connie and John. The strangers, of course, had no reason to be on edge. They remained completely unaware of what and who the Earthlings were. It seemed to me that this thought would ease the aliens' minds. Nonetheless, the tension stayed.

I glanced about the new room before stepping out into it, allowing Soare-a and her new family take the lead once more. John was holding his wife's hand tightly, the woman visibly shaking. As we strolled further, I quickly patted Riven's shoulder, making a nigh unnoticeable gesture with my head toward the humans in front of me. The boy appeared confused at first, but swiftly realized that I meant for him to move forward.

He almost leapt, bumping against Connie in his rush to be the new leader of the group. The small collision successfully took the woman's paranoid gaze from those journeying around us, as she rested it on the kid, who excitedly spun around upon catching up to his mom, continuing to walk backward and smiling at me. Lifting one side of my mouth, I showed him another motion toward Connie, causing his grin to falter momentarily until he realized what I wanted this time.

The boy made a silly face at his cousin, sticking out his tongue and crossing his eyes. I heard Connie giggle in response before putting a hand in a strange placement over her face to, I assumed, make a face of her own. John had turned his head enough for one eye to study me. I remained in my stoic demeanor, not making notice of him, and he instantly returned himself. At that point, we had made it to the garage, and the doctor appeared to have calmed. Soare-a put down her device so she could instead find her way to a rover to take us home.

Our 'cars' were not based upon wheels for movement. Instead, they used magnetic pulses which fought against the natural magnets of the planet to create a false flight effect. The bodies of the machines hovered low in the air, and traveled by sensing the objects beneath them, acheiving a smooth and steady path.

This also allowed for collision detection beforehand, so as to avoid the situation or lessen the damage if the other was impossible. They were charged using electricity and ran on a tiny amount of Ahlversian, piloting themselves at any given speed without need of a driver, although manual override was possible. Aesthetically, they were similar to Earth vehicles. Why wouldn't they be? It was a simple, efficient design.

We approached a purple colored vehicle with two rows of three seats and a third row of two. It was half covered on the front, but the last seats kept an open roof. Riven was the first to command the machine open, jumping into one of the second seats, as John laid a hand on the door to the final row, and Connie awkwardly stepped forward with him.

"But I want you to sit with me," the young boy protested as his mother took a spot in one of the first chairs.

Soare-a groaned and unloaded herself from the vehicle to shoo her son out of his seat, in order to get in beside him. However, the moment the first door had slammed, a new voice called her name.

"Soare-a, sweetie!"

I stopped where I stood, twisting to see a large woman in a puffy green tunic scurrying away from a group towards us. *Ugh*. I recognized them. They were the husbands and wives of four men that worked beneath Malook.

Soare-a craved their affection because within that circle, she was of the highest social status. That meant their fawning over and catering to her since they were also shallow, no doubt bragging to others of their highly ranked friends. She closed the door next to where her son sat and stepped away from the machine, ignoring Riven's frowning whimper.

"Dear, you almost missed Temir's gathering!" the fat woman, Typher, said as she halted just feet from our company.

"Oh, I know!" Soare-a's voice matched her plastic concern, "We had a bit of trouble, but don't worry- I will be there to celebrate your brother's new year!"

"I'm glad to hear it! Temir will be too! The rest of us just finished here, if you'd like to come with us to the grove," Typher's beam started to fall upon seeing that I was watching them.

Soare-a picked up instantly that attention had been taken from her, and followed her friend's eyes over to me, "I'm going to be out," she glared at me, "I'll let Malook know that I relieved you of me."

She stuck on me a moment more before putting a grin back on and trotting away with Typher. As I watched them regroup with the other men and women beyond, I dropped my hand to my side, detaching a device similar to hers from my leg, and reaching it up to my ear. I didn't trust her to say anything to Malook. I'd let him know myself, so he could make this relief formal. Speaking his name, I waited for an answer.

"Sulru?"

"Your wife has relieved me," I gave flatly, "I'm taking Connie, John, and Riven home."

The man's frustrated sigh sounded through the phone, "I'll put it in. Thank you, Sulru."

With the press of a button, I ended the call and put the com back on my side, whilst stepping to the vehicle and making myself the fourth and final passenger for the trip. "Riven," I called to the second seat as I activated the machine, "Show your cousins where their safety straps are."

The boy, though upset by his mother's disappearance, was happy to be able to help, which I had figured. After they were all properly set up and the rover was off the ground, I carefully looked into the panoramic camera in front to make sure it was safe to go, before I sped the machine out of the spot and toward the garage's exit. I would have control over the vehicle until we were on the main road; then the auto-pilot would take over to best handle the high speeds of that stretch.

Once out of cover of the building, the full bustle of the city was seen and heard. I didn't look back, but did study the screen to keep an eye on Connie and John. Both seemed excited. It was an emotion that I had seen on the woman, however, not yet on her husband. Seeing the man portraying such a simple and pure feelingwas somehow encouraging.

Contuin was a shiny spectacle, largely made up of synthetic materials that were constantly cleaned and buffed to keep the environment pristine. This deep into the city, there weren't any natural parks or clearings, though many trees lined the roads for the sake of vanity. Firsthand experience of modern Earth dwellings wasn't something I had. From what information Malook had shared with me, I gathered that they were nowhere near as clean and healthy as ours.

It was about an eighteen mile trip from the station to Malook's home: a nine minute drive. The residence was among several built between the shops, stations, and other places of business, as well as the recreational outposts on this side of the Black Forest. Although each home had minor differences, all were basically the same structure. Three stories high and, once more, circular in appearance. Some were divided into more than one residence by floor, but Malook owned his in its entirety.

The vehicle reverted to manual mode as we neared the house, letting me take control and slowly ease the machine into an open, covered area at the bottom of the building. As the humming ceased and we were lowered to the ground, Riven and I unlocked and removed ourselves from our seats. The Earthlings followed suit, their faces full of obvious thrill, which made me chuckle.

"Enjoy the ride?" I asked.

"Yeah," Connie laughed and John shook his head, looking downward as if to hide his grin.

Riven had already gone to the entrance in front of where we parked, and put his little hand on the panel to order it open. Just as he ran inside his home, I gestured with my hand for the human adults to go as well, then I went after. Once securing the three inside, I would have been free to leave and see Teylof, had it not been for Soare-a's disappearance.

With nothing against them, I couldn't leave Riven in either of the Earthlings' hands. On the outside, it would have been acceptable since Connie was Malook's family. However, given the actual circumstances beneath those appearances, I wasn't going to leave them alone. Having them watch over Riven would be tantamount to him being alone as well. They were not acquainted with Galdelier enough for something like this yet.

So instead, I went inside and waited, watching the boy run to the lift, presumably up to his room. What had seemed from the outside a modest abode, had an extravagant interior. Surely even with differences in culture, the alien couple were able to see this.

The floor dipped down lower than the ground outside so that the walls were almost twice as tall. Silver lined arches, leading off into the other circles of the house, shone brightly between marvelous paintings of lakes and mountains. The largest room on the first floor had held many gatherings and dances over the years. Just as I thought, I found Connie and John gawking as they journeyed further in.

"Oh, I-we didn't mean to be rude," the woman spoke suddenly, taking a few paces back to where I was.

"The bedroom and family rooms are on the higher floors," I explained. "Everything down here is more or less public."

Connie nodded, once more putting a comfortable distance between us.

"I have a question," John turned around and pointed at the door, "No key?"

"No need," I informed, "Only registered hand marks will allow access, and the person who opens the door is put on record with the time."

"I see," John mused, "Interesting."

Chapter 33: John

I let Connie be the first to explore after Sulru's permission. The main area we had been in was circular and lacking of much anything, though I assumed there were more of the hidden furniture we had been introduced to on the ship. My wife stepped into a smaller room off to the side. This one was rectangular and had couches and chairs, all arranged in a sort of rectangle themselves, facing each other.

The seats looked very cushy. They were a dark brown color that contrasted with the beige walls. Walking up to them, I laid a hand on the back of a couch to find that they were, indeed, quite plush. This den, I guess, was apparently on the very end of one side of the home, as there were no other openings within it and no panels to suggest any were hidden. Connie strolled around the furniture, not sitting, but instead turning around in the midst of the pieces and studying the room.

"Sulru? Are there TVs here? Do you have anything like that?" Connie stilled her gaze just behind me, so I twisted to see the vampire as well.

The woman had followed us, stopping in the door frame and leaning her back against it. She looked extremely tired and I could tell her thoughts were elsewhere. She hadn't even been watching us, though when Connie spoke, she turned her head our way.

"TV?" she asked in her usual monotone.

"Television," my wife clarified, enthusiasm lessening upon realizing Sulru's state, "Like to watch movies? You know, people acting out stories?"

"Right, right," Sulru replied half-heartedly, "Onkar," she spoke into the air loudly, not aiming her voice at either of us.

At the sound of the unusual word, the lights in the room dimmed and shapes of plants and people popped into view, distorted around where Connie and I stood. Holograms. Not simple translucent forms, but ones of full color as if other bodies had actually teleported into the area with us. They had turned the room into a forest where two humans where standing, their eyes shifting nervously about.

Directly beside Sulru, some sort of massive, angry creature, reminiscent of a rhino with an enormous jaw full of rows of spiked teeth, burst into view and hurdled toward the fake people. Even knowing it wasn't real, the movement was startling. Fortunately, there was no accompanying sound. Perhaps the volume was down. The scene projected into the room shifted then, to follow the characters.

"This is really..." I chuckled, looking from the Earth woman to the Galdelierian, "It's awesome."

Sulru smirked, yet said nothing. Once more, her aura spoke that something was bothering her; it showed through her normal stoic unresponsiveness. She had told us to forego formalities with her, however, my mind couldn't get past the feeling that I should leave the matter be. Connie did speak up though.

"Sulru? Do you live here too?" she asked.

"I do not," the woman answered simply.

"Why don't you go home? You're obviously tired," my wife pushed, and I instantly knew she shouldn't have.

Sulru lifted herself from the door and turned to fully face our direction, dark eyes setting heavily upon us, "Derkar," she commanded the holograms around to disappear and the lights returned to a bright setting. She took no other action than to stare at us.

"I didn't mean-" Connie began again awkwardly, realizing too late her blunder.

I looked back apologetically at the soldier. My wife had unintentionally insulted Sulru's honor as a warrior, and her pride as a person, in a single concerned suggestion. I was certain that the alien woman was aware that Connie was still getting used to this new world and the second rate citizen that Sulru was considered.

She had forgotten that the soldier was likely required to stay here and therefore couldn't just go home and rest. However, the glare in the vampire's eyes had me on edge. I hadn't seen this gaze since we had become allies and it had my heart reacting as if I should ready to fight off the creature, despite being told by logic that such a scenario wouldn't occur.

I shifted where I stood, choosing to ignore the incident rather than confront it, "What is onkar and derkar?"

Sulru tilted her head toward me, an eyebrow raised, "They're just made up words. The company that first created this ES found it better to have words which meant nothing to control the system so that casual conversation would not disrupt it or cause it to come on when unwanted."

"ES," I muttered, "Does that mean-"

"Entertainment System," she clarified, the intense look in her eyes waning as my own inquiry reminded her of what we were. She blinked a couple of times, dropping her vision to the ground and turning her head away once more. The vampire twisted her torso and looked back to where we had come before stepping to the side and speaking, not returning her attention to us, "I have to go check on Riven. Stay inside."

And then she was gone, quickly pacing to what looked like an elevator. Although the machine was smaller than that we had used when first arriving on the planet, it was equally modern and trim in appearance, and it blended perfectly with the walls of the home. Connie came to my side as we observed Sulru until she was aboard the lift and out of sight.

"Shit, John," she whispered with a disheartened expression, "I think I hurt a vampire's feelings."

Most likely it was her intent to outline the fault on her part, but it came out comical. It also, with the help of those black eyes returning to fight mode, made my mind recall the events on Earth. A vampire. I had- we both had worked to look past the slaughter to see just another soldier doing their job, but we still needed to remember what that soldier was capable of. Sulru was right. We must be careful who we trust.

"Don't worry, sweetie," I pulled her close, kissing her forehead, "You didn't do anything wrong."

She grumbled under me, taking my affection before pulling away, "I guess we can keep nosing about," she shrugged.

"Yeah," I smiled.

After grabbing her hand, we walked into the large open area which held the door to the house itself and the one that the kid and Sulru had vanished behind to go upstairs. It appeared to be a sort of ballroom and was somewhere in the neighborhood of eighty feet squared. Studying the colorful stone floor, I couldn't tell if there was hidden furniture like I assumed or not.

The spirals, streams, and blots of varying hues that the rock consisted of was what kept detection of anything nearly impossible. Connie, on the other hand, was not focused on these little details. She had begun dancing in a swirl, circling around the room, throwing a grin at me with every turn. I watched the light-hearted woman until she spun to a stop, curtsying, and then skipping her way into the next circle on the opposite side of the den and the ES.

Just the same, this room was rectangular inside and much smaller than the one in the middle. Two

348

walls were lined with containers like there had been in the storage area on the ship and the other two had them as well, but only partially. They were topped with counters and the wall above these tops had multiple small windows decorating it. Toward the center of the room was a square island. Everything was a silvery color and gave the place a clinical feel.

"It's a kitchen?" Connie wondered in minor confusion, "Well...is there a sink or..."

I strolled up to the island counter where I had noticed an ovular outline on the middle of two sides. Laying my hand on one of these, I waited in expectation of it opening, yet nothing happened. I lifted my hand and then lowered it once more, letting my palm touch it. Still nothing. Standing there in thought for a few moments, I raised my second hand and put one on either side. There was a low beep and the panel slid away, revealing a metal half-sphere.

"Found the sink," I threw a smirk of success over my shoulder.

My wife left the other counters where she'd been gazing out the windows and took position beside me. Her eyes started wandering around the spot, as did mine. We had the same thought: *where was the spout?* It didn't take long to figure out, since we had begun to get used to the design of the alien technology and wares. There were small black dots lining the rim. Putting a finger on the largest one caused a faucet to rise up out from underneath the rim and extend into shape.

From that point, it could be slid around by the other dots. It seemed to work on a sensor basis: how high or low your hand was beneath the spout determined the amount of pressure in the stream. Just as we were finding this out, Connie's smile fell and she startled, giving a small yelp while staring at something beyond me. I twisted my body immediately and took a defensive stance, only to be greeted by a loud chortle.

"Jumpy John," Sulru was leaning in the frame of the kitchen entrance, a sneer on her face that showed fangs.

Something was creepy about the way she said my name, but Connie continued the dialouge before I could respond, "You're quiet," she laughed, "We didn't realize you were back."

The vampire kept her expression, "Sorry. It's not me, though. You were preoccupied and our machines are quieter than the ones you are used to."

The admission that it was no skill of hers, only circumstance, was strange considering the offense at what had been said earlier, so I sufficed it to say she was over the misunderstanding. Nontheless, she remained seeming a bit off and at arm's length. Obviously, I wasn't going to ask about where her mind was. The woman was sensitive in her own way; she desired no formal gestures yet wasn't entirely personable or open either.

Chapter 34: Malook

I normally tolerated Cartef pretty well, but his attitude and even small mannerisms of his were grinding on my nerves today. Perhaps it was due to my paranoia concerning this whole situation. Add that to the exhaustion from the ordeal, and it would naturally account for a dive in my usual tolerance.

Sulru did not care for him at all so I was glad there wasn't that extra tension of having her present. I didn't know why it was Cartef that she picked to have it out for. We had met so many more deserving of her hatred and mistrust, yet it was him who had gained her focus.

The sound of tapping suddenly struck me from my thoughts. I looked up to see my assistant typing rapidly on a thin tablet held before him on an posable cord extending from the device's case on his leg. His attention hadn't strayed far from the handheld since we had departed the docking bay, and even though I knew he was working, it was infuriating me. I refrained from speech though, sighing instead as I put attention back on my own work.

A large part of the paperwork had been authorizations for executions, or rather vampire feedings. The death penalties were largely decided by Empress Naiker herself, however, handling which vampires were to take care of them fell to me.

Generally it was just a schedule: whose turn it was. Sometimes when a vampire had sustained damage, they were allowed extra feedings to better aid in recovery.

Other times there were complications where sentences were changed last minute or an officer otherwise had to forego a feeding or other such discrepancies. It was part of a General's job to be certain every vampiric officer was properly nourished, as well as allot an appropriate amount of the sentenced inmates to the academy meant for training their young.

Although not a favorite duty, not carrying the disdain against the vampires took away much reluctance toward fulfilling the task. No, I understood that they required blood to sustain themselves. This was no fault on their part. My problem lay solely with the deaths themselves. Unlike the typical carnivore, vampires didn't need to kill to eat.

I'm sure if the world were different to where we didn't work together, as it were, or they were as animalistic as many seemed to think, that they would find it easiest to kill or otherwise subdue their prey, yet as it stood, this was not so. It baffled me that a grand majority of humans still did not realize these things, or either they chose not to believe it. It wasn't as if it were often taught. Our leaders and most government officials certainly did not care for it to be common knowledge.

After the final form was signed, I exhaled sharply and stretched my back straight, pushing it against the chair I sat in before slicking back my hair with my hands and standing. I took hold of the pile of folders and papers I had been working on for the last hour or more and strolled over to Cartef, who, upon noticing I had gotten up, bent the metal arm protruding from his leg back into place and grudgingly relieved his eyes from the screen of his device.

"Finished?" he observed.

My only reply was a nod as I handed him the stack and continued past him on my way out of the office, down the hall beyond. I heard a short sound behind me coming from the man shuffling the paperwork under his arm and stepping quickly after me.

"Would you like me to escort you home?" he asked.

Maybe fear was playing in, but I found the offer strange. It wasn't something normal for him to do, considering it wasn't his job and neither were we friendly. We worked with each other; he had been to my home a handful of times as a guest to gatherings. That was the extent of our relationship. At least it was until Soare-a and I had begun planning our vacation.

Not long prior, come to think of it, Cartef had made himself present more frequently. I accredited it to the trip, that he was readying himself for extra tasks during my absence as much of the added company had dealt with discussing work and even getting ahead of a few things to keep all smoothly running. Nonetheless...

"No, thank you," I said as I skipped forward to command the elevator open. It was apparently in use because I had to wait. Cartef hadn't made a move away from me yet, as if he was waiting on me for something. To keep from growling in agitation, I decided to further this bit and turned to him, "Why do you ask?"

There was a brief pause while he registered the question, "It's just that your guard isn't here to meet you and it's late."

I glanced out the window as the door in front of us opened. He was right. It was already becoming dark. My routine when leaving normally included calling for Sulru to pick me up though today, I hadn't. Mostly because the odd events had me off kilter, but I also knew I'd want her with the aliens for the time being anyway. It wasn't as if I was incapable of driving the short distance to my home. It was a precaution per my standing- one that was all except legally required. Moreover, I longed to spend time alone with her.

"No, that's not necessary ," I said, warming the button for the main floor as well as the one where his files were meant to go.

There was a slight hesitation in him when I did so. However, he remained quiet and the elevator began moving downward. I felt he was wanting something else from me or at the very least to speak more. I was too tired and too frustrated to care enough to know so instead, we took the ride silently.

When we at last had reached his destination, he spoke again, "Do you have your spra, then?"

"Hm? Oh, uh," I stammered, realizing that I was not, in fact, carrying the weapon, which *was* against the law for me to be without it.

"Here," Carter reached a hand down to his side and unclipped a cylindrical metal piece.

I took it with an awkward grin as his expression became cynical, "I am rather tired," I offered.

The man chuckled softly, "Take care, Malook."

I gave a slight nod just before the door slid shut. The rest of the descent, finding my way to a vehicle, and getting to the main stretch of road seemed to drag on, each step becoming increasingly difficult. When I finally laid back in the rover, letting auto pilot take over, my eyes fell to the weapon in my lap.

Spra batons. I hated them even though I understood their need. It was our main defense against vampires as humans, other than other vampires. A strike from one would destroy a human within minutes or render a vampire incapable of function with eventual death if not reversed. The device was crafted to shoot a heavy spear into the target, the tip of which then released hundreds of tiny machines that traveled in no set pattern inside of the body.

These nanos constantly tore and cut the tissue, organs, even bone, of the victim. It was designed with vampiric regeneration in mind. To me, it was tantamount to torture. But I also knew that without it, a lone human, or even a few, had no chance against an attacking vampire. Regardless, I did have a definite soft spot when it came to the race.

Sulru wasn't the only vampire who had saved my life. There were two others before her: Laal and...Toka. It was actually Laal sacrificing himself to save me that allowed me to meet Sulru. He was my guard prior to her. We didn't have the intimacy that she and I did, but he was aware of my unyielding compassion for his people. We were on good terms. I liked to think he considered me more than just a boss or another human. Either way, it was a vampire that murdered him; one I subsequently killed by use of a spra.

It was an unexpected battle one evening as the two of us departed from an ambassadorial mission to our sister nation. It was he and I, walking toward the harbor where we would board a small vessel to bring us back to Gelvin. It wasn't crowded since travel between the countries was not a common occurrence. It was a trip most would never be able to take. Laal was also the only vampire in the vicinity until the rogue showed and assaulted him.

It was another man. His sudden strike surprised me, but my guard had seen it beforehand and parried. The others around us ran away from the two, and I also took my distance, grasping onto the baton at my side and aiming it in the direction of the attacker. Laal and the other vampire fought hand in hand, neither one getting any real blows in. Unfortunately, the enemy eventually got the drop on my partner, slashing his throat deeply, leaving gashes that even a vampire would have difficulty healing.

And he did not stop there.

When Laal staggered off, he was met with a sharp stab to his chest. I was certain that in all my time serving, I had never seen so much gushing blood. The rogue vampire was colored crimson, his clothes drenched. Somehow I was able to shoot him twice with my baton. As he fell, I saw that reinforcements were coming around...but it was too late for my friend.

The Department of Behavioral Regulation handled most affairs dealing with vampires. They fed there, all concerns were voiced and incidents reported there, and it was where those who monitored their children, before life in the academy, were located. In addition, the staff performed many other tasks involving the race as.

They were originally set up to make humans feel more comfortable when approaching the courts or otherwise processing legal matters, as it lessened the vampiric population about them and made those courts more human-oriented. The department was also responsible for assigning vampires to their new roles, which was why I found myself there after Laal had passed.

I had Riven with me that day. His mother had a date that was set weeks prior and was unable to take him with her. Despite awareness that our home's security system was of the highest caliber, meaning that even in the worst case, he should have been safe there alone for the extent of the two hours it would take me to put things in order, I still did not want to leave him by himself at such a young age.

Humans did generally avoid the Department of Behavioral Regulation, though, as per codes to keep vampire groups below a certain number, the majority of the employees were human. There were only a handful of vampires who actually worked within their walls. As well, times did call that humans should need use of the offices, such as it did for me that day.

So, I had gone behind an office door to initiate matters, leaving my son in the lobby on the other side. I hadn't been gone ten minutes, and still it was enough time for him to make a friend. When I was back in view, I saw that he was chatting with a young girl who was a bit taller than him, yet had to be close in age. Her skin was extremely pale and she had long, straight, jet black hair. They weren't facing my way until Riven caught a glimpse of me out of the corner of his eye. He then excitedly grabbed the girl's hand and pulled her along with him to meet me.

"This is Teylof, Dad," he beamed, "She's a vampire."

Of course, I had already come to that conclusion. Even so, I felt a momentary dim in my being, thinking of the danger of the situation. Not of the girl hurting him, but rather the repercussions my son could face from his own people for acting so kind to her. Age was not a factor in this terrible prejudice.

Everyone was of the mind that children should be made to act same as us adults. My concern as a father wanted to override the fact that he was in the right, and tear him away...I just didn't have the heart. I was thrilled that he had a loving soul. If Soare-a had been there, she would have been irate. Thankfully, she was too busy to care for her son that day.

"Oh?" I prompted.

"Yeah, the people in the hall were being mean to her, but I told her it was ok and brought her in here with me," Riven's head rose with pride at having saved the little girl.

"Hello, Teylof," I greeted her, kneeling down to the kids' level and looked into her bright onyx spheres.

The young vampire gave a toothy grin that showed her fangs were just beginning to come in fully. Vampires had baby teeth and adult teeth similar to humans. As children, they had six or eight pointed teeth scattered in their mouths nearer to the front, and as they grew older, more grew into place, their size depending upon the age when they came out.

After large ones started protruding, then the initial smaller ones were finally forced from the gums. This process continued until they had a row of strong fangs on both the top and bottom jaws. I glanced from her to the hall where I saw two women and a man nosily peeping inside the room, doing nothing to conceal their condescending demeanor. My sight fell back to the vampiric child. My heart dropped. Her face was so sweet and innocent, exactly how Toka had been...

Shuffling from the other humans along with a snorting sound, then the thud of footsteps made me raise my head. A vampire woman had appeared in the doorway and she walked directly up to Teylof and Riven, picking the little girl up and holding her tightly against her body. The girl said something to the affect of 'What's wrong, Mama?' to which the woman shushed her and put her gaze on me as I returned to my feet.

"I'm sorry if Teylof was bothering you," she said curtly before letting her daughter slide down her side to stand by her. She then she took her hand and turned to leave without anything more to say.

The young vampire glanced at Riven, who waved at her while tugging my clothes with his other hand. I tilted my head to see him face me with an expression that told me he wanted his friend to stay. So, not really thinking about it, I moved a pace forward, reaching my hand out to the woman's shoulder and stopping her from leaving.

"She wasn't bothering us at all," I said, retreating my hand when the woman vampire spun back around.

She hesitated with a response, the scenario definitely strange to her. Instead of speaking or gesturing, she only stood there, beautiful dark eyes piercing into me as she silently judged who I was and what exactly I was doing. Her face was soft in appearance and yet she had a strong jaw and nose.

Her eyelashes were long and perfectly curled; she was barely taller than me, her body lean yet muscular.

"My name is Malook and this is my son, Riven," I said delicately to be sure my words sounded neither angry nor haughty.

"I'm Sulru, General," the vampire replied in a cold tone, "I thought you looked familiar. This is my daughter, Teylof."

The little girl grinned up at me with the mention of her name. I could sense her mother was aching to get out of there, yet something was making me desperate for her to stay. It was more than just her beauty. Her energy was intoxicating. Even though she'd done nothing against codes of conduct, I could tell that she was a proud being.

She held herself high. My rank and definitely not my humanity made her feel uncomfortable or less than the wonderful, important creature she was. Her entire being was stunning me. However, after a few moments of quiet contemplation, soaking in her aura, I gave a dismissing nod. There was no explainable reason for me to keep her longer.

When the vampires had cleared our line of sight, Riven had a question, "Can she be my friend, Dad?"

Not removing my sights from where Sulru had vanished, I smiled, "Of course she can."

And as simply as that, Sulru became my new guard.

Chapter 35: Sulru

I had left the humans a few times to keep an eye on Riven, who was entertaining himself in his room. It was while with him the third time, that I thought I heard a noise outside and went to one of the bedroom windows to investigate. A vehicle had pulled into the yard below.

"Your father's home," I told the boy.

His head shot up and then the rest of him did as well. He ran to his door and skipped to the lift, waiting patiently for me to catch up before making it descend. His energy had slowed as it was nearing the end of day for him, yet he still remained in constant movement, his expression phasing between showing enthusiasm and sleepiness.

When the elevator stopped, I stepped out to stroll toward the door as he faltered behind, like he had been taught to do when I purposely went in front of him. I saw Connie and John, in the den watching the ES, turn heads my way when the two of us appeared. I stopped a few feet from the entrance and watched it slide open, Malook instantly entering with an apology.

"Sulru, I'm sorry you've had to stay," he said, "Has Soare-a not returned?"

"No," I replied flatly.

The alien couple had lowered the volume in the other room, the man standing and slowly making his way to the oval passage to become part of our group. I don't think he realized it was rude. I looked to the Earthling, head tilted, brow raised, and he took the hint, reversing toward the couch and recovering his former position.

"Dad, is it fortmeal yet?" Riven produced himself from behind me.

"Uh," his father sighed, "If your mother isn't home soon, we'll go ahead. Give me a minute with Sulru, OK?"

The young boy shrugged on his way to sit down with his cousins, as Malook took us a few casual paces away from everyone else. I crossed my arms, keeping sight on the man, not expecting there to be an important reason for his separating us from the others like this. When he spoke, that was disproved.

"Thank you, Sulru. I know you're anxious to see Teylof," he put simply.

"I am," my head cocked to the side, "So if there's nothing else-"

"Actually it's them," he made a slight gesture with his chin in the Earthlings' direction, "Are they allies to you?"

I paused, taking advantage of my eyes' coloring in studying the humans without making it obvious that I was. They were letting Riven switch the shows. "You mean in regards to the faction?"

Malook's silence was his answer.

"I think they could be," I continued, removing my sight from them and giving it to the man beside me, "At the very least, I don't think they're a direct risk to exposure."

He nodded, shifting his vision from the topic of our discussion to me, "And as far as duress...well we can't be certain what anyone would do in that case."

"Hm," I thought, "If they were put in such a situation, your worry would be greater."

The man's soft green eyes became confused, "What are you getting at?"

"Secrets, Malook," I pointed, "If captured as part of our company, the following investigations would turn up some pretty shady things about your cousins."

"They may be just as likely to be found out on either street. So long as we keep the trust of the defectors, I don't see how bringing Connie and John in will create more problems. Those among us should be understanding in the event they discover the truth about the Earthlings. Above anyone, they would understand the need for secrecy."

"Perhaps,"" I murmured, "Speak to them, then. And speak to Otahn," I removed my arms from my chest and began to stride away, "Update me next time."

"Give Teylof and Kivela my regards," he called softly after, to which I simply raised a hand without bothering to glance backward or cease my walk.

Passing between the two vehicles parked in the garage, I slid into the second, smaller one that

Malook had brought home. The machines worked similarly to the system of the home which had been explained to John. The General had a handful of them at his disposal. Besides himself, Soare-a and I were registered users, rendering them unusable by any others. All that was required was a brief scan of the hand and I could set the course I wished.

My destination was on the other end of the city, next to a small nameless wood that acted as part of Contuin's limits. The building itself was approximate in size to my boss' home, although obviously not as luxurious or well kept. I lived on the top floor along with Teylof and her father's father.

On the stories below were eight others, but my daughter was the only child throughout. These people were all agreeable to other vampires. Humans, however, not so much. One man even liked to jab at me for being a 'human sympathizer.' In the end, he was harmless to my family so I didn't pay him any heed.

When I arrived, this charming guy and another from the residence were standing outside under the light on the front entry which was on since the day hours had ended. I pulled the rover up next to them, parking it in the drive because there was no covered area for it. The two vampires studied me as I let the machine settle and hopped out of it.

"*Tawsey!* Why have you been gone?" the delinquent shouted as I approached.

"Watch your mouth, Mote," the other growled at him, then turned to me with a kinder voice, "You have been away much longer than expected. Humans been here."

I paused in front of them, ignoring the insult as my eyes narrowed with worry, focused on what Poit had said, "About Teylof?"

He nodded, "Don't worry. She's still here. We made sure they knew who her mother worked for."

"What?" I pondered.

"If they'd seen her, you know they'd have come back to get her," Poit pointed, "Didn't know when you'd be back. My mates told them that the General had her seen before you left so not to remove your focus from work."

"And they believed you?" my doubt displayed.

"More or less," Mote scoffed, "She also happened to be out with her uncle at the time."

"She doesn't have-" I began, then what he meant dawned on me and I returned, heated, "You *took* my daughter out?"

He backed off, mockingly, "Yeah, you're welcome."

Doing my best to hold back anger, I breathed sharply while shaking my head, then kept on past them and stormed inside. Gratitude should have overridden being mad at this taken liberty, knowing full well I would never trust him with Teylof, however in the moment, it was difficult to feel thankful. There was a small area on the other side of that door with two more passages leading to apartments, and a panel concealing an elevator between them.

I rushed to it, commanding a lift up to the third floor. Once sealed behind its entry, I closed my eyes and steadied my breathing, stilling emotion and remembering my daughter was waiting for me. When the elevator dinged open, I deliberately made my pace toward our apartment casual, raised my hand, and waited for the door to slide away. The moment I was inside, I was met with the cold gaze of my father-in-law, his form barely visible in the dimly lit room.

"You know we have electricity," I said, vision sweeping briefly over the candles around the room.

"We also have candles," he replied with a smirk, not moving in the deep blue chair he sat in.

Our voices alerted Teylof to my presence and she scurried into the den from her bedroom, which was hidden in a short hallway behind Kivela. Upon seeing me, she smiled, quickly dropping her eyes to the floor and pausing, in order to cease her excitement before coming toward me in a reserved strut. It was hard for me not to chuckle, but I didn't because I knew it would insult her.

Once she had started to become capable of understanding the world better, including the existence of the vampire academies, she had picked up mannerisms and attitudes of the other, older vampires around her...namely me. Otherwise, she had always been a rather timid child, quiet and preferring to stick to herself, though not easily frightened. After passing by her grandfather though, he grinned wildly behind her field of sight.

"What took so long?" she asked, trying to be stoic, though her face spoke a different story. She missed me and was dying to show it.

"Do I get a hug?" I counter-asked, lifting a brow.

I watched as she attempted an annoyed expression first, then gave up and moved forward with open arms. Kneeling down, I took her pouty embrace, happy to feel her squeeze tightly back against me, "I'm sorry. It wasn't supposed to." I held her for as long as she would allow me before she released, both of us falling back into our stances.

"Was there trouble, Sulru?" Kivela dipped back into the conversation, his voice incredibly raspy.

"Something like that," I murmured, setting my eyes on him, "And here?"

The old man picked up on the accusatory tone instantly, "I see you've heard about Mote. You owe him one for being here while I had to leave...which I wouldn't have had to, had you been back on time," he growled.

"Don't fight, you two," Teylof's voice broke in, adamant, yet soft.

I grinned, but cleared my throat and straightened my demeanor into a bow to the little vampire, "Of course," I looked again to Kivela, "Thank you for keeping an eye out. When will they be back?"

"Hm... They didn't say," he scratched at an scar that covered one cheek, "I'd talk to Malook. I don't know if they'll check up on anything that was said."

My response was a simple hum.

"Am I going to go away soon?" the twelve year old girl's innocent inquiry broke my heart, even though she had always assured me of how ready she was and how everything would be fine.

"No doubt," Kivela gruffed.

Teylof's head shot toward her grandfather and then returned to me as I growled menacingly at him, "You never learned to mind your own damn business, do you?"

The ancient vampire scoffed as he stood from his chair, striding past us and to the door, his long black robes floating gracefully against his aging frame, "Maybe when you learn to stop being selfish, I'll give it a shot," he threw back nonchalantly, leaving me dumbfounded and not giving me enough time to contemplate a reply as the apartment entrance slid open to let him walk out.

Teylof was superbly adept at sensing the auras of others. She always knew when someone had shifted into sadness or anger or even happiness. Therefore, she easily felt my fury then, one that had been growing the entire day with no relief. My daughter cowered away from her determined persona, shying from me while simultaneously trying to calm me with a sweet, delicate voice.

"I don't think you're selfish, Mama," she said, "If I were you, I wouldn't want me to go either."

My claws extended and retracted a few times at my sides. Initially the repetition only furthered my agitation, but next to the sound of my daughter's concern, it became soothing. Finally, I retracted them one last time, closing my eyes and taking a deep breath. As I exhaled, I lifted my lids once more and looked over to Teylof. My body seemed to fall into a smaller form of itself, the trip, the disturbances, all the emotions catching up with it and making my own weight nearly impossible to carry.

"Have you been watching the stars?" I asked her gently.

She beamed, regaining some outer strength, "Yes. Every night."

It was something that her father and I had always done. We'd sneak out to the woods or the forest when twilight had settled, find a spot, and gaze at the sky, counting, naming, and charting. Sometimes we wouldn't even talk. Just look and feel the air, the ground, the trees...let the nature surrounding us envelop our very existence.

We took the simple moment to enjoy having each other, even if that was all we had. After our daughter had been born, I continued this tradition with her. Teylof...it had been Lotac's favorite star. He said he first saw it the night we met. It was one of the brightest in the sky and always visible...*if you were steering the right way*, he said.

"What's it like?" the words shook me from my trance.

"Hm?"

"To feed on a human," the young girl clarified.

I had explained to her what the academy would be like: what would be expected of her, how she would get a job, and most importantly how to act in order to get that far. Yet we had never spoken in much detail concerning being an executioner. It was not a pleasant topic- even more undesirable than the others.

At least for me.

I was aware that many were either too used to it for it to bother them, or they legitimately had no quarrel with killing those humans...my vision flashed with the remembrance of conversations with Mote... I, on the other hand, loathed it. Our little ones weren't expected to do this themselves. Adult caretakers were allowed to take blood from their assigned humans as part of the process in order to feed their children.

"Well," I sighed, turning away from her and stepping toward the window to our side, "It's...confusing." I glanced from the view outside to her, retreating back to it when I saw her awaiting a clearer explanation, "It's as if everything that feels weak about you suddenly isn't anymore. And at the same time, you feel vulnerable."

"Why?" she breathed with anticipation.

My fingers twitched at my side, "Because you feel them dying...and you know they don't have to..."

"Can you really feel them? Like who they are?" her voice had grown a bit more solid.

I hesitated at first, then nodded, "The blood itself almost tastes different and it tells your mind what kind of person they were...but more than anything," I turned to her, "You feel that fear of dying...of losing everything and wondering what happens next."

There was a short silence in the room where all I heard was the wind wailing against the glass in front of me.

"Mama," Teylof took slow paces until she stood with me by the window, "Does it scare you?"

I twisted my neck, lowering my gaze onto her and ordering myself not to shed a tear, "What scares me is all this taking you away from me."

The child offered a weak grin and inched even closer so that she could lean against me and stare out the cold glass to the sky, "I'll always come back," she whispered.

I bent my spine and kissed the top of her long black hair. She didn't understand my meaning, not that I had honestly expected her to. However, I didn't want to discuss it anymore. This time would pass and her journey would begin. Sadly, she would soon come to the realization of that statement. For now, I just looked up to the stars with her. They appeared so frail...

Chapter 36: Malook

I had wanted to speak with John and his wife about our dissenting group the past evening after Sulru left, but during the day's last meal, Soare-a had returned. Although she was somewhat aware of us, it was more an abstract idea to her, or at least that's how I'd left it. I certainly didn't trust her full knowledge of our affairs; neither did I expect her to agree with us except for in part at most.

So instead, I'd shut my mouth and tried to keep small talk. I'd have to bring the Earth man in immediately anyway to prep him for work, since our society did not look fondly upon those without careers. One homemaker per family was respected. Otherwise everyone was expected to contribute to the community in some form. I would talk to him about it before I introduced him to the workforce. In the meantime...

I looked down to the communicater on my desk. Sulru had informed me that morning on our way in, that representatives had been to her home for Teylof and her neighbors had fabricated a story concerning me. She told me in case I were put in a situation where I needed to know. Of course, I would back up the lie without question. But the news set in mind for me that it was over. I had no more time to come up with a plan to protect the girl. I had to act now.

Taking in a breath with heart heavy, I clicked a button on the device before me, causing a hologram to flicker to life. My pointer finger trailed through some of the different images there and then I leaned back in my seat, waiting for an answer. I watched the pictures change into a green wave that rose and fell to depict the hold between my request and someone on another machine elsewhere to connect. After a few moments, the wave turned to a red color, the image once more shifting; this time to the outline of a man's face.

"Malook? It's been quite some time," the man smiled, "I was sure you'd forgotten about your old teacher in your new success."

"Of course not, Ansel," I forced a grin. Simply the sight of him made me ill, "These days are just busy, you know."

The hologram chuckled, "Right they are. So, to what do I owe this reunion?"

I swallowed hard before attempting to deliver the words I had prepared, "A favor, actually. I wondered if you might help me out with something."

"Hm, must be something, uh...very specific to my area of practice if a General is invoking my aid," the man's head tilted back in curiosity.

"It is in regards to a young vampire, my guard's daughter," I tried desperately to seem devious, but all I could feel was disgust.

"Oh?" Ansel's smile returned.

"She's come of age," I continued, "It's time for her to be sent to academy and I was hoping your division would take her on."

"I see. You have a special interest in this one?" he questioned.

"Indeed," I leaned forward, resting my elbows on the desk with my hands laced together just under my chin, "She reminds me of...someone special."

Ansel Luten's lips grew into a large devilish smirk, "I've heard things about you, General. About you sympathizing with these filthy parasites," the man's pause was just long enough to frighten me. If these stories colored his view of me, then coming to him might have sealed Teylof's fate. I was relieved when he continued, "And I admit that I almost believed them. However, I know you, Malook. I know how dirty your hands have gotten to get you where you are."

"So you understand me, then," I lifted an eyebrow, playing along as this past version of myself.

"Entirely," he purred, "Send me the information. I'll have someone out to get the pup and I'll keep an eye on this pet of yours."

"Thank you, old friend," I choked on the words, "I will want to see her from time to time."

The 'professor' chuckled, "Of course. I know you'll make it worth my effort, yes?"

"Without a doubt," I breathed, "I will wire you the address immediately."

"I'll be in touch," he replied before turning off the com on his end.

Once the holograms vanished, I pushed away from the table, my chair rolling slightly backwards as I grabbed my head with both hands. The air I'd been holding in my lungs tried to force its way out, only making a hissing noise as it hit against my teeth and closed lips. I lowered my hands to my lap, instantly raising them again to wipe against my face, pulling the skin downward until they were returned to rest on my thighs.

I was not that person. Not anymore... Ansel knew a me that no longer existed, but he was right about one thing: It had taken more than dedication to the empire to become General. Toka was a perfect example of how different I used to be.

It was rare for a person not to begin on the lowest tier within the ranks of officer prior to climbing to another position. Since I had come from a long line of military personnel, I should have had the advantage of this special preference when officers were chosen for promotion. Should have.

However, my family had also been known for their soft nature. Too compassionate to be taken very seriously as anything other than simple workers. To others, my relatives didn't have the guts to make difficult decisions so my privilege turned into a handicap, one I had been determined to break out of and rise above...at all cost.

I had been out one day with a few of the humans I worked with. We were all in our early twenties. I wasn't even the oldest, but nonetheless, I had been the group's unofficial leader. Although we hadn't meant to be working at that time, we'd heard that a vampire had fled the academy. I saw taking the liberty to bring this lost student in as my way up. It was certainly nothing my family would have taken the initiative to do, being sympathizers themselves.

I talked to these three, convincing them to leave our leisure to look for her. Toka couldn't have been older than fourteen. She had apparently snuck out during the sleeping hours and her absence wasn't noticed until morning. My posse had been poking about the wooded areas for a couple of hours when we came across her.

She was thin and looked sickly for a vampire. There was no tone to her form beneath the traditional garments she wore, and she moved as if disoriented. Upon seeing us, she tumbled backward, breathing heavily as black eyes darted back and forth between us. Grinning, I stepped forward, ignoring the fear on her face.

The girl managed to get back up, stilling her stance and glaring at me, "I'm not going back there. You can kill me now."

"Don't you fucking order me," I growled, looking to my sides to see that my three friends were stepping around to help me close in on her.

Toka's eyes fell, once more her vision cycled over the humans who surrounded her. I had been scared at first with the prospect of confronting a rogue vampire, even a young one, but when I saw how terrified and tired the creature was, any doubt of my strength left me and I had strut forward with purpose. My goal was to become somebody and that frightened little runaway was going to help me get there.

Though young and frail, she stood fairly tall, as most vampires did. Their height was one of the first features grown into. As I approached, she backpedaled. It had somewhat disappointed me that she wasn't eager to defend herself, yet it wasn't until I took hold of her shoulders and she tugged away, that her lack of drive began to anger me. Rather than pull her back and have one of the others cuff her and just keep on our mission, I threw her to the ground with as much force as I could.

"You're really pathetic, aren't you?" I yelled at the girl scrambling to her feet, "You want to die? Give me a reason to kill you."

Two of the others had started laughing at the sight of a vampire portraying such weakness. I chuckled as well while we baited her to come at us. I could tell even so that Toka didn't have much fight left. She bolted at me with hands up, her adult claws mostly in. The sudden burst of speed caught me off guard and she latched onto my throat, her grip making me falter as she dropped her jaw to reveal already nicely developed fangs. Likewise, I reached my hands to her neck, pushing against her and finally winning.

She was on the ground again and my three allies cornered in around her, taking her arms and holding her down while she kept struggling. I went to her and leaned down, only for her to break an arm free and swipe at me with her claws. The attack just barely cut me, though it did prompt one of my buddies to egg me on.

"Damn, Malook. Looks like you need to show this blood-sucker her place," he smirked.

After wiping the few drips of blood from the small wounds on my cheek with my sleeve, I set my gaze on the little girl while I pulled a retracted blade from a pocket on my side. I switched it open without even glancing down. My parents had given me the knife when I first began work.

Despite my resent for their compassionate natures, I never went far unless the gift was on my person. In a single stride, I was above the young vampire. I squatted at her feet and inched myself closer until I was hovering above; then I lifted my weapon in the air. I let the blade hang there for a moment before thrusting it down on her, yanking it over her tunic to tear it open.

She squeaked in shock as her pale skin was exposed, even though her body had not been harmed. Those beside me quieted while I reached to pull either side of the fabric away from her. I laid my blade to rest beneath her neck and placed my other palm flat on her undeveloped chest.

She jumped at my touch, which I answered by digging the tip of my knife into her throat. A thin trail of crimson left the spot and flowed quickly to be absorbed by the black fabric right above my hand on her breast. The others with me tugged tightly on her arms and Toka began flustering her legs under me. I let myself fall onto my knees so that my weight pressed against her groin and legs, debilitating her. I could still feel her continue to wiggle beneath my body. Removing my hand from her, but keeping blade in place, I let my chest fall onto hers.

She turned her head to the side as my face came close to hers, yet I still whispered maliciously into her ear, "It's not like you're going to be spared anyway. Nobody wants a vampire around. Definitely not one that can't follow orders."

I lifted myself slightly, only enough that I could see her face. She stayed turned, refusing to look at me, though her vision remained open to the dirt at our side. I had expected her to cry or beg me to leave her alone, but she did nothing. She just laid there. Didn't even struggle anymore.

The others with me had started laughing again, "Ha! Fuck her, Malook! Looks like she wants it!"

My own body had become thrilled with having her powerless to me and I was certain I was within a proximity that allowed her to feel that I was stiffening. After an instant though, I relented and removed myself from her, pushing back onto my feet and then rising to stand.

With one last huff at her, I spun on my heels to carry on with her capture. However, I was met with the sight of two men standing several feet from my group and I, watching us. Both wore uniforms denoting a rank higher than myself. They were also armed with spra batons, a weapon I hadn't then had access to outside of a work environment.

"Don't let us interrupt, boy," a younger Ansel Luten commanded, "It seems you were in the middle of teaching our little student here a valuable lesson."

I hesitated at the man's words, unsure of how to respond and fearful that my actions could be seen as misconduct. The woods around us were silent enough in that moment that I heard those restraining the vampire shift nervously in their positions. When I didn't immediately respond, Ansel walked over to me, his eyes boring into mine.

"Was finding this escapee your doing?" he demanded.

"Y-yes, sir," my voice was weak, though I somehow managed to hold his gaze.

"Then finish what you started," his eyes slit with the gruff, "These creatures have to be taught who their masters are. Discipline is a must or else they begin to slide out of control."

I looked from the man back to Toka, who had put her attention on the new scene unfolding. She was breathing rapidly, the terror clear on her face as she tried to pull against those holding her down. Suddenly, I felt hands on my upper arm that shoved me toward the young girl.

"Don't be weak!" Ansel barked, "Follow through or prove yourself as useless as that soulless beast."

His words infuriated me. I was not weak. I would do what needed to be done. I assumed the stance I previously held over her with our bodies close, the weight of mine pressing her into the ground. She once more chose not to look at me as I retrieved my blade and cut open the lower parts of her clothing. I felt her body tense when my hand dropped the knife and reached to my own tunic, slithering my hand inside it and grabbing hold of myself, adjusting so that our bare parts touched each other.

She jerked and I promptly responded by using my free hand to grab onto her throat. The men around me were all but motionless, yet I could feel their heavy, sadistic expressions upon me. I trailed the tip of my hardness along her mound and lips until I found her opening and instantly thrust myself inside her, letting go of my hold there as soon as her walls kept me firmly in place. She yelled at the abrupt sensation. It must have hurt as I felt a warmth coming from her cold body and looked down to discover slow red streams dripping from her.

Only then did she began crying, really sobbing...tears falling from her dark eyes and down her cheeks. At first, they were almost screams, but gradually lessened as my movements slowed then stopped. I held firmly onto her neck the entire time...

The next day, I received my first promotion on good recommendation from Ansel Luten. He then became a sort of mentor to me. It was a dirty and disgusting relationship that thankfully ended as my greed was eventually overcome with ethical logic.

Chapter 37: Sulru

Malook hadn't been upset when I shared how Poit had brought him into matters concerning Teylof, as I knew he wouldn't be. However, when I spoke of it, he got that look in his eyes that meant he was contemplating something important. I didn't talk about my daughter often, but he was well aware of my distress at having to send her away, and I had begun to feel that he'd taken it too much upon himself to help with the situation.

I drove the man to work that morning and dropped him off within the protected walls of his office before heading to the Department of Behavioral Regulation. My feeding on Earth had obviously gone unreported. Therefore, I was scheduled to feed that day since returning from our trip. I easily found my way to an elevator inside and went down to the basement floor.

There, a human woman rested behind a desk concealed with tempered glass. She barely glanced up at me while I waved my hand across a monitor between us, letting it scan my identity. She responded to the new screen that opened on her side of the glass with a few taps of her finger, which caused the machine to produce a keycard. I grabbed the slither of plastic and trotted further down the hallway.

"Sulru?" a voice called from behind me.

Slowly, I rotated to set eyes on an old friend: Zofra. We had known each other since our academy days. He, Lotac, and myself had been like a little family. At one point, we were even all romantically involved with one another. However wonderful that three-way relationship had been, it devolved into just Lotac and myself once Zofra became focused on his career. He was, after all, the eldest. Even so, we always looked out for each other despite the change and Zofra's disdain at it.

The man approached me smiling, despite the strained friendship. After Teylof's father had died, He had come around more often and as much as I'd like to think it was just out of sincere worry, I knew he wanted to be together again. He never directly said so; I read it in his actions. I *had* thought upon it, yet I never was able to commit to trying such a partnership with him. He had, though, been part of our secret faction for quite some time, so he had met Malook and I was always fearful of his judgement should he discover how close the human was to me.

"Are you alright?" he asked, head tilted to the side.

"I'm only tired," I assured him.

"Hm. If you say so..." his features lifted and dropped, showing disappointment.

I stepped forward, closing the distance between us and placing my hands on his shoulders. "Come by later," I offered, "We can talk then."

He smirked, "Alright. I'll leave you be. See you tonight."

The vampire stepped out from under my palms, giving a small nod before strolling to the lift that had brought me to the basement. I tore my gaze from him as he waited on the machine and began on my own trek past the receptionist. On the way, I looked down at the key in my hand.

Printed on it was the marker K14. I quickly came to a closed door in the middle of that corridor which opened with the presentation of the plastic. I journeyed deeper into a broader hall with small rooms along either wall, hidden on the other side of more door panels. Outside some were armed human guards. This denoted what cells were in use.

I strolled casually to the one with the same number as on my key. There was a young man standing outside who must have been new. Not just because I didn't recognize him, but due to the way he fumbled trying to take the item from my outstretched fingers. He managed to slide the key into a device beside the door he guarded, though no matter how desperately he tried to hide his nerves, I could almost smell the apprehension. I had been trying to remain reserved so not to upset the poor thing, yet as he moved to the side, I accidentally let him see me shake my head.

Ignoring my faux pas, I stepped forward through the space now cleared at his side. Beyond was a sight I knew well; we of the vampire race all did. It was a room just large enough not to be described as cramped and it was bare, save for the presence of a single person sitting in the center of the floor, facing the opposite direction.

The human was dressed in a plain white robe, their hands and feet bound, which made for a more rapid process. I waited for the entrance to this cell to shut again before lowering my eyes to the man sitting there. Or at least I thought xe was a man. I couldn't really tell for the formlessness of the attire. The voice, when the person spoke, didn't settle this either. Not that it really mattered, I supposed.

"I don't deserve this," xe said softly, not turning to look at me.

My feet took me in a semicircle around the human, eyes staying on them. Once I was in front, I knelt, "This isn't my fault either."

The human must have sensed some sort of warmth in my reply, for xe looked up to me then with rich brown eyes that matched their skin, "What's your name?"

I cocked my head curiously. Normally I didn't entertain conversation with those I was directed to kill. I had never seen the point in putting off the inevitable. Nonetheless, for some reason I answered, "Sulru. Why?"

"You don't seem like a beast to me," their vision squinted with the statement.

I gathered from the inflection that xe hadn't much experience with vampires. Xe did appear quite young. "Thanks, I guess," I said flatly.

Xe chuckled, then sighed, "I won't bore you any longer, Sulru."

I lifted my chin and gazed upward at the camera in the top center of the cell's door. The room had fallen silent as I looked back at the human. What could xe have possibly done to warrant this demise? I would likely never find out. Instead of worrying on it, I crept to them, gently grabbing their hair and tugging it to the side and back so that the neck was exposed to me.

Their inhale echoed in the tiny chamber. It didn't matter how careful I was, this was going to be painful so all I could do for them was get through it as fast as I could. I threw my jaws apart and rushed to sink my teeth into the soft flesh before me. The person let loose a pitiful scream as my fangs extended past the usual length they appeared. Xe struggled against the restraints, remaining unable to move far from their original position due to the bonds' connection to a rod and link in the floor there.

I had to alter my normal method in order to keep from hurting my gums where the Earth doctor had extracted my damaged teeth, however it still was a might painful. As I removed my fangs slightly to begin sucking in the blood, I felt a drop of moisture hit my cheek. Rolling my eyes to the side, I realized that it had been a tear falling from the human.

They were watching me, trying not to fight, but the intensity of the situation made that impossible. If I could have, I would have killed them more mercifully. Unfortunately it was the beating heart that made the plasma flow steadily. All I could do was hold tightly and continue to drink.

When the stream started to slow, so did their body weaken and fall nearly limp in my arms. Xe was still alive, yet wouldn't be for long. I pulled my teeth back into my gums and removed my maws from their throat. Doing so left behind multiple, deep puncture wounds, though only a small bit of crimson trickled as I studied the injury. Practice had made me quite capable of properly hitting the correct arteries necessary for murdering in this fashion.

The vital muscle whose pumping kept the body alive soon stopped pulsing and the undeserving human was dead. I placed their corpse on the ground beside me and then rose to my feet, wiping my face with a black sleeve prior to departing without placing any further attention on the scene. The guard on the other side of the door shakily handed the keycard from earlier back to me. This time I had been able to ignore his rookie demeanor.

My day was far from over. Malook wanted me to return to his home to retrieve John and bring him to the office so he could inform him of what the two of us discussed, as well as set him in his intended work. In the meantime, I'd return once again to keep an eye on Connie and Riven. S

oare-a, as always, remained up in the air as to if she'd stay in my company or go about on her own. My boss made it clear when I began working that my first priority, when not accompanying him, was to care for Riven. He had said that his wife was very independent and she would likely decide to not invoke my aid. Now that the Earthlings were in the picture, I had them to focus on in addition to Malook's son.

It didn't take much time to leave the department and gather John. I had to assure him how rapidly I would be back to protect her in order to ease his expressed discomfort at leaving her alone. He reluctantly agreed, giving the woman a kiss and a hug and then coming along with me. The return drive was quiet despite how I could feel his anticipation. I gave him props for not showing it though.

It wasn't an often occurrence that I took the lead while working with humans, but since John had not yet been processed, he was without access to the office building. So I was the one to guide him through the halls. Malook was setting into place an identity for the new Galdelierian, which would include allowance for him to be within the building as long as family was employed there.

He would also need ID in order to use any scanners anywhere on the planet, even at home. This system was required by law and production of any program that did not work under this database was considered an act of treason. Once outside the door to my boss' area, I had my palm read and the door there instantly slid open, meaning he had been waiting for us.

The device worked in a matter that eradicated the need for a secretary to alert the person called upon to any visitors.A scan told them personally who was outside and if they were whitelisted, then they would be let in automatically. Otherwise, they'd be given the signal to wait until the person they sought audience with was ready for them, or in some cases, that their request was denied at present.

"John, Sulru," Malook greeted from behind his desk as we entered.

"Malook," John replied in the same plain manner.

"John," the General put his eyes on the man, "Can you wait outside? There's a matter that requires our attention first."

"Of course," the Earthling nodded, politely turning and going back out the entry still open behind us.

Likewise, I twisted to command the door closed as he exited, prior to replacing my focus on Malook, crossing my arms and waiting for him to explain what he needed. The dark-skinned man stood from his desk and walked around to my side, where he leaned against the sturdy frame, resting each hand on either side of him.

"Sulru," he started, gaze downward at first as if he were gathering strength, then put fierce green orbs on my own of equal caliber, "I've talked to an old friend. I-I've gotten them to agree to keep an eye out for Teylof at the academy."

I took an unintentionally menacing step toward him, "Is she-"

"No, they haven't picked her up yet," he interrupted.

"When?" I breathed.

"Tomorrow."

I took in a deep breath and nodded.

"I'll be able to talk to her on occasion as well," he continued and I could tell he really didn't want to be having this conversation.

I glanced away from him and shifted my weight between suddenly aching feet, "Thank you, my friend," I put steady sights onto him with the words and dropped my arms from my chest.

He lifted himself from his spot to take a couple of paces so that he and I were almost touching. Raising his hands, he put one on each of my shoulders as he gazed into me. Obviously, his desire was to embrace and comfort me. At the same time, he knew how fragile the situation was and didn't want to chance angering me.

Neither of us spoke more specifically due to the fact that even in these confines, there were audio recorders, should ever an incident occur. Many places had visual as well, though the General was fortunate not to be monitored this closely. So I could have allowed a hug, but I was not in the mood to have the human comfort me in such a manner.

When I didn't react other than to stare at him, he blinked and ducked his head a bit before returning to his seat, "I'll be done early today, so make sure my son is not out for long," he instructed, lifting a knowing eyebrow. The order was not actually that, but rather telling me he'd be certain I'd have time with my daughter that evening.

"Sir," I confirmed, spinning around and leaving him once more.

Chapter 38: John

Whatever detail they had been attending to didn't take long. Sulru walked out of the office only minutes later with a stern glance my way, which I took to mean 'go ahead.' When I was back inside with Malook, he clicked something to his side that apparently closed the office shut after me. I found it a bit unusual that there was no decoration, no photographs, not even a window in the little room. Then again, the alien planet, however like ours, still had many differences.

"Sit down, John," he commanded casually, not looking up from his spot.

I traipsed awkwardly over. I hadn't seen a chair during my first time in, neither did I see one then. This hidden furniture deal was widely used, it seemed. I stopped in front of his desk and tapped the floor with my foot. A contraption similar to that on the ship appeared and constructed itself. It was larger though and sitting, I found it to be more comfortable.

The other man had put eyes on me and wore a grin with how easily I had become acquainted to these new things, "I have some forms for you to go over so you can begin work."

I said nothing as he touched the side of a screen that was angled in front of him. The action caused a second monitor to produce behind it- this one facing me. I then studied the information displayed upon it. I had taken some time at Malook's home to better adjust to reading the alien symbols, so I hadn't found it too difficult to understand what I was seeing.

Mostly, it was a lot of details about me. Descriptors, past positions, addresses... There was even something regarding my recent termination. After I'd taken in everything there, I rested my vision on him. He seemed to have been watching me for a while, yet it wasn't until I acknowledged him that he slid a tablet-like device along the table in my direction. Glancing over, I saw a message scribbled there.

"Tap to erase, then place your hand, palm flat on screen. Don't speak."

I did as it instructed. The device lit up in response to my touch. Malook reached out with his own then, so I removed my hand, using it to push the tablet back. He took it and connected it to the machine with my information. Vision returned to the form, I saw that new data had been placed. It read oddly, but it was no doubt my new ID. Shifting my gaze to the General, he motioned for me to sit in front of the screen and look at it. Another subtle change and a new visual: my photograph.

He handed the tablet to me again and there was a new message. I swear I hadn't seen him write anything, *"I need to speak with you. I trust you the utmost secrecy."*

I handed the device back to actually see him use a stylus to make more notes this time before it was slid to my side again, *"There is an uprising coming. We wish for many changes. Can I count you as our ally?"*

Scrunching my face, I gave him an odd look, then shook my head and tapped on the screen. The words disappeared as I set the stylus on it and wrote, *"Not that I disagree with your cause, but it seems a pointless question,"* and sent it his way.

Reading it, the man shrugged his shoulders, scribbled, and returne, *"I felt you needed to be aware without forcing your loyalty. Sulru, you can trust. Assume everyone else will be against you...even my wife. You will be working with two men in our order. Do not share even with them who you really are."*

I looked up and confirmed compliance, handing the tablet over to receive one last message. Instead of giving the little computer to me this time, he only held it in the air between us for me to read, *"We hope for many changes that I have no doubt you and Connie will support. More details will come. We should hurry."*

I gave an obvious nod and he instantly dropped the tablet, erasing what he had said, and then removed from its side another piece that looked like a microchip, which he promptly crushed in his fingers several times before rotating his chair to place the dust inside what must have been some sort of trash receptacle.

"I just need you to switch to that next page, place your hand, and sign," he kept on aloud about the paperwork originally brought up.

I swiped the screen and wrote the alteration of my name that I had been given back on the ship, *Jun,* and let the computer scan my print. Malook made a few flicks and passes on his own screen and the files in front of me disappeared. He then took several minutes to read a handful of pages that did not display on my end. I waited patiently until finally, he sighed and stood from his position.

"Come along," he said, gaining a friendly expression, "It's midday. We can go to meal together before your new coworkers show you about."

I smiled as well, figuring that he could tell me a few more things there to help me act as naturally as possible before starting my career. I was a bit unsettled at how fast everything was moving, but I was also skilled with handling change so it wasn't a huge worry.

The building, I had surmised from pieces of dialogue, its appearance, and Malook's part within, was for offices and other such data storage and deskwork. It definitely had the feel of the typical pencil pusher stations back home. It was, however, more clinical as it all had the exact colors and layout everywhere we went. Just like the General's office, no sort of decor or variations were about to give the mind something to focus on.

We had only passed a few others, who all appeared human, by the time we arrived at what I could only describe as an intimate sort of cafeteria. There was a long counter at front with employees bringing forth dishes and laying them down while people on the other side picked them up and walked off to booths in the larger part of the area that resembled synthetic caves.

Malook did just as the others and I copied him. It was curious to me that there was nothing friendly about the atmosphere even on break. Nobody acknowledged each other, even the General who, as it was explained to me, was above everyone here.

"What's on your mind, John?" the man asked once we were both seated.

I hesitated, unsure if we were still being recorded. The man had apparently predicted this concern, "It's alright to speak vaguely," he said, poking at a diced orange food on his plate. I had only briefly glanced at our meals, but I had noted there were small portions of colorful items. "But with discretion," he added, "No need for monitors outside of business quarters doesn't mean no one is listening."

"The atmosphere is strange," I stated, tilting my head to study the food before me. *Ugh.* A good portion of it, judging by the hues, were fruits and veggies. Then there was another item that appeared to have been scooped onto the plate, although instead of a circular mush, it was square in shape, "I've also noticed that your attire doesn't set you apart from the others."

"Such a thing is unnecessary," he shrugged, "Those who need to know who I am, know what I look like. My authority lies in ordering Commanders who will deal with anyone else below who may not recognize me. Otherwise, I have no greater power than an average citizen rather than, perhaps, influence among certain groups."

"I see," I murmured, picking up a utensil that was similar in looks to a butter knife. Examining what was laid before me, I saw nothing else more helpful such as a fork or even another knife to use the two like chopsticks.

"The command is under your thumb," Malook informed, acknowledging my struggle.

Curling my fingers away from the device, I saw there was indeed a small indention which I had already learned indicated a sort of button on the alien technology. I assumed it would shift the flat stick in my hand into something more useful, but still, I glanced over at my companion to see if I could witness it in action prior to using it.

Following my eyes, Malook obliged this silent wish and put his...whatever the hell they called it, close to the dish on his plate that I hadn't been able to identify. Pressing the contraption, two small beams of light came off either side of the tip, circling so rapidly that my mind barely kept up with the process. Immediately after, a spike hardly larger than a toothpick poked out of the space between where the lasers had been and stabbed the brownish food that was firmer than I had anticipated.

I repeated the action on my own, "What is this?"

"It's a common dish here called talu. More or less an exterior made of moist grains with various bits of meat inside. As far as atmosphere," he rapidly reverted to the last topic, "All things inside work environments, from conduct to aesthetics, are designed to increase productivity."

"Anything else I should know before I start working?" I asked, shoveling a bite of the odd-looking rice and a small piece of something of a darker, more maroon color into my mouth.

The outside did taste more or less like brown rice, while I could taste a hint of blood in the flesh which was surprisingly savory, much as a proper slice of venison. The strangest part was that I couldn't place any sort of oils or grease in the meal, something that was highly uncommon for most lunch foods, and certainly cafeteria plates, on my planet.

"Not really," he replied, gazing up to me before something beyond caught his eye, "Just keep on as you have been. You will be at a post different from your previous. Ask what questions you need about the job. I trust you'll realize what cultural misunderstandings you must skim over."

He motioned with his chin so I followed his focus to a woman fast approaching from where we had come. She was closer in color to me and fairly short. Her head was entirely shaved with black markings on the skin there. Tattoos, maybe.

According to Malook, there were no races so they couldn't have been tribal markings. She wore a tighter type of tunic in a dark color that resembled a uniform. Stopping at our table, she gave the traditional greeting, aiming it at me, so I returned it.

Although Malook did not, he did start a new conversation with the woman, "John, this is Iitel. She will show you around this afternoon and bring you home after. You will start work with her and Zofra tomorrow."

"I may be early," she said, "But we are ready whenever you are, John."

She had large blue eyes that were set inside a shadowy brow. It was an odd combination of features to come off as exotic as they did. Just like any good officer though, it was obvious her concern was not on her beauty.

"I'm actually good," I glanced at the General who gave a slight acknowledgment, "Not very hungry."

"I will see you this evening then," Malook watched me as I stood, flicking fingers casually in the direction of my plate and shifting his eyes to the counter.

I grabbed the plate and walked away. Iitel went with me as I replaced the food in its original spot. An employee immediately took it, taking me slightly off guard, but the woman I was meant to travel with kept on without pause. I had to make a few quick strides to catch up with her as we entered the hallway, traveling silently to the elevator and downward.

The quiet felt somewhat stiff, like she wanted to talk, but was instead keeping to formality. I, too, wished for a release from the odd sense in the air. To initiate a friendship with my new coworker did not appear to be something forbidden. At the very least, I had managed to decipher the dates on my file and a short lie certainly would not complicate matters, while having the potential for betterment.

"I appreciate your patience. It's been a little while since I've been in commission," I spoke with a reserved tone, my stance within the lift matching.

The woman turned to me and smiled, "Of course. Our General is an upstanding person and he has spoken highly of you and your wife."

"The General is more than kind," I returned, "He's opened his home up to us without hesitation during a dark time."

Iitel chuckled, "You speak eloquently, don't you John?"

I laughed, rotating my position to see her just as the elevator started to let us out at the garage, "Not usually."

The woman stepped out first, leading us out to one of the machines that was already hovering. Standing next to it was a man who stood a head taller than myself. His side was to us, arms behind him as he stared along the line of vehicles. I had assumed this was Zofra, though I didn't realize he was a vampire until we reached him. He shifted to place us in his sights, black eyes as cold as Sulru's.

Chapter 39: Connie

It seemed that as soon as Sulru had left with John, she had returned, and I couldn't tell if I was happy about it or not. I had started wandering around the house and had found what appeared to be a sort of library on the same floor as the bedroom we had been given. Except instead of paper bindings, it was all electronic.

There were lines of cases in likeness to thin CD albums, each with a different title, photo, and description on them. The only problem was my inability to figure out how they worked. They didn't seem to open nor were there buttons or anything that responded to touch. I nosed about and ended up discovering a handful of devices displayed on a small table next to a few chairs that appeared to be earbuds, except without any wires or other attachments.

When I couldn't decipher them either, I gave up and went downstairs where I ran into Soare-a, who had maintained a distasteful attitude. I didn't want to retreat to the bedroom since I had even less to keep my attention in the extremely plain resting quarters. Besides a bed that was a grand amount larger and more comfortable compared to those on the ship, there was a window, a table, and a chair. I had taken a few moments to study the interesting pictures on the walls, but staring at paintings wasn't going to be satisfactory for my busy mind.

Nonetheless, back on the first floor, it was as if I could feel Soare-a's aggravation of me growing every time I moved in the slightest, and I was afraid that speaking to her would only make it worse. Sulru's presence at first offered a way out of this predicament, then I remembered that she had a long established rocky relationship with the woman where it was possible that in my case, it was simply the novelty that Soare-a hadn't gotten used to.

John was so much better at diffusing awkward situations and reading people... I really wished he hadn't had to go off. The first thing the vampire did when she entered was look past where I stood oddly in the middle of the open room, and to the den where Soare-a sat watching a hologram.

"Is Riven still in bed?" she asked.

"Mm," was the only response the other woman offered, not even glancing from her 'movie.'

Sulru immediately put her gaze to me, "You look misplaced."

"What?" I asked with a quizzical expression rivaling her blank one. Part of me was happy for the distraction while the other was still uneasy of all the tension in the air, "I guess I'm just kind of bored. I don't know what to do," I admitted.

"What would you normally be doing?" the vampire   mused.

"You mean back on Earth?" I clarified, "Well, I have

a job there. I work a lot...I don't really take much free time, to be honest."

The conversation had suddenly turned into an unintentional reminder of how isolated I had become in my life. It was a strange thing, considering both John and I had always been extroverted, but it seemed that the older we got, the less we worried with friendship. As well, neither one of us had family ties outside of my sole sister, who we may or may not hear from for months or more at a time.

At first, we blamed it on being that we preferred each other's company over anything else, so why bother? However, we had gotten to a point where our focus wasn't even directed on either of us and instead was on our individual thoughts and interests. I had pondered enough on the situation to conclude that things wouldn't be that way if we had been able to start our own family.

"I don't know how much use you are in the kitchen," Soare-a's voice cut through my thoughts as she decided to interject herself into the dialogue, "But we have a guest coming over for midmeal soon. You'll at least have some company then."

Her words were thick, making me feel less like she was offering assistance and moreover that she felt obligated to inform; perhaps alerting me so I was prepared not to embarrass her...or expose the reality. I remained hopeful that the statement was an awkward attempt to become familiar with me, even though I didn't like the idea that another person's presence would remove the informality with Sulru. A new person meant I'd have to be my alias instead of speaking freely.

Either way, I replied as best I could, "I look forward to meeting your friend, but I might be weird company for you until I become more acquainted with Galdelier."

Soare-a, head turned in my direction and partially resting on the back of the couch she sat on, laughed, "It's really not as difficult as you're making it seem. Just don't refer to your planet, really. You know enough about our customs and society. And in any matter, you've already met him."

My ears perked hearing this last tidbit. I'd met him? Was she talking about the guy that was there when we landed on the planet for the first time? I guess it was a meeting, even if nothing was said. I had almost blown it with my stupid handshake too. *Shit.* Seeing him while remembering this blunder was only going to make me overly anxious. Sulru crossed her arms and glared at the woman on the couch. I expected her to open her mouth and clarify the situation somehow, yet she did nothing, so I decided to say something myself.

"You mean the man on the landing platform?" I asked.

"His name is Cartef. I don't suppose you caught that," her reply was snippy.

"No, I- uh, no, I didn't," I stammered as I looked back at the silently perturbed vampire.

I had, however, caught what this guy said about Riven's liking of Sulru, a beyond demeaning

404

statement. I had honestly hoped that the prejudice wouldn't be as obvious as we'd been told, but that short exchange crushed such hope. On the other hand, Sulru's clearly angsty display now made me wonder if maybe his blatant insults were out of the norm. Otherwise, she'd have remained calm if it was typical, right?

"I hope you understand that I will be present, as per Malook's command," our guard said in a low monotone. Her arms falling to her sides as she spoke.

The woman on the couch shot her own glare, lips pursed when she finally decided to stand and stroll over, a short laugh in my direction, "They're not giving you enough credit, my dear," she cooed, "You'll be perfectly fine."

She placed a hand on my shoulder as she smiled directly at me. Somehow it was far more discomforting when she played nice. Her words were thick like they were letting it be known she had a hidden meaning without revealing what said meaning was. She *was* right about me being able to handle myself though, which urged me to simply agree. If it weren't for Sulru's antagonizing demeanor acting as a reminder that something might be off, I probably would have gone along with what Soare-a said too.

"I'd actually feel better with her around anyway," I admitted. More than wanting to prove my capability, I didn't want to mess things up. If Malook thought it best, then it no doubt was the safest route regardless.

Soare-a removed her hand from my shoulder and gave the vampire a grim glance with a short breath before directing herself to me again, "It's not like Cartef is going to demand anything of you. He's quite the gentleman."

"Indeed," Sulru scoffed, the word completely eradicating any kindness left in the other woman.

"You have no right to-" the human started in on the vampire, having completely removed any focus on me. However, she was interrupted by a small electronic sound. "Wave him in," she growled at our guard, who was still standing in front of the home's entrance.

It surprised me when instead of ignoring or arguing, she obeyed the order with a raised claw to the panel next to the door, causing its lights to brighten and slide the passage open to reveal the man we'd been discussing. He was dressed in the usual tunic, though his seemed more form fitted and had a sort of yellow belt alongside.

The suit itself was a navy blue and had a few notches down the chest that I was unable to determine if they served a purpose or were just for decoration. They were somewhat reminiscent of the stripes on Earth military personnel. The vampire instantly moved to the side to allow him to pass, but she kept a stiff pose and eyes heavy upon him as he entered, taking no notice of her whatsoever.

"Good morning, my lady," the officer greeted Soare-a sweetly while striding toward her to five a tight hug and a kiss on the cheek.

From how the culture had been taught to me, along with the brief dealings we'd had with the public ourselves, I didn't expect such an intimate greeting between the two, even in the almost private encounter. The people's rigid formality seemed like it would have overridden such an embrace between friends unless...

"Ka'ney!" the man had let go of Malook's wife and was grinning at me.

I opened my mouth to say 'hello,' half-expecting him to come toward me and offer the same greeting he had given the other woman. I was thankful when he didn't. His gaze upon me, however, was steeling and kept any sound from coming, leaving me awkwardly parting my lips and closing them again as I smiled back. I caught sight of Sulru standing a bit behind him, her hand lifting and making a circular gesture as if to say 'go on.'

"It's nice to see you again," I managed, "Our first meeting was rather short."

"Quite right," he replied, "Perhaps this time we can actually get to know each other a little."

I tried to keep my vision still, yet my eyes kept darting over to Sulru in case she was to give me any more cues. Cartef quickly caught on, acknowledging it by letting his grin fall and addressing the vampire himself, "Don't you have somewhere to be?"

"I do," she responded flatly, "I'm there already."

The man muffled a growl and strolled further in, making his way to the kitchen with Soare-a following closely behind as she shook her head angrily. The seemingly adamant attitude both she and Cartef had regarding the vampire's presence was not helping my unease at all, but it did firmly back my feeling that there was some hidden intent or desires.

The hug and kiss steered me in direction of it being an affair. Sulru was clearly close to Malook, so maybe they wanted her gone in order to free them from having to act a certain way. Although, I'd still be around and they weren't doing anything to discourage my presence. Then again, why would he trust me over his own wife and assistant who he had known for far longer?

I nervously went after the couple, but only made it two paces before I felt a cold hand and soft pricks on my upper arm. Twisting abruptly toward the sensation, I saw that Sulru had taken hold of me. I stopped, eyes leaving her grip and finding her face. Her vision was still upon the other two while she spoke under her breath, "You are not required to stay here, but I am required to go with you if you leave."

After that last word left her lips, she released me and returned to her sentinel stance a foot or two away. I wasn't sure how to respond because I didn't know exactly what her point was. It took a few moments of contemplation for my mind to find her reason. I looked from the vampire to the kitchen where Cartef had taken a position leaning forward onto the island, and Soare-a was gathering items from the shelf-containers.

The man, smiling, set eyes on me, saying nothing. He only watched and waited for me to react. I swallowed hard and strolled into the other room with them, trying to see Sulru out of the corner of my eye. I couldn't, however, and didn't want my attempt to be blatant so I simply continued on my way until I stood at the counter opposite Cartef.

"Is there anything I can help with?"

"No," Soare-a sighed, setting several pieces of produce down next to me, "I don't think you've gotten to know your way around my home yet. Maybe in a minute," her explanation seemed to outline the fact that I was an outsider, not a true part of the family and unwanted.

"Well, actually, I asked because I was thinking I'd rather go out and have some time alone," I mumbled, quickly adding with an intentional glance backward at Sulru, "Mostly alone, I guess."

Soare-a immediately rose from where she had been crouched beside one of the larger containers near the floor, and put an odd glare on me, "Don't be rude, Connie. Our company just got here."

My heart skipped and palms began to sweat as my eyes shifted nervously from her to Cartef and then repeated the cycle, "I-uh... I didn't mean to be rude..."

"Ah, don't be so hard on her," the man spoke in what sounded to be a genuinely compassionate voice, "She's had a lot to deal with." He turned away from Malook's wife, "But I assure you, I'm not difficult to get along with. I might even be able to lift your spirits, huh?" he added with a wink.

I chuckled awkwardly, "Maybe."

"Sulru," the other woman chimed in, transparent kindness returning, "Go get Riven for me."

I spun softly, placing my gaze on the guard and almost shaking with the thought of her leaving. She hesitated. Even in her stoic, pitch black eyes, I could tell there was a message for me. However, after a moment of inaction on my part, she slowly turned toward the lift and started the trek upstairs.

I am required to go with you if you leave.

"I just," I didn't bother to force calmness, "I can't do this right now!" I cried, throwing hands up to my face and almost running from the area, to the door that I fumbled with re-opening, before jumping into the garage.

Only when I was out of sight, did I slow down and begin to take in my surroundings. Outside of the style of the buildings and how clean and ordered everything seemed, the place didn't appear very alien. It could have been due to the fact that the only plant-life around me was the grass that was nigh identical to what I was used to.

"Subtle," Sulru's inexpressive voice startled me.

I briefly tilted my head to see her behind, instead keeping my eyes focused on the neighborhood. There didn't seem to be many cars or 'rovers' as everyone had been calling them. I spotted one in the distance, but other than that, the roads stayed quiet.

Initially, this struck me as strange since it was the middle of the day. Then I was reminded that Galdelier was of stringent structure compared to Earth. A greater majority of the citizens likely had the same routine. Even if employees came home for lunch, er- midmeal, they'd all have done so at the exact time and movement would have already ceased.

"I panicked, ok?" I finally twisted around to look at the vampire who was staring blankly at me. "What the hell is going on?"

"Other than you freaking out?" Sulru's voice was the same, but an eyebrow raised.

I paused and took a couple of breaths before speaking more quietly and calmly, "I just felt like something else was going on. Like something besides my nerves," another short pause, "Why don't you like that guy?"

The woman blinked, keeping her stance, seemingly unsure of answering, "I find him untrustworthy. He and Soare-a get along too well."

"Oh," I said under my breath, "So they *are* having an affair..."

"What?" her tone lilted with its first hint of inflection for the day.

"Soare-a is cheating on Malook with Cartef is what I meant," I clarified.

The vampire's forehead cringed momentarily and then her expression was soft again as she emitted a thoughtful noise from behind closed lips, making me realize that it hadn't been what she meant at all, "I wouldn't be surprised," she murmured.

"But I don't understand why they were so eager to have me there," I continued. "At least it felt they were."

"No," she agreed, "I thought so as well. Soare-a is not kind. I wouldn't put it past her to wish to make you uncomfortable for the simple fact that she doesn't care for you."

"Yeah, I didn't think she liked me very much," I sighed, "Malook said otherwise though."

"That's because he *is* kind," the General's friend pointed.

"You two are really close, aren't you?" I observed absentmindedly.

The question seemed to catch the vampire off guard. She hesitated with responding and shifted on her feet, "Yes, we've worked together for quite some time."

Her dull, reserved voice settled out into an almost warm hum as she replied. I knew I wasn't the quickest to pick up certain cues in social situations. I most certainly was no good in psychology or reading people. Nonetheless, I did have one skill within those realms: romantic relationships. Maybe it was something to do with the way my brain was wired as a stereotypical western culture Earth woman or maybe I had a bit of a romanticized mindset myself, but I always did tend to be right about these matters.

The thing with Cartef and Soare-a was a definite possibility. Studying Sulru now and remembering everything about her interaction with Malook that I had witnessed thus far, made the chance that they were more than coworkers or friends even greater. He had been adamant on calling her family from the beginning. In this society, such a relationship was surely forbidden. It did make me wonder if a couple like that could produce offspring. I mean, surely there was a vampire and human at some point who had sex with each other.

"You still want to see those horses?" Sulru's words interrupted the silence and my thoughts, "I'm assuming you don't just want to stand outside and wait for him to leave."

"Oh. Um, no," I chuckled, "I'd love to see the horses."

Chapter 40: Sulru

"I didn't realize Malook had family. Well, at least any that still talked to him," Zofra mused from his position across from Kivela over a small table in our den.

He had come over immediately after I had been relieved of my duties. Although she didn't get to see one of the horses, Connie did seem to greatly enjoy the time at the farm, meeting the assortment of creatures. Most of them, she said weren't very 'alien' looking, but there were a few that piqued her interest.

She had described the farm as a 'petting zoo,' which apparently is a collection of small, generally docile animals. I was surprised and a bit disheartened to find Malook and John were already done at the office by the time I returned with Connie. Zofra and Iitel had accompanied them and from there, so had Zofra accompanied me home, where we had been spending time with my daughter and her grandfather.

"Yes, neither did I," my father-in-law agreed, "Quite odd-timing for you to pick them up, as well. After the trip and all."

"I suppose so," I sighed, walking closer and leaning over the table to hand Teylof the ofpa I had prepared for her.

The girl straightened up in the seat between the two men and took the ware from me, offering a slight bow of the head as thanks before sinking her growing fangs into it. Ofpas were developed specifically for vampire young. They were much like cups though wider like a bowl.

Blood collected for feeding was placed inside and warmed. Then a thick, malleable top was placed tightly around its opening to simulate skin for the child to pierce and drink from, just as they would once they started to feed on live prey.

Many vampiric children, as they grew, became resistant to using them, viewing them as babyish and unnatural. Both of which were true. Nonetheless, it was how things worked. My daughter was no exception to this. She was doomed to inheriting stubbornness, having both myself and Lotac as parents. The girl had once become ill for refusing to eat and unfortunately, I was not aware until after she had let the blood stay out and stagnate.

I had to petition for an emergency serving and thankfully was awarded it with Malook's influence on my side. I had known of those in similar situations being denied because the child didn't meet the requirements for severity until days before the next scheduled feeding. Vampires were already meant to function on strict feeding times that kept several used to a constant pang of hunger since many factors were not taken into account. The entire construct was extremely ill-compassionate.

This evening was different, however. There was no tension about her drinking the meal. She didn't fight or pout, or complain that I was hovering to be sure she didn't neglect the nourishment either. Regardless of the fact that no time spent with my daughter was unpleasant, I wanted this evening to be as stress-free as possible.

Therefore, I had begun it by informing her that she would be sent to academy the next day. I had already told this to Zofra on our ride to the residence. I was certain he would take it as reason to place further attention on me, though he had enough decorum to place none of it upon me now, instead allowing my full focus to be on Teylof.

I watched as she suddenly stopped drinking, lowering her cup and awkwardly thumbing it, "Mama, will I get to say goodbye to Riven?"

Her inquiry gave me pause. The day had happened so quickly that this detail had honestly not occurred to me. The boy was a bit younger than her and definitely not as mature...or should I say as knowledgeable about the real world.

While Malook taught his son kindness and respect, he often neglected to expose him to any bitter truths. I didn't know if Riven even knew about vampire academies and that he was likely never to see his friend again. Not that they were often together as it was.

"I don't know," I reluctantly admitted, "I wouldn't count on it. I can try to contact Malook, but-"

"It's ok," the girl interrupted, looking up and offering a smile, "He's already put himself out there for us. I understand that."

I beamed proudly, making a mental note that I would contact him anyway, "Ok, sweetheart."

"What do you make of them, Sulru?" Kivela hummed after a silent moment assured that his granddaughter had nothing more to say at the moment.

"They seem to be decent people," I answered plainly as I took a seat across from Teylof, completing the circle.

"Iitel and I got the same sense about John," Zofra agreed, "He appears to be mostly unprejudiced, wouldn't you say?"

"Hm. I believe his only apprehension towards us is due to his own physical weakness and not for any feeling that vampires are less than him," I answered as best I could without revealing that I knew he wasn't prejudice, just in his world, he wasn't used to handling a creature of equal intelligence, but greater strength.

As well that his first experience with such a being was far from positive. Despite completely trusting both Kivela and Zofra. I remained aware that it was in everyone's best interest that the secret about our visit to Earth stay so for as long as was possible. Not just for the safety of the involved, but others too. "You'll find that his wife does not share this wariness; sometimes even to a dangerous degree, as I understand."

"I spoke to Saelok," Kivela informed, "He told me of a discussion with Otahn concerning this John after meeting with Malook. It is his intent to bring his cousin's spouse into things."

"I'm aware," my mind was hardly on the conversation. Instead I had been focusing on my daughter, who was clearly enthralled with being included in the adult affair despite keeping to silently sucking on her ofpa, bright black eyes darting between the three of us. Each time her eyes caught mine, she would give a quick half smile and look away. "Any other word from Saelok?"

"He says Otahn is considering a move," Kivela answered, breaking the pyramid his hands had been forming beneath his chin, simultaneously leaning backward and raising an eyebrow at me to his left.

This thought brought my attention and I took sight from my daughter and placed it on the old man, "Is that so? In what way?"

"I'm unsure, but it would be discussed with Malook after tomorrow's festivities," Kivela continued.

"Ugh. I had almost forgotten about that," I groaned.

Zofra laughed, "Don't worry about it so much," he rested a gentle claw onto my knee, "I will be there too."

I slowly rolled my eyes over to him, being careful to keep any reaction reserved. I wished I knew whether he was sincere or trying to put his foot in the door, so to speak. I felt maybe it was both, yet my mind seemed easily swayed to believe he was simply trying to win me over. I was absolutely certain of his romantic interest in me.

Even thus, I kept my response in the middle ground, not showing affection while also remaining friendly, "It's not even Temir himself. The man is quite politely formal. It's knowing that his sister, Soare-a and the rest of those shallow-minded prisses are going to be there."

"Humans are entirely too self-absorbed," Zofra nodded.

Where he was right, I took an offense to the generalization. I shifted my legs, causing him to retreat his hand, "It's not just the humans. I'm tired of vampires being content as drones or just outright despising humanity altogether when there are good humans too."

Before my friend could recover from the slip up, which he clearly understood he committed by the look on his face, my father-in-law stepped in, "Much like your boss, hm?"

My gaze instantly grew threatening. He was privy to the relationship that Malook and I shared, and it wasn't for my own admission either. He was one of those wise elderly types who read the smallest signs that the average person would not even realize were there. I knew, though, that this information stayed with him.

Undaunted by my frustration aimed upon him, he continued, "I believe the largest problem with the humans isn't hate or selfishness, but ignorance."

Zofra and I settled back into our seats and waited for his impending monologue. Teylof likewise put down her ofpa and respectfully placed full attention on her grandfather.

"Our rulers have mandated a system of laws and culture over the past centuries that feed into the superiority of humans over vampires. In this pursuit, very little about vampires is actually discussed, other than the prevailing ideals that the Alhverseir family wishes to be accepted. Those would be primarily that we are dangerous, without concern for human life and that we need to be controlled.

"This all, of course, is to aid in their own control of the people. Anyone who has fought the system in the past was done away with as a lunatic and a criminal. So that today, questioning society is not something normally thought of. I wouldn't find it surprising if at this point in time that even Empress Naiker and Emperor Inton were ignorant, having been drawn into the constructs set forth by their ancestors and kept by their people.

"Why worry with changing something or learning more when there are no prevalent problems with how things currently run? This can be said of vampires as well. The misunderstandings of our kind, in place originally by humans, is what created the hatred of their kind. Vampires do not always see that these people are simply ignorant and actually are not spiteful by nature."

"Our collection has certainly shown that some have learned past, or are at least willing to learn past, the prejudices ingrained within our peoples over the years," I mused, "I'd say it's a step in the right direction."

"Perhaps," the younger man chimed in, gently scratching his jaw line with two points extended from a claw, "Though I still wonder how much these humans are on our side for our brute strength or for need to keep loyalties with those of us pre-partnered with them."

My eyes rested on Zofra as I allowed the full meaning of those words to settle into my brain, "Are you suggesting that Malook only agrees with helping our people so that I wont turn him in for looking to overthrow our government?"

The man dropped his claw and gazed intently upon me, seemingly more confident this time in his criticism of humans, "Not Malook necessarily, but yes."

I contemplated his suspicion for a few moments, staring at him the whole while. I couldn't say that the idea had never occurred to me. When I was initially approached, my first thought was that it was a trap to get rid of vampires, to show that we were the ones plotting, in order to have a valid reason to do away with us. Even since then, I've had my doubts upon meeting with the other humans involved, even Otahn himself, who had been the leader of it all.

However, logic steered me to the fact that if these humans were against us and wished to become greater powers, they would instead press for eradicating our species. With as rampant as prejudice against vampires was and how small a population we were, finally getting rid of our kind would seem a better way to rally support from the vast majority of Galdelier so as to further their own agenda.

In the end, I felt even if turning against us was an eventual goal, letting all of us know which humans were involved proved a fatal flaw in such a plan. Therefore, I did not see Zofra's suggestion as probable enough to worry about.

"I don't think Malook is like that," Teylof spoke up, her voice soft, but her will strong, "It wouldn't make sense after everything he's done for us and how he and Riven have always acted."

I saw Kivela's lips curl into a sweet grin out of the corner of my eye, "I don't think he is either, child. But your uncle's thought should be kept in our minds as a possibility, even if not with Malook, with others." The old vampire turned his eyes to me then, "It would be unwise to give any benefit of the doubt in such grave circumstances as this."

I inhaled sharply as I met his gaze. He was right. Everything should be considered until definitively proven or disproven. It was a dangerous situation as was. We needed to take all precaution, especially being part of the unloved minority in this world. I glanced from him to Teylof, and then rested my vision on the window behind Zofra. It was starting to get dark. If I was going to try to get in touch with Malook, I'd need to do so soon.

"Teylof, are you finished?" I asked, rising from my seat to loom over the company.

The girl nodded, taking hold of her drink and handing it out to me. I took the ofpa and strolled away from the group to the small storage area that typically served in place of a kitchen in vampiric households. There was a small dip on top of one of the cabinets where I opened the cup and swayed the two pieces, so that a stream of water spurted from the top of one side and washed the dish clean.

As I set the dismantled ware to rest when the water was off, I reached into a pocket on my leg and retrieved a small handheld. But before I could press in the order to contact Malook, I realized that I had a message. The device had been off to allow me to keep my full attention on my daughter so I hadn't heard any alerts.

It was from Malook: *CHT*.

I had gotten this code from him several times. He had apparently been more clear minded today than I had been. I looked at the time it had been sent. Not even half an hour ago. I quickly tapped in and sent my answer: *EN*.

His response was almost immediate: *HY*.

I ordered the screen off and replaced the device before returning to the den and looking at my daughter, "Let's go, Teylof. Malook sent a message for us to come over."

The girl's face brightened suddenly and she jumped from her chair, squeezing her way out of the circle and skipping behind Zofra and over to me. I couldn't help but to grin at her enthusiasm and the moment she saw I was, she lowered her smile and slowed her energy.

My stomach fell. I wanted to tell her it was okay to be excited and to show it, however the horrible truth was...it wasn't. Not for vampires. Instead I just sighed and put my arm around her shoulders to pull her into a side-hug before letting go again and leading the way outside.

"Would you like me to wait here or should I leave as well?" Zofra called after us.

I twisted my neck to see him, "Go home. I'd like to have some time alone with my daughter when we return."

The man nodded, "I will be absent then."

Teylof and I went downstairs in silence and loaded into the rover I had driven home. Malook and I had long ago decided on this shorthand code for handling meetings of a non-business nature. It wasn't illegal for us to meet up outside of work; it was just that neither of us wanted any extra trouble. This was especially true after we had allowed sexual and romantic encounters. The bit about our children being friends could definitely prove a headache as well. For him more than me.

Teylof knew the drill. She had to remain quiet and do nothing until I instructed her otherwise. Knowing not only how well she understood the gravity of these scenarios, but knowing how seriously she took them and how closely my order was followed, ensured me that she would do fine in academy on that account. Moreover, it was her kind nature and her spirit that worried me. I didn't know if they would survive what she would endure within those walls.

We made it to Malook's home easily where I parked in the normal space inside the garage. I quickly jumped out and swiped my hand across the command to lower the door and seal us from sight. In instant response, the home opened and my boss showed himself. He grinned at me and went back inside, motioning for us to come after. So I gave my daughter a silent instruction to be at ease.

Chapter 41: John

The day with my new teammates came to an abrupt end. Iitel turned out to be a very straight to the point, no nonsense type of person. After she showed me around and briefly acquainted me with my duties, she instantly snapped it all to a close with, 'Well, let's get you back to your family.'

It was the vampire, Zofra, that actually paused the woman to make sure I understood and see if I had questions. I didn't, but the awkward movement of my hand I gave in response drew attention to the injury I had sustained from the battle with Sulru. Upon seeing it, Iitel slowed herself long enough to inquire as to whether it would affect my work. Of course, I once again said no.

I honestly hadn't thought about the wound that had been seared shut since the day it had happened. I didn't know if there was something else...some sort of medication that was burned into it, but it had stopped hurting rather quickly, and seemed to be healing well. I pointed it out to Connie when I got back home. I guess this was home now...

She said it was probable, considering the strange method. Though it was also likely that a lot of the nerves were damaged and I just wasn't feeling it very well or at all in some places. Looking up from where I sat, I saw my wife still had her head stuck in the holographic book she had picked up once Malook had been able to show us his library.

Apparently, Galdelierian books came in dual format: audio and script. There were CD like devices that held the story and were activated by a separate piece, which either caused the book to emit displays of words or could be inserted into the ear for the novel to be narrated. What was really incredible was how a person could switch between reading and being read to at any point, and the device would know exactly where you had left off in the other format.

As I watched Connie lift a finger and tap the air beside the lights in her lap to 'turn the page,' I realized that I had no idea what was going on in the story I had *not* been listening to. It started out explained to be concerning a man who was fired from his position as some manner of officer on a false claim. He then decided to seek revenge on everyone he thought was involved. I think I got to the part where he was about to be fired when my mind had started to wander.

Malook's day had been short as well. When Zofra and Iitel took me back to him, he was readying to leave, so they escorted the both of us home. Neither Sulru nor my wife was around when we arrived. According to Soare-a, Connie had 'stormed out and the vampire followed her.' I didn't have too long for worrying fortunately, as the two women came in a handful of minutes afterward.

Soare-a had rolled her eyes on the sight of them and loudly traipsed to the lift, presumably up to her bed. I noticed that nobody in the room acted oddly about it either, except for Connie who shrunk into herself and averted her gaze. The rest seemed to take it as par for the course, although I wasn't sure if they were just silent, or silently judging...

I had given my wife a tight hug as she walked up to me with a breath of relief. Malook had made no notice of his own wife's behavior and instead instantly set attention upon his guard, asking her with a smile if the day had gone well. She answered positively while retaining her usual flat affect, her boss wasting no time in discharging her.

Zofra had then dismissed himself and joined her, and Iitel went on her own way after a short conversation with the rest of us humans. Once she was gone as well, Connie shared what had happened in our absence. Malook shared his anger about how Soare-a had invited Cartef over, saying that she knew he had specifically removed Connie from regular contact with others until things had become more stable.

Honestly, I found it inspiring how well his logic overrode his emotion. I would have instead been upset that my wife had invited a man into a private situation while I was not present or had known about it prior. When we parted ways with our host for the night, Connie told me she felt the same way, and moreover that she had a sneaking suspicion that Soare-a was having an affair with the man, which apparently, though Sulru hadn't confirmed, seemed inclined to believe it too.

Knowing that this all had transpired on the first day I was away from Connie had me a bundle of worry about leaving her again. I kept telling myself that she had handled the situation and that Malook would have words with Soare-a, yet still I couldn't help to remain anxious.

His wife didn't strike me as the kind of woman who would take heed to anything someone else had to say, especially considering her now obviously turbulent relationship with her husband. I wondered what effect all this would have upon her keeping our secret. I had thought I would become more settled with the passing of time. However, granted not much time had passed, nothing had calmed my nerves.

Connie glanced up from her book and caught sight of me, "Are you alright?" she asked with a frown.

"Tired."

She instantly knew I was lying. Leaning forward, she placed the small book onto the table between our chairs, "What's on your mind, John?"

"Just anxious, I suppose. I feel like everything is far too fragile," I admitted.

"Well," her lips curled, "We're doing all we can. Malook seems to know what he's doing. And if this rebellion is as big of a deal as it seems...we have that in our favor, right?"

"Hmph. Yeah, I guess. I just feel unsettled. There is no comfort zone right now. There's so much uncertainty," I tilted my head back on the chair and clutched my hands around its arms, then let them go and sighed before lifting my head again, "When it comes down to it, we are both nobodies here. Nothing. How am I supposed to keep you safe?"

The woman scoffed and picked herself up from her seat, inching in my direction. I stiffened when she slowly fell to her knees in front of me, crossing her arms on my lap and resting her head on top, deep brown eyes peering upward, "You worry too much."

I had known the woman long enough to also know what she was thinking. Even after nearly a decade, I still found her as sexy as hell. She constantly complained about her fat thighs and how they were disproportionate to her breasts because she had gained weight after leaving the military, but her body was perfect. I grinned at her and began stroking her mid-length locks of a color that matched her eyes perfectly.

Her comforting smile turned devious as she crept closer to my face, sliding her chest close between my legs and onto my torso, purposely grazing my groin with her fingertips as she did so. I noticed the subtle excited shift in her expression when she realized that these new, tighter forms of dress with their loose overlay, allowed for a better feel than my usual jeans or uniform slacks.

"I think we could both use a little relaxation," she whispered into my ear, letting her body lay on top of mine.

My nerves concerning our predicament tried to take the back burner with the sudden increase in hormones. However, it was still too much for me to be able to properly give her my focus or to enjoy anything sexual myself. Besides that, I wasn't sure if we would unintentionally commit some cultural insult by enjoying coitus in our host's home.

So instead, I bent my neck and kissed her forehead, "I'd like that, but-"

I was cut off by two fingers suddenly in my mouth and pressing down on my tongue, "Trust me," she smiled coyly before removing her fingers and returning to her feet.

I remained still and watched as she trailed her outline with her hands and then used a single finger to point at me before curling it in a silent order to come near. I followed the command and rose. She took my hand, passing a knowing glance my way, taking deliberate steps to show off the curves that I loved, as she led us around the furniture and into the hallway toward our room. I knew the floor was guest and private family rooms and not ours, but since we were the only ones who had been making use of it since our arrival, it was a nice feeling to have it to our own.

When we reached the bedroom's entrance, Connie let her grasp on me fall and hurried faster inside, calling behind her, "Close the door."

I once more obeyed, taking an extra precaution to make sure it was sealed before I turned around and found my way to the bed. The woman was standing on the opposite side of it, smirking. As soon as I laid my eyes on her, she pulled off her tunic and let it drop to the floor, exposing her small chest. I gazed at her naked top and slowly my vision found the outline of her hips, hugged perfectly by the tights she had worn beneath the other clothing.

The seductress eased herself onto the mattress that was of a material I had yet to know. Laying on her side, facing my way and with one hand propping up her head, she beckoned me near. I did as she wished, grinning when she used the the voice commands we had been taught to shut off the lights.

In the darkness, I found my way to the bed and pushed my body snugly next to hers. As she leaned in, wrapping her lips sensually around mine, I felt my worry fading in that moment of expected ecstasy. However, just when I placed a hand on her breast and hers found my groin, there was a knock at the door.

We both jumped, our hands retreating to more decent areas of the other's body. A small, muffled voice sounded after the noise, but it was too quiet to understand. Exhaling with returned concern, I ordered the lights on and gave my wife an apologetic shrug, her face expressing greater disappointment than my own.

Standing and strolling to the door, I glanced backward to make sure Connie was able to put on her tunic again. Only when I knew she was dressed, did I open the sliding mechanical entrance. I was met with Malook's excitable son and his adorable grin.

"Hey, whatchya need, Riven?" I asked.

"I wanted you to meet my friend," he grinned proudly, "She's downstairs. Dad said I could see if you wanted to."

As much as I hated to deny such a simple request from a kid, I probably would have in order to try and save the interrupted moment with the woman I loved. That is, if I weren't already so uncertain about the possible rude or lewdness of the act. In either case, Connie was standing behind me, eager to speak to the child herself. She loved kids. I stepped to the side as she pushed in.

"We'd love to meet your friend," she beamed, bending at the waist just barely to be closer to Riven's level, "What's their name?"

"Teylof," he answered, "She's Sulru's daughter."

That revelation was enough to peak genuine interest from both of us. Connie rose again, her mouth emitting a quite silent 'Ok' as the boy scurried off. The two of us exchanged curious glances while stepping into the hall and traveling to the lift after the boy.

The machine was barely large enough to fit the three of us and had me wondering if that many people were supposed to be on it at once. Nonetheless, Riven pressed the buttons to make it shut and slide down to the bottom story without hesitation. The boy hardly contained himself enough to not begin rushing out before the elevator was fully stopped.

He ran out of the box as soon as possible, heading through the largest room and to the smaller den on the other end. Connie and I sauntered casually after him, finding that he had taken a place on one of the couches next to a child easily a head and a half taller than him.

As we neared, the black-haired girl turned to face us, coal eyes and pale skin that matched the other vampires, though she wore a look somewhat more expressive than Sulru and Zofra. It felt as though she hadn't quite learned to hide her emotions like they did.

"Hi," my wife smiled, unaffected by the sight of the miniature vampire, "I'm Connie. This is my husband, John."

The girl nodded her head slightly, otherwise remaining motionless, "Teylof," was all she said.

"Connie and John are friends," Sulru's voice sounded suddenly from behind us.

I turned to the side to see both she and Malook had come upon us. I was about to survey the floor to see where they were when they showed themselves. Malook's face was pleasant, yet Sulru seemed to keep cold. I thought it was strange that she used such a demeanor around her daughter. Still, I tried not to judge it prematurely. My wife took no notice as she continued the meeting with a compliment usual of Earth.

"She looks just like you," she smiled at Sulru, who tilted her head, confused by the woman's words.

I put the nuance in my head's store, realizing that this casual statement was not a normal thing to say, since the vampire did not seem to know how to react to it. However, there wasn't time for Connie to pick up on it, or anything to be said as Riven was speaking again.

"Teylof's gotta start school tomorrow so she can get a job," through his innocent words, something in his tone changed when he shared the detail, leading me to believe it was a severe statement.

"And she will do well with it," Malook interjected with a strong beam at both his son and the little girl.

Teylof took the encouragement with a flicker of movement in lips that seemed to wish to mirror the man's smile. Instead she nodded, greeted by a more enthusiastic nod from her young friend. My vision caught my wife in its corner. She had become silent after realizing I had started reading into the subtle body language and shifts of the others.

She could tell I had picked up on something, yet, unsure of what it was, she decided it best to err on the side of caution. I felt that Malook would soon remove us in order to clarify the meanings hidden behind the random encounter...so I patiently waited.

Chapter 42: Connie

There hadn't been much time for rest since landing on Galdelier, like I had hoped. The second day, my first without John around, had even ended with a reminder from Soare-a that today was some important event.

She had come downstairs during Sulru's visit with her daughter. It was about the time that the vampire academy was being explained to us. I couldn't tell if she was unaware that the vampires had come by or not, but it was pretty obvious either way that she didn't like it. She had made a show of glaring over at the children in the den before facing us and answering her husband's inquiry as to 'what's wrong?'

Fortunately, the children hadn't seen her anger and kept with watching some kooky characters on the holograms. After Soare-a lifted an eyebrow and gave Malook the reminder, along with an order to act lively at said affair, she returned upstairs without waiting for a response. I was glad when she was gone; more so that the couple had yet to actually fight in front of us and less so with the thought that the next day would not be restful either.

Not only were all of us expected to show at this birthday celebration, an Earth term replaced by Galdelier as the person's new year, but since neither

John nor I had our own wardrobe, Soare-a was tasked with taking us shopping beforehand so that we may be presentable. At the very least, my husband had been present during the trip to the unreasonably large store. In addition, both men would be at the party.

The only reason I thought the size of the store was incredulous was because of the undiversified clothing line that Galdelierians seemed to possess. I didn't see the use in such a large place when everyone mostly wore the same thing in different colors with minor aesthetic changes. I found out that the store included clothes, bags, shoes, food, jewelry...even a park. It was like a mall without the interior walls, and was apparently singularly owned and not, in fact, an outlet of several shops.

What fascinated me was how a person chose their size of clothing. There was a booth that you could step into which electronically took every measurement and then spat out a palate of colors explaining what would fit you as well as *how* it would fit. The shades I received were some odd mixture of yellow and purple whereas John received a basic lining of orange hues.

The whole time we were out, I dithered between trying to make kind comments to Soare-a and just remaining silent and waiting for the trip to be over. Neither seemed to do any good, so I settled for only speaking when I was absolutely curious about something that might help later on for me to know. This included the pricing of items and how currency worked, which she reluctantly and briefly explained.

The currency was a credit and not an actual piece that could be touched. The credit, somewhat creepily, was registered to handprints. It seemed most everything on the planet was used this way. At the same time, it made sense since it must be safer.

Either way, every citizen was allotted the same amount of credits simply for existing and staying out of trouble. To earn more, a person had to work. According to Soare-a, the base amount was barely enough to feed oneself and live in an open communal area with several others. She scoffed saying, 'even the vampires live better than humans who don't work.'

I attempted to point out that all vampires *did* work though, due to law, and that also, they had fewer expenses as per their diet and overall health. She didn't like this statement and it had been the end of our dialogue until we reached the dress robes that she wanted to choose an outfit for me from. I noticed every item there was easily three times the cost of the casual tunics; surely not something afforded to most.

In addition, they were all extravagant in appearance. Compared to clothes back on Earth, there were items similar to silk dresses, such as the stereotypical red carpet designs, as well as things looked to be crafted by edgy runway artists or musicians. I saw Soare-a placed deepest interest in the, uh...crazy designs, so I kept trying to steer her back towards something that seemed more basic to me.

John, my savior, saw my worsening distress and finally butted in. Clever as he was, he put eyes on one of the pieces that the woman had seemed to linger on the longest. Smiling, he said that he thought it would look ravishing on her, but that 'Connie would do best in something that drew less attention.'

If I didn't know the man as intimately as I did, I wouldn't have reacted well to the flirt. However, I knew it was fake and he probably thought the clothes were just as hideous as I did. The creature that was Soare-a gobbled the compliment up and quickly let me take one of the simpler pieces. It didn't take long to pick out my husband's attire, even with all the annoying passes at him by Malook's wife during the process. What a slut.

I laughed thinking about the insult as I stood in front of the bathroom mirror back at the home. The formal tunic that had been purchased for me was beautiful in its own right. It was just far more revealing than anything I had ever worn in public. Ironically enough, the pieces that Soare-a fancied had literally covered everything.

I stared at myself in the blunt sapphire cloth hugging my chest, falling down loosely on both sides to cover my crotch, butt, and thighs, while leaving my shoulders, back, abdomen, and calves exposed. Then I looked down at the black sandal type shoes I had gotten with it.

They had slid onto my feet simply despite how intricately laced the material seemed to be. I had seen shoes before with strings meant to be tied around the calf several times, and then in a bow beneath the knee. These were similar, except instead of two simple strings, there were pre-laited pieces that fit tightly above the ankles both in front and on back, connecting to each other with a perfectly hidden snap.

"You look lovely," John stepped up behind me and whispered in my ear.

As he put his arms carefully around my waist, hugging me and kissing my neck, I grinned, "Now let me see you."

The man sighed, then chuckled as he stepped away and allowed me to turn around and look at his outfit. It was strangely more feminine than what I was used to seeing men wear. It was a lighter blue that seemed to both compliment and clash with my own.

It, too, was form fitted around the chest, but thankfully also the stomach. It fell loose at the waist and extended down to his ankles like a typical Earth woman's dress. The stranger part was that the back of the piece was also entirely open, barely covering the butt just like mine. His shoes were a silver color but otherwise plain, covering the whole foot.

I could tell he was uncomfortable and waiting for me to laugh. Part of me wanted to, but the other part was confused. The outfit...actually looked really nice on him. He was a sturdily built man and I had always admired his broad shoulders and tapering back. The dress showed these features off well while the light color and otherwise feminine feeling seemed just to accentuate his strength of body and of mind.

After I waited too long to react, he asked in an accusatory tone, "What?"

Cocking my head to the side, I crossed my arms with one hand thoughtfully resting below my lips, "I think I like it."

He squinted, unsure if I was sincere or not, but quickly realizing I was, "Huh," he glanced past me and into the mirror to give himself a once-over before shrugging, "Alright then."

We exited our bedroom and journeyed downstairs where we waited only momentarily before Malook joined us. He wore an outfit of a light brown, reminding me of the first time I had ever seen him. Just as it did then, his deep skin tone looked extremely handsome against the softer version of it. Instead of a dress, however, his piece was a straight pair of pants with a top seemingly made of multiple shreds of cloth hanging from his shoulders.

They covered his torso, but not his arms. As he moved, I couldn't figure out if there was a shirt beneath the shreds or if it were possible to wriggle one's hands through them and touch his skin. As he neared us, I saw that he was wearing makeup as well. Nothing extraordinary. Some minor highlights to the eye including what looked like a small yellow flower on his right temple. Had he loosened his hair from its usual tie behind his head, the decoration might have been hidden.

"Before my wife has a chance to complain," he said as he approached, "Let me give you your masrels."

"I'm sorry, what?" John asked.

Malook took one finger and pointed at the flower on his face. In his hand, I could see what appeared to be eyeliner pencils, "It's customary for friends to wear a yellow masrel in honor of the anniversary," he explained.

"Oh," I smiled, "That's so sweet."

He lifted his hands, motioning for me to let him make the drawing. I complied and h painted my face without any response or smile. The pencils he pressed onto my temple were extremely cold and wet, though they dried instantly. When he was through with mine and moved onto my husband, his focus lessened mildly and he finally explained this tradition.

"It's extremely poisonous," he informed absentmindedly, "And only blooms once a year at random. My father used to tell me when I was a boy, that anyone who was born on a day that a masrel was in bloom, was of the rarest of beings, destined for something grand."

It was the first time I had heard direct mention of any family member outside of those that had been on the ship that crashed in the Milky Way. For some reason, I felt it wasn't the best time to open that window. I observed as he stepped away from my husband, giving one last look at has work.

"Have you known anyone like that?" I asked casually, "Whose new year was when a masrel bloomed?"

"Sulru," he replied bluntly before snapping his eyes back onto us instead of the flowers, "Now, Soare-a should be done shortly and we'll be on our way."

He beamed politely, acting as if the previous dialogue had not occurred at all. John glanced at me, quietly confirming that I should not further it. We ended up following our host to the den and sitting for a few minutes until his wife showed up in her ridiculously accentuated attire.

It was poofy in all sorts of strange places while the tight sections showed off parts like her groin and midriff. Even the colors were wild...at least compared to everyone else as there were four different shades instead of just one. Even thus, I complimented her along with the men right as we all rose to leave.

It probably shouldn't have, but seeing that Sulru was waiting for us when we got outside surprised me. She was wearing her typical black tunic and was also painted with the flower. What Malook had said made me grin, although I remembered not to express the thought aloud. Instead, I greeted her as I normally did, instantly rejected by her emotionless gaze. I hung my head. *Shit.* It was one of those dreaded times...

The ride was short, as they always were. The building we stopped at didn't appear much different than where we'd been living either. The only changes seemed to be minor, such as the color. There were several people standing around outside and I found myself taking deep breaths in order to remain calm while Sulru parked the rover maybe thirty feet from the garage.

We all hopped out and headed indoors. While Malook and John wore friendly expressions, Soare-a was the only one of us who seemed truly happy. From the moment we arrived, she had been turning her head every which way as if searching, though she didn't stray from our group. Was she looking for Cartef?

Within the residence, it varied more from Malook's. The entire bottom story was a large ballroom. In the center was a platform with three people playing what I guessed were instruments. They all looked liked keyboards with attachments. One had tubes, one had some sort of colorful holographic display that its member was poking about in, and the last had something akin to horns, not appearing to be currently in use.

As we strolled, we were stopped briefly by two men who were a couple and then by a single woman. The last person to speak to us was a quite excitable older gentlemen who pointed off in the distance at a younger man and woman, chattering about how his wife and husband were being so fussy that evening. After he left as well, I wanted to inquire about polygamy on Galdelier, but didn't have the chance to as the person Soare-a had been waiting for came by.

She beamed when her suspected lover showed, letting go of her husband's arm and walking up to his assistant instead. I noted from Malook's expression that this wasn't normal behavior. Furthermore, Sulru appeared to be on alert...and she wasn't alone. As Cartef halted in his position, gently shooing the human woman to the side, a second vampire stepped toward us, causing our guard to trod up to him, blocking his way.

"Stand down, vampire," Cartef growled from the sidelines behind his own vampiric associate.

Three more officers showed themselves beside the human when Sulru disobeyed the order. My heart began racing, vision blurring in grim anticipation. John had taken a firm grip on me, pulling my body slightly behind him to act as my shield. *What the fuck was going on?*

"Cartef? What is the meaning of this?" Malook moved forward, barking at his assistant, but was held from approaching by Sulru, who threw a hand sideways onto his chest and pushed him back into our little group.

"You are all under arrest for high treason against Galdelier and her people," Cartef smirked with evil intent.

Chapter 43: Sulru

Of all the low-down...

My claws twitched furiously at my sides while I desperately attempted to stifle my anger. Even though I knew that woman was slime, this was unprecedented. Damn it, I should have paid better attention! Malook was too close to the situation to be of much use, but I had known this relationship could only be trouble, having sensed beforehand that she must be up to something, albeit this wasn't what I had foreseen.

My eyes scanned across the three officers who accompanied Cartef and had since stepped forward between he and I. The General, to my side, was clearly fighting the urge to push back against my hand and approach them. He no doubt had already surmised that simply speaking would do no good now, as such an arrest and override of his command would not have been done easily.

Cartef didn't have such authority that he could call upon anyone to assist in any matter, certainly not one of this gravity. Therefore, since they were here, it wasn't on his word alone. There were no Galdelierian soldiers who would agree to aid simply for having been presented with whatever evidence he could have gathered on his own.

Even friends, if the scumbag actually had them, surely wouldn't risk their jobs, livelihoods, and even lives by pulling such a stunt without the command of someone much higher on the ladder. However, it was equally doubtful that the man himself had attempted to bother the Empress directly.

That left the most probable explanation to be that he was working with another General. Within our faction, there were two: Malook and Otahn. That left five possibilities and I knew of none among them who favored or disfavored Malook any greater than the rest.

My vision was carefully placed so that I was able to take in every movement of the two vampires and two humans in front of me, as well as watch my friend, who had finally taken a foot back, allowing me to have free reign over both my claws again. I didn't recognize the armed three nor did they have anything on them that might have given a clue. All were male and wore basic uniform tunics in dark blue with no markings denoting their rank or title.

"I said, stand down," Cartef repeated, glaring from behind his human counterpart at me.

My eyes shifted momentarily to see that Soare-a had cowered behind him, a false expression of fear on her face. I couldn't help except to glint, lips curling into a snarl, "My job is to protect the General and his family," I stated coldly.

"The General has been relieved of his duties," the former assistant mocked, "And therefore, so have you. Do as you're told and we'll make it known that you cooperated which might...help your evaluation."

He lilted sarcastically with those last words, knowing full well that he would do nothing to help to get me off the hook as an unknowing victim if Malook was tried. It didn't mean a damn thing anyway. Even if I had been unaware of treasonous acts performed by my boss, there wasn't a thing this filth could do to keep me from standing by him. I was nothing if not loyal.

"You'll have to forgive me," I continued, "For my own hide, I'd need to see some sort of confirmation of this order," I turned my glare pointedly at the first vampire and then to the second as I continued speaking, "Wouldn't want to unintentionally choose the wrong side."

There was a subtle shift in the man I was looking at. It was in his throat...a swallow. Glancing back at the first, I saw him blink, but nothing more. Once again, my sight settled in the middle, readying myself for when the encounter would turn into battle.

I wasn't really trying to put off the inevitable. My sole intention was to gather more information about the ordeal if I could. Cartef wasn't an idiot though, so I questioned if it was a futile attempt even before poking. However, it was obvious that he didn't anticipate anyone escaping, which *was* stupid.

"You can take upon the word of your fellow *vampires* here," he gestured to the men standing to my front and to either side, "As you are aware, they would not be here without said proof."

I scoffed. Thought so. I kept my gaze a moment longer. We didn't know what it was Soare-a had led them to, but it had to be one of two things: the faction or the Earthlings. Logic would suggest that it was the latter. This move would warrant something concrete and there was nothing for it on the side of the rebellion. Even between trusted members, meetings were carefully planned and monitored for discretion.

Nothing to do with our group was physical. No contracts. No recordings. The number of members allowed to be together in one place was even greatly limited. Connie and John on the other hand...their very existence was evidence of what they were. Doctored documents and erased data could only go so far and since it *had* existed tactile at some point, there was room for error, for retrieval, and most clearly, betrayal.

I tilted my head so that my voice was aimed in Malook's direction and whispered, "Get out of here."

The man didn't have time to hesitate because my words set the fight into motion. One of the enemy humans instantly lifted the spra baton he carried, but the speed of the vampires to either side of him kept him from attacking first. As one jolted past me, I managed to throw a hand, catching my grip on his upper arm and tugging with enough force to pull him backward, while simultaneously parrying the second vampire's extended claw with my other just before he struck my cheek.

The hand clutching the runner's arm retreated quickly as I spun to the left to dodge the human fighter who had suddenly sprung around his ally to get at me. This movement, however, landed me directly in the path of another oncoming blow from the vampire, as well as put me further away from the one that ignored my tug and kept after Malook and the others. Having turned in the spin, I was able to see that the three humans I had been guarding had been able to push through the parting crowd and were almost passing through the home's threshold.

His claw barely scratched my back. I was quick enough to reach my hands over my shoulder and grab it, sinking the tips of my own claws in and drawing my enemy's blood. He tried pulling away from me so he could use the closeness of our bodies to his advantage and hold me in place for his human counterpart to strike me. However, instead of maintaining my grasp, I let go and put my attention on the man whose weapon would send me to the ground, should I let it hit.

Jumping upward with a kick backward into the vampire's stomach, I caught enough air to rise above the baton's wielder and remove myself from his range before flying inches above his head, curving my body so that I fell to the floor hands first, rolling the length of my spine, forcing my weight onto my feet at the end so that I was returned to my feet. Once I stood, I burst into a sprint, chasing after my companions without looking back at the attackers who had no doubt begun pursuing me.

When I had spotted them at the door, I had also seen that the second vampire was upon them. None of them were armed in any fashion. With my guaranteed presence, even the General had not carried his own baton. I fortunately had no guests to wade through on my way, for all of them had moved to the sidelines as soon as the battle had started.

Despite being unarmed, there was no citizen who was going to put their neck on the line to uphold the law and aid in our capture. On my account, I could understand. But Malook, Connie, and John were human. It would not have taken much effort to slow them and assist.

Slipping through the exit, I felt a tug on my sleeve, and then heard it rip when I instinctively hopped to the side, barely dodging the other claw of my pursuer. His new position blocked me from my planned path away from the residence and toward the forest.

Growling, I extended my blades to their full length and threw them in the air, aiming for either side of his neck. One cut deeply into his shoulder as he twisted it to catch the potentially fatal blow, and he was able to grab my other wrist between his two hands. Even so, I left a nasty gash on that side of his throat.

With a slice out of his shoulder to send a second attack, I was knocked down when he exerted pressure on my captured wrist, attempting to curl it strongly enough to break the bone. Although he was unsuccessful, I did feel a twinge of pain when I overcompensated to evade. However minor it was, the feeling enraged me. I hadn't the time for this. Barring my teeth, I reversed two paces, rearing my shoulders behind me so that each arm fell full circle at my sides, claws bloodthirsty.

I then bolted forward and swung each hand in a sweeping motion that left my opponent confused for only a second, but it was all I needed. Each blade sliced into the fronts of his shoulders to the side of the collarbones. From there, his hesitation served to be a terrible flaw by allowing my claws to tear down his arms, digging as deeply as possible. Even as his crimson spewed my face, I continued the attack until I had accomplished my goal: ripping up his hands so that his weapons were too damaged to be effective in battling me.

The vampire screamed. It sounded to be of pain, I knew better: he was aggravated.

I attempted to remove myself from him and make chase once more...however, he realized that at that point, his best chance in subduing me was to keep my body close and use strength. He ripped his hands away, finishing the shred, and worked to wrap them around my torso. It was obvious his idea had been to hug my arms to my sides and then, probably, start tearing at my neck with his fangs. Too bad for him that I was the better fighter.

I anticipated the move and easily denied its fulfillment, instead cutting his throat as he flailed awkwardly at my chest and waist with his injured arms. Although I delved far enough into him to expose the hole of his esophagus, he persisted through gagging plasma in a nearly hilarious attempt to kick me to the ground. His foot hit my groin with hardly the force of a human punch and I merely stepped backward, not bothering to keep the feud going as I huffed and ran around him.

It was my failure, however, to reach Malook in time. Just as the fallen vampire was behind me and out of sight, I came upon the unfortunate scene of my defeated friends in the lawn of the home on the other side of the street.

It seemed that at least Connie had tried to resist the officer. The three sat in the yard, Malook with knees bent under him and John on his ass with legs straight out, but it was the woman who was laying face first to the ground with the other vampire standing above her, a leg on either side of her hips and hand grasping her hair.

The action was unnecessary as far as I could determine because just like the men, she wore a binding bar on her wrists. She wasn't speaking, but her husband was yelling at the officer to leave her alone and I could barely make out that Malook was calmly trying to relax him. I sped across the road, finding myself curious as to why the vampire was harassing Connie. When I stopped to stand perhaps five foot from the soldier, I discovered the reason.

"The others are coming up behind you," he whispered, "Get out. Get help."

His words jostled me, causing my body to still. One more glance toward the party-goers informed that the armed human and Cartef were both nearly upon us. The second vampire did not delay in jumping from his spot as they approached, sending a weak attack my way. He cut his eyes to reiterate his prior command while allowing himself to fall short of his supposed aim. It was enough to shake my mind to proper thinking and I dodged, instantly skipping to the side, and then running away at full speed.

Chapter 44: Connie

Staring blankly through the glass panel of the cell where I'd been locked, I released a heavy breath. I had tried pressing my face against it to see more than the white corridors beyond. I had even placed pressure on the entrance and rammed it with my body before finally just yelling random insults and pleas. None of it had done any good. I hadn't received any response even to 'shut up' or a guard coming by to glare at me.

I had never been a prisoner before. Not without consent, that was. I shifted in my position, tugging against the restraints that held my wrists firmly behind me on my lower back. It was quite a different feeling to know it wasn't in fun and that your captor might quite literally torture, kill, or keep you forever.

This was entirely unpleasant and completely frightening, especially with the added bit where I could not even sit or lay comfortably while pondering my fate and that of the others. My guess was that we had all been given similar accommodations except hopefully Sulru, who appeared to have gotten away. It was my understanding that if she had been caught, her judgement would be swift and unfair.

The cell itself was plain; the floor cold and black, the walls slightly padded and a lighter, not quite white color. At first, I had thought it strange that only three walls had cushioning while the ground and the glass entrance door were as they were; not too effective in keeping whomever was contained from hurting themselves. Then I realized that more likely, it was just to help with sound-proofing.

Despite this awful predicament, my mind couldn't help but bob from thought to thought. Maybe it was ADD or maybe resistance to confront what was really bothering me. A vision of John, reserved and fighting reaction, being prodded, kicked, and punched, kept flashing across my mind. Even as they dunked his head under water and made him struggle for breath, my husband would never betray his home.

However...now I was in the picture and I had no idea what my partner would consider the best move in protecting me, something he had always made abundantly clear was his priority. And what about Malook? Sitting alone in his prison, side propped on the wall as he realized that his life had been taken from him.

Not even in the literal sense necessarily, but rather his title and standing, his associates and livelihood, what was left of his fragile relationship with his wife- perhaps even his son- and certainly Sulru. A sorrowful sight indeed to see this of the kind man I had come to care for so rapidly. He didn't deserve this horrific betrayal and I couldn't help except to feel responsible.

If I hadn't run after them...jumped onto their ship... True, my leap had been in an attempt to save my husband from the grip of his assailant, yet knowing Sulru, had I not entered the fight, she would have just dropped him as they rose. Though the fall might have caused injury, it'd have been temporary, and right now all of us would be at our individual homes, safe.

Soare-a's character had been apparent to everyone and still somehow nobody had predicted this outcome. I had picked up on the affair with Malook's assistant, and Sulru had said she had never trusted their relationship. We both were aware of the fighting with her husband as well, so why hadn't at least one of us put together that she was formulating a way to keep her high standing while getting out of the precarious situation?

Everything about what was going on had me feeling stupid. It was difficult, but I tried to steer my brain power toward determining the best course of action in moving forward. It was what John would be doing, no doubt, yet it was hard to ignore my emotion. I suppose I did have a bleeding heart after all. My lips suddenly became weak and I could feel moisture swelling in my eyes.

I just wanted to be home with my husband- to feel his arms around me and know everything was going to be okay. Now, in addition to our own misfortune, I had that of four other innocents on my shoulders: Malook, Sulru, and their children, all because of my senseless curiosity. Hanging my head and slouching so that my legs fell in their bend to my side, I allowed tears to fall. However, the moment I began sobbing, I felt a gush of air in the tiny room.

Jerking upward and inhaling deeply to hold back my cries, I saw that the abrupt wind came about from the door's release as it slid open, thickening half of the glass and creating a hole for two humans to walk through. Both were dressed in white robes slightly different from the usual tunic. The woman carried a small metal case and the man, a rifle of some sort.

"Sit still," he ordered, stepping in first and circling around me.

His weapon stayed aimed on me during the motion, causing me to fight the urge to grab for it and fight. It was an exceedingly idiotic idea, seeing as I was bound and hadn't a clue as to what to expect outside of this jail. When he was finally behind me, he stopped. I couldn't see what he was doing, however, after a brief silence, I felt the tip of his gun pressing against the back of my head. Gulping, I did my best to remain still.

The woman, with what I presumed was medical equipment, came in next, kneeling on the floor beside me. She set her case on the ground and opened it to confirm my guess. Inside was a tiny gun, not unlike those Sulru had introduced us to before, except this one had a large, singular needle at its tip. It was the size of one typically used on Earth for biopsies and tissue sampling.

The device had a compartment and vials attached to its other end. Upon this note, my palms became sweaty, hoping it was not her intent to use it for such purposes right then and there. I was relieved when, after fidgeting with the instrument's settings, she reached her free hand to my cheek and tilted my head to the side by the jaw line.

Again, I resisted the urge to fight. I couldn't win and it would only antagonize. When my throat was exposed to her, she placed the gun on it, quickly threading the needle into my vein. I knew it would be more painful than the usual CBC, as per the needle's girth, yet it proved painless just the same. A small wince was my body's only response.

Only a handful of seconds passed before she had retrieved the metal from my skin and let go of my face as well. I looked down from her stoic expression to see that those vials were filling. One stayed completely full of my blood while a second had a line that was slowly rising. The line of a third was instead going down, a smaller bottle next to it filling with a yellow liquid. If my inklings were correct, it was a surprisingly efficient system and I wondered if it worked so well on a larger scale.

Platelets were a type of cell in the blood and basically their job was to heal wounds. When separated from the rest of the plasma, they presented as a yellowish color. It would make sense that, knowing we were of a different world, they'd be curious to know how well we regenerated. Likely they'd wish to be certain we were more like their humans than like vampires. Humans should definitely pose less of a threat.

After studying her equipment and seeing that it had functioned properly, the woman carefully replaced the gun in its case, latched it shut, and stood. There was no word or even a glance at me and the man as she casually strolled back out of the cell. She didn't even wait for her companion prior to continuing down the hall.

Somewhere between her reaching the door and walking away from the chamber, the barrel poking at the back of my skull fell and I heard heavy footsteps begin circling me again. I twisted my neck as they picked up, and I watched the man repeat his movements from before in reverse. He kept his stance strong, eyes intent upon his target, yet he said nothing as I met his gaze and glared. Just like the woman, he remained emotionless.

Recalling when he had spoken, I realized he had not barked. Aggressive measures, I had expected, and where their actions may have been, their demeanor had not matched. My vision stayed glued to him until he had exited the cell and sealed it once more. After he had disappeared, my dumbstruck attitude dawned on me.

From what I had come to know thus far, vampires were extremely reserved. The humans, however, even officers, were not. At least not overall. So the stoicism of the two tasked with monitoring a prisoner, strangely gave me a slimmer of hope. Maybe we weren't as disposable as John had thought.

I stretched my legs so they were straight and did what I could to stretch the rest of my body as well. Galdelier's version of handcuffs were restrictive compared to those of Earth. They reminded me of more ancient methods with their bars, yet I knew they were anything except primitive. I had seen the vampire from the party throw a piece at Malook which initially appeared as a bundle of black metal bars.

However, when it hit his arms, the bars shot into their full length as what I could only describe as mechanical cable ties wrapped around his wrists. Alongside them, the bars formed a restraint that extended from wrists to shoulder blades so that the arms could not be bent. A second pair of rods separated hands by the palms to ensure they were unable to grasp anything.

All in all, it was an admirably efficient method of restraint, despite how utterly frustrating being their victim was. My back was sore from only having shifted between staying straight and slouching as I sat. I had tried standing several times of my own accord or by pushing against a wall, unsuccessful in reaching my feet for more than a moment each time. The weight of the bars wasn't incredible, but it was enough to royally fuck with my balance.

So soon after having all that lab work wasn't the time to try again either so my focus was on getting into a decent position and resting. I shuffled about, rotating to lean on the pads with the side of my shoulder, then its back, and lastly its front.

After that, I fell onto my spine switching over to my side and finally giving up to lay on my stomach, eyes cut toward the entrance as thoughts of escape returned. It didn't take long for them to be over-shadowed by guilt though, and I found myself laying cheek on chilling ground with arms painfully strapped behind me, emitting soft whimpers.

Chapter 45: John

After wasting my rage shouting at the vampire, who had jumped on top of my wife during our capture, only to find out he was on our side, I had kept silent the rest of the ordeal. At least mostly so. I did speak to Connie and Malook in the spare moments we were together and I was able.

Largely, the officers had commanded us to quiet while prodding us around. My words had done little to console me or my wife, and Malook more or less told us nothing other than that we were best served to be compliant. He didn't actually speak toward honesty, but something about what he had said gave the impression it was his meaning.

The three of us were transported via a larger, slower version of the hover-vehicles we had gotten used to traveling in. It was completely covered like a van and there were no windows that we could see. The vampire from the arrest also boarded the machine and kept a watchful eye on us the entire way.

He had let Sulru escape, so he must have been someone she knew. From what he had said to her, I guessed that he was a part of their secret faction. Even with how self-evident it was that this should not be acknowledged, I found it tasking not to point this detail out to my wife in my attempts to soothe her. I continued with the hope that we would be confined together, despite its improbability.

Given the amount of time it took us to reach our destination, I felt we had to have journeyed past the limits of Contuin, although I could not be certain just how far if it was even so. In addition to the vehicle having a different speed set than the others, the tactic of switching paces, directions, or drawing out the time in order to confuse occupants could have very well been used. Before we were released from its confines, our vampiric guard stood, withdrew small devices from his pocket, and approached Malook.

Sliding these pieces between two fingers, he used a retracted claw from his other hand to grab one and then poke it in the space between the General's brows. What at first seemed little thicker than a cut of cardboard, covered over the man's vision with circular shields popping out to fully encase his eyes.

I hadn't been sure how the blindfold stayed in place until one was placed on me. It was a pairing of suctioning the skin and spikes, which had to have been nearly microscopic, protruding into the flesh. It had been uncomfortable, but not painful. Literally and figuratively progressing blindly, I took that instant to mutter an 'I love you' to my wife, whose voice cracked when she reciprocated.

I had discovered it had been the best decision to do so since it had been the last moment we were together. After a trek containing a lot of prodding and the introduction of weaponry, my sight was returned to see I had been relocated to a cell, out of touch and out of sight of my companions. My first focus was on calming my heart. The second was to understand the restraining bars holding my arms against my back.

I hadn't been left alone to accomplish much before two human women entered the prison to draw blood from my neck and apparently shoot me if I struggled, which I didn't. Just as my angry yells had done nothing earlier, I knew that there was no point in resisting at present. I simply let them do their job, as Malook had suggested.

It could have just been in my head, but neither of them seemed too enthused with the task. After sensing this, I had asked what tests they were running, only to be met with silence as if they hadn't even heard me. My mind told me that it was part of their roles to stay calm and detached, yet my gut told me there was something else. At any rate, once they were gone again, I returned to analyzing every detail available to me and contemplating the likeliest turn of events from this point out.

I had only shifted position once, from sitting straight with legs bent at their knees and laced over each other in front of me, to stretching them out and leaning the tops of my shoulder blades against the wall behind me. I started with the basic outline of Earth protocol, more specifically US procedure, and plugged in the similarities and differences I was aware of between there and Galdelier.

There weren't many of great enough extent to worry about. The ones that were, included the vampires, the leap in scientific advancement, and that the entirety of Galdelier was under rule of a single family. That simple division of the planet was still the strangest out of anything I had witnessed. Even with the difference in population and in the physical size of the space rocks, it seemed so unattainable to have this small system of governing.

I suppose a large part of it was to due with how divided my home planet was. I needed to account for the fact that there was a completely different chain of evolution and development of culture, therefore the possibility, if not the truth of, a vastly varied way thinking, concreted over decades, centuries, or more.

I could only assume that there would be further study of our alien forms and likely some kind of interrogation, even though it felt probable that these people were neither interested in nor trusting of what we could say. I got the sense that speaking to us might be deemed a pointless endeavor in that what might be learned wasn't worth the hassle of uncovering it. Beyond that, I couldn't come up with a reason they would keep us alive since we hadn't anything to offer.

We were useless in terms of gaining proper intellect, should an invasion of Earth be desired, and we were clearly of no grand worth to our own planet to use as a bargaining tool for cooperation; definitely not surrender. Even if it was considered that we were, it could easily be found out otherwise. Simple tests of our knowledge would permit sufficient proof that we were useless in that fashion, as well as showing our people had no higher engineering abilities than the Galdelierians already possessed.

My spirit fell with the certainty that we would be executed quickly, which for this world meant death by vampire. An interesting way to go for someone who only weeks prior knew that such creatures did not exist. The idea of this demise, or of torture, honestly caused me minor anxiety at best.

My only fear was of my wife's torment. I hadn't the strength to think of her enduring any such pain and yet, I was utterly helpless to prevent it should my suspicions of this danger be correct. It left me despondent, physically aching from the sorrow of this nasty truth. As I sat unwillingly envisioning her subjected to cruel treatments, I berated myself for focusing on nothing but gloom.

My brain was programmed for logic and rational conclusion based upon known facts. However, my wife had always given me the light of hope despite hardship. And the thing was, she hadn't always been wrong about it either, even when her emotional faith contradicted my cold reason. Connie wouldn't give up because failure appeared to be the likeliest or only outcome. She was the type to see the conclusion she wanted and fight for it.

Closing my eyes, I inhaled deeply, then exhaled slowly. I wanted for both of us to come out no worse for wear. I wanted to remain free, even if that meant to live in hiding. I just wanted to be with my wife and know she was safe. This meant I would have to do whatever I could to appease our captors, and to hold my courage and brute capabilities should I be faced with annihilation. No matter what, I had to come out on top, locate my wife, and get the fuck out of here.

Get out.

My sights shot open as I recalled the words that the vampire who arrested us had spoken to Sulru. He let her go and she might have...no, she *had* gotten away. She wouldn't hide, nor would she abandon Malook: that was abundantly clear. The both of them had at least one other General, as well as many vampires and human officers working to overthrow the current regime, including the one that had let her slip through his grasp.

Maybe there were more members than the brief allusions I had heard too. Perhaps that vampire's boss was also a member, and it was their facility where we had ended up. If any of these things were true, Malook couldn't have told us. There hadn't been a chance. Suddenly, my heart picked up its pace again. I had found it. Not only the hope that Connie had no doubt already put together, but a logical argument to back up its possibility.

We weren't over yet.

Chapter 46: Sulru

I knew I only had a small sliver of time that I was guaranteed to be free from pursuit, though I didn't know exactly how long it would be. If no other vampire came after me immediately, the time it would take any humans to physically catch up, or a course of action in finding me to be decided and ordered to any officers, human or otherwise, was the amount I was working with.

The first places they would look would be the obvious ones: my home, Malook's, and of course, his office. Zofra might be the next person to be looked into since Cartef certainly was aware of our companionship at the very least. My old friend, however, had been at Typher's anniversary gathering, so I could trust he would stay scarce until he was able to get in touch with me in some way, lest he inadvertently lead forces to me and therefore also incriminate himself.

There was no doubt he had immediately learned of my escape. Many party guests had been outside and would have carried word to the others in the ballroom, if they hadn't already shifted in that direction themselves once it had become safe.He would be able to inform Kivela of what had transpired after finding me and, as part of our resistance, both would remain in contact to know what was needed moving forward.

That eliminated my need to go anywhere near my home, which was a positive, as it left me to focus on getting to Otahn rapidly and undetected. The chance that it had been him who Cartef had contacted was nonexistent, due to several reasons, including that he was the closest of all the Generals to have any sort of known relationship with Malook.

Therefore, he was the most likely to give my boss favor. Apart from that, he had also never made any remark or indication of negative feelings toward vampires, which might as well, in the minds of most, mean that he saw us as equals even though it didn't warrant any 'blood-sucker lover' rumor as Malook had dealt with for his own words and actions.

Cartef was of enough mind to look for his best shot in completing his mission, meaning he would have looked for a General of more common ground with him than his target. As I traversed the Black Forest, bounding from the ground, ricocheting my body from one tree to another, then sprinting, skipping, leaping, and ricocheting again with soles of my shoes scratching off the bark, I searched my memory for any recollection of meetings, work, or other sorts where Cartef had made the acquaintance of any other General.

With the duty to protect Malook, accompanying him to meetings with the other Generals, and then of course being tasked with helping the other guards protect all of them at said gatherings, I had learned the names and faces of each of Gelvin's seven sub-leaders. It gave me only a shallow store of information about them, though, so wasn't much use.

Otahn would have more insight into these men and women as individuals, but what would be most helpful is his access to data regarding such an undertaking as the arrest of a fellow General, since our world's system thrived on the strict legal obligation of recording pretty much everything.

I had always been a fantastic runner in regards to speed and stamina, even among my own people, yet the overwhelming danger of my current situation had me in a constant state of fear that I wasn't working fast enough. This prompted me to continue forcing myself to increase my pace and never slow until, when I finally made it past the forest and reached well into the back alleys of the vampiric neighborhood of the next city, I had pressed myself to the point of over-exertion.

I hated to do it, yet was incapable of keeping myself from easing up. I absolutely refused to stop moving altogether however, so I kept walking, doing my best to regain my breath while not drawing any attention. Otahn was meant to be at Typher's anniversary, yet he had been absent. This was why I was heading through the next district and into his territory.

Past Contuin and the Black Forest, there were three cities before I would reach his home town. By the time I was ready to dash into another sprint, I had nearly crossed to the second. I thought I had been thorough in staying aware of my surroundings.

However, just as I began to lunge forward, two claws grabbed me by either arm and I found myself twisting in a circle with another body as they yanked me behind a nearby building. When our motion came to rest, I had ended up freeing one arm and had its blades extended, bearing down to slice the attacker who had let go of me entirely in order to stop my claws before they fell onto his face.

"Mote!?" I growled upon recognizing the other vampire.

"Yeah, tawsey," he spat back, addressing me with his favorite insulting petname, "Lower your fucking voice. You're gonna get us caught."

Only then did I realize I had spoken loudly. Clearing my throat, I jerked my hand from his grip, retrieving their claws as I shoved him against the structure hiding us, stepping backward to glance around, "The hell are you doing?" I demanded of my typically unpleasant neighbor in a whisper.

"I ran into Zofra," he picked himself up and glared at me, "I came to help, though I can't say I'm not offended that I wasn't made privy to this bit of information."

I cut my eyes at him, "The fuck are you talking about?"

"This 'rebellion,'" he threw hands up in a mocking gesture.

I scoffed, "Yeah, because you are definitely a prime choice when it comes to friendly relationships with humans."

He lifted an eyebrow and crossed his arms, "I'm here, aren't I?"

Staring him down, I sighed. As much as it pained me to admit, the punk was good at keeping secrets and had come to my aid multiple times without reward, "Did Zofra tell you-"

"He said you'd be looking for Otahn, a General, right?" my new companion cut in.

I nodded, eyes still shuffling about us.

"It's best to save your strength," he smirked as he began walking the length of the building in the opposite direction of where I had been heading.

Reluctantly, I followed, but quickened my pace to hurry him along, "What?"

Along the coming curve of the structure, a rover was parked. Mote walked up to the driver's side and opened the machine, "Get in," he called over his shoulder.

But I halted. Vehicles were only government property or privately owned by humans. In either case, it meant they were easily tracked, which was why I had judged traveling on foot as the best option. He could have only acquired the machine by taking one he was registered to use at work or by getting the human who did own it to give him permission for it's use.

"I don't have time for this sort of idiotic-" I began protesting, only to be interrupted once more.

"You really don't give me any credit, do you?" the vampire seemed genuinely offended as he spun around and barked at me, "I know you think I'm some simple-minded lowlife, but you never stopped to think, 'hey, maybe the shady guy knows something unconventional?' I mean isn't that kind of the whole idea behind being shady is that you don't-"

"I understand you're making some grand point, but can you hurry it along?" I grew increasingly anxious with every second the guy was rambling.

"Per my lowlife ways," he growled in a rush, "I reprogrammed the system so that this particular rover, which has no connection to me, is unmarked or rather, owned by a human that no longer exists."

My brow furrowed as I contemplated what he had said. I walked closer to the machine and glanced inside, "How were you able to control it without registering your print?"

"Bypassed the system. I'd explain better," he grinned, "But we're in a rush, so get in," he repeated, returning to sliding inside the vehicle.

"Wait," I ordered, skipping toward where he stood and gently pulling him from his position, "I'll drive."

I didn't give him the choice to resist, and he seemed to be aware that no more time should be wasted, because he simply skidded his ass across the hood of the machine and took the passenger seat instead. As I situated myself in the rover and clicked it into drive, I began marveling at Mote's apparent capabilities.

I was considered amongst my peers to be intelligent, yet the skills he had shown made me feel dumb, especially considering I had been oblivious to them. Upon initiating our little adventure, I had doubted his story and his reasoning for helping me, wondering if he was working under some sort of bribe or threat.

I couldn't help except to trust it, though, because however much he put me down, I was still a vampire, as was Zofra and a large number of our faction's members. He may not care for humans, but Mote was racist to the point that he'd do anything to aid in the well-being of his own kind. Besides that, he had no connections, nothing viable to be used against him, and the only people to know about Otahn's involvement would not have sent a dangerous individual to me.

The vehicle definitely cut my trip short and the break it gave my body was well-appreciated. The journey from Elter to Otahn's home town of Thelevaid was simple enough. The extra set of eyes also decreased paranoia of getting caught and we were soon on the outskirts of the residential area. Parking the vehicle in a discreet location before beginning the trek toward where Otahn lived, I noted that it had started growing dark. Even if it had been work that kept him from the party, the General should be at home now.

Mote and I crept close to his building. The meeting was unplanned and therefore the utmost caution had to be used, should I accidentally lose us both Generals currently dedicated to the cause. As I contemplated the best approach, being unable to see into the windows or the garage that was closed, my companion suddenly poked my arm.

Quietly, I turned to him to see that he was handing over a black cloak. I took it, curiously, and unfolded it to see that it was quite long with full-length sleeves and a large hood. I glanced back to see him putting on an identical fabric, pulling it well over his head and then zipping it close to hide his face. I copied, silently waiting to see what he was up to.

Once covered, he instantly jolted to the residence, making a leap upward to grab the ledge of a window on the second story. Hanging there, I observed him pull himself up and crouch precariously, holding onto the top of the indention with one hand and using the other to fiddle with something in his lap.

My eyes shifted about nervously while he continued with whatever it was he was doing. We were at the rear and there didn't appear to be anyone nearby. After a few moments passed, I saw the glass beside the vampire give way, allowing him to climb inside and disappear into the home. Unsure, I dipped after him, making the same sprint and jump.

I half-expected an alarm to be sounding when I entered, but it was quiet. Mote had done something to disarm the system before cutting into the window and forcing it open. He stood on the opposite side of the bedroom, smirking at me as my brain pieced together what had happened. As eager I was to know exactly what had been done, I didn't waste any time with questions.

Instead, I assumed the electronic device, about twice the size of a standard phone, that he waved at me, was the culprit. Stepping forward, we searched our way out of the room and down the hall, listening for any hint of who else was present. When the elevator slid open, I could just barely hear soft music playing downstairs.

Nodding first at Mote, we boarded the lift and sent it to the first floor. The music became quiet with the sealed door, and then grew louder than it had been at the start once we had reached the bottom story. Readying ourselves should we need to fight, we slipped out of the machine into an empty parlor.

The music was coming from the other end, so we slunk along the walls, all the while studying our surroundings to stay clear of any surprises. Inside the kitchen, Otahn stood over a counter, slicing into a fresh cut of meat. Seeing the blood splurge from it as he pushed his knife down was a deliciously tempting sight.

The man didn't notice us until Mote stepped to my side and led us near. The General dropped his cutlery in shock, quickly retrieving it and holding it up at us in a defensive stance. I only then remembered the masks over our faces. When I unzipped the hood and pushed it away from my head so that it rested on my back, the human's expression became confused, his weapon remaining in position.

"Sulru? What in the world are you-" he began.

"Malook was just arrested," I answered rapidly.

"What?" he said in disbelief, pointing his knife at Mote, "Who is that?"

The other vampire had not lowered his hood. Angrily grabbing at the cloak, I forced him to expose his face. He growled, replacing his focus on the human.

"Mote is a friend. He came to help," I informed.

The General gave the new individual a critical look before laying down his blade and strolling past us, heading for the elevator. We followed him unquestioningly and once more boarded the lift.

"Arrested?" he repeated, "On what charge?"

"Treason," I answered, "They arrested Connie and John and attempted to do the same with me."

"And Soare-a?"

"Was the one that ratted us out," I hissed.

"I see," Otahn continued, "It was my understanding that she wasn't aware of our goings-on. What did she give as evidence?"

I hesitated. I was sure that it was the ordeal with Earth that was the downfall, yet if it wasn't, I didn't want to be the one to reveal it. As the elevator stopped, door coming open and the man in front of us getting out, I simply answered, "I was hoping you could find out."

"Hm. It should be in my system," he agreed, "Though I cannot interfere, you understand."

I should have known it and yet I had still anticipated his help, "Malook is in trouble," I argued, "We need-"

"Sulru," he cut me off just as we reached his private quarters on the third floor, "Malook has been an important asset to our cause, but I cannot let your emotional attachment to him put us in any more jeopardy than we already are. If there is something I can do, I will do it, but I won't lead anyone to my position."

He stopped at a desk in the corner of the room and unfolded a slim computer, ordering its screen to life. I was angry with his resistance to help despite knowing he was right. He had to look at the bigger picture and, unfortunately, if aiding in Malook's release would point to him as a conspirator, then it just couldn't- or shouldn't be done.

He typed in several commands, including scanning his print, and rather quickly found the reports. From our spot about five foot away, I watched the man's eyes flutter, reading the screen before suddenly, they grew wide. He reached a thoughtful hand to rub his chin for a moment, and then turned to face me with crossed arms.

"What's really going on, Sulru?" he inquired threateningly, "Why were they arrested?"

The response was all that was needed to confirm my suspicions. I stared back at him, nervous about speaking. Mote picked up on the odd turn in the conversation and raised an eyebrow in my direction. My pause was long enough to prompt further word from the General.

"Illegal use of a spacecraft, tampering with government record, erasing sensitive data, invading alien space, and conspiracy against the throne of Galdelier?" his tone was harsh and his voice was shaky. I couldn't tell if it was only anger or a mixture of that and disbelief.

"Alien space?" Mote inquired in an almost mock.

"We have not begun any sort of attack to warrant acts such as these," Otahn accused, "What's Malook been up to? You must know, if only for the fact that you were with him on the craft specified."

"I..." I mumbled.

As a General, Otahn was aware of the wormholes our scientists had discovered, as well as the information collected from the drones sent through them. If Soare-a had told Cartef about the aliens, he could have pieced together evidence to prove Malook's family were actually extra-terrestrials. Then again, if he hadn't been able to, should I reveal them? Otahn was an ally, but...

"There was an accident. On the trip, we ended up in one of the alien systems that the scientists had been monitoring. The ship malfunctioned and we were forced to land on the nearest planet," was as vague as I could get and as direct as I was presently willing to be.

There was more than one planet with breathable atmospheres amongst those discovered, so I could have been referring to any of them. I couldn't tell if the human believed or disbelieved me, though I had begun to feel that he was going to accept the information I gave as was...until the loudmouthed vampire beside me spoke.

"Hold on," Mote laughed awkwardly, "This so-called family, are they...?"

It took every ounce of strength not to punch him in the face. For such a dumb creature, he was certainly smart. The flurry of anger in my eyes was enough to show the General that my companion had hit the mark. As Otahn lifted a single brow, I gave in, "By the time they had gotten aboard, there was no safe way to send them back. We had to hide them."

That moment was the first time I was fearful of another member in our group. Observing his glare while tapping the back of his elbows with arms still across his chest, I thought perhaps he would turn on me...and on Malook. Our members relied on absolute trust and I felt that we had broken it. The gravity of our illegal actions concerning the aliens had unnecessarily put the rebellion in danger and Otahn was undoubtedly furious that I had approached him when the issue was not about the faction.

"I understand," he stated abruptly, halting my thoughts. My own brow furrowed, uncertain whether it was a forgiving understanding he had given, or a reluctant one. Letting his arms fall to the side, he sighed, "Some things have to be kept secret for the good of all. That being said, you know I cannot interject myself into this matter."

I dropped my jaw to retort, but he kept on, appearing to want to shut down the topic quickly.

"There is little I can do to help, that he has not already tried. And, if I were to be found pulling the same things, where would that leave us? Without a General at all, our movement would be severely stunted. As it stands," he glanced back at the screen, "He is in the hands of Generals Shief and Alg, neither of which I know too personally. If I am brought in or something should change, I will get word to you. I'm sorry, Sulru."

Chapter 47: Malook

Even within my mind, I was speechless. I had known my wife was both selfish and devious, but not to this extent. I would have gladly set her up- given her whatever she wanted- just in exchange for leaving us alone. She held contempt for all vampires, probably especially Sulru, and she had never bothered herself with strangers. She hated me, certainly, but how powerful was that anger to put my life at stake? and not only mine, but the Earth people and possibly others as well?

And Cartef...she had done all this...with him. Had she *been* with him? Were they lovers and if so, how could I have been so blind? Sulru...she had tried to warn me. She told me the man was untrustworthy and I had just dismissed her concerns. There was no way I could forgive such treachery. On Soare-a's end or even on Cartef's; certainly not my own.

If I were fortunate enough to get out of this, they would both do well to never cross my path again, because I would destroy their chances at ever having the success they seemed to desire so much. Moreover, I'd *never* doubt anything from Sulru at all. What she had to say and what she needed would always come first, like it should have been from the start. She was the only one I could trust. The only one.

I softened at the thought of the woman. She had been able to get away, but she wouldn't stay gone for long. I didn't know in whose power we had been left, which would be the first thing she would seek to discover. Otahn could no doubt answer this for her, though I doubted his further involvement.

As important a member as I was, he'd have to look at the larger picture. If the two of us were in switched places, I would not interfere unless I had a direct, and preferably positive, connection to whomever was holding him. Otherwise, I'd likely have to leave it be. Sulru would not be happy with such a plan of action.

Her loyalty was concrete; she had pulled me through affairs multiple times against her best interest. She also continued to comply with my wants, to work with and confide in me beyond her call, definitely beyond what was wise for any casual relationship. This was not something I had witnessed her do with anyone, having others confirm this as per their own knowledge of her.

As much as her dedication and partnership was appreciated, I wished for her to only do what she needed to survive. Even if it meant my isolation or death, I wanted nothing greater than for Sulru to be free. I found myself chuckling as a grin spread across my face. That's not what was going to happen, was it? Stupid woman; I love you so much.

The door to my little cell slid open, jarring me from the pleasant, yet somber thought. A man and woman in uniform showed, one armed with a rifle and the other with a shock baton. It was the first contact since being locked away, and neither seemed too amused. In fact, distant was a better word. It wasn't an attitude usual for those in their position. These officers were taught to keep a grave, even threatening demeanor. Yet here they were, seemingly robotic.

"Get up," the woman ordered.

I silently complied. Rising to my feet with the bars behind my back was a difficult maneuver, but I accomplished it well enough. She stepped to the side, motioning with her gun for me to keep walking until the man took hold of my restraints. He slipped his baton so that I could feel its tip digging into my back. A simple press of a button on his end and it would send electricity though my body powerful enough to instantly drop me to my knees.

I went with them out of the cell, down the first corridor, and onto a second. I recognized the layout of the building: it was an advanced containment unit. There were seven facilities like it in Gelvin, one for each General. They weren't always in use, but rather left for only grave matters or, most commonly, official meetings between Generals without the presence of the Empress.

They weren't particularly large, despite the importance of the criminals kept therein at any given time, nor for the safety of these leaders. They were each surrounded by many security measures though. Most of which were digital, however, obviously, living guards were present as well. The area I was taken to was surprisingly meant for meetings and not for interrogating prisoners. I couldn't tell whose station it was since each of these facilities were identical from the inside out.

That is, I couldn't until the woman standing on the opposite side of the room turned around to face me. Her name was Sheif and I'd had the opportunity to speak with her on a personal basis just once. She never came off to me as anything other than genuine, albeit extremely work-oriented. That wasn't all and all a negative thing either. It just left much of her a mystery. I did know she was one of the few Generals who had ever chosen a human guard over a vampiric one. Speaking of, it didn't appear he was around...

"Malook, I've been informed of some terrible things," she stated plainly as I approached, with no hint of expression on her person.

I answered in a similar manner, "I'm sure you have."

The woman locked gazes with me for a brief moment before waving off the two standing with their weapons on me, "Go check the others."

After a brief hesitation, they obeyed, leaving me alone with the General. My arms were still bound, so it wasn't like I had much chance of harming anyone anyway. Sheif's eyes followed after the guards until I heard the *whoosh* of the door slide close again. Then, her sight was returned to me.

"I don't rightly believe it, though," she continued with the same affect.

"And what is it you don't believe?" I countered, somewhat antagonistically.

The denial to incriminate myself was obvious, drawing a short chuckle from the General. She turned her head to the side and began to stroll away from me. I wasn't sure if she meant for me to follow, but either way, I stayed where I was, simply watching as she rested herself gently against the front of a desk. When she was facing me again, about six foot away, I expected another vague push towards getting me to speak. However, she didn't take that route.

"I wasn't the only one informed of these crimes. General Alg is on his way as well. It has been left with us to decide whether or not to take your case further, but," she glanced down beside her where a screen lay displayed on the table she had leaned onto, "With all this, it will be hard not to."

She lifted a stare, waiting for response. When I did not oblige, she simply shrugged and kept on, "Alg is extremely interested in your unauthorized trip to the alien space. It would appear that it's been his desire for our programs to focus more on actually entering and exploring the other side of these wormholes...but that's not what got my attention."

Another pause, seeing if I would react.

"Your assistant seems convinced that there is an uprising being formed and that you are a part of it. Something to do with liberating the vampiric species. Now, there isn't any evidence of such a thing. Hearsay at best. Though should I or other Generals press for it to be snuffed out so that we can be certain the empire is safe, I imagine it would at the very least cause a lot of trouble for those involved."

Try as I did to remain blank, I felt my brow furrow. Where was she going with this? Although the last bit was surely meant as a threat, revealing everything known, and furthermore what wasn't known, against me was a move of either stupidity or friendliness. And I knew better than to think General Sheif was an idiot.

"I do not know what you are looking for," I finally spoke, my confusion already evident.

"Well," she grinned, "Your status definitely makes you a valuable member to this rebellion, if not the most important. I want to know about it. It seems to me a change in the system is overdue."

It was a surprising turn in the conversation, yet I wasn't convinced of its legitimacy, "You're assuming that such an uprising does exist."

"I suppose I am," she had stopped smiling, expression becoming solemn, "And I suppose it would be tenuous for me to do so upon Cartef's word alone. However, this is not the first time I've heard rumor of such a thing. More non-concrete sources...though it's less that and more of your guard that has me believing."

My flat affect bloomed into one of anger. Even in my predicament, I would not take kindly to anything foul being said of Sulru. I swallowed hard, palms sweating at my back, knowing I couldn't do anything except for be enraged, should the General's threats turn to my partner, "And what do you mean by that?"

"Only that I have never seen such tenacity in a vampire when it comes to a human, even their superior. So tell me, Malook," Sheif's eyes grew as fierce as mine, "What have you done to earn such loyalty? What have you done that Sulru should give her own life to in such a foolish attempt to save your freedom?"

My chest had begun to heave and simply breathing was difficult. Heat filled my face as I desperately tried to refrain from speaking. I had gotten entirely fed up at that point and I wanted nothing more than to tell the woman off for daring to speak about Sulru like she knew anything about her! But I refused to do anything to further agitate my partner's standing. I knew my anger stemmed from the fact that the situation had been approached as if Sulru were already dead.

"You're getting needlessly upset," the General raised her brow after taking in my state.

My glare strengthened.

"You doubt my sincerity," she stated bluntly, "It only makes sense that you would. Tell me, do you know *why* I chose not to have a vampire guard me?"

"I do not. Neither do I know why he isn't present," I replied, hoping that even if it wasn't what I wanted to say, speech would help ease the tension within me.

"I'm not very good with people, you see. I'm not like you. If my guard were of the species, I'd have no idea how to make them think right of me," her words came out oddly, but I was sure I understood their meaning, "When I worked as an officer, my personality left others to judge me cold and arrogant. You can imagine that such an attitude did not sit well with the vampires."

"Are you trying to tell me that you took a human counterpart because you didn't want a vampire to think poorly of you?" I surmised.

"Indeed," the woman glinted, "Because I don't think poorly of them."

There was a brief pause.

"Why are you saying all of this to me?" the thought was a growl in my head, yet somehow when it left my lips, it seemed innocently curious.

"You are well aware of gynts, yes?" the jump in topic threw what was left of my rage away and put me fully puzzled. When this became clear to the General, she tilted her head to the side and glanced at something across the room from her.

I, too, diverted my vision and saw that she was pointing out a small device attached to the side of the wall nearest me. It was, in fact, a gynt, an item meant to disturb frequency so that within a certain radius, nothing could be recorded. They were contraband and of course, I owned one myself. Most probably the majority of Generals and even many lower officers did.

The disruption of record was not enough in itself to be safe since lack of audio would lend suspicion. Normally the device was used in adjacency with altering the recorded times of events or with another device that simultaneously inserted pre-selected dialogue when there was no way to explain the absence of a recorded session altogether.

"I'm not interested in the misuse of spacecraft," Sheif was speaking again, "I've told you what I want. I've also informed you that there is nothing to prove you guilty of it nor anyone else for that matter. My interest lies in rewriting the laws with which we don't agree, as well as personal advancement. I would assume that that is the desire of most."

Suddenly, there was a small electronic sound coming from the desk. She reached over and picked up a handheld, reading a message on its screen before attaching it to a holster on her leg.

"General Alg will be here shortly. You can rest assured he has no positive feelings for rebellion and won't care if you are taken down for treason on the other accounts," she took a couple paces toward me, "You have two choices. You can inform me of what is going on- who to be in contact with- and I can aid in your release. Or you can leave it to chance. If you don't work with me, I won't work with you...and that means Sulru too."

A flash of fury recharged my being with the sound of her name.

"Your friend is already on her way to execution. It's up to you to give her a fighting chance," the woman added these last statements with a nod toward the door behind me.

I hadn't even realized that it had opened until the two officers from before reappeared at my sides, silently pushing and pulling me into the same position I was in when first brought to the General. As they tugged me away, I watched Sheif retrieve the glynt and return to the spot she had been in upon my entrance. She took a similar stance as she had then, but this time kept her eyes on me as I was led from the room.

"Time's wasting, Malook," she reminded, completely void of emotion.

And yet I felt like time had slowed. All I could hear was my heart thudding in my chest as I was forced to the exit, over the threshold, and out into the hallway. Every inch of me was fighting with a million different thoughts and possibilities...although they would all come about by either one of two choices:

Tell her.

Don't tell her.

In that instance, I found myself without concern for anyone except Sulru. I had to help her. That realization should have made the decision easier, but it didn't. If I opened my mouth, it may help or it could also lead to her death...a fate she might evade without my interference.

If I did and Sheif's words were untruthful, then it would not only end my friend, it would destroy what she had worked to create: a hope for her people.

On the other hand, if I said nothing, the probability of her remaining free, whether through hiding or not was slim. What if talking to Sheif was the only chance she had?

By the time the door slammed shut in front of me, I hadn't made up my mind. As I was dragged back to my cell, I stayed equally unsure. The encounter with the General had simultaneously made me feel like she was an ally and an enemy.

Her personality, as she had said, definitely did not do her any favors if she was trying to be friendly...which made me think that she wasn't. In the end, I realized that it was all out of my hands. I couldn't do anything without some semblance of rational thought, but that same logic told me that either choice was just as harmful as the other.

At least I wouldn't have to live with myself for long.

Chapter 48: Sulru

Speaking any further to Otahn would have been futile. The man had made up his mind and although logically, I couldn't argue with his decision, I wondered what exactly could be done to warrant his attention on the matter. Sheif or Alg calling him in or if something were to happen where the information came to his notice in a casual way would allow him to take part.

My mind instantly began contemplating in what instances such a thing would not seem conspicuous. It didn't matter what I could come up with though, because even being able to say he was aware, there was nothing he could do to remove Malook and the Earth people from the situation, outside of somehow convincing the other Generals that my friend had been framed. He could perhaps vouch for leniency.

Even then, depending on what more evidence was presented and the mindsets of the other Generals, this would do little, unless Sheif and Alg were in full agreement and dismissed all proof entirely. The chances of that were not even small, I doubted their existence altogether. Otahn would absolutely not risk such an attempt; not when there was no immense or imminent threat to the faction and at present, there was not.

Everything in the system had to do with the alien affair. Mote and I had left the General's home the way we had come, after alerting him to the damage on his property. He seemed slightly aggravated at the news, but I assumed it was less to do with the break-in itself and more with my having bothered him overall.

"So what's the plan?" Mote's tone was casual as we boarded the rover once more.

"What do you mean?"

"What. Are. We. Dooooing?" the man stretched out the rewording deliberately in order to sound as if he were speaking to an idiot, knowing it was only going to piss me off.

"I would assume," I growled, "That you would go back home." To be honest, with as much as he enraged me, the thought of him tagging along was actually comforting, even if I had naught a clue as to my next move.

The vampire paused, turning a stare on me as we both settled into our seats and I readied the engine, "Well, I would *assume*," he threw the phrase back at me, "That you would like help freeing your boss."

I inhaled sharply before twisting my neck so that I faced him, "Why are you doing this?"

Mote gave an obvious shrug, "Why not?"

I scoffed, "You must have a reason. Nobody puts their life in this much danger without good cause."

Another shrug.

"I hate the system," he answered plainly, eyes forward while leaning back and curling his arms above him in a relaxed pose.

I shook my head, "That may be so, but springing Malook isn't going to bring about change. And if you're seen, you'll be put to death alongside me."

"Stupid tawsey," he grinned, staying in his position, "Expecting to get caught is just setting yourself up for failure."

My gaze kept on him, desperately trying to bore into his mind and see where his real thoughts lay. Out of all his indiscretions and the sketchy ordeals he had been a part of, he had never once, to my knowledge, endured negative repercussion. I did know that he had lived in many different cities before settling in Contuin.

For a vampire, this meant that he had been transferred numerous times. That, of course, usually coming from being needed elsewhere or being rendered inefficient at your current post. He had maintained the lowest rank, pointing to the latter being the truthful reason behind his relocations.

My gaze returned to facing forward. Chattering voices carried on the wind, alerting us to the presence of a citizen couple walking across the sidewalk in front of the buildings we had parked behind, the small space visible from our spot. The two didn't even glance back or hesitate, completely oblivious of the strange sight of two vampires without human escort in a rover in their neighborhood.

"I'm not sure where to go from here," I admitted, having no choice except show this weakness.

"You said you're not sure," Mote pointed, "That means you have some idea."

I growled at how he picked apart my semantics. Nonetheless, he was right. Sheif and Alg were my only idea. Each General was given control of a type of facility for their grander duties, such as meeting with other Generals, holding the highest of criminals for interrogation, or storing certain irreplaceable items which had been entrusted to them by the Empress.

Malook, Connie, and John *had* to be at one of these. There was nowhere else it would make sense. That meant they were within the walls of either Sheif's compound or Alg's. I didn't know which one or where they were, but I knew who would. I glanced over at Mote. If he could hack into the computers of both this vehicle and Otahn's home security unit, perhaps he could also break into these prisons.

Erasing whatever data had been accrued...would that even do any good? Like Otahn said, Malook had already tried tampering with data and it had been found out. It probably would have gone unnoticed if nobody had known what to look for though, so since there were now a handful of people who did know, deleting or changing the information would only send up more red flags. Unless...

"Mote, is there a way to re-route in the government records to make it appear as though a certain individual is responsible for the presence of different info?" I asked.

My passenger lazily looked over as a devious grin crawled onto his face, "Who are you wanting to point the blame on?"

"Who else?" I snapped rhetorically, "Does that mean you can do it?"

"I don't see why not," he shrugged, "But don't you want to first make sure the only evidence they have is digital?"

My mind returned to the electronic pages of information regarding Malook's arrest that Otahn had shown me before dismissing us. Mote hadn't been allowed to see it, but thinking on this detail now, I realized it was a moot point on the General's end considering the vampire's apparent capabilities. Not just that, but that he was working with me and likely to come to know of these things anyway. Perhaps the General had simply lent enough trust to me to decide what to reveal to my new companion.

"The spacecrafts automatically record length of time they are powered up as well as the coordinates and dates. There was no way for us to wipe the information manually. Well, not all of it, apparently," I explained.

"I would think such a newly advanced machine like that would have a very hard print," Mote mused. My expression must have told him that I wasn't following because he expanded the thought, "Basically, it records things to internal memory so powerfully that it leaves a trace of everything even if it's deleted. I expect they are closely monitored to make sure the systems are not worn down by this."

"Alright," I continued oddly, "Along with that, it looks like they have picked up on John's false identity and that Malook was the one to alter it. The prior careers he was given...those in charge of the areas at the time are denying his presence and some of them even have alternate stores that show he was not there. It seems that the exact crimes they can presently prove are being in alien space, having unauthorized passengers on the ship, modifying John's record, and trying to cover these things up."

"*Conspiracy against the throne* meant what then?" Mote quoted the offense, speaking with an annoyed chuckle, "Just doing something they don't like?"

"That part was thin. It could be referring to verbal accounts against him regarding conduct to do with the whole ordeal, or the rebellion, but yes, basically..." I hummed, "Criminal activity while being a General is treated as far worse than being an ordinary citizen."

"Or being a vampire," my friend said angrily, "That's why you're in such deep shit."

I wanted to growl, to rebut his prejudice, except in this instance, he was completely correct. Had I been a human in the identical circumstance, I would have been questioned to prove I had no knowledge of my boss' actions, and then put back to work immediately. Fighting and fleeing had no doubt made me look guilty, yet surrender was not an option.

True, it might, MIGHT have saved my hide after strenuous trial if Cartef or others didn't work against me, but it would have all ended with my degradation. Malook would have not been found innocent which meant he, too, would be demoted. It followed that we would not be allowed to work alongside each other if the two of us did survive.

This outcome was not acceptable to me. I'd rather die than not have him in my life. Teylof was strong. She was independent and she no longer needed me. Not that there was anything I could do at this point to help her even if she did. Outside of them, I had no one. No reason to continue. I was one vampire without whom, the rebellion would do just as well.

As it stood, even if I could wipe Malook's slate, there was only an ever-so-slight chance for my own liberation. I had still disobeyed the law by defending him against arrest. It would be said that regardless of the General's guilt, there was no appropriate excuse for my actions.

If you have nothing to hide, you have no reason to fear, right? Fighting officers on duty and fleeing the scene was tantamount to confessing guilt of dubious behavior. My mission was to keep Malook free. He was far more important. I'd try to stay alive for as long as I could, should my services be needed in some way. Other than that, I was resigned to my fate.

"Well, with knowing that," Mote picked up again after several moments without response, "I'm not sure steering things toward Cartef will work."

I tilted my head, "Because you can't do anything with the ship if it works that way?"

He confirmed with a nod, "Though if I can get into the files of the department that maintains the hardware, I might be able to make a report stating that the parts were transferred from elsewhere to test after a malfunction. That should be a good enough explanation for those discrepancies."

"So what do you need, then?" I asked, my eagerness to start moving returning.

"To go back home for more equipment. Then, we'll need to get access to Malook's personal outlets for accessing the system," the vampire's brain had become so focused that, even with his gaze directly on me, I could feel that he was looking straight through, "Had Cartef been the one to frame the General, he would have gone directly through Malook's links as it'd be easiest to both to get into and to pass off on his boss. Cartef's background would suggest that he has a somewhat expert grasp of technological workings."

"His home? His station?" worry was settling in, "I can't get you access and even if you could get in, you know those places will be on high alert right now *and* most likely shut down inside."

"Right. Hmm..." Mote diverted his sight.

He didn't appear bothered at all. His entire demeanor had remained relaxed while he kept contemplating options. I shouldn't have been shocked at the lack of concern. It had been our species' expectation for countless generations to stay reserved and keep an emotionless state. Nonetheless, it upset me further.

My life was ending both figuratively, and soon after, literally. I refused to die without saving Malook. Life and death had not ever been something that gave me pause. I had grieved for my mate after his passing. I would be torn if my sweet Teylof were hurt. Yet overall, life and death were just passing moments occurring all the time. Something about this predicament, however, I knew I could not let my last hours be rendered worthless.

"A doubt," I breathed as a thought struck me, drawing my ally's gaze, "It doesn't even have to entirely eradicate Malook as a suspect. Just something that would cast concrete doubt on the case and send it in another direction. Visual proof. A recording of the true mastermind."

"Yeah, that'd be great," Mote rolled his eyes, "But I'm no video editor and you're not going to get Cartef to-"

"No," I sighed, "Not Cartef...me."

The man next to me twisted in his seat, throwing one

arm over the back of it and the other on the dash. He stared incredulously, "What the fuck are you talking about, tawsey?"

"With several testaments against the validity of John's identity, there's nothing much to keep him from being exposed as a fraud, though as an alien would be a stretch," my eyes glinted, "Connie's set as a house-maker all her life within Malook's family who, as you know, are mostly all dead. She's in the clear. Let's not create Cartef as the enemy. If it's John and I, then I can let myself be recorded breaking *him* out instead of Malook. The pieces would fit together. A man with a false identity being sprung to leave and take another fake life?"

"You are...absolutely insane," Mote shook his head, "No wonder I like you."

My head was cocked again and I grinned, "Oh?"

The man scoffed, rotating so that he was in a forward facing position. He rest his right arm on top of the door beside him and forced the smile from his face while his vision settled onto the town before us, "So now you just have to find those facilities and see where your John is."

I kept my smirk and ignored his attitude, "You know Kivela was once a guard and he has an impeccable memory."

"Looks like we'll be heading home after all," Mote replied, "I'll get the old man and my stuff. I assume you'll need me to get you inside."

"Hm," I agreed with a small grunt before commanding our vehicle to hover back onto the streets and quickly into the forest beyond.

Chapter 49: John

"Who are you? It's a simple question. Give an honest answer and I assure you this will all go much more smoothly."

After what I best estimated as three hours, the man had come into my cell and said it in the same instant. There had been no introductions, no once-overs, no time wasted at all. He simply walked in with the armed woman from earlier, and started in. The suddenness had taken me off-guard, though I did well in not showing it. I only stared back at him from my spot on the ground, leaning against the back wall while I thought.

The woman kept her rifle trained on me and maintained the same indifferent demeanor as before. She stood directly to the side of her counterpart, who did not seem to share in her apathy. Instead, he seemed fixated upon me, almost eager for me to deny cooperation.

Although that would normally speak that he was of a cruel mindset and wanted a struggle, it actually set me at ease. It wasn't that I was unafraid; it was just that such treatment was recognizable. It was something common on Earth and my being was oddly comforted by the familiarity.

That being said, it was easier to then contemplate how I should respond. Malook had suggested that we be honest and work with them. As logical as it was that I should trust the General since we were in his playing field, I just couldn't seem to relent to speaking freely with my captor. This wasn't for some sensible train of thought either.

It was a gut feeling. My instinct, I suppose. Connie rarely worked with rational logic first. She was emotional and mostly did what 'felt' right to her. Under such grave circumstances was probably the worst time to try out her way of doing things, yet even when my brain tried to put details together to formulate the best approach, I couldn't ignore this unknown urge in my psyche to resist.

Maybe it was because my wife was in danger and I could not reach out to touch her and comfort either of us. Maybe the soul was real and mine was connecting to my mate in order to use her strengths during my time of uncertainty...or perhaps something more tangible such as the inkling that they did not realize I was an alien. In any matter, I gazed back at the interrogator standing in front of me, kept somber and kept silent.

The man, whose uniform was identical to the woman's, smirked. His blue eyes appeared false next to the mocha complexion of his skin, which somehow added to his aggressive stance. He stepped forward and placed a boot on my ankle too quickly for me to retrieve it. The shoes he wore were extremely heavy, probably weighted with steel or a similar material.

I had noticed that most Galdelierian attire was light or at least was in Contuin's region. I had seen one or two of the humans at the station, where I was meant to work, wear boots similar to this and still I hadn't guessed how massive they were. He tilted his body forward and pressed the entirety of his weight down upon my leg.

I attempted to pull away, yet somehow could not manage, so I instead focused myself on not letting it show that I was bothered. Despite having a high tolerance for pain, this guy was quite large and the added pressure of his nearly spiked boots on my joint was testing my strength. The annoyed look on his face assured me that he wasn't getting what he was aiming for, which pleased me.

I returned a grin.

He suddenly lifted his foot and I allowed my eyes to cut over to the woman, whose attitude had changed from indifferent to uncertain. It was another thing I had witnessed in my career: an order was being disobeyed or, at the very least, smudged. My attention was soon upon my attacker again as he lunged forward, downward, and grabbed hold of my tunic. His brawn was evident in how easily he lifted me from the ground and slid my body up the wall.

My smirk shifted to a glare when his lips curled in a wicked smile.

The man opened his mouth like he was about to threaten, yet just when I thought he had readied an insult to sling, the light in his eyes changed. The look of sheer determination to break me switched to one of shock. My confusion was only momentary, disappearing when claws suddenly showed over the top of his head. The blades pressed down into his flesh, drawing strings of blood as the fingers attached to them grabbed his short tufts of hair and yanked him backward.

"Sulru???" my voice was a hushed shout.

The vampire had become visible as I was dropped. My mind rushed to assess the new scenario, spotting a second vampire, a male, with her. He was smaller than Zofra. Shorter than Sulru as well, his body stout and even more human-like in appearance with his less prominent features...though the coal eyes were a dead give away as to his species. He was standing over the female human, who lay unconscious on the floor, still gripping her rifle.

Sulru had also done away with the human she had attacked, the one who had been intent on me, by the time I had caught up with what was happening. At first, I had pictured that the hold she had on him would end with her jerking his neck and breaking it.

So I was relieved when instead, she had only spun in her place, taking him against her body before ramming his skull into the glass of the wall behind her. After she was finished, she carelessly let him fall next to the woman before twisting and skipping up to me.

"Hey!" I complained when the vampire reached her hands around my waist, taking my binds and trailing me in a circle so she could better see them.

Curving my neck to see what she was doing, I saw her companion had come forward with a device that I recognized from my brief training. It was a tiny computer, about the size of a pager, with a thin metal bar extending maybe an inch from its base.

Calculating a command within the machine would send electric pulses through that bar to release different kinds of restraints: an electronic key. The moment I heard its tiny hum, I tore my wrists apart, rubbing each with my hand as I rotated to face my saviors and then rapidly found my feet.

"I didn't expect you to get in so quickly," I admitted to Sulru.

Her vision lingered on me for a moment, but she said nothing. It was still difficult to read the vampires, especially with how they were made to act stoically, yet somehow, I was certain that I saw guilt in those eerie eyes.

My brow furrowed, not understanding. She didn't allow me to respond either. She simply rose and turned to begin walking out of the cell. The other vampire huffed at the sight of my confusion and leaned to take the rifle from the fallen guard.

"Here," he said, shoving it at me.

This one wasn't reserved and he came off as having an outright hatred of me. Or rather not me, but my kind. Humans. I suppose that was warranted, therefore I didn't question it. It wasn't a time for questions anyway. No doubt peril was close, so I merely went with him as he followed after Sulru.

In the corridor, we were met with a third vampire. Also male, though he appeared much older. He seemed as healthy as any other; the only hints toward his age were the wrinkles on his face and the air he carried: unworried and without haste.

"They're coming," he stated plainly, unperturbed.

It was only then that I was able to speak, "Where's Connie? Have you already-" I started, only to get cut off by Sulru.

"Shut up and just come on."

Her words sounded angry and frustrated. More than that, they gave the sense she was trying to silence me in order to keep something secret. Although, of course, that did not set well, I forced myself to ignore it. I was not yet more than novice here and did not wish to run the risk of fucking the escape up.

I knew that Sulru would have worked to free Malook, but had realized that surely to her, my wife and I were only secondary. That meant since she *was* breaking me out, she had already succeeded with the General and moved on to us. Connie was definitely her favorite, so had she needed to go in any certain order with us, I would have been last. For the time being, that was all I needed to know. Everything else, I'd just have to trust her.

As the four of us journeyed down the hall and turned the second, I kept expecting an alarm to sound. However, nothing ever came. We were finally met with resistance upon entering the third passageway. A shot rung out from the distance, along with an unintelligible yell. Those leading me shuffled backward to take cover on either side of the corridor where we had just been.

"Do you know how to work that?" Sulru's emotionless words were pointed at me.

I glanced down at the gun I carried. I knew I was expected to understand its function whether I actually did or not, so I was unsure of why she had asked. Then again, it was a heated situation we were in. Covers went out the window when safety was threatened.

Nonetheless, it sent me wondering as to what exactly had been found out about us, or what she had been forced to reveal to her teammates. Fortunately, Malook had shown me a government weapons manual in his library which I had studied well enough to have a grip on the workings of Galdelieran armory. This particular piece, an energy-based weapon, was used by pressure on the trigger pad.

I nodded.

"Kill if you must, just don't aim to," she added quickly, her attention back on the enemies.

I felt that bit of information was apparent. However, I *was* an alien. I had learned much of Galdelier, but she had been taught less about Earth. Better safe than sorry... I couldn't guess what the plan was after we made it out. Galdelier, as I had learned, was nearly entirely mapped and the majority of activity was closely monitored if not recorded. Their faction must have decided on a route forward which certainly meant war.

Although I wasn't keen on the idea of indefinite battle, there wasn't much choice at this point and as long as Connie and I were together, maintaining some sort of freedom, it didn't really matter. Sneaking a look at the people in the distance, I noticed something strange. There was a group of five, that I could see, yet there were no vampires.

I opened my mouth to speak on it, immediately remembering that anything I might have said could seem either idiotic or racist or both...so I altered my question, "Is that all of them?"

"For now," it was the old vampire who answered, "But if we take too long, they'll have sent for vampiric reinforcement."

He didn't look at me, yet his wise tone alone seemed to understand my hidden questions. I didn't know who he was and I had already grown to liking him. He seemed a perfect middle ground as far as judgment was concerned...completely removed from any squabbles about species and hatred.

A few moments passed with neither the enemy group nor our's moving. The hesitation would not have normally made sense. However, our group was mostly vampires and theirs entirely human and I had learned that close combat against a vampiric opponent was not only considered most efficient, it was typically the only way to go about fighting one.

But why were Sulru and her companions waiting if reinforcements were surely on the way?

"That should be good enough," the younger male standing next to me stated randomly, his gaze lifting from a handheld as he reattached it to his thigh.

With that, he and Sulru bound toward the humans, leaving their elder with me. I looked awkwardly over at the old vampire for instruction. He didn't speak, but I took his lack of movement to mean I should stay back as well.

We watched while the two other vampires grabbed at the humans around their spra batons, narrowly dodging them as their wielders managed to maneuver expertly around their claws. These officers were clearly trained at a more elite level than the common rabble I had been introduced to.

"Keep a sharp eye, Jun," the man next to me warned suddenly and I noted his verbal interpretation of my name's pronunciation was more akin to how I had been told to write it, "There will be a surprise. There always is during an ordeal like this. My daughter is just too singularly focused right now to pay much heed."

Daughter? My eyes shot to Sulru, who had just taken a baton from one of the men and struck him to the ground with it. I grimaced alongside his scream. Knowing how the weapon worked, I could only imagine the sheer agony he was currently in. Fortunately, it wouldn't last long. As the hundred tiny blades tore through his innards, a blow that would incapacitate a vampire, he'd soon be destroyed from the inside out.

Chapter 50: Sulru

Kivela, the stubborn bat that he was, had insisted on accompanying Mote and myself to the center to retrieve John. It hadn't been a verbal dispute either. He simply rose from his seat and began leading us to General Sheif's compound.

When I asked for the location, he had remained silent, loading himself into our pirated rover and waiting for us to do the same. I had long learned that arguing with my mate's father was futile and I hadn't the time to waste with trying. If the old man wanted to put himself in this death trap, it was on him to do so.

Mote had brought Kivela to the spot where I had been left with the machine, after he'd gotten a few devices from his own partition within the residence. The first two looked to be handhelds, though one was larger as if it were an older model. The third, I didn't know what to make of.

I didn't bother with asking him how they worked; we only discussed the plan for getting inside and back out. Kivela and I were both well acquainted with the interior layout of the Generals' facilities. To ensure the best protection of criminals or paraphernalia kept therein, it was created in the form of two spirals. At the center of one were the prison cells and the other, storage.

The halls leading to these middles spun around in a circle until gradually, at their ends, were four large rooms in each corner of the oddly square building. These four areas were separated from the next with locked entries. Every wall was considerable in its depth in order to soundproof and protect.

In the corridors were occasional blocks as well, to amp up security, and the final surveillance measure, as far as the blueprint went, was the circumference, which was made up of a massive stone wall with two towers where the main guard kept a watchful eye on the place from the monitors in his station. The largest hurdle of entering illegally was this wall.

The entirety of the structure was settled in an isolated area, a thick row of trees outlining it to keep it from casual view, while just on the other side, it lay completely bare until the barrier. Such an open spacing made sneaking up on the guard towers challenging. Being that Mote was the one meant to hack us through the system, he decided he would be the first to creep toward it.

Kivela and I remained in the wood-line, anxiously awaiting word from our companion. The tool that had been unknown to me, was apparently for boring through the stone block. He had to work quickly, using the smaller of the handhelds to call upon the electrical wiring within the wall soon enough to stop it from triggering an alarm.

If, he had said, *it's not in good time, I'll just hush the signal and send an error report back.* This was what had ended up happening too, so we rushed to scale the gate with him before anyone was sent out to investigate.

We knew that officers would be on our tail starting from the moment Mote touched that wall, meaning we were well aware of how rapid our rescue would need to be. Yet for it to do any good on Malook's end, we also had to delay our movement so that everything was recorded by surveillance properly. We therefore decided to focus our efforts on stealth and speeding to free John before any hesitations were made for the cameras.

It felt like betrayal using the Earth man to ensure my goal, but I had already seen that his identity was causing dangerous suspicion. Leaving it alone would only force them to dig further, incriminating him, his wife, *and* Malook, while breaking him out would alleviate such proceedings and offer a solid excuse for the fake records.

After retrieving him from his cell, I didn't have time to explain this all to him and even if I had, I couldn't be sure he would leave Connie behind to accept his future in hiding as a criminal outcast. Since his cooperation was vital, I opted for commanding him silent as Mote and I rushed to our small group's defense. He hadn't any choice except to obey.

Luckily, we hadn't been caught onto until making it to the prison. Kivela had patiently waited outside to listen for enemies. They would begin locking down every interval of the passageways soon, but if we could handle this batch quickly, Mote could halt the blocks. The old vampire protecting John let me keep my attention on the fight.

Fortunately, being a leader-oriented facility, it was human-trafficked: no vampiric officers kept on site. However, with each lunge, the humans successfully parried or evaded. I wanted this to go without blood shed, yet as the moments continued to pass without a successful strike from either Mote or myself, I grew too frustrated to hold back.

Grabbing one of the spra batons thrown at me, I yanked the weapon from its wielder, spinning and forcing the man to the ground with a released shot. I ignored his pained cries as he convulsed. He would die, but I didn't care. I couldn't.

There were more important things at stake than another mindless drone carrying out unquestioned orders. This was life or death; not for me or my companions, not for John or his wife, not even for the man I loved. No, I understood that it was more than that. They *needed* Malook...the innocent people...*my* people...no. Not even them.

Me.

I needed Malook because he would save Teylof. His place in the rebellion would give her a future or at least the hope for one. That was what this was about, wasn't it? If all these humans died, if John died...none of it mattered as long as the General was free and retained his power. That was all that mattered...and I wouldn't fail.

Mote seemed to take my last attack as approval to up his own aggression: something he appeared thrilled to do. He likewise easily relieved a woman of her weapon before raking his claws into her abdomen, instantly pulling out and twisting to throw them across the face of a second human closing in on his back. I jumped out of the line of one blow, dropping to a crouch and sweeping my leg under the attacker to take them off their feet.

Instantaneously, I was up again, sending my foot full force down upon his neck and crushing his esophagus. It had been quite some time since I had battled like this. These humans, as per their position within a General's ranks, were of the elite.

Fighting them was almost as taxing as sparring with a properly trained vampire. I felt a light thud on my back as I finished the blow. My torso twisted to see Mote had reached out and taken the last guard by the shoulders as she had tried to hit me.

Pulling her against his body, his jaws sprung open and a claw left one shoulder to yank her head to the side so his barred fangs could sink into her flesh. While he began sucking on her neck, I reached out to pull her baton away, idly thumbing it in my hand as I spun around to make certain that was the last of our enemies for the time being. I glanced to the side and saw Kivela and John hurrying towards us.

"Come *on*, then," I barked at Mote, who had lifted his fangs from the woman to make a more critical tear into the front of her throat before casually releasing her, letting her fall, grasping her wound and choking for breath.

"Fuck!" John had skipped toward the scene and started kneeling near the female guard.

Annoyed, I stomped over, grabbing the top of his robes and pulling him back to stand, "We don't have time for your sympathy," I growled, our faces almost touching, "Take this, and pay attention!"

He reluctantly took the spra baton from me, simultaneously shuffling the rifle he had been carrying over his shoulder and onto his back by its strap. I cut my eyes from him and looked at Mote. The vampire was dripping with blood, having unabashedly fed in the company of others.

And an ally human too, for that matter. I reminded myself that John had not yet seen such a thing; neither had he yet become quite accustomed to the existence of people like us at all. Recalling the events on Earth, what he had just witnessed probably shook him back into his own unpleasant first encounter with our species.

I tried not to concern myself with it, but part of me wanted to bitch at the asshole for at least not cleaning himself. Nonetheless, I put my focus on the escape. The bitten human had gone still, though she was not yet dead.

Almost as if in response to our small victory, massive steel doors slid downward, the rush of air and the heavy thuds onto the floor below them easily felt. Our human friend remained silently even with his clear startle from the sudden motion. He merely watched with the rest of us as Mote strolled to the closest door.

The vampire curled one hand into a fist and banged on the panel next to our sealed exit. It only took two hits for the casing to bend. He extended a single claw, slipping it under the metal and prying the compartment open. Having already retrieved the small device attached to his waist, he began connecting it to the exposed wires.

As he worked, I stole another glance at John and Kivela. The old man remained unphased and it seemed the human was starting to settle into the role expected of him at present. A negative sound from the computer between Mote's claws, followed by a thoughtful groan from his lips, sparked my discomfort. Peering over at the screen, I could make nothing of it, other than it was code.

I had only seen programming perhaps once. It wasn't a common thing to be familiar with in any way. The scientists who were taxed with such things weren't allowed to teach about it unless set forth by the Empress or Emperor. Furthermore, all intelligent men like those who studied technology were closely guarded. Not to protect them, but rather to keep that knowledge from spreading.

This, of course, wasn't free information either. I was privileged to be close to a General who was willing to share everything he knew with me. Mote's own intelligence piqued my curiosity. Where could he have achieved it? He would be a valuable addition indeed...

I broke my thoughts from these questions as well as his apparent trouble, and cast my eyes downward, allowing my vision to fade and my hearing to sharpen. It was impossible to pick up on anything on the other side of the block, and yet I tried. With each passing moment the door was down, the chance of resistance waiting behind it increased.

It was difficult to remain calm despite knowing that not even a handful of minutes could have passed before Mote emitted a hum that drew my gaze. His eyes were on me. I tilted my head to see the rest of our group. The Earthling nodded at me, having caught on that we were ready to proceed.

I turned back to Mote, eyes lingering only a second, and then my body instinctively took a combative stance, staring at the door like a beast waiting to be let out of its cage. It was called for, because the instant the entry was open, two pairs of guards were charging at us, all wielding batons. I noted that in the distance, a fifth human stood with an energy rifle aimed.

Blasts from the gun itself would burn and that was about it, though a well-placed one in say, the eye, would grant enough pause for a fatal blow to come from the officers nearest us. However, if we were able to keep our movements constant, such a strike would be exceedingly challenging to land, especially with the risk to their fellow man.

In many high priority cases, friendly fire was acceptable if it meant taking down the enemy. Even if it was authorized now, it would do more harm than good, considering the necessary teamwork of using both the energy rifle and the baton together to take one vampire out. Otherwise, injuring one of their own would only help us.

I found myself spacing out during this next round. My motions were instinctual, unplanned. I circled around my younger partner, who was gaining far too much joy in taking down our evolutionary inferiors. It may have bothered me more if I wasn't struggling with my own hatred.

Not of human kind, really, but of sentient life in general. Humans, vampires, these aliens...all creatures of superior thought were cruel and controlling and I was taking my dissatisfaction out on these drones. I was dead alive so what did it matter if a few more joined me?

My eyes flitted from human to human, occasionally glancing to Kivela or Mote or John, frequently and briefly, just to see they were still part of the battle. My father-in-law had joined the fight this time while the Earthling looked to have taken paces in reverse, his vision trained on the only other person holding a gun.

I had given him the spra, but had doubted he would actually want to use it. Turned out, I was right. I wondered how sharp his eye was...if he would be able to take the shot if one presented itself through the muddle of us close-combat fighters.

Peew!

I discovered John's capabilities soon, as Mote threw his victim into the opposite wall and I grabbed onto the last standing guard. The energy rifle's shot, charged to its full power, rang past my head, flying toward the man at the other end of the hall. I forced my eyes to stay on the person in my clutch instead of looking to see if he had hit his mark.

I pulled our bodies backward, pressing myself against the wall behind me, growling at my captive when they fought for the grip on their weapon. As I spun, rolling against the structure so that I could pin her body to it, I caught sight of Mote having taken hold of the man he had thrown, to begin ramming him into the wall once more.

Another shot came, this one from the opposite direction...and then a third from John's side. I had gotten the baton from the woman beneath me, striking her temple with it without activating its full capacity. Her eyelids fluttered as the second blow drew blood, but I struck her one last time before letting her be.

Rotating, I saw first that the person John had been firing at was on the ground, though was unable to tell if they were dead. Next, I saw that Mote held the human he had been fighting. Despite being in his arms, lifeless, he continued the attack.

My brow furrowed, curious at how the seemingly simple-minded creature that had always stayed generally positive, engaged in such vicious overkill. I didn't see an immediate point in stopping him. They were already gone; it wasn't as if he was actually hurting them anymore. Kivela, as always, was reserved. It was John who demanded the vampire cease.

"That's enough!" the Earth man yelled, flinging arms around the vampire's shoulders, grabbing each of them and attempting to pull him off.

I stepped forward, expecting Mote to resist our ally in his distraction. Shockingly, he did not. I halted mid-track, interested, and simply observed as he ceased his frustrations and dropped the corpse. John's eyes flashed momentarily to the body, then were back upon the vampire.

Mote turned, his lips and chin stained crimson, spots of the same liquid dotting the rest of his face. He stood motionless, glaring at the audacious man. I knew he wouldn't attack. I had come to understand that he was not, in fact, an idiot. I didn't know what his plan was as far as after leaving the compound, but he wasn't going to jeopardize his success against the humans.

I could sense a fleeting unease in John under the weight of the vampire's stare, the human impressing me when when he didn't falter. He even spoke again, halfway ordering the gruesome creature staring him down.

"Let's just get the fuck out of here..." And with that, the man simply walked away, his gaze staying on the vampire a moment longer before he put it on me, expecting me to lead the way.

Chapter 51: Malook

Once again, guards were in my cell to take me to the General, presumably. Alg had likely made it to the compound directly after my visit with Sheif and now that another hour or more had passed, they'd no doubt discussed the situation and come to a conclusion on how to proceed.

I didn't imagine this meeting would go well, though I had decided if Sheif was indeed positively interested in the cause, she would do something, however slight, to steer Alg away from suspicion of rebellion and towards the other parts of my case.

She had basically described the man as disagreeable, so if a true supporter, she wouldn't lend any aid to his focus on our faction. As well, even if her reasons were selfish, doing this would still show me, who she was convinced was involved, of her willingness to aid. From what the General had told me, I felt it wouldn't be a difficult feat anyway.

I took what she said to mean that Alg was more scientifically focused or, at least, politically. Stressing scientific advancement did not necessarily mean an individual was concerned with helpful progression. Knowledge was powerful. Not only did it breed technology which meant weapons and domination, but heightened understanding allowed for manipulation and control.

Most definitely in a world such as Galdelier, where the public was kept uninformed, science had even greater strength. I remembered during a conversation with Connie, I had learned that largely, advancements in science, technology, and the like were released freely to the Earth's population. I hadn't honestly believed it at first.

However, thinking about how chaotic their planet's governing systems were, I ended up figuring they were probably telling the truth. Not that I thought they would lie; it was just I felt they *thought* they were let in when they were really very uneducated...like most Galdelierians. Then again, I was sure not *all* information was given to them. Humans just didn't work that way. And all in all, their humanity was nigh identical to ours.

After the three of us reached our destination, a room conjoined to the first I had been taken to but that was indeed meant for interrogation, I saw that the second General was standing with the first, an amused look on his face as he laid eyes on me. Sheif, on the other hand seemed slightly less reserved than before, though I couldn't tell what the difference in her was.

To her side was her human guard, wielding a shock baton and carrying both a rifle and a spra. On Alg's side opposite, stood a vampiric guard, armed with nothing except her own brute strength. My two officer escorts nudged me forward until I was standing in the middle of the room, a comfortable distance from the Generals, before they slowly took paces back, retreating from the room.

They would stay nearby on the opposite of that wall in case they were needed, but such proceedings were only allowed to be witnessed by the Generals involved and, of course, their personal guards. Once the door fell shut behind me, Alg was the first to speak.

"Your assistant has made quite the fuss over you," he grinned wickedly.

I sighed inwardly. I didn't need to have much experience with the man personally to know the type. His goals were most assuredly personal gain. There was no nobility in his quest for knowledge.

Arrogance ebbed from his being thicker than the heated blood my heart was currently pumping with much labor. This might end up quite painful, but so be it. I wouldn't bow to the likes of him...or of Sheif for that matter.

Ignoring his words, I kept a placid expression and actually allowed an audible exhale this time. As expected, it angered him. His smirk fell, as did his brow, and he turned a glare. While he took a step toward me, my vision cut to his guard. The vampire expressed herself just like the multitude of her species, by not expressing herself at all. It was idiotic, but I realized I only gave her my attention because I was thinking about Sulru.

Other than pale skin and black eyes, this woman looked nothing like my partner. Even with the same stoicism, she acted nothing like her either.

The guard had noticed I was looking at her yet she remained unchanged.

Sulru, in the same position, would have had some subtle shift in her energy, a nuance showing she not only wasn't intimidated, but her mind would challenge anyone who dared to even think she was less, as such an obvious glance from a human like me usually appeared.

During my distraction, I had unwittingly frustrated Alg further. My brain quickly brought me up to speed in knowing that the man had spoken to me again. Once more, I was glaring at him, entertained by how easily agitated he was. It was a bad time to be toying around, yet I couldn't help except find myself eager to upset him.

"You're wasting time," Sheif interjected, drawing my gaze, "This Cartef, though he may have had some good intel, is obviously pushing," the woman lifted an eyebrow, slightly twisting her neck so her sight rested more on Alg than me, "Don't tell me you can't see that."

General Alg, who had come close enough that he could have clutched my tunic, let his face fall as he considered her words, "Hmph. Perhaps you're right," he murmured to the side before talking at me, "Then we should indeed focus on what exactly you were doing out of Trind first."

Even Sheif saw the man's simple mind and was using it to her advantage. It seemed that whatever I had missed was to do with Cartef's accusation concerning the rebellion, and she *was* indeed steering him from the topic. Interesting. Maybe she was a possible addition to the cause after all.

The realization was both uplifting and disheartening. Had I discussed with her earlier, I may have helped my friends', if not my own, standing. Nonetheless, I was where I was and logically, I could not have known. Even now, there was doubt. It was all likely that the pair was attempting to manipulate me.

"This John...who is he?" was Alg's next question.

It wasn't the line of inquiry I expected, so I gave a simple answer as I tried to put together his thoughts, "My cousin's husband."

The man in front of me smiled, "Strange that nobody except for you and your cousin has heard of him before now, yes?"

Silence.

What did they think John had to do with the trip? Surely they hadn't yet put together who he was. From what Sheif had revealed, there was no suggestion of it. Then again, she may have not told me everything...may not have felt it important since it meant nothing to her, as per her confession of not caring for anything except government overhaul in her own vision.

After our gazes remained locked for several moments, he casually tore away, nodding at his guard while retreating to stand next to the other General. The vampire strolled closer to me, taking his place and then getting even nearer.

Unlike the human, she did take hold of the fabric at my chest, slowly lifting me from the ground, her black eyes void as she suddenly jerked in a motion that threw me up slightly higher, and then forcefully throwing me onto the hard floor. The brunt of the impact was upon my spine and if it had been just a little more painful, I would have wondered if the vertebrae had been injured.

Not to say it didn't hurt. I couldn't contain a moan as I rolled over in time for the vampire to crouch over me and take hold of my clothes again. As my eyes shot open, I saw that she had only one hand grasping my tunic with the claws of her other extended, her arm reared back ready to strike...but she paused. A slight tilt of her head alerted her boss that something was halting her.

"What are you doing?" Alg demanded.

She didn't need to answer. At that moment, an alarm sounded from the door, accompanied by the same noise from both of the Generals' handhelds. I was dropped to the floor again, without intent, when the guard decided to leap from me to her superior's side.

Whatever danger was approaching, her priority was to protect Alg, not ensure my captivity. I imagined that in this instance, such a thing would anger the man, should his safety not be at immediate risk. Everyone's attention jumped to the entrance when a heavy thud was heard through it, the crash causing it sending the steel sliding upward, revealing a violent scene...one welcome to me.

Sulru, Kivela, John, and another vampire I had only heard of in passing were on the other side. Mote retrieved his claw from the neck of one of the humans that had brought me into the interrogation, letting her spurting body collapse to the ground just as I saw him. The human's counterpart was already on the floor, struggling to reach his feet. Mote didn't allow him to, slicing his throat in one swift motion.

The older vampire was flanking John who was further inside, making careful shots at more officers who were coming upon the group from the compound's main entrance. My eyes quickly found Sulru, where she was maneuvering around a handful of others. She fought with the tenacious determination that I admired her for.

A few of the incoming humans took off to the side, rushing into the room with the three of us Generals, preparing to fend the intruders from coming any closer to us. It was, however, a poor choice. This Mote...I hadn't properly met him before. The one time I had had the chance, he gave a dirty look in my direction and ran the opposite way.

Sulru had informed me of his hatred for humans. I had truly hoped I could convince him that we weren't all terrible, but it hadn't panned out. She had spoken of their mutual contempt yet...I had never expected such fury. This vampire was relentless. He made no hesitation in swiftly executing each human he saw. It wasn't his actions alone that painted him depraved either. The look in his eyes, the way they glinted with joy as his lips curled in a playful smile...

Alg's own rage had grown. As Mote ravaged through the human officers, he commanded his guard to go after the unhinged vampire. She did so as he neared, her interference saving the life of one of the officers about to be caught in his grasp. Sulru's attention left her current struggle, shoving the woman in her arms absentmindedly away as she set course for her companion.

Instead of joining his fight, she skipped by them, heading for Alg and forcing his guard to retreat from Mote and chase after mine. During this time, what few officers made it by the furious male vampire had circled around me and Sheif with her guard, focusing on protecting the General and the prisoner.

"Mote, GO!" Sulru yelled loudly, pushing against the other female vampire, their claws interlacing each other and cutting into their unflinching opponent's skin.

I questioned if the man would actually follow her order. Fortunately, he did, rushing back for Kivela and John just as the older vampire was forced to enter battle with the humans left behind by his daughter. Mote barely dodged a blow from one of the humans he lept past. However, he was tripped from another motion from a second officer.

I watched him fall to the ground, instantly jumping to his feet and grasping onto the baton of the same man as he lunged at the fallen vampire. Sulru's pained screech sounded and my sight was instantly returned to her, witnessing her rival successfully driving her claws into my partner's abdomen.

My stomach fell when witnessing her distress. I must have emitted a worried sound of my own because her obsidian spheres cut to me, her weak expression immediately regaining its power. She clutched onto her enemy's wrists, yelling loudly as she ripped the blades from her.

"TAWSEY!"

I recognized the vampiric insult that Sulru had taught me. It was from their original language and was a racial slur for vampires to use against others of their kind. At its base, it meant 'betrayer.' The word had come from the entrance where Mote had taken to, though I had no idea what the plan had been. There was movement in the side of my vision.

Looking to it, I saw it was Sulru, fleeing her struggle and making her way for her teammates. Most of the human officers had either been killed or were standing their ground around Sheif and I, while some had begun rushing to Alg upon seeing his guard having to leave his side to fight. Kivela remained within hand combat with a human who had stayed dedicated to stopping the invaders. John was standing at Mote's side and Sulru had just reached them.

I stepped forward, immediately held back by a tug on my binds, "Sul-" I whispered.

It was enough for her to hear. The vampire's head turned, eyes falling heavily upon me. They may have seemed emotionless to the common person, but I knew the woman. I saw what she was hiding: she wasn't here for me. What...what was happening? I didn't understand any of it.

My eyes fluttered from her to John as she grabbed his shoulder, yanking him away from the entrance as Mote simultaneously jumped in order to join them. He twisted as he bound, landing a kick on the human that Kivela had not quite done away with.

As the group fell back, an explosion came from the doors where they'd been gathered. I knew that reinforcements should have been directly outside in this instance, and was curious as to the intruders plans for dealing with them. Apparently that was it.

The rustle was loud enough to shake the immediate vicinity and all of us within. The blast crumbled the metal of the entrance and was also powerful enough to cripple the majority of the humans crowded outside. Mote instantly leaped through the rubble and past the few officers attempting to regain themselves. Likewise, Sulru threw her arms around John, picking him up as she made smaller hops out of the mess.

But one teammate didn't make it.

Just as those who had been around me and the Generals left to chase after the threat, my vision caught sight of Kivela and Alg's guard within each other's grasp...but the woman had the upper hand. She had allowed him to strike her shoulder to distract him as she spun, her own blades shooting around his throat. Sinking her claws into his flesh, the old man wasn't fast enough to keep her from twisting his neck in an abrupt motion that both cracked it and shredded the flesh.

I forced myself away from those holding me then. It was only momentary, but it was long enough for me to near Kivela, his body lifeless on the floor of the battlefield before I gazed after where Sulru and the others had fled. There was no sight of the three...only the havoc they had wreaked...and me...

Chapter 52: Connie

"What happened?" I asked, unsure if it was rebellion or normal legal procedure that had freed me.

The woman who had entered my cell pulled the metal from around my arms, clicking the device to retract the bars into its more compact setting, "You have been cleared with General Malook."

She spoke matter-of-factly as she put the cuffs onto a spot on her uniform. It wasn't really in an apologetic or calming way, but something about it seemed warmer than the previous receptions I had received.

I didn't know how long it had been since we were arrested. It had to have been longer than a day...perhaps longer than two. You'd think that with my own experience in the military, I would have picked up on some semblance of an internal clock.

The officer helped me to my feet before I could start rubbing my wrists within my palms to ease the discomfort that they had been in. There was a second person who waited at the door and to be honest, I couldn't tell their gender. They stood with a rifle, not aimed at anything, but resting in preparation for easy use in front of them. The individual stepped to the side, allowing the two of us women to pass through, and then they followed behind.

"You'll be processed by our medical staff before you leave to be sure you are in proper condition," my escort continued, gaze never leaving from the path ahead.

I simply nodded my head. I didn't know what to say or if it would be deemed strange for me to speak. I was sore, tired, and hungry. I had spent the last many hours fighting between screaming and crying, shifting endlessly from hating myself to hating those around me and then back again.

I had only been visited a couple of times, leaving me in a state of pure uncertainty. Sleep had been nearly impossible and I had become so cramped that the slightest movement made my bones feel like they were cracking. I didn't even want to recall the bathroom situation.

Therefore, in that moment, I was exceedingly happy. We had been released. It may end with more red tape, more suspicion, and whatever else, but at least we were free again. I cherished the thought of feeling my husband's embrace. It was needless for me to worry on it since he was even tougher than me, yet I couldn't stop myself from hoping his imprisonment had been as plain as mine or better.

Our trio stopped at the end of a spiraled hallway upon reaching a barred entrance. The woman beside me took a larger pace forward, issuing a series of quick commands into a panel on the wall, causing the heavy passageway to open. On the other side was a large room, lined with what my best guess were types of medical equipment...or torture devices...it was hard to tell. I had not yet been introduced to Galdelieran hospital atmospheres.

The officer turned to me and gestured inside toward a man who stood near the middle of the room. He was dressed entirely in white, much like the stereotypical doctor on Earth, so that's what I assumed he was.

I gave another small nod before walking away in his direction, instantly hearing the door fall shut behind me. The sound was startling, causing me to jump and see that my two escorts had disappeared.

"Connie?" a familiar voice sounded from where the strange man had been standing, his focus on a table in front of him, though it was not the voice I wanted to hear right then.

I looked back inside the room and saw that Malook had emerged from around a partition therein. I gave him a smile and hurried closer, almost throwing myself into his arms. I did hug him, which seemed to take him off-guard as he awkwardly allowed his own arms to return the embrace. But he soon put his hands on top of my shoulders instead, and slowly pulled us apart.

"Sorry," I muttered, seeing the confused look on his face.

"No, it's not-" he started softly, cutting himself off as his eyes leapt to the other man coming near, "It's ok," he finished with a half-smile.

My own vision left him and began scanning the room as the doctor reached out and took my hand. Normally I would have retreated at the unannounced touch, but my mind was elsewhere. While he wrapped something akin to a blood pressure monitor around my wrist, I put my attention on Malook again, "Where's-"

The General stopped my question with an abruptly loud order, "Be still so the doctor can finish up quickly."

The words came out harshly. However, gazing into his gentle green eyes, I knew he was only protecting me in John's absence. Nonetheless, I was worried and once more, frightened. Something was off; I could feel it.

Malook knew what I was about to ask and he had hushed me. Was John...was my husband ok? My expression definitely betrayed my emotion, for the man who had shied from my touch, reached his hand out and took hold of the one of mine that was still free.

As he grasped it tightly, offering me a comforting grin, I wondered if he realized the intimacy of the position. I didn't fight it, even though it was not something a stranger or even most friends should do with someone in a relationship. I knew his intention was not sensual, so I assumed that perhaps it wasn't considered any more intimate than a hug here, which we had already shared.

The offered support actually had the opposite effect. I found myself focusing on reminders that there was nothing wrong about letting him hold me like that, which did well to distract me from working myself up worrying about John...for the most part.

"You appear to be quite fine," the doctor had already retrieved the wrap on my wrist and pricked it with a second tool, drawing blood, "General, if you would like to ready your transport, this last scan will take no time."

"Hm," Malook agreed, releasing me from his grip, but turning a raised eyebrow at me before strolling out of the room, as if to remind me to stay reserved.

"Come over here," the doctor gestured at me as he walked to the wall on our right.

I remained behind long enough to watch Malook finish leaving, and then followed the man dressed in white. He motioned for me to stand in the middle of an outlined circle on the ground and as soon as I had, he stretched a hand above me, grabbing onto a thick greyish colored curtain, pulling it so that I was completely hidden behind it on every side.

"Stand still," he called.

Even with his bedside manner completely lacking, I did what I was told without fuss. Like Malook had said, compliance would get me out of here faster; then he could tell me what the hell was going on. A small sound encased the curtain around me almost like static vibrations I could feel. As quickly as it came, it left, and the sheet was removed.

The doctor gave no further instruction, yet when he had made it far across the room again, I decided I might as well go after. I observed him flip a few screens on a computer on the desk he had first been studying when I entered the room. After a few seconds, he wrote something into the machine and then turned his gaze upon me.

"You're in perfect health," he nodded, offering a smile- the first hint of kindness from him, "And you'll need to file an appointment with your regular physician when you get home."

My head tilted, "I thought you said I was in perfect health. Why do I need to see been seen again so soon?"

The man's grin grew, "To schedule for your implant to be re-inserted."

I opened my mouth to say something else, but instantly shut it and took a minute to think. I had to seem dumb simply standing there and blinking. However, he had spoken plainly as if I should immediately know what was meant. Remembering Malook's subtle command to be careful after he left, I wasn't going to risk saying anything, even if it did make me look like an idiot.

Implant. What type of implant would just be so typical and casual that-

My eyes shot wide. Birth control. I remembered learning about the implant every citizen was required to receive as means of population control. The scan must have shown I didn't have one and that meant...my palms began to sweat. If I didn't have one, that meant I had been trying to get pregnant.

"I'm... Am I..." I stammered.

"It's very early, but yes," his smile continued, "You'll need to begin prenatal care."

Even though I heard the *whoosh* of the door coming open off to the side, I couldn't seem to tear myself from the man in front of me. I could feel someone approaching us and taking a place at my side.

"If you're done, we'll be on our way now," Malook's firm voice commanded, rather than inquired.

The doctor's smile fell and he departed to return to his spot back at the computer. The General's arm reached around my shoulder, pulling me closer to him. Only then did I finally look his way. His expression was concerned, eyes boring into mine, intent on making sure I was alright. I shook my head once, oddly, forcing myself to give a small nod to assure him I was fine.

He didn't seem convinced, but it got me walking so it was enough. Outside of the room, there were four human officers and they all accompanied us to what I surmised to be the building's exit. As two of them moved forward to open the way, a voice came from the opposite side of the structure. I twisted with Malook toward where it had come to see a man and a vampire approaching.

"Malook, please take Kotur here with you," the human said.

"I don't think that's necessary," Malook answered flatly, giving me the feeling he didn't like the guy. Likewise, I didn't think I did either. His grin seemed fake and his words were thick.

"With all that has been done against you, I think it is," the man retorted. *Who was this ass?*

"General, I understand your concern," my friend returned the false attitude and I assumed he was going to deny the offer again, but he paused, and then simply said 'thank you' under his breath.

I glanced over at the vampire, not judging anything from her before Malook tugged me back toward the exit with him, nudging me to just go along. The outside of the compound actually appeared similar to most prisons back on Earth. We were escorted by two humans to a covered rover where the vampire instantly took the driver's seat, waiting for us to situate ourselves in the rear.

The ride to Malook's home was frustrating, though not as long as the trip to the facility had seemed to have been. It was only aggravating because he refused to speak in Kotur's company, keeping me in the dark even longer, though he once more tried to comfort me by placing a hand on my thigh.

Chapter 53: Malook

We both walked into my now hollow home. I would have preferred informing Connie of what had transpired during the trip since I could have focused enough of my attention on driving that I didn't have to look at her as I knew she would be hurt...something I didn't feel I could handle more of right then.

Unfortunately, I also didn't feel like fighting with Alg or being in his presence any longer, and I couldn't trust Kotur. My strife had grown into hatred and anger. Even as I ordered the door closed behind us, moving to take a seat on the couch as I ignored her cautiously saying my name, I fought the urge to snap.

"Malook? What's happened? Is John- is he-"

"He's fine," the answer came out cold, the best I could muster despite knowing she was undeserving of my frustration. Just hearing her voice and dreading the coming conversation was annoying me, "He's alive anyway," I clarified.

"What-" she began pushing again, but I threw a hand up, ordering her to silence.

I sat with my head hung and retrieved my hand from the air to rub my chin before letting it drop hard onto my knee. I had been confused at first, not understanding why Sulru was with this character she hated, someone who wasn't part of our faction.

He couldn't have been because she, and therefore I, would have known. And he wouldn't have made it through Otahn's discerning discretion...not with how the vampire had conducted himself during the events from days prior.

Initially, I felt betrayed, being left behind by none other than the one person I deemed worthy of my implicit trust while the Earth man, basically a stranger, was saved. But I had learned over the years to control my temper and I quickly shook that feeling away. I knew there was something more.

Mote's presence told me that the three of them were *not* working under instruction of Otahn or with the rebellion's aid. Sulru had persevered even without our allies' assistance. That was why she worked with this man she hated. I guess the only incentive he needed was the promise of being able to slaughter humans. It was indeed another testament to my needing to take Sulru's intuition of a person to heart.

I finally realized that she had to have received some help from Otahn or she wouldn't have known where I was or that they had caught on to John's alias. Smart woman. She had used their suspicion to point the blame on him and make it seem as if he were the one behind it all, as if John had framed me.

She knew it would give them an answer as to who he was without revealing that he was alien. To the other Generals, it now appeared that John had created a false identity to worm his way into my family and use me as a scapegoat to press his own agenda, one actually similar to that of Alg's: scientific advancement.

I couldn't help a grin at the thought of her. Sulru was indeed a rarity...someone to be prized and appreciated. Connie took sight of the curve in my lips to mean I had calmed down. She strolled closer and took a seat on the cushion beside me. Close enough that I could feel her, but not so much that we were touching.

"Um," I began with an odd laugh while forcing away the fond thoughts of my partner, "Sulru and John made it out of the prison. They'll be in hiding. I don't know how long...but there will be officers searching for them," I looked up at the woman who was clearly fighting to remain relaxed herself, "I may have to help with these searches myself," I added.

"But...but um...you won't...I mean," she was stumbling, her chest having started heaving.

It looked like she was about to cry, so I leaned over to wrap my hand around her shoulder. I had been surprised when she had hugged me in the medical wing, but it told me that she needed physical comfort so I had done my best to give it to her. She had always been so kind to me.

However, she jerked away from me and jumped to her feet, emitting small, confused sounds. Her eyes kept darting back and forth. Each time they were on me, I saw a flash of anger in them. Watching her pace the floor in front of me, her mind trying to understand what I was telling her, I couldn't decide if I should try holding her again or just let her be.

"Of course I'm not going to do anything to actually help, but I may have to pretend," my brow furrowed, "Connie, it had to happen this way," I tried to explain better.

"No! None of it had to happen at all. It's all so fucking stupid!" the woman screamed at me, throwing her fists up, and then back down as tears started streaming down her cheeks.

I didn't know what exactly was bothering her besides the obvious. Her statements insinuated deeper thoughts, deeper guilt, and I saw that simply discussing the situation wasn't going to help her. I stood from the couch and took slow paces forward. When I had gotten close to her, she stepped back.

"Don't touch me!" she screamed again, but I ignored it, closing the gap between us and forcing my arms around her.

She fought against my embrace, trying her best to get out of my grasp. Her yells became cries as she pounded her fists onto my chest. I only kept holding her, letting my head fall to rest on her shoulder as one hand grabbed the back of her hair and pushed her to lay under my collarbone. Then...she was sobbing, still resisting holding onto me, but not trying to get away.

I rubbed my palm against her locks and whispered into her ear, "It's okay. We'll get him back. We'll get both of them back," I told her as her loud crying grew weaker and she finally gave in, letting her hands find their way from her sides and up my back, clutching my tunic.

I continued the hug, rocking our bodies softly by shifting weight from one foot to the other. After several minutes, the woman in my arms had quieted so I loosened my hold and lifted my head to look down at her. She didn't move from my chest.

"Do you know what you're doing, Malook?" her voice was barely audible.

Pausing to consider the question, I at last assured her, "I know what I'm doing. They're going to be alright."

The woman sniffed one final time, "I trust you."

Coming Soon

Borrowed Loyalty

Visitor's Blood: Book Two

by

Sahreth 'Baphy' Bowden

For all updates concerning the Visitor's Blood
Series
and other works by Sahreth 'Baphy' Bowden,
visit baphy1428.com